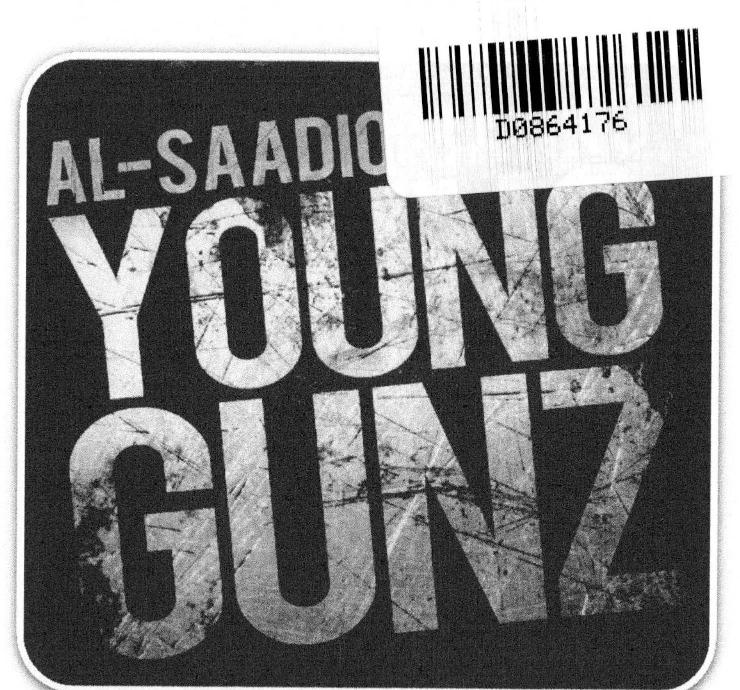
D0864176
YOUNG
GUNZ

True 2 Life Publications Presents:

Young Gunz

All rights reserved © 2013 by Al- Saadiq Banks
No part of this book may be reproduced or transmitted in any form or by any means, graphic, electronic, or mechanical, including photocopying, recording, taping or by any information storage retrieval system, without the written permission of the publisher.
This novel is a work of fiction. Any resemblances to real people, living or dead, actual events, establishments, organizations, or locales are intended to give the fiction a sense of reality. Other names, characters, places, and incidents are either products of the author's imagination or are used fictitiously.

Author: Al- Saadiq Banks
ISBN: 978-09740610-9-2
LCCN: TBD
Editing/Typesetting: www.21StreetUrbanEditing.com

Contact Information
Mail: True 2 Life Publications
PO Box 8722
Newark NJ 07108

Email: alsaadiqbanks@aol.com

Twitter: @alsaadiq

IG: @alsaadiqbanks

www.True2LifeProductions.com

"Better to have one woman on your side than ten men."

Robert Jordan – The Great Hunt

CHAPTER 1
APRIL 2002

The waiting room inside of Newark's Penn Station is packed, with not one available seat. This is quite normal for such a beautiful Saturday afternoon. All walks of life are here in this one room, from families on their way to New York City to enjoy an outing to the homeless people who live here. The vagrants actually stare at the people with disgust. They stare in disgust because they feel that these people are invading their homes.

In the distance, a train can be seen racing up the tracks. All the people in the waiting area get up hurriedly and bombard the door, especially the ones who have been standing all the while. In no time at all, the ramp is filled with people, just waiting for the train to get there. The moment the room empties, the five homeless people spread out and make them selves comfortable.

The train comes to a complete halt, and the doors slide open slowly. Just as fast as the doors open, the train becomes crowded. Everyone rushes to a seat, leaving a few standing. The doors close, and the train pulls off. The sound of a baby's loud cry breaks any peace that anyone could have expected to get during this train ride.

For some reason, two young men, who stand side by side against the doors, stick out like sore thumbs. The way that they are peeking around in a sneaky manner could easily make one feel uncomfortable. One man holds a shopping bag in his hand with a shoebox inside. The other young man is empty-handed.

In the far corner, a young Spanish woman tries her hardest to calm her crying baby down, with no success. A middle-aged, balding man looks up from his newspaper and looks down through his bifocals at the young woman. His look makes her feel quite uncomfortable. The thickness of his eye glasses makes his eyes look tiny and beady, but, as tiny as they appear, agitation is clearly evident in them.

Just as the man lifts his paper and begins to read again, the baby screams at the top of her little lungs. The man lowers his paper and stares deeply into the woman's eyes as she pats the baby's back. He grabs his eyeglasses by the taped corner and slides them to the edge of his nose. The young woman looks up at him with a cheesy smile as she lifts the baby into her arms.

"Shhh," she whispers into the baby's ear as she unloosens the buttons on her blouse. She peeks around with discomfort on her face before sticking her hand into her blouse and fumbling with her C cups. The young woman looks up at the man with an embarrassed grin on her face, raising her eyebrows before shoving her breast into the baby's mouth. The crying stops automatically.

The bifocal wearing man looks away from her with shame before walking away and leaving her with what he feels is privacy. He stuffs his newspaper underneath his armpit. His plaid dress shirt, polyester slacks, and thick, rubber soled shoes give him a Steve Urkel/ Pee Wee Herman type of feel.

As the train comes to the next stop, the man stops in the middle of the train and grabs onto the bar. He peeks around at the new people that have gotten onto the train. As the train pulls off, the man leans against the bar and lifts his newspaper from his armpit. He commences reading again. Every few minutes, he lifts his beady eyes over the newspaper and peeks around sneakily.

Over his newspaper, he peeks at the two young men who are standing at the door. They are indulging in a deep conversation in low whispers. The man looks at their mouths as if he's trying to read their lips. His attention is diverted to the left of him as an older woman gets up from her seat, preparing for the train's next stop. Just as the seat becomes available, the young man by the door dashes over and fills it, leaving the man with the shopping bag still standing.

The man stares through his bifocals with rage in his eyes as he stares at the man who just filled the seat. The young man looks him up and down with a goofy smirk on his face before looking over at his friend, who is wearing the same goofy smirk. The man watches the young man, who is sitting down, not paying the least bit of attention to his friend. He rolls his eyes in disgust before looking down at his newspaper again.

One stop and a few empty seats later, the man with the shopping bag takes a seat diagonally from his friend. The man with the bifocals walks with his face buried in the newspaper until he gets to the empty seat next to the young man. He takes the seat, barely taking his eyes from the paper. He wiggles into the seat, in between the two passengers. The young man slides over with a sign of aggravation on his face.

A sudden tapping on the young man's side causes him to jump. He looks down to his side where he sees a small pearl-handled handgun pressed against him. In total shock, he sits there before looking over to his left. He and the man stare into each other's eyes through the bifocals. The man leans closer to the young man to conceal the weapon, and he raises the newspaper a little higher, so no one can read his lips.

"Dig, don't even think of making a move or a sound," he says as he nudges the nose of the gun into the young man's gut. "You see your man over there?" he asks.

Just as the young man looks over, he notices that his friend is wearing a look of nervousness on his face.

"Look at both sides of him."

The young man looks to both sides of his friend and notices two baby-faced teenagers sitting there with stone-cold looks on their faces. As they both are looking at him, they slide over a little, allowing their guns to be seen. Their guns are glued to his side as well.

"Short and brief," the man whispers as his beady eyes shift from side to side. "I'm on this train peeping niggers who are going uptown to cop, and you been peeped. With your foot, slide that sneaker box over to me slowly. Keep looking at me as you do it," he whispers. "Go against it, and we gonna blow you and your man off the map," he threatens with sincerity in his eyes.

While looking straight ahead, the young man slowly kicks the bag over, closer to the man.

"See how smooth that was?" the man asks as he flashes his pearly white dentures. "Now, follow my instructions. Sit here and don't move. Move and your man loses his life," he says as the train comes to a stop.

As the doors slide open, the man tucks the gun into his pocket, grabs the shopping bag, gets up, and makes his way to the door. The young man sits there, staring straight ahead at the two young men who are still sitting next to his friend. Both of them stare at him with coldness in their eyes. The doors of the train close, and the train departs. The man stands on the ramp, holding the bag, as he watches the train speed off. Once the train is out of sight, he gets onto the escalator and goes on about his way.

CHAPTER 2

The two teenagers sit across from each other at the raggedy, lopsided coffee table. Wustafa, the bifocal wearing terror, sits on the edge of a worn out leather recliner, at the head of the table. This basement apartment is a complete wreck. The walls have huge holes in them, the ceiling hangs from excessive leaking, and the floors are warped from flooding.

Even though this apartment is a disaster, Wustafa is happy to call it home. After being incarcerated for a total of twenty-five years out of his forty-two year old life, he has the ability to make himself comfortable under the worse conditions. As raggedy as the apartment is, he keeps it neat, clean, and organized, just as he did his prison cell for all the years that he served in there.

Wustafa, born Grover James Watson, took his first trip to jail at eleven years old for arson and has been going back and forth ever since. He's more comfortable in jail than he is at home. In fact, jail feels more like home to him, and, anytime that he's on the outside, it feels like a vacation for him. His charges range from petty theft and burglary, wherein he's spent a year or two in prison at a time, to aggravated assaults to murder charges.

As a child, the Newark school system classified him as a special needs student, and he went through elementary school enrolled in all special education classes until he finally dropped out in sixth grade. Everyone believed that he had a learning deficiency until, as an adult, he had more than enough intelligence to defend himself in superior court on three separate occasions on three different murder charges. Singlehandedly, without the use of an attorney, he was able to outwit the system and was acquitted on all three charges.

After such close brushes with losing his freedom forever, one would think that he would walk a straight path, but crime is all he knows. His last brush with the law was a petty burglary charge that cost him a third of his life because of his extensive record. Only home two weeks after a fifteen year prison stay, he's back at what he thinks he does best.

A few piles of money are stacked on the coffee table in front of Wustafa as he counts through the last of the loose bills. Wustafa looks up from the money and stares at the teenager to his right.

"Seven thousand, five hundred," he says with a goofy smile. His nephew looks at him and tries hard not to laugh at the slightly retarded look of his face. "Not bad for a few minutes' worth of work."

The teenager to his left is his one and only nephew, Lamar Watson. This is his only sister's only son. His nephew idolizes him so much that he named himself after him, calling himself Lil Wustafa. All of his life he's heard so many treacherous stories about his uncle that he wants to be feared and respected just like him. Lil Wustafa is a small framed, intelligent, fifteen-year-old kid who has never done anything outside of the right thing until he linked up with his uncle.

The other teenager is Lil Wustafa's best friend, Leonard. This clumsy, 6 foot 3 inch kid has always been the biggest kid of the bunch and, by far, the goofiest. His tall and lanky frame has earned him the nickname Lurch. Over the years, he's gotten used to the teasing and mockery. The only thing that he hasn't gotten used to is the physical abuse. Being big and weak has gotten him bullied on by the older kids for most of his life.

The cool kids in school don't consider these two cool. In fact, they are labeled nerds or, even worse, rejects. As much as they hate not being accepted by the popular crowd, they have gotten used to it and learned to stay in their lane. Up until now, all of their free time has been spent on the basketball court. Lil Wu has spoken so highly of his uncle that his friend, Leonard, feels privileged just to be in the same room as him.

Most would consider these teens too young, since they're only fifteen, to be involved in crime, but Wustafa feels that they are the perfect age to be groomed. He sees something in them that no one else can see. He plans to give them the battery charge they need to bring the beast out of them.

"I told y'all that plan works every time. There's always gonna be somebody in there on their way to cop. We could sit there all day and pick 'em off one by one and come off crazy, but you don't want to blow your cover. That will be the spot we save when everything's slow and we need to make a quick move, dig me?"

Both teenagers nod their heads in a trance like state, listening to his every word.

Wustafa hands a stack of money over to his nephew. "Your earnings for the day. Count your money."

Wustafa looks at his nephew closely as he sifts through the hundred dollar bills quickly.

"How much you got?"

"One thousand, two hundred and fifty dollars," he says with a bright look in his eyes.

Wustafa, then, hands a stack of money over to Leonard.

"And here are your earnings. Now count your money."

Wustafa waits until the kid is finally finished counting. Then, he asks, "How much you got?"

"Five hundred," he replies with a look of disappointment in his eyes.

"Do you know why you got less?"

Leonard shakes his head from side to side with curiosity in his eyes.

"You were brought into this organization by Lil Wu, who was born into this organization. Two fifty of your earnings went to him and two fifty goes to me."

Frustration sets on Leonard's face as he shakes his head from side to side.

"You got a problem with that? If you do, the door is right there," Wustafa says as he points. "You can walk right out the door the same way you walked in." Wustafa looks at him with his beady eyes shifting from side to side. "So, what is it gonna be? You out or you in?"

Leonard looks up, still shaking his head from side to side. "I'm in."

"Okay. That's more like it," he says as he raises his fist high in the air. Leonard bangs his fist against Wustafa's. "Don't worry, though. After a few vicks, your dues will be all paid, and you will get the same amount of money as everyone else at the table does. The bigger the stings, the faster your dues will be paid." Wustafa stands up and drops a stack of bills into his pocket. The other stacks, he dumps back into the shoe box that they were originally in. "This four grand, we invest into our business. We buy artillery."

He raises the small pearl handled .22 into the air.

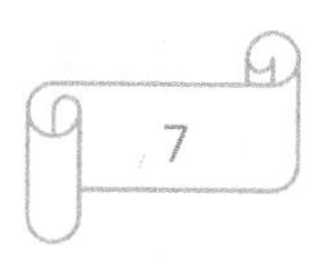

"This isn't gonna be enough."

He lifts the guns that sit in front of the teenagers and aims both of them at their foreheads. They both sit there, shaking and frightened to death. He stands there with a cold smile on his face. Slowly, he squeezes the triggers, and both teenagers close their eyes and take their last breaths.

Click. Click.

They both open their eyes with shocked expressions on their faces. They look up at Wustafa, who wears a huge smile on his face.

"These two ain't gonna cut it," he smiles. "Relax, y'all. They're just starter pistols. I didn't tell y'all that y'all had starter pistols because it may have affected your confidence. Y'all pulled it off," he says with a grin. "Now that we got money, we can get real and bigger guns. Bigger guns will get us bigger jobs. Y'all ready?" he asks.

They nod their heads simultaneously.

"Let's get it then!"

CHAPTER 3
DAYS LATER

Lil Wu and Leonard stand closely behind Wustafa in the dark, abandoned house. They watch Wustafa with admiration as he takes total control of the meeting.

"Listen, we are all businessmen, and, if you don't trust us, then maybe we should take our business elsewhere," Wustafa says as he looks the old man square in the eyes. "We take it as a total insult...y'all requesting that we be pat down and searched as if we are savages. That's a clear indication that you don't trust us. For all we know, you could be scheming on taking our money, but never did we feel the need to pat you down. I trust you; we trust you," he says as he points to his young accomplices.

"We trust you, and all we ask is for the same. We got a few thousand dollars in here," he says as he opens the duffle bag for them to see the money. He hopes that will bring them some type of comfort. "We're here to purchase goods, and that's it. Now, can we get on with the business that has brought us all here on this beautiful day?" he says with the most charming smile that he can muster up.

The old man looks over to his partner and gives him a head nod. The man walks over hesitantly, carrying a duffle bag of his own. The second he gets there, he opens the bag and starts to unload. The young boys watch with amazement as they set their eyes on the shiny, brand new handguns that are presented.

"What all you got there?" Wustafa asks.

"This is the last of the shipment. All we got left are five seventeen shot Smiths and two of these," the man says as he unfolds a bulletproof vest and holds it in the air in front of his chest.

Wustafa looks back at his accomplices with his eyebrows raised high, giving them the head nod of approval. In the blink of an eye, he turns around with his .22 drawn and in the air.

Pop, pop, pop!

The old man ducks for cover, rolling onto the floor.

"Take it all, Wu! Just don't kill us," he cries.

The other man dives onto the floor as well. He holds the vest on top of his head for protection.

Lil Wu and Leonard watch with great surprise as Wustafa stands there with a devious smile on his face, still holding his gun high in the air. He laughs a cynical laugh before walking over and snatching the vest from the man. He holds it in the air, examining it closely. The three bullet holes are set dead in the center with a few inches between them.

He flips the vest over and rubs his hand over it slowly.

"No penetration whatsoever," he says with satisfaction. "Get up from there."

He helps the man from the floor. The other man stands up slowly while looking down at his chest, praying that he hasn't been hit. "Give us a price and be reasonable."

"Wu, you fucked up," the man says, still trembling with fear. "That's why nobody don't do business with you now. You're crazy," the man utters as he tries to get himself together.

"I'm not crazy," Wustafa replies. "I had to see if they work, and they do. Now, let's do business."

CHAPTER 4
A WEEK LATER

It's a beautiful spring day, and, instead of the tranquil sound of birds chirping, the only thing that can be heard are teenagers shouting curse words. A huge crowd of school kids gather in the middle of the street, shouting and jumping up and down with excitement.

"Ooh!" they all shout simultaneously.

Inside of the circle stand two teenagers brawling it out. The bigger teen is twice the size of the smaller teen.

The smaller one is taking a brutal beating, but he just won't give up. His vision is quite blurry. Both eyes have been swollen shut by the painful blows that he's absorbed. He peeks through his half-closed eyes, holding his guard high. He throws a sloppy haymaker, praying that it will land on target.

Surprisingly, the haymaker catches the bigger kid directly on the chin. The blow has no effect whatsoever. In fact, all it does is excite the kid. He rushes the smaller kid and yanks him by his collar, lifting him into the air with ease. He hooks his arm in between the kid's legs and lifts him high over his head.

With extreme force, he slams him onto the ground. He, then, commits to stomping the kid abusively.

"I told you to go ahead. You too little for me!" the monstrous sized teen says as he stomps the kid over and over. The teen on the ground curls up in an attempt to protect himself.

A crying girl runs over, enraged. She feels she has to come to her younger brother's defense because the beating that he's taking is a result of him coming to her defense. While walking home from school, the bully pinned her against the wall and groped her perversely. Her jealous and overprotective younger brother witnessed it all and couldn't just sit back and watch his older sister be disrespected, regardless of the fact that the bully is four years older and one hundred pounds bigger.

"Watch out!" the crowd warns.

Just as the bigger teen turns around, he's greeted by a weak sucker punch. He eats the punch with a smile before palm gripping the frail girl's face and shoving her to the ground. Now, the brother and sister tag team both lay on the ground, side by side, while the crowd cheers away. The monstrous teen walks away as they get themselves up from the ground.

A minute later, the crowd that follows the bully disperses as the kid and his sister come running at full speed. He grips a long 2x4 as best that he can in his little hands. He can barely carry it, let alone get a controllable swing. His eyes are full of bloody tears, and his nose is full of snot.

"Watch out, Bull!" the crowd warns, but it's already too late.

The 2x4 crashes into the back of the boy's head. The impact sends him tumbling forward. He lands on the ground face first.

Wustafa, Lil Wu, and Leonard have front row seats to the action as they sit on Wustafa's porch. "That kid has a lotta heart," Wustafa says as he looks over at his nephew. "I like him. You said you know him, right?"

"I don't know him, but he's in my math class. He's new to the school. He's kind of quiet and weird," Lil Wu says with jealousy in his voice. He hates the fact that his uncle is giving praise to someone other than him.

"Whoa!" Wustafa shouts as he stands to his feet in awe.

Just as the 2x4 wielding kid stands over his prey, preparing to finish him off, he's caught by a sucker punch from one of the spectators, which sends him to the ground once again. He loses his grip on the 2x4, and it falls to the ground a couple of feet away from him. While the kid is on the ground, the bully gets up from the ground. He quickly runs over to the kid, snatches the 2x4 from the ground, and raises it high in the air, ready to attack.

"Yo! Yo!"

The monstrous sized teen turns around and peeks over his shoulder.

"Don't swing that!" Wustafa says as he points at the bully in a threatening manner.

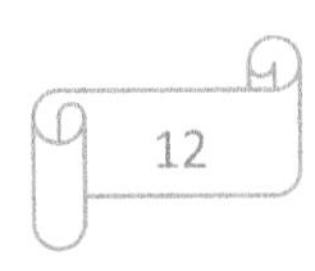

The bully looks Wustafa up and down, and a smirk pops onto his face as he judges Wustafa by his goofy looking appearance. The bully lifts the 2x4 into the air again.

Wustafa walks up to the teen and looks up into his eyes. Wustafa's beady eyes pierce through the bully's soul. As small as his eyes appear through the thick bifocals, the bully still sees a coldness in them that he's never seen in another person's eyes before. The teen lowers the 2x4 before, dropping it to the ground.

"It's over. That's it. Y'all get on away from here," Wustafa demands.

A few kids mumble under their breaths with rebellion until the bully commands them all to leave as instructed. Wustafa walks over to the kid, who gets up from the ground in despair. Defeat is all over his face. Wustafa places his hand onto the kid's shoulder.

"You alright, kid?"

The kid nods his head silently. Wustafa extends his hand toward the teenager.

"I'm Wustafa. What's your name?"

The kid returns the handshake. "Anthony," he whispers.

"Anthony, this is my nephew Lil Wu, and this right here is Leonard. We saw the whole thing, and we like how you came to your big sister's defense," he says as he points to the girl who stands there still crying with rage and fury. "You got a lot of heart. They got you this time but only because he was bigger and stronger than you. Plus, he had something that you didn't have, and that's a team. Notice how I said what you didn't have?" Wustafa wraps his arm around the kid's shoulder. "Trust me. Now that you have a team, that will never ever happen to you again."

CHAPTER 5
DAYS LATER

Leonard stands against the wall inside of Wustafa's apartment. Terror bleeds from his eyes as he stands there, petrified. Wustafa whispers faintly into his nephew's left ear as he stands behind him.

"Focus. Aim," he whispers.

Lil Wu tries to aim, but his hands are unsteady with nervousness. Wustafa slaps the back of his nephew's head.

"Hold your hands steady," he says aggressively as he reaches over and wraps his hands around his nephew's hands, which are clasped loosely around the .9mm. "Tighten your grip. Now, squeeze," he barks. "Aim at his throat, and you will hit his head. Hold your breath and squeeze."

Lil Wu stands still as his heart races with fear. Leonard stands on the other end of the room with his eyes closed tightly.

"Squeeze, I said!" Wustafa never raises his voice, so, when he does, it brings his nephew great alarm.

Lil Wu closes his eyes and squeezes the trigger.

Click!

Both Lil Wu and Leonard open their eyes at the same time. The looks on their faces display surprise. Lil Wu stares at the gun dangling in his hand. Wustafa snatches the gun from his nephew's hand.

"Relax, y'all. It's empty," Wustafa says with a smile. He reaches behind himself and digs inside of a duffle bag, which is on the bed. He pulls out two more handguns. He hands the gun back to his nephew first. He, then, tosses the second gun over to Leonard. The third gun, he hands over to the newest member of the crew, Anthony.

He, then, reaches inside the bag and grabs hold of three cartridges. He passes them out one by one. He paces the room slowly like an army drill sergeant.

"This game is all about timing," he whispers faintly. "If you slow, you blow. It's all about who beats who to the draw. Now, all of you tuck your weapons, and, when I give the command, I want you to draw," he says as he stands in front of them.

He gives them a few seconds to tuck their weapons before shouting, "Draw!"

They all draw slowly and clumsily.

"That's too slow. It's all about speed," he says as he shakes his head. "Now, tuck."

Wustafa takes a few more steps before shouting again. "Now, draw!" He looks at the three teenagers, studying them closely. "That's a lil better. Now, load!" he shouts. They raise their guns in the air, pointing to the ceiling. They slam the clips into the butts of the gun in sync. "Now, release!"

The boys hit the levers on the side of their guns and the cartridges slide out smoothly. "Hands under the butt," he says as he pays close attention to them. "In a gun battle, be sure not to leave anything behind, just in case your prints or DNA have been left on anything. You are to guard an empty clip the same way you would guard a loaded clip," he says, staring them all in their eyes, one by one.

"Load!" he shouts aggressively. "One in the chamber! Slide!" He nods his head slowly. "Practice makes perfect, and we are gonna practice this until you all have reached perfection. "Release! Now, reload!"

CHAPTER 6
LATER THAT NIGHT/12:48 A.M.

It's a beautiful spring night, and the streets are as peaceful as the cool breeze, which blows comfortably. Very little traffic seems to be on the street for such a beautiful night. A gleaming BMW pulls into an Exxon service station. Not another car is present throughout the entire parking lot.

The BMW pulls into the parking space in front of the telephones. Once the headlights are turned off, the area becomes pitch dark. The young driver gets out and slams the door shut behind him as he walks through the darkness toward the convenience store. He steps around a panhandler, who stands in his path.

The young man walks into the store and commences a mini junk food shopping spree. Wustafa walks into the store, holding a few loose bills in his hand. He walks straight toward the back of the store and pretends to be looking at the potato chip rack. He peeks over the rack as the man gets into the short line. Without being noticed, Wustafa eases out of the store.

The young man walks out, holding his shopping bag tightly in his right hand. In his left hand, he holds the remote to his car, which he presses to unlock the door before he gets there. He grabs the door handle, not paying the least bit of attention to the person standing at the phone booth with his back facing him. Just as he pulls the door open, he hears, "Don't move!"

Anthony says this with the most threatening voice that he can muster up.

The man stands there, in shock, as he slowly raises his hands in the air. Leonard raises his lanky frame up from the passenger's side and dashes over. He stands directly behind the man. Lil Wustafa pops out from behind the dumpster just as Leonard wraps his arms around the man's neck. He presses the gun against the man's back.

"Move, and I'm blowing your whole back out," he whispers as he peeks around.

Anthony aims the gun at the young man's head as he uses his free hand to search his pockets. He finds money in every pocket. What he finds, he tucks into his own pocket.

"You got anymore?" Anthony asks. "If I find more, you in trouble," he says as he continues to search him thoroughly.

"Lay him down," Wustafa says in the backdrop.

"Yeah, lay down," Leonard demands.

Wustafa dives into the car from the passenger's side. Quickly, he looks through the glove compartment for anything of value. He, then, flips the visors down and opens the middle console. He dives onto the floor, looking underneath the seats. His eyes light up with satisfaction when they land on the shopping bag, which lies under the driver's seat. He snatches the bag and opens it.

"Bingo," he utters to himself as he sees stacks of money.

Wustafa gets out of the car and slams the door shut.

"Throw me the keys," he demands.

Lil Wu snatches the man's keys from the ground and throws them over the roof of the car to Wustafa, who catches them in mid-air. Wustafa leans back, and, with all of his might, he launches the keys high into the air. Wustafa runs over to the driver's side. He kicks the man in the rib cage.

"Get under the car," he says aggressively. He kicks him again but this time harder. "Hurry up," he barks.

Leonard stands over the man, who wiggles under the car as fast as he can. Once his entire body is underneath the car, Anthony and Lil Wu take off running in the same direction. Leonard and Wustafa, then, take off in opposite directions.

In less than five minutes, they all link up with each other several blocks away. Their guns are tucked, and they're walking as normal as can be. Wustafa, who leads the pack, looks back to his crew with satisfaction in his eyes and says, "Job well done."

CHAPTER 7
THREE DAYS LATER

It's after midnight, but, judging by the abundance of foot traffic on the block, one would think it was the afternoon. A line of twelve people wrap around the stoop of the apartment building. The young dealer stands at the top of a small flight of stairs. He distributes the vials of cocaine openly, as if it's legal. He holds the brown bag full of crack vials in his hand as he fills the order of every customer one by one.

"Can I get two for eighteen please?" the woman begs.

Without a verbal response, the dealer digs into the bag. He, then, drops two vials into the palm of her hand. She turns around and takes off, skipping the entire flight of stairs.

"One," the man says anxiously.

The dealer drops one vial into the man's hand as the man hands him several singles. Just as the dealer scans the bills to get a count, the man holds his fist in the air. "Here."

"What's that?" the dealer asks.

"Three dollars in quarters."

"Oh, hell naw," the dealer says with attitude as he snatches the vial out of the man's hand. "I don't take change. Cash that in and get back with me."

"Please," the man begs desperately. "Where can I get cash at this time of night?"

The dealer pushes him out of the way arrogantly.

"Next! How many?" the dealer asks as his next customer steps up to him. "Yo! How many? Hurry the fuck up!" the man shouts as the customer pats his pockets in search of his money. "Yo!"

"Sorry," the man apologizes as he nods a dope fiend nod.

The dealer becomes agitated.

"Yo! Get the fuck out of my line!" he says as he puts his hands onto the man's chest and shoves him.

The man grabs hold of the dealer's hands and pulls him toward him. Leonard steps out of the back of the line with his gun drawn and aimed at the dealer and the male customer, who is Wustafa.

Anthony dashes out of the alley on the side of the house, gun waving and aiming at the porch.

"Don't nobody move!" he says as he points to the customers. "Everybody! Empty your pockets," he says as he snatches the money and goes into every customer's pockets one by one.

"Lay down!" Leonard shouts. "You know what the fuck it is," he says as he runs up the steps and starts digging into the man's pockets.

Wustafa peeks over his shoulder and sees that Lil Wu is in place as well. Lil Wustafa stands across the street in front of the abandoned house. He stands there, discreetly overseeing the action, while holding his gun close to his thigh. Wustafa backpedals down the stairs and stands to the side where he has a clear view of everything. He watches with admiration as Leonard shakes the man down like a seasoned professional.

Leonard holds the gun against the young man's head. While digging into his pockets, he does not miss a thing.

"I want everything," he says aggressively as he stares coldly into the young man's eyes.

Leonard snatches the bag. He backs away from the man while still aiming his gun at him. He backpedals down the steps and continues until he gets to the alley. He cuts into the dark alley and dashes through it at top speed.

Wustafa slowly eases away from the action and makes his way up the block. He peeks back and forth, just to make sure everything is intact. Anthony waves his gun randomly.

"Everybody, lay the fuck down!" he says.

Everyone dives onto the ground and lays on their bellies. Once they're all situated, Anthony backpedals away as well.

As soon as the men appear to be out of the way, the dealer pops up hysterically.

"Fuck that!" he says angrily as he jumps down the steps and runs toward the small car that is parked in front of the building.

Lil Wu stands in the cut without even being noticed. Just as the young dealer gets to his car and grabs hold of the passenger's door, Lil Wu raises his gun and points to the sky. He squeezes two shots into the air. The people scatter like roaches at the sound of the gunfire. As the man ducks for cover behind his car, Lil Wu disappears into the alley next to him without being seen. Wustafa stands at the corner out of the way, just watching how his plan has unfolded.

CHAPTER 8
THIRTY MINUTES LATER

Wustafa and the crew have just met back up at "the headquarters" as he calls it. They all sit around the coffee table as Wustafa counts through the earnings. They all sit around in suspense, wondering what their share of the score will be. Wustafa smacks the last few bills onto the table.

"Twenty-two hundred and thirty-six dollars," he says as he looks around the room with shifty eyes.

He counts through the bills once again. He first hands Leonard a small stack of bills.

"That's one hundred, twenty-five for you," he says as he grabs another small stack.

"And that's one hundred, twenty-five for you," he says as he hands Anthony the stack of money. "And this five hundred goes to me. The extra twenty-five comes from the dues the two of you paid," he says as he points to Leonard and Anthony. He completely overlooks Lil Wu, as if he isn't even sitting here. "The rest goes into the pot, the reserve tank," he says as he slides the rest of the money to the edge of the table.

Wustafa gets up from the table and walks over to the end of it where Lil Wu sits. Wu's face displays confusion. Wustafa stands close to him without saying a word for a couple of minutes. The tension becomes thicker and thicker by the second.

Wustafa stares Lil Wu square in the eyes as his temples pulsate. "Let me guess, you are wondering where your cut is, correct?"

Lil Wu shrugs his shoulders, palms up while nodding his head slowly. Wustafa walks off and starts pacing around the room. His pacing makes Lil Wu even more nervous. They all know, when he gets to pacing, something is weighing heavily on his mind.

"What was your job description?" Wustafa asks as he stares at Lil Wu from across the room.

"Stay there until," Lil Wu manages to reply before Wustafa interrupts.

"Speak up!" he shouts in a voice that they're not used to hearing.

Lil Wu jumps nervously. They've gotten accustomed to hearing his light whisper. Now, whenever he yells, they damn near fall into pieces.

"Stay there until everybody was outta sight."

"Correct," Wustafa says in his normal light whisper. "My further instructions were for you to fire shots as we were fleeing the area just in case someone had the balls to come behind us and retaliate. Your shots would buy us more time to get away. Is that correct?"

Lil Wu nods his head with innocence in his eyes as he replies, "That's what I did."

A smirk covers Wustafa's face.

"That's what you did, huh? So you're gonna sit here and lie to *us*, the organization, stating that you did what was instructed?"

"I'm not lying. That's what I did."

"No, that's not what you did," he says before banging onto the table loudly. They all jump nervously. "Yeah, you fired two shots but not at them. You fired two shots at the sky. In the air," he adds. "You wasted two rounds. Aiming at nothing," he says as he steps closer to Lil Wu. "Our lives were in your hands, and you're wasting shots, shooting in the air? What? Were you too scared to shoot over there and possibly hit someone? Is that why you shot in the air at nothing?"

Lil Wu shakes his head before lowering his eyes with shame.

"Something tells me that's what it was," Wustafa says with a smirk on his face. "You were scared. We out there on the frontline with our lives in the hands of a scared man," he smiles with anger. "We could have lost our lives out there depending on you."

Wustafa takes his attention off of Lil Wu and looks at Anthony and Leonard. "I'm totally proud of you two. You both adhered to protocol as instructed." He looks back to Lil Wu. "You," he says as he points at him, "are a pure disappointment, an embarrassment to the organization. Where's your gun?"

Lil Wu withdraws his gun from his waistband and shows it to Wustafa. Wustafa holds his hand out. "Surrender your weapon," he instructs.

Lil Wu holds the gun in the air and hits the lever on the side, causing the clip to fall out of the butt of the gun. He catches it in the palm of his hand, gripping it tightly before handing the gun over to Wustafa. Wustafa walks off and starts pacing again.

As pissed as Wustafa is right now, it brings him great pleasure to see that his teachings are not in vain. Wustafa has emphasized over and over that they should never give a man a loaded gun. The fact that he not even trusts him with a loaded gun lets him know that in no way is Lil Wu slipping, mentally, that is. He knows, if he doesn't trust him, he will not trust anyone.

"You will get your weapon back when you earn it. You will earn it by following instructions and learning to respect the lives of the members of this organization as you respect your own." Wustafa stops short. He looks back at Lil Wu. "Remove yourself from your seat."

Lil Wu stands up as instructed.

"Leonard, take his seat," Wustafa instructs as he points to the empty seat. "You sit over there on the couch. Until further notice, we will not meet at the table with you. You are to be present at every meeting, but you are not to say a word, unless you are spoken to by me."

Lil Wu takes a seat on the far end of the couch with watery eyes. He's crushed right now. All of his life, he has looked up to his uncle, and all he's ever wanted was his approval. Right now, he feels as if he's let his uncle down, and that makes him feel as if it's the end of his world.

Wustafa sits back at the head of the table and proceeds to speak.

"Again, I'm proud of you two," he says with sincerity in his eyes. He looks from Anthony to Leonard, back and forth, totally ignoring Lil Wu's presence. "Twenty-two hundred is a fairly decent sting but nowhere near the magnitude of a score that we really need. We need to take our show on the road. Plus, we can't keep attacking at home. Eventually, we will create more enemies around here than we can go to battle with at this time. Don't get me wrong. I know we can go up against the best of them," he says, trying to build their confidence. "And eventually, I'm sure we will go up against the best of them," he says with a sinister look on his face, "because I got a plan that will get us some real money."

CHAPTER 9
TWO WEEKS LATER

Anthony steps into the dark playground. He looks to the far end of the playground where he sees two young men sitting under the lights of the basketball court. His heart starts to pump with fear as he continues to step toward the center of the playground. He quickly looks to the exit to the right. Seeing Wustafa peeking his head in gives Anthony all the confidence he needs to carry him through this. He, then, peeks to the exit to the left where he sees Leonard standing in the darkness.

The closer Anthony gets to the basketball court, the more visible the images of the young men become. One young man is rapping as the other one bangs on the wall creating a beat. The smell of marijuana blows in the air. The young man stops rapping as he peeks through the darkness, trying to see who is walking up on them.

Just as Anthony gets right in front of the young men, Wustafa and Leonard make their entrance. "Oh, not you again," Bull says sarcastically as he laughs in their faces.

Anger quickly replaces Anthony's nervousness. His mind plays back to how the bully groped his sister. He, then, thinks back to how he was embarrassed out there. He draws his gun and holds it close to his thigh.

Wustafa stands to the right of Anthony as Leonard stands to the left, while the bully and his friend look back at them with nervousness in their eyes.

"What's... What's up?" the bully asks as he stares at the gun in Anthony's hand. "It was just a fight."

He has the urge to run but realizes there is nowhere to go. They have them trapped.

"Just a fight to you," Wustafa says sarcastically. "You like taking advantage of those that you feel are weak, huh? How does it feel to be helpless? How does it feel to be dominated? How does it feel to be oppressed? Tell me?"

"I'm sorry, man."

"Too late for sorry." Wustafa looks to Anthony. "Remember how you felt that day? Remember I said you would, one day, get your get back?" Anthony nods his head in silence. "Well, the day has come. Now, get your get back."

"No, please!" the man begs. "I'm sorry."

Boc!

The first shot misses by a long shot. Wustafa peeks around with caution.

"At the throat," he whispers.

The young boy backs up with fear. Anthony stands there with his hands trembling. He stares at the boy's throat, aims, holds his breath and squeezes.

Boc!

To his surprise the boy's neck snaps backward violently, indicating that he's been hit. He immediately falls onto his back.

"Finish him," Wustafa commands.

Anthony stands over the boy, who is squirming helplessly.

His friend attempts to take off in flight, but Wustafa snatches his collar, flinging him backwards.

"Ah hah, don't go nowhere." Wustafa looks over to Anthony. "Finish him!" he shouts.

Boc!

Anthony stands there in shock as he stares at the lifeless boy. Wustafa shoves the other man in front of Anthony. "Leave no witnesses."

"No!" the boy cries. "No! Please!" he cries before two slugs cave in his forehead.

Boc! Boc!

Wustafa, Anthony, and Leonard all take off in opposite directions, leaving the two boys lifeless on the asphalt.

****Twenty Minutes Later****

Leonard sits on the couch next to Lil Wu. That was the closest to a murder that they've ever been. Leonard stares in front of him with a blank look on his face in a trancelike state. He's in a state of shock as his mind replays the murders over and over. He can still hear the cries of the young boys. Their last facial expressions are stuck in his head. The stomach turning smell of the fresh blood is stuck in his nostrils.

Anthony is on his knees, bent over the toilet, throwing his guts up. Wustafa pats his back, trying to bring him comfort. Wustafa laughs with no compassion at all.

"Go ahead," Wustafa says. "Get it all out. Don't worry it gets easier and easier each time."

CHAPTER 10
TWO DAYS LATER

It's just a typical Sunday here at the headquarters. They're doing what they've been doing ritually every other Sunday since they've formed as a group. The only difference is, this Sunday, Lil Wustafa sits to the side. He listens in on the lessons but can't involve himself.

The alienation from the organization has gotten the best of him. It's been almost three weeks, and Wustafa still hasn't said a word to him. Leonard and Anthony talk to him at school, but, here, they treat him like a total stranger. At first, Lil Wu was angered by it, but, as time crept by, he's begun to understand what it is all about. He's learned a valuable lesson from this. One thing that he knows for certain is, when he finally gets the chance to redeem himself, he will not hesitate in going all the way out. Wustafa knows that as well, which is why he did it in the first place.

Wustafa paces in small circles with his head hanging low. Suddenly, he looks at Leonard. "Leonard, law number five?"

"So much depends on your reputation. Guard it with your life," Leonard replies loudly, clearly, and quickly.

Wustafa nods his head in appreciation. He looks over to Lil Wu.

"You hear that?" he asks as Lil Wu drops his eyes back to the floor.

Lil Wu just absorbs the mockery with a blank look on his face. Over the days, he has gotten quite used to it.

"Law number two, Lamar Watson," Wustafa says.

Lil Wu pops his head up quickly, and his eyes zoom right into his uncle's. The sound of his name catches him by total surprise. He doesn't mind the fact that Wustafa called him by his government name instead of his nickname. He's just happy to be called on. On top of all the other teasing, Wustafa has been calling him by his birth name ever since that night. Just another form of humiliation.

A look of disgust covers Lil Wu's face as he thinks of the law in his mind.

"Never put too much trust in friends," he says as he lowers his head in shame. "Learn to use your enemies."

He drops his head in shame.

"True story," Wustafa says before looking away and taking a few more steps. "Law fifteen, Anthony!" Wustafa shouts.

"Crush your enemy totally!" Anthony replies rapidly.

"I see y'all been studying," Wustafa says with a big smile. "Reading is key. They say, if you want to hide something from a black man, put it in a book. My mental library consists of over 4,000 books," he says as he taps his right temple.

"Reading stimulates the brain and keeps it sharp. All my reading is the reason that I'm standing here today. While others were watching BET music videos and reading urban novels, I spent my time in the law library reading anything that I could get my hands on. And that's why I was able to beat three murders that I was caught dead to the rear on," he brags. "In jail, big time attorneys would visit me and request me to help them with cases. That's how I was able to feed myself in there and also send my family money out here when they needed it. With all of their schooling, I still knew more than them. A man should never stop educating himself. Knowledge is infinite. The more we feed our brains, the stronger they will become. The stronger we are, the more money we will make." He smiles. Then, he says, "Leonard, law number thirty-three!"

"Discover each man's thumbscrew!" Leonard shouts. "Every man has a weakness!"

Wustafa nods his head, followed by a wink of the eye. "Indeed, they do, and it's up to us to find that weakness and capitalize off of it."

CHAPTER 11
SATURDAY 3 P.M.

It's an abnormally hot spring day. It's a record breaking 103°F, 90°F in the shade. The sun beats down on the street vulgarly, almost melting the asphalt. For it to only be the end of May, it feels more like July.

A teenage boy stands in the center of the intersection, looking around attentively as he holds off the traffic coming from both directions. He steps back seconds before a 5 Series BMW comes speeding through the intersection, doing a hundred miles an hour. All the kids on the curb cheer, as if they're at the Indianapolis 500.

The cars at the intersection speed through fearfully, just hoping to get through before the BMW returns. Just as the intersection clears up, the BMW comes back at an even faster speed. All the spectators watch in suspense, wondering what stunt the driver will do next. Just as the car hits the intersection, the driver slams on the brakes, causing the car to hook slide.

The driver proceeds to do doughnuts in the middle of the intersection, circling three times, before peeling off, leaving the intersection smoky and smelling of burnt rubber. Just as the driver is speeding up the block doing eighty-five miles an hour, a pedestrian is crossing the street, not even a half a block in front of him.

The driver slams on the brakes to try and break the speed down. His heart beats with fear as the pedestrian gets closer and closer. The driver skillfully cuts the wheel and swerves around the pedestrian, barely missing him. The pedestrian stands on the yellow line, flagging the driver down, as if he's trying to get him to stop.

The driver skids past him a few feet before the car comes to a complete stop. The kid hangs his head out of the driver's side window.

"You old, dumb motherfucker!" the teenager barks venomously. "Why the fuck you gone stand your goofy-looking ass in the street? You see me out here," he says as if he's supposed to be driving like a maniac.

The man looks at him calmly.

"First of all, watch your mouth when speaking to me," the pedestrian says. "And, second of all, this is a residential area. You have no business speeding up and down this block. I live here," he says as he points to the raggedy little house that sits across the street.

"Who the fuck is you to tell me what the fuck to do? You must don't know who the fuck I am!"

The crowd that has now formed at the scene shoots the young driver's ego to the sky. He feels as if he has something to prove, and he's willing to prove it.

"I have no clue who you are and really I don't care to know," the pedestrian says with a blank look on his face.

"Oooh!" the crowd sings in an attempt to hype up the matter.

Suddenly, the car door pops open, and the kid gets out with a small handgun exposed. He walks toward the pedestrian, expecting the man to show some type of fear, but, to his surprise, he wears the same calm expression. He's now quite confused, not knowing what to do next.

The teenager stops in his tracks after not getting the reaction that he expected.

"Stop running your old-ass mouth before I do something to you," he says as he points the gun in the man's direction. The pedestrian still doesn't flinch. The teenager wears a false sense of confidence, but his ego is crushed.

The pedestrian walks toward the kid. The kid backpedals a few steps nervously.

"I'm telling you, don't walk up on me," he threatens with fear in his eyes.

"Or what?" the man asks.

The kid takes a few more steps and peeks back, only to see that he's trapped with nowhere to go. Leonard, Anthony, and Lil Wu are all stepping behind him.

"Or what?" Wustafa repeats with an evil grin on his face.

They have now formed a circle around the kid. Wustafa stares him in his eyes, piercing the kid's soul.

"You drew. Now, pull the trigger," Wustafa says with an arctic look in his eyes. Wustafa lifts his shirt slightly, allowing the kid to see the .9mm. "If I pull mines out, I'm blasting mines. You don't want that, do you?" he asks with a smirk on his face. The kid looks with fear in his eyes. "Do you?" Wustafa asks as he puts his hand underneath his shirt.

The kid shakes his head. "Nah," he mumbles under his breath.

"I didn't think so," Wustafa says. "I'm not about none of that, but I'm with all of that," he whispers as he lowers his shirt. "Now, put that gun up before it costs you your life. I'm gonna let you slide with that for now," Wustafa says before looking over to the curb full of spectators. "Y'all go on and clear this up. The show is over."

The kids disperse with no backtalk at all.

After the kid tucks his gun, Wustafa extends his hand and say, "I'm Wustafa. What's yours?"

"Speed," the kid replies as he returns the handshake.

"Listen, Speed. Park the car right there outta the way. I got a proposition for you."

The kid gets in the car, but he doesn't park it. He sits in it while double-parked in the middle of the street.

"Dig, you got a lotta talent, but you wasting it speeding up and down the street, showing off for a bunch of nondescripts. Ain't no future in that. All you gonna do is hurt somebody and end up in jail for joyriding. All that talent is senseless if you're not generating a dollar for yourself from it. I got a plan on how you can capitalize off of that talent."

The kid is now all ears. "How?"

Wustafa digs into his pocket as he peeks around cautiously. He peels three hundred dollar bills from his neat stack. He sticks his hands inside of the car and hands the money to the kid.

"Here, this is just a little something to show you that I'm serious and not just blowing smoke. We can make a lotta money together," he says as he swings his hand around the circle, emphasizing all of them. "Take that three hundred. It's yours. Park that around the corner and walk back around here and politic with me. Alright?"

The kid looks at Wustafa with confusion on his face. He's gone from about to kill him to talking business. He's not sure if he should even trust him.

"Alright," he replies hesitantly.

He cruises off while the crew watches him ride away.

Wustafa and the crew cross the street, walking toward the porch of the headquarters.

"You should've rode with him," Leonard says. "What if he don't come back and just beat you for three hundred dollars?"

"If he doesn't come back, I just bought his life for a lousy three hundred bucks," Wustafa says with no sign of emotion on his face. "Simple as that."

CHAPTER 12
THE NEXT DAY

Another Sunday at the headquarters. All are present except Anthony. It's not like him to miss a meeting, so all are quite curious as to why he's absent. He's normally the first one to report for every meeting, but, even in his absence, the show must go on though.

The apartment is pitch dark, peaceful, and serene. Wustafa lays back on his cot, in total relaxation mode. Lil Wu and Leonard sit back in their seats as well with their eyes closed. The sound of Narrator Don Leslie's voice seeps through the stereo, soothing their ears. They listen and attempt to memorize *The 33 Strategies of War* as he not only reads them off but breaks each one down so that even a small child can comprehend.

"Create a threatening presence," the narrator says crisp and clear. "Deterrence, build a reputation for being a little crazy, where fighting you is not worth it. Uncertainty can be better than an explicit threat. If your opponents aren't sure what attacking will cost, they will not want to find out," he says before a tapping on the door sounds off. Their concentration is broken, and they all open their eyes on alert.

They all sit up with caution in their eyes until they hear their secret knock. They exhale with ease, knowing that it can only be Anthony. Wustafa gets up from the cot and shuts off the stereo before making his way over to the door. He opens it with his face showing agitation. To his surprise, he finds Anthony standing in the rain accompanied by another. Wustafa can't really see the other person's face on account of the big hood, which covers the individual's head.

"Peace," Anthony greets.

Wustafa replies only with a head nod.

"Peace," Anthony repeats.

Wustafa looks him square in the eyes.

"You know I will never greet you with peace if I'm not at peace," he says as he looks the person over from head to toe. "What's up? Who is this that you are accompanied by?"

"This is one of my best friends that I want to talk to you about bringing into the organization."

"Step inside," Wustafa says as he points to Anthony. "Excuse us one second," he says as he slams the door in the face of the person. Wustafa stares coldly into Anthony's eyes. "You break my peace by bringing a stranger to my rest? You should get a man's permission before bringing a guest to his home. Not invite them yourself. A man's home is sacred. Never ever bring a stranger to my rest," he says with rage in his eyes.

"Sorry, I know, but this isn't a stranger. It's my best friend since kindergarten."

"So, you trust this person?"

"With anything I have, even my life," Anthony says with sincerity in his voice.

Wustafa pulls the door open slowly.

"Come in." Wustafa closes the door and leads the way. "This way."

Anthony takes a seat and so does his guest.

"Ah hah," Wustafa says. "You don't take a seat in my house until I offer you a seat. Stand right here," he says as he points to the area next to the coffee table. The crew observes their guest closely.

"The first thing that I'm gonna need you to do is to remove that hood," Wustafa says as he draws his gun. "You're making me nervous, sitting in my house with a hood on your head. Where are your manners? Take the hood off and state your name and your reason for being here."

They all watch with full attention as the individual slowly removes the hood. To their surprise, thick curls bounce as her hair lands on her shoulders. The young girl snaps her head back to remove the long hair from her face. They look her up and down, in total shock. Dressed in a black hoodie, black cargo pants, and black boots, it's hard to recognize that this is a female. They all now pay attention to the voluptuous curves that are hidden under the baggy attire.

"My name is Sameerah, and I'm here because I want to be a part of the organization," she says loud and clear with no sign of nervousness.

Wustafa looks at the members of the crew with a smile before looking at the girl.

"So, you think you want to be a part of this organization? What makes you think that you have what it takes? Do you even know what we are all about?"

"I don't think I want to be a part of it," she says. "I know or else I wouldn't be here. And I, also, know I have what it takes because I know me," she says with her lips puckered up sassy-like.

"I like your quick answers," Wustafa says. "Makes me think you know exactly what you want. How old are you?"

"I'm fifteen, going on sixteen," she replies quickly.

"As you see, there are no girls in this organization. I'm not sure if you can handle all that's required to be a part of this organization. Don't think that, because you are a girl, you will get special treatment. Every person in this organization is required to hold his or her own weight."

"Don't look at me as a girl," she replies. "Block that out and accept me for me. Just give me a chance. If it don't seem like I can handle it, kick me out."

"So, you mean like a probationary period?"

"Exactly," she replies.

"You know what?" Wustafa says. "I'm gonna honor that."

His mind races, thinking of all of the advantages there are to having a female member. He thinks of how easy it will be for such a beautiful and innocent looking girl to get in certain situations that they would never be able to get into.

"We have room for another member." Then, Wustafa looks at each of the members and says, "All in favor? Anyone have anything against my decision, speak now."

No one says a word. They shrug their shoulders with uncertain looks on their faces.

"Okay. You're in but on a probationary basis. Make the cut, and you're all the way in, or fall short, and you're out. Fair enough?" he asks.

"Fair enough!" she agrees.

"Just like that?" Leonard asks with attitude. "We all had to be initiated in, and you're gonna give her special treatment because she's a girl? How do we even know that she can be trusted?"

Sameerah looks at Leonard with hatred.

"He's right," Wustafa says. "It wouldn't be fair to bring you in just like that when all of them have given something up."

"What do I have to give up then?"

Wustafa looks at his crew, who all seem to have the same thing in mind, except for Anthony. Lust is clearly evident in their eyes. Lil Wu and Leonard stare her up and down with perversion.

"Oh, nah. I know what y'all thinking. Y'all ain't fucking me in," she says with massive attitude.

"The language," Wustafa interrupts. "We don't use profanity. Only people of limited vocabulary use profanity as a way to get their point across."

"I apologize, but I know they didn't have to fuck to be in, and I ain't getting fucked to be in. Sorry, again," she says with no sincerity.

She rolls her eyes away from them and focuses on Wustafa. She looks at him with a look of confidence in her eyes.

"Just 'cause I'm a girl, they trying to pull that on me. Fuck that. I bring more than that to the table. I know I'm more gangster than either one of them!" she says as she points to them and looks them up and down with disgust. "I beg you not to let me in because they want to have sex from me. Bring me in for what I can do for the organization. I guarantee you, I got way more heart than them, and I'm way more gangster than them! Just let me prove it to you! That's all I ask."

Wustafa looks at her with a smile on his face. He likes her spunk and her attitude and believes he can channel that energy into something fierce.

He replies, "You said you want the chance to prove yourself? Well, you will have your chance, and then we all will see what you're really made of."

CHAPTER 13
FRIDAY 11:12 P.M.

Wustafa and the crew step out of the door of the headquarters into the alley. All of their hands are covered by white latex gloves. They walk to the backyard where the stolen Cherokee Sport is parked. The Jeep is courtesy of Speed.

Speed trots to the driver's side. Leonard opens the back door on the driver's side and slides in. Anthony, Lil Wu, and Sameerah all stand there in confusion, wondering how all of them will fit inside. Wustafa looks at them and gives them a solution to their problem.

"Lamar Watson to the back," he says as he points to the back of the Jeep.

He walks to the back and lifts the hatch open. With agitation on his face, Lil Wu climbs into the hatch and squeezes into the tiny cramped space. Wustafa slams it shut and walks away, leaving Lil Wu watching him through the dark tinted glass. As dark as the glass is, Wustafa can still feel the hatred penetrating through the glass.

Sameerah slides into the middle seat before Anthony gets in and slams the door shut. Wustafa takes the front seat. After closing the door, he straps the seatbelt over his chest. Speed looks over at Wustafa as he's starting the Jeep. He falls out in laughter for seconds.

Wustafa looks over at him with a clueless look on his face. "What?"

"You really putting a seatbelt on in a stolen car? I never seen that before," he says while laughing hard. "You breaking the law by being in a stolen car, but you follow the law by putting your seatbelt on? Crazy!"

Wustafa turns away with attitude. "It's not about breaking the law. It's about my safety."

Speed cruises down the narrow alley. As soon as he reaches the street, he turns wildly onto it, making the tires screech loudly. He reaches for the volume and blasts the stereo. His favorite song rips through the speakers. Wustafa braces himself in the seat by holding on and gripping the side.

He looks over at Speed with his eyes damn near popping out of his head with fear.

"Yo! Slow down," he pleads. "Take it easy, will you?"

"What's wrong? Why you acting so scary?"

"You don't have to drive like that," Wustafa says.

"That's how I drive," Speed claims.

"That's how you drive when you joyriding, but, right now, you're working. You're gonna have to drive like you got some sense. Can you do that?"

"I don't know," Speed answers honestly. "Never did."

Wustafa shuts the stereo off. "And how do you concentrate with all that hippity-hop stuff banging in your ears?"

"That's how I concentrate. The music gets me going."

"Well, it breaks my concentration. We are working, and I need to concentrate to get the job done properly. I need to think."

"So, we just supposed to ride in quiet?" Speed asks.

Wustafa looks at him with a solemn look on his face. "Yeah."

For twenty minutes, they ride in complete silence, and Speed hates every second of it. He's never driven under these conditions. He feels like he's taking a driving exam. Wustafa has him cruising the streets moderately, stopping at stop signs and actually obeying traffic signals.

Wustafa sits firmly in his seat, hands gripping the chair tightly. He stares straight ahead, holding his head erect. His tension can be felt throughout the Jeep. At every corner, his foot damn near bangs through the floor as he steps down every time he thinks Speed should hit the brakes.

"Whoa, whoa!" Wustafa shouts fearfully. "You don't see that car in front of you?"

"Yo! I can't do this!" Speed furiously shouts. "That car's a half a block away! I see it! You drive since you think you can drive better than me," Speed says as he pulls over on Martin Luther King Jr. Boulevard in Jersey City. He opens the door. "You take the wheel!"

Wustafa looks at him with a terrified look on his face.

"Nah, nah," he stutters. "You drive. That's what you do."

The crew is shocked at how Speed is talking to Wustafa. They sit back, waiting for the repercussions, but, to their surprise, there aren't any. For the first time ever, they witness him in submission.

Speed rolls his eyes as he shakes his head from side to side. He slams the door closed.

"Well, sit back and be quiet and let me do what I do," Speed says as he slams the gear shift into drive and mashes the gas pedal to the floor. He speeds through the street recklessly as Wustafa sits quietly in his seat as he's been instructed to do. He sits there as stiff as a statue.

After ten minutes of riding in silence on high alert, Wustafa finally speaks.

"Right there," he says as he points up ahead at a young man who stands in the doorway in the middle of the block. "He just made a sale. See the lady walking away from him?"

As they approach the young man, his eyes are buried into the huge wad of money that he counts through.

"Right there?" Speed questions.

"Yep," Wustafa confirms.

"Say no more!" Speed replies anxiously.

"Anthony, he on your side. It's on you. You ready?"

Anthony says not a word. The sound of one being slid into the chamber confirms that he's ready. He quickly grabs hold of the door handle, just waiting for the moment. Suddenly, Speed mashes the gas pedal and busts a wild turn onto the sidewalk. Anthony forces the door open and hops out just as the young man looks up.

The young man stands there, frozen stiff, as Anthony runs over to him with his gun aimed.

"You know what it is!" he shouts as he snatches the money from his hand.

Anthony shoves him into the door and immediately starts checking his pockets. He finds another wad of money in his back pocket.

"Lay down!" Anthony demands, while aiming his gun at the young man's head. The young man dives onto the ground without wasting a second. Anthony backpedals all the way to the Jeep with his gun still aimed. He backs into the seat, and, before he can even close the door, Speed backs off of the sidewalk and peels off.

Not even five minutes pass before Wustafa has his eyes on more prey.

"Look. The corner to the left," Wustafa says as he points up ahead.

At the corner, not even a half a block away, two young men stand in front of a chicken shack. "Leonard, you're up."

Leonard sits on the edge of his seat at the sound of his name. He grabs his gun from his lap and prepares for his attack. Speed turns the lights off and cruises with moderation, trying not to bring attention to themselves. As soon as Speed hits the intersection, he swerves to the left.

The Jeep bounces onto the sidewalk. The nose of the vehicle has them damn near pinned against the wall. Leonard jumps out of the backseat. Before he can even get both feet onto the ground, both men take off running in different directions.

Leonard stands there, confused. He's not sure if Wustafa would want him to chase after them or let them go. He stands there for a few more seconds before aiming at one of the moving targets. He aims, holds his breath, and squeezes.

Boc!

The sound of gunfire only makes the young man run faster.

"Let him go!" Wustafa shouts from the passenger's seat.

Leonard runs back to the Jeep, full of discouragement. He closes the door and hangs his head low. Feeling like a total failure, he waits to hear what Wustafa has to say. He's sure that he's quite disgusted with him.

Wustafa looks into the backseat.

"We're not going to get them all," he says. "There will be more to get. The night is young."

CHAPTER 14
TWO HOURS LATER/1:15 A.M.

After over two hours of work and about ten consecutive vicks, Wustafa feels it's time to make their way back to Newark. He feels they should end their spree even though they haven't scored anywhere near what he projected to score for the night. He's sure the word has been spread throughout the city that they're out here lurking. He, also, figures anybody who's still on the streets at this point will be ready for them and make their job harder. More importantly, he's sure that the police are out in search of them by now.

"Hold! Hold!" Wustafa shouts. "Y'all saw that?"

He looks over to Speed as he sits on the edge of his seat, looking over his shoulder.

"Come back around the block."

Speed circles the block, while anxiety fills all of their guts. They wonder what it is that Wustafa saw that sparked his interest like that. He hasn't been this excited all night.

"Stop at the corner. Don't turn," he instructs.

Speed stops at the corner, while Wustafa peeks up the block. They all look up ahead at the brightly lit canopy which reads RINGSIDE.

"See up there? That's a sports bar where all the Big Willies be," Wustafa says with a devious grin. "Look at the dude standing in the front. When we rode by, I saw a lotta ice. Let's defrost him. Melt him right on down."

The man stands there with his ear glued to the phone. His jewelry glistens brightly for over a half a block. Adrenaline races throughout their veins. Leonard and Anthony draw their weapons and prepare to go to work. Wustafa looks into the backseat in between the both of them.

"Sameerah, you said to 'give you a chance' to prove to us what you're made of. Here's your chance."

Sameerah's heart starts to bang through her chest. Wustafa snatches his gun from his waistband and hands it to her. As she grips the cold steel in her hand, her heart begins to pound harder.

"Anthony, let her out."

As Anthony gets out, Sameerah holds the gun, pointed to ceiling.

"Is it one in the chamber already?" she asks nervously.

"Mines always got one in the chamber and off of safety, so be careful."

"We going with her?" Leonard asks.

"Nah, she handling this one on her own," Wustafa says with a cold look in his eyes.

Hearing that makes Sameerah even more than nervous. She's now terrified. She slides out of the seat. She snatches her baseball cap off of her head and drops it onto the floor. Her big curls bounce onto her shoulders. She quickly snatches her hood sweater off and throws it back into the Jeep. She brushes her fingers through her hair to bring life to it. She looks herself up and down.

"I'm good to go?" she asks as she looks at Wustafa for his approval.

"Good to go," he confirms. "Look. We are right here if you need us," he says in an attempt to build her confidence. "And remember your initiation rides on this."

"Got you," she replies as she tucks the gun into the pockets of her cargo pants and starts walking toward the corner.

They all watch in amazement as she makes the transition from tomboy to sexy right before their very eyes. She switches with a sexy aura that they have never seen before. The curves that she manages to conceal normally now reveal themselves with each ground shaking step that she takes. For the first time ever, since they laid eyes on her, they're reminded that she's a *girl*.

"Bend the corner and be ready to go, just in case we need to bail her out," Wustafa instructs.

Sameerah's adrenaline is pumping, and her heart is simultaneously racing with fear. She understands that everything is riding on her performance. With that being understood, she plans to go all out and make a lasting impression on Wustafa.

The closer she gets to her prey, the harder her heart beats. Finally, she gets within a hundred feet of him. She gives him a quick and discreet look from head to toe. He appears to be in his mid- twenties. Just as Wustafa stated, his neck and wrists are as icy as a deep freezer.

As he talks with the phone glued to his ear, he takes a long look at her. Sameerah lowers her head with her normal, shy demeanor. She peeks up and notices him walking toward the convertible Mercedes sitting on chrome rims. As Sameerah gets closer, she hears the quiet engine purring like a kitten. The young man walks over to the driver's side, snatches the door open, and stands there while continuing on with his conversation.

Sameerah quickly tries to put a plan together in her head, but her thoughts are suddenly interrupted.

"Got damn, lil shorty! You thick as shit," he says as he looks her up and down perversely. "Yo, let me hit you right back, my nigga," he barks into the phone before ending the call.

He walks in front of Sameerah, cutting off her path.

"What's your name?" he asks.

Sameerah looks away from him, totally ignoring him. She attempts to walk around him, but he steps in front of her again.

"Damn, shorty! Why you being so rude?" he asks as he grabs her hand.

She stops with a look of aggravation on her face. She places her other hand on her hip as she looks down at their clasped hands.

"Could you let my hand go, please?" she says with sassiness.

"Nope, not till you tell me your name," he says with a charming smile. "You a bad lil motherfucker. How old are you?"

"Too young for you," she replies.

"How you know that?" he asks. "How old are you?"

"Sixteen," she replies.

"Got dammit," he says with a smile.

"See, I told you I was too young for you," she says as she cracks the very first smile of their brief conversation. "Now, let my hand go before I have you arrested. I am jail bait, you know?" she says with a seductive look in her eyes.

"Age ain't nothing but a number. You may be young, but you're ready," he sings in his best Keith Sweat impersonation. "Ready to learn," he adds as he swings her hand and pinches her cheek. This puts a big smile on Sameerah's face.

"Where you headed, though, lil shorty? Let me take you there. It's too late for your lil ass to be out here traveling by yourself."

"Nah, I'm good. I'll be alright," she says as she peeks at her surroundings. She realizes that she has spent way too much time here as is, but she doesn't know exactly how to make her move. She steps away from him. "Nice meeting you, though."

"Hold up! Hold up, shorty! Don't just leave like that. Let me, at least, get your number."

Sameerah stops short.

"Give me your number, and I will put it in my phone," she says as she looks around cautiously.

"Alright. Where your phone at?" he asks anxiously.

"Hold your horses, Mr. Impatient," she says with a bright smile as she digs into her pocket. She grips the .9mm in her hand tightly as her heart pounds through her chest. She quickly pulls the gun from her pocket and aims it at his throat.

"You know what it is," she says with a fierce look in her eyes.

She's expecting him to fold and show fear. Instead, he flashes a goofy smile. He pauses to see if this is part of a joke. He looks around before speaking.

"Shorty, knock it off. You kidding me, right?"

"I'm dead-ass serious," she says while peeking around. She now aims the gun at his face while reaching for his necklace.

"Run that chain!"

He backs away from her, while smacking her hand down to prevent her from touching his necklace. Sameerah peeks over her shoulder quickly, and, before she knows it, she's mashed the trigger.

Boc!

The sound of gunfire brings alarm to Wustafa.

"Go! Go!" he shouts to Speed.

His heart races, not knowing what's to come next. Speed steps on the gas pedal and reaches the scene in no time. Just as Wustafa is about to hop out, he realizes that Sameerah has the situation under total control.

Sameerah looks at her prey who stumbles backwards. He falls against the wall before sliding down it slowly. He stares into her eyes with a delirious look in his. Sameerah snatches the chain from his neck. She peeks around once again before dumping one more into his face.

Boc!

She trots a step or two before running back over to the man who lies there, squirming in a pool of blood. She snatches his car keys from the ground next to him. She races to the Mercedes, snatches the door open and hops in.

Just as she's pulling off in the Mercedes, she hears someone yell, "Yo! Somebody call 911!"

She looks over her shoulder and sees that the front of the bar is engulfed with people. The sound of the gunshots must have brought them all outside.

Sameerah cuts in front of the Cherokee her crew is in and mashes the gas pedal, leaving them in the dust. She extends her hand high out of the window, signaling for them to follow her.

"Oh, my God!" Wustafa says in a hyped manner that they've never gotten from him. "Did y'all see her in action? Now, that's how it's supposed to be done! No instructions or nothing. She played it all by ear. I hope all y'all was watching because y'all can learn a thing or two from her."

Thirty Minutes Later

Wustafa examines the necklace carefully as the crew sits back, awaiting his response.

"This chain has to be worth, at least, a hundred and fifty grand," he says as he looks at Sameerah. A tapping of the door interrupts Wustafa. Wustafa looks over at Anthony. "Open the door for Speed."

Anthony opens the door, and Speed walks in, juggling the keys to the Mercedes. Wustafa looks at him with concern and asks, "What you do with it?"

"I stashed it in my secret spot," he replies.

"You sure no one will find it?"

"Positive," Speed replies confidently. "First thing in the morning, we will go over to Elizabeth and get rid of it."

"How much you think they will give us for it?" Wustafa asks with greed in his eyes.

"At least, five thousand," Speed replies. "I'm gonna tell them the rims ain't for sell, and we can sell those on the street for another three thousand."

Wustafa nods his head, satisfied. "What they gonna do with a stolen car?"

"They ship them over to other countries. I dump all my exotic cars there."

"Oh, yeah?" Wustafa asks as his eyes light up. "That's good to know." Wustafa switches his attention over to Sameerah. "Excuse my French because I never use profanity," he says in an apologetic tone. "But you a cold-ass bitch," he says with a smile. "Your first score, and you scored the biggest."

Sameerah turns her head as she blushes from ear to ear. She looks back up him and asks, "So, am I in?"

"In there like swimwear," he says, sounding corny.

Sameerah jumps up for joy.

"Yeah," she says as she points down to Leonard and Lil Wu who sit side by side. "I told y'all motherfuckers I was bringing more than pussy to the table. Now, motherfuckers!"

CHAPTER 15
THE NEXT DAY

Lil Wu and Speed step into the headquarters, and Wustafa shuts the door behind them. Leonard, Anthony, and Sameerah all lounge around quietly. Speed drops a mound of money onto the coffee table, and all their eyes zoom in on it.

"So, how we make out?" Wustafa asks as he stares deep into Speed's eyes.

"Five large," Speed replies. "Just as I figured."

"Is that so?" Wustafa asks as he peeks over at his nephew Lil Wu.

Lil Wu turns away and becomes quite fidgety. Lil Wu's body language sends off a signal that something isn't right.

"Yep," Speed says with a straight face, while looking Wustafa dead in the eyes.

Wustafa stares back, studying his eyes and his body language. Speed stands there firm and confident with sincerity in his eyes. Speed's aura is completely different from Lil Wu's. This baffles Wustafa. He feels that he must get to the bottom of what's going.

Wustafa quickly counts through the money and divides it all up accordingly. After it's divided, Wustafa holds fifteen hundred dollars in his hand.

"For the organization," he says as he holds the money high in the air for them all to see. "Lil Wu, do me a favor and go in the bathroom and look under the sink. Grab that box of rubber bands for me."

Lil Wu takes off and disappears into the bathroom.

After a few seconds, he shouts out, "Where at? I don't see them!"

"Right there in your face," Wustafa shouts back.

"Nah," Lil Wu denies.

"Phew," Wustafa sighs. "If you want something done right, you have to do it yourself," he says as he makes his way toward the bathroom.

The group begins to indulge in meaningless conversation just as Wustafa steps into the bathroom. Lil Wu is bent over looking underneath the cabinet when Wustafa taps him on the back.

"I still don't see it," Lil Wu says as he stands up.

"Shhh," Wustafa whispers as he presses his index finger against his lips. "What's up? Everything alright?" Wustafa whispers. "You're acting strange."

"Yeah, everything cool," Lil Wu replies while looking away from Wustafa.

Wustafa steps close enough to Lil Wu that they could kiss.

"So, five grand is what they gave him?" Wustafa asks. He goes in straight for the kill with no further hesitation.

Lil Wu shakes his head and answers, "I wasn't gonna say nothing because I didn't want you to label me a stool pigeon. And I know how you feel about stool pigeons, but Speed don't know that I know they gave him seven thousand for the car."

"Oh, yeah?" Wustafa asks with a shocked expression on his face. Wustafa leans closer to the doorway before yelling out, "I'm sure that I put the box in here somewhere!" He, then, leans back closer to Lil Wu and says, "Yes, indeed. I despise stool pigeons, but this is different. We are supposed to be a team, but, if it comes down to it, it's me and you against them. It's about us. Don't you ever forget that. We are family, and we should never let one of them," he says as he points to the wall behind him, "get one over on us. Never," he adds. "If you didn't tell me, I would look at you totally different. If he will steal from the team, there's no telling what else he will do."

"When it was time to break off the money, he stepped outta the room, so I wouldn't see how much they were giving him. He still don't know that I heard the man counting the money out loud. Please don't tell him," he begs. "I don't want the rest of the crew to think I'm a tattle-tale snitch."

"I would never throw you under the bus," Wustafa claims.

He slowly turns around, facing the doorway. He looks out at Speed, staring at him with frustration in his eyes. What bothers him the most isn't the money that he's stashed away from them. It's the principle of it all. The fact that Speed is capable of lying to him with a straight face and eye contact bothers him. He's usually great at reading body language, but Speed would've been able to throw him off if it wasn't for Lil Wu's uneasy body language. That means one of two things. Either his senses are staggering with his old age, or Speed is just that good at deception.

"This will stay between us," Wustafa says. "It's good to know that he can't be trusted. That's half of the battle. Now, I know to keep my eyes on him," he says as he taps his glasses. "All four of them."

CHAPTER 16
LATER THAT NIGHT/ 11:17 A.M.

The pearl white BMW stops short at the intersection here on Irvine Turner Boulevard just as the light changes from yellow to red. The driver looks over to his female passenger.

"You shot the fuck out," he says with a charming smile.

Just as he looks up at the light, he sees a black Jeep bouncing wildly toward him in the intersection. The element of surprise leaves him no time at all to react. The Jeep cuts him off, and both of the back doors pop open. The sight of the chrome handguns paralyzes him with fear.

Leonard runs over to the driver's side with his gun aimed at the windshield, while Anthony runs to the passenger's side. Leonard snatches the door open and drags the man out of the car. Anthony flings the girl out of the passenger's seat with very little energy. Sameerah dives into the driver's seat and pulls the door shut.

Speed backs the Jeep up a little to give her enough space to pass, and she does. As the BMW races up the block, Anthony and Leonard backpedal to the Jeep, leaving the man and his female passenger lying in the middle of the street, face down. They hop into the Jeep, and Speed peels off recklessly.

"I told y'all this is as easy as taking candy from a baby!" Wustafa shouts from the passenger seat of the Jeep. "As long as these niggas buying these fancy cars, we're gonna have us some money! At six grand a pop," Wustafa says with sarcasm as he stares at Speed.

He clearly knows that the car was sold for seven grand. He just threw six out there to see how Speed reacts. Plus, he knows that, if he says seven, Speed will know that Lil Wu must have given him up. Speed sits up tensely at the sound of six grand. His guilt shines through.

"I mean, five grand a pop. That's mo money, mo money!" he sings. "And mo money!"

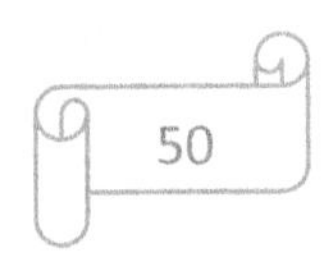

Deep down inside, he's infuriated at Speed for getting over on them.

CHAPTER 17
ONE HOUR LATER

Lil Wu steps quietly into his room a few minutes after his curfew. Up until just recently, he's always adhered to his curfew, but, since running around with the crew, he's deviated. Several warnings have been given to him by his mother along with a few threats. Tonight, he practically begged Wustafa to excuse him early on account that he didn't want to hear his mother's fussing tonight.

Wustafa would have excused him with no problem at all if he had known that his being out late was causing a problem, but he didn't know. The last thing that he wants is to his hear his sister's mouth as well. Lil Wu has been keeping it from Wustafa out of shame. He is embarrassed to admit it in front of the crew that he has a curfew.

Wustafa explains that they had a long night ahead of them. The carjacking is only the start of the night. It is then that Lil Wu realizes that he must speak up. The last thing he wants is to be many miles away because it will take him forever to get home. That will be automatic trouble at home. Luckily, for him, he makes it home just a few minutes after curfew.

Lil Wu reaches into his pocket and grabs the few dollars that he has folded neatly inside. He, then, bends over and reaches underneath the bed and grabs hold of a sneaker box that sits at the far end. He opens the box, and, to his surprise, it's completely empty. He stands there in confusion for a few seconds, wondering where his money could be.

"Looking for this?" Lil Wu's mother asks from the doorway of his room.

Lil Wu turns around slowly. His facial expression turns sour as his eyes set onto the few stacks of money that she holds in her hand. He, immediately, lowers his eyes onto the floor. His mother walks up to him quickly. She doesn't stop until she bumps into him, breasts against his chest. He backs up until his back touches the wall. Finally, he looks up at her with a scared and goofy look on his face.

"What?"

"What?" she repeats sarcastically. "You know what. Explain this money to me. That's what. Where did you get this money from? I'm the only one in this house with a job, and I don't have this much money saved up. I work fifty-five, sometimes sixty, hours a week, and, still, I live from paycheck to paycheck. I give you an allowance of fifty dollars every two weeks. Now, if you've managed to save up three thousand dollars from the fifty dollars I give you twice a month, I need to know your secret," she says as she stares into his eyes, awaiting an answer.

Lil Wu stands there with not a single answer for her. This has caught him totally off guard. Nothing he can think of will justify this amount of money.

"Hmphh," he sighs just because he can't think of anything else to do or say.

"Well, I'm waiting," she says as she puts one hand onto her hip. "Where did you get this money?"

Lil Wu shakes his head from side to side for seconds before the words exit his mouth.

"It's not mines," he whispers. This is the only thing that he can think to say.

He knows that she will next ask him whose it is. He needed something to tell her just to buy himself some time. He hasn't predetermined an answer for whose it is, but he's playing it as it comes.

His time clock runs out quickly.

"Well, whose is it?" she asks.

"Huh?" he asks as if he didn't hear her.

"If you can huh, you can hear," she says sarcastically. "You heard me perfectly well. Last time I checked, you were not hard of hearing. If it's not yours, whose is it, and why is it under your bed?"

"It's Leonard's," he lies. "He, he, he asked me to hold it for him."

"Why are you stuttering? Why can't he hold his own money? And where did he get three thousand dollars from?"

Lil Wu realizes that saying it's Leonard's money is the equivalent of owning up to it himself. With them being together every day, she knows for certain that whatever Leonard is involved in, so is he. He is really left with no choice. The last thing he can tell her is that the money belongs to Wustafa because he knows all hell will break loose from there.

Lil Wu shrugs his shoulder slowly.

"I, I don't know," he whispers.

"You're a bold faced lie!"

"I'm not lying. It is his."

"I will not tolerate any more of this from you. I have never had a problem with you lying to me or going against my rules until you started hanging out with that no good uncle of yours. I will not watch you throw away your life like Grover did. If this is Leonard's money, then I'm ordering you to give it to him and let him hold his own damn money. This ain't no damn bank over here!" she shouts, enraged. "And, as far as that uncle of yours, if you keep on following him around, both of you will end up in the same jail cell together," she says as the tears creep into her eyes. "I promise you one thing. You end up in jail, and you can bet your bottom dollar that I will not be there to visit you. My name will never be on another prison list," she says as she taps her chest. "Not even for my own son's, so don't even count on it or even call on me to come get you. I will disown you just as I have disowned him many years ago. This is my first and only warning to you. I pray to God that you take heed."

CHAPTER 18
TWO DAYS LATER/ JUNE 3RD 2002

It's eleven in the morning, and Wustafa sits in the room with the shades drawn tight, so no sun can peek inside. He sits in the corner of the dark room in complete silence. He's in the corner, eyes closed, and legs crossed in a yoga position. Every morning, before he starts his day, he indulges in deep meditation. This has been his practice for the past ten years. His motto is, "A man will never find peace in anything until he finds peace within himself".

Suddenly, his soul is awakened by a tapping on the door. His eyes pop open, and he sits on alert until the secret knock sounds off. He's reminded of his age as he attempts to pop up from the floor. He fails on the first attempt but finds success in his second attempt.

He walks over to the door and opens it slowly. He's greeted by his favorite girl, Sameerah. "Peace," she greets with a saddened look on her face.

"Peace," he replies as he opens the door and welcomes her in.

Sameerah drags into the apartment and plops onto the couch with her head hanging low. "What's up, Babygirl?" he asks as he stands over her.

"Nothing new," she says as she reaches over and grabs the television remote. She presses the power button. "The same old shit. My fiend-ass mother getting on my fucking nerves as usual," she says as she flicks through the channels.

Wustafa places his hands over his ears until she finishes speaking.

"Your mouth, Babygirl, is filthy," he says with sternness in his eyes. "I don't need all that negativity in my spirit this early in the morning."

"Sorry," she apologizes with no sincerity at all.

Wustafa reaches over and snatches the remote from her hand.

"Oh, no," he says as he shuts the power off. "We don't do the idiot box in here. All the times you been in here, have you ever seen it on?"

Sameerah shrugs her shoulders. "I don't know."

"Never," he barks. "I never indulge in such foolishness. The only reason it's in here is because it came with the apartment. I use it for decoration," he says as he rubs his hand over the old thirteen inch screen. "You can't trust anything on the boob tube, not even the news. The media uses television to control our mindset and our way of thinking. It's all mind games that I refuse to have played with my mind."

Sameerah looks at him with confusion on her face. All that he's saying is going way over her head. "Oh, okay. I just wanted to watch Maury," she says with a look of innocence on her face.

Wustafa throws the remote onto the couch and asks, "What's up with your mother, though?"

"Tripping, as usual. She knows I got a couple of dollars, and she will beg and beg until there's no more left. I'm not selfish! I take care of my lil sisters whenever I can. I bought them sneakers, and I been feeding them every night," she says as the tears build up in her eyes. "She called me selfish. I'm not selfish. I'm just not spending my money on drugs for her fiend ass! I hate her!"

"Hate is a strong word, Babygirl. You don't hate her; you just dislike her ways."

"No, I hate her! You don't know the half. I just can't wait to get eighteen, so I can get the fuck outta there and take my little sisters with me. They been through too much already. I have to save them before they are fucked up in the game like me," she says as the tears now drip down her face.

Seeing her like this touches Wustafa's heart. He stands there, confused, not knowing what to do. He feels compassion for her but doesn't know how to show it. He's been hiding his emotions so long that he can't tap into them even if he tries. He pats her on her head like a puppy and reassures her, saying, "Don't worry, Babygirl. It's gonna be alright."

Sameerah wipes her eyes dry, sucks up her sympathy, and holds her head high.

"I know," she sniffs. "I know it's gonna be alright because I'm gonna make it more than alright. I have no choice. My little sisters are depending on me," she says as she wipes her nose on her sleeve. "So, what we into today?" she asks as she tries to change the subject. She's

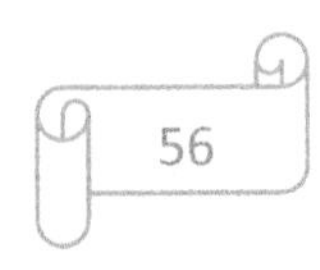

now embarrassed that he's seen this side of her and wishes she could take it all back.

"Haven't put a plan together yet. Wait a minute. It's nine in the morning," he says with a look of agitation on his face. "Why aren't you in school?"

She shrugs her shoulders and puckers her lips. "I don't know."

"You don't know? You know everything else. Why don't you know the answer to that?"

"I just stopped going," she whispers.

"What you mean 'stopped going'? Stopped when?"

"I don't know," she says with attitude. "Like last year."

"Last year!" Wustafa repeats hysterically. "How you just gonna stop going to school? So, you just stopped educating yourself? Technology advances every second. How do you plan to keep up with the rest of the world when you already a year behind?" he asks with the first sign of emotion that he's displayed throughout the entire conversation. "A woman with no education will get nowhere in this world, Babygirl. With no education, you will be forced to submit to a good for nothing nigga who knows you need him, and, because he knows that, you will be forced to accept whatever he feeds you."

"I ain't accepting shit nobody feed me!" she interrupts. "I don't need no fucking nigga! I been feeding myself since I was twelve fucking years old!" she barks. "I ain't never gon' depend on a nigga for shit!" she spits with determination in her eyes.

"I'm gonna make sure of that," he says as he sits on the edge of his cot, putting his shoes on his feet. He gets up and snatches his keys from the table. "Come on, Babygirl," he says as he leads the way out of the door.

"Where are we going?" she asks. Wustafa ignores her as he steps through the alley.

"Where are we going?" she asks again as she trots, in attempt to catch up with him.

****One Hour Later****

Wustafa and Sameerah sit inside of the principal's office here in West Side High School.

"I'm sorry that I can't get her enrolled into the regular school curriculum, but her tardiness and excessive absences leave her no other option but night school. Sorry," the principal apologizes as she looks over at Sameerah, who rolls her eyes with disgust. "If you would have come a few months earlier, maybe, I could have done better, but, with the school year over in a few days, it's rough. She can just attend night school over the summer months, and, depending on how well she does, maybe, we can get her on the regular roster."

"I totally understand," Wustafa replies politely. "But as I've stated, I take full responsibility for her behavior. My unfortunate situation has affected her in more ways than I knew, but the lesson has been learned on my part, and I can assure you that this will not be the case in the future. I'm home now," he says with a smile.

"We have been reunited for a little more than three weeks now," he says. "I'm in her life to stay, and we will pick up the pieces. Right, daughter?" he asks as he looks over at Sameerah, who totally ignores him. He places his hand on her shoulder and asks again, "Right, daughter?"

Sameerah looks at him with a sarcastic smile before rolling her eyes away from him in disgust.

"I sure hope so," the principal says. "She's such a bright, young woman. She grasps everything all so well. I see she's a straight A, B student and excels when she's present. She has such a bright future ahead of her if only she would come to school and apply herself."

"And that she will do," Wustafa says with great confidence. "I promise you that."

CHAPTER 19
TWO WEEKS LATER

Sameerah sits in the passenger's seat of the Acura Legend. She stuffs her mouth with French fries as the driver cruises along Central Avenue in Newark. The driver is a young man she met a few days ago while walking home from school. He called her a few hours ago practically begging to see her. She was under the impression that he came here all the way from Plainfield just to see her, but she now realizes that he has other business here.

"What's up, though? What you got planned for the rest of the day?" he asks as he looks over at her.

"Shit," she replies as she shrugs her shoulders.

"So you with me for the rest of the day then?"

"With you where?" she asks defensively.

"I'm gonna take you back to the field with me. Get some smoke and just chill at my spot," he suggests. "You with that?"

"I don't care," she replies.

"Cool. I just gotta get with my man, and we out," he says as he pulls in front of the Exxon station's convenience shop. He picks up his phone and dials. In seconds, he speaks, "I'm here."

He ends the call and lays the phone on the dashboard before leaning over and digging underneath his seat. He retrieves a bag, in which, he digs inside of. He pulls out three hefty piles of money and begins counting through the bills.

Sameerah sits there, staring out of the window as if she isn't paying the least bit of attention to him, but, in all reality, she's counting through the money right along with him. As he counts through the last stack, she has it estimated at just a little over twenty-five hundred. He leaves the money laid out on his lap while he looks over at her. He wants so badly for her to see the money with hopes of impressing her.

Sameerah knows exactly what he's doing, which is why she pretends to be the least bit impressed.

"You alright?" he asks.

"Yeah, I'm good," she replies as she turns to look out of the window.

Finally, he loads the money back into the bag and lays it on the floor.

"I'm gonna run in here and get the White Owls while we waiting on my man," he says as he opens the door and gets out. "You want something outta here?"

"Nah," she replies.

Sameerah watches him as he walks toward the convenience shop. He steps into the store and immediately starts junk food shopping, preparing for the munchies that he expects to have after smoking. Less than a minute later, he's stepping toward the counter. He peeks over his shoulder as the clerk slides a few items to the young man through the opening in the glass.

Sameerah's 20/20 eyesight allows her to see not only five White Owls, but she, also, sees a blue box of Trojans. She shakes her head from side to side with anger as she thinks about what he has planned for them. She watches him as he attempts to discreetly slide the condoms into his pocket. He shakes the bag open and dumps the rest of his items into it.

He grabs his change from the counter and tucks it into his pants pocket before walking to the door with his head hanging low. Just as he's forcing the door open, he sees Sameerah climbing over into the driver's seat. He stands there in shock for a second, just wondering what it is that she's doing. Sameerah looks over, and they lock eyes just as she slams the gear into the drive position.

"Yo!" he shouts as he runs toward the car. Sameerah mashes the gas pedal, and the ass of the car drops before taking off with great speed.

"Yo!" he shouts again as he chases behind the car as fast as he can. His heart pounds with fear as he watches his car leave him in the dust. After being left a half a block behind, he finally stops.

He stands there with a look of defeat on his face as he looks around for help that isn't there.

"This bitch!" he says as he slams his bag onto the ground with rage. He quickly thinks of his money that's in the car. As he realizes that she

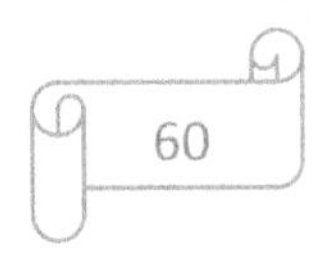

got away with the last money that he had to his name, he becomes even angrier.

"Fuck!" he shouts. "Lil, dirty-ass bitch got me!"

CHAPTER 20
DAYS LATER

"And as for these," Wustafa says as he digs into a brown paper bag.

He holds a handful of tiny glassine envelopes in his hand. Inside the envelopes are rocks of crack. He lifts his hand high in the air for the crew to see before slamming the little envelopes back into the bag with disgust. He snatches the bag from the table and walks over to the kitchen area.

Wustafa and the crew have just returned from a quick local robbing spree. The spree was nowhere near as lucrative as he hoped it would be. They only rounded up a couple of grand from six spots, which averages out to not even four hundred a job. The most valuable spot seemed to come from luck. They just happened to catch the workload coming into the building. Apparently, they had just punched the clock because they didn't have a single dime in possession, only work.

Wustafa stops short at the trashcan next to the sink. He steps on the pad, and the lid pops open. "In the garbage, where it belongs," he says before dropping the bag into the can. He lifts his foot and allows the lid to close.

"But," Sameerah says as he looks upward at Wustafa with confusion on her face.

"But what?" Wustafa asks.

"That's over six hundred pyramids in that bag. At twenty a pop, that's close to thirteen thousand for the organization."

"Let me tell you something, Babygirl. I will never be the cause of the further destruction of my people. That poison has destroyed our people. It has set us back even further than we already were. That poison will never come out of these hands," he says as he holds his hands high in the air.

"Shit," Sameerah sighs. "It ain't gotta come outta your hands. My big cousin got a spot on 15th Avenue doing a thousand dollars a day," she says as if they will be impressed hearing that. "I can give it to him, and we will have the money back in less than two weeks," she suggests.

"Negative," Wustafa replies. "There's no compromising when it comes to this. It goes against everything I believe in. I hate drugs. I hate those who are weak enough to use drugs. And I despise those who sell drugs," he says passionately.

CHAPTER 21
TWO WEEKS LATER

The small storefront is packed with a total of ten men who stand around, while a young man shakes the dice that he holds in the palm of his hand. He slams the dice against the wall.

"Agghh!" he barks with disappointment as he shakes his head with despair. "Damn!"

With frustration on his face, he hands a few bills over to the man who now shakes the dice vigorously. The young man reaches over and wraps his arm around Sameerah's shoulder. He pulls her closer to him and plants a wet kiss onto her lips. She stands there completely irked, yet she manages to keep a fake smile on her face. The wetness that is plastered onto her lips disgusts her to no end.

"Which way is the bathroom?" she asks as she tries desperately to keep her lips from touching. The last thing that she wants is for his spit to marinate in her mouth.

"Straight to the back and make a right," he says as he points in that direction.

Just as she turns away from him and steps away, a hard smack on her rear catches her by surprise. Her body tenses up as her right cheek is squeezed and groped. Feeling totally disrespected, she continues to walk away without looking back. She's livid, and her face shows it, which is why she won't turn around for him to see.

Sameerah hears back and forth bickering as she steps toward the room where the gambling men are. As she gets to the doorway, she realizes that it's just friendly competition. She makes her way across the room and stands side by side with the young man who brought her here. After throwing the dice against the wall, he watches in suspense. As the dice land, a look of defeat sets on his face.

"Damn!" he shouts as he peels off the bills that he holds in his palm. Once he's done paying out, he's left with about four twenty dollar bills.

At the beginning of the dice game, Sameerah noticed that he had approximately fifteen hundred dollars. Now, he stands here, holding onto his last eighty dollars.

"Game over for you!" a man shouts in mockery.

"It ain't over until the fat lady sing," he says. "Just roll."

"Nigga, the fat lady done sung and went home and took her fat ass to sleep, just as you should," he says before falling out in laughter. All the men laugh as well, which makes the young man even more furious.

"Okay. Fuck it! Since you insist," the man says as he starts shaking the dice in his hand. "I will humor you. How much money you got left?" he asks as he peeks into the young man's hand.

"Come on," Sameerah whispers. "I have to go."

The young man totally ignores her.

"None of your fucking business how much I got! Just roll the fucking dice!"

"Okay. Eighty dollars you got. This game for seventy dollars. I'm gon' spare you that last ten, so you can have enough left to get your pretty, little girlfriend a happy meal," he says, laughing.

The man rolls the dice and slams them against the wall. The first two dice land simultaneously. The numbers read three and six. The third dice lands shortly after, reading an additional three.

"Yes," the man cheers as he clenches his fist and yanks downward. "Your turn."

The young man rattles the dice in his hand for longer than he normally would. He blows in his hand once before shaking the dice again.

"Motherfucker, roll the dice already for crying out fucking loud!" the man shouts, causing everyone to laugh. "You stalling like this the last meal before the chair. This ain't the last money you got to your name, is it?"

"Fuck you," the young man says as he slams the dice against the wall. The first die lands, showing a four. The young man stands on his tiptoes with anticipation. The second die lands and stops spinning. Another four is revealed. His heart begins to pound with excitement.

Please, God, he thinks as he watches closely. The last die seems to spin for hours before stopping. The young man's heart drops with despair as the lousy one reveals itself.

"Pay up motherfucker and get the fuck out!" the man shouts with a smile as he points to the door. "Good fucking night!" he laughs.

The young man looks at the man with deep fury in his eyes. He's lost all of his money, but the jokes are only adding insult to injury.

"Come on, babe," Sameerah says as she hooks her arm around his. "Let's go," she says as she pulls him away.

He puts up a little resistance before following her lead. They walk to the door slowly.

Just as they reach the door, the man shouts out once again.

"Yeah, take his broke ass on outta here! This spot is for niggas with real money, not that little Monopoly money you got!" the man shouts, causing everyone to laugh hard.

This is the final straw for the young man. He can't take another slick remark.

"Suck my dick!" he shouts over his shoulder as he reaches to open the door.

The laughing comes to a complete halt. The whole room seems to freeze. That is until the man takes four giant steps toward the door. As Sameerah and the young man turn around, they are greeted by the man, who now has a gun gripped tightly in his hand.

The older man snatches the young man away from Sameerah. With one hand wrapped around his neck, he shoves the gun into the young man's mouth with his other hand.

"You invited me to your penis?" the man asks as he force-feeds the barrel of the gun into the young man's mouth.

The young man gags as the barrel touches his tonsils.

"Back up, lil mama!" the older man demands as he pushes Sameerah out of the way. He grips the young man's neck tighter. "Go ahead and pull it out! I'm gon' suck it for you. Go ahead, motherfucker!"

"My bad," the young man says as he trembles with fear. "My bad."

"Your bad, nuffin, nigga! You wanna show off for your little girlfriend? Get on your fucking knees!" the man demands.

The young man pauses for seconds, which infuriates the older man. He slides a bullet into the chamber and points directly at the center of the young man's forehead. "'Get on your knees,' I said!"

The young man drops to his knees with no further hesitation, while the older man stands over him with his gun resting on the very top of his head.

"Do I look like a fucking homo to you?"

The young man looks upward with fear in his eyes, and he shakes his head.

"So why the fuck you inviting me to your dick then?"

The man looks over at Sameerah, who stares back at him not knowing what she should expect. She feels no sympathy at all for the dude for the simple fact that she barely knows him. They've only known each other for a few days. Her fear comes from the fact that they came here together, and, if the man murders him, he may feel as if he has to murder her as well.

The gunman looks back down at the beyond terrified young man. He knees him in the face, busting his nose wide open.

"Now, apologize before I pop your fucking top!"

"I, I apologize," he stutters.

The older man snatches the young man by his collar and lifts him onto his feet. They stand nose to nose.

"If you ever invite me to your dick again, I will murder you and everybody that loves you," he says as he looks over to Sameerah.

Sameerah shakes her head in attempt to let the man know that she doesn't love him the least bit.

"Matter of fact, if I even hear through the grapevine that you told anybody to suck yo' dick, I'm coming for you," he threatens with sincerity. He, then, looks over at Sameerah once again. "You better get this motherfucker outta here, before I change my fucking mind," he says before shoving the young man over to her.

Sameerah fumbles with the door lock clumsily as she grabs hold of the young man's hand. She snatches the door open, and, as soon as it's parted, she's greeted by a huge Desert Eagle .9mm, which is being shoved in her face. She stops in her tracks as the door is pushed open with great force. She's snatched by her shoulder and quickly placed into a Full Nelson.

The masked gunman places the gun against the side of her face.

"Move, and I splatter her brains!" he threatens as he pushes her further inside.

The older man stands there in awe while holding his gun at his side. Just as he thinks of reacting, the sight of two more gunmen making their entrance forces him to reevaluate his thoughts.

The man stands there, petrified, as both guns are aimed at his head.

"Drop it!" the gunman closest to him shouts as the other one closes the door behind them.

The man slowly bends over while looking up at the gunman.

"Okay. Okay. Don't shoot, please," he begs.

"Don't nobody fucking move!" the third gunman shouts as he waves his gun recklessly around the room.

The other three men stand completely still, as instructed. The gunman who holds Sameerah speaks.

"Everybody on the floor," he instructs. "Shorty, this ain't got nothing to do with you. I'm gonna open this door, and you're gonna step outside. I got three men standing on guard on the other side of that door. You are to stand there until this over. Make one false move, and you will not live to talk about this day. Understood?"

Sameerah nods her head in a trancelike manner without uttering a word in response. "Everybody else, lay down and place all valuables beside you. And that means guns, too," he adds. "If I search any one of you and find a gun, I'm murdering everybody," he says as he reaches behind himself and opens the door.

The gunman shoves Sameerah toward the door as he keeps his eyes on the room. Quickly, her body is sucked through the cracked doorway before it is slammed shut from the outside.

"Now, let's get it!" the man says, giving the signal for his accomplices to go to work.

Minutes later, all the men lay face down with their hands on the back of their heads. They have been rid of every penny that they had on their persons. They have been stripped of their valuables as well. The three gunmen stand with their backs against the door, preparing to make their exit.

"It's been fun!" the gunman shouts. "Y'all come back now, y'all hear?" the man says sarcastically before opening the door and fleeing the room.

In seconds, the men reach their getaway car. Once they're all seated inside of the Suburban, they begin peeling off their masks.

"Let's go!" Wustafa says from the passenger's seat.

Speed peels off at the sound of his command. Wustafa peeks back into the backseat where Sameerah sits—cool, calm, and collective.

"Babygirl, you deserve an Oscar for that performance. Good job as usual. Your little friend will never have a clue that you were in on it all."

CHAPTER 22
DAYS LATER/ 9:32 P.M.

Anthony places his soda and chips onto the liquor store countertop as Lil Wu stands at the freezer, deciding which soda to grab. The young Hispanic man stands not even a foot away from Lil Wu. He stares at Lil Wu like a hawk, in fear of him stealing something.

"One dollar, papi," the older Hispanic man says to Anthony from behind the counter.

Just as Anthony digs into his pocket, Leonard walks into the store. He looks to the back of the store where he sees Wustafa reaching into the beer freezer. Wustafa peeks around to make sure that everyone is in place before he gives Leonard the signal.

The man behind the counter watches Leonard with suspicion as he stands at the door. He looks back into Anthony's direction only to have a .9mm shoved into his face.

"Don't move!" Anthony says aggressively.

The young man standing next to Lil Wu takes a step toward the counter, attempting to sneak up on Anthony. Lil Wu snatches him by the collar, while placing his gun against his temple.

"Don't even think about it," Lil Wu says as he backs the man up against the wall. The gate is pulled down from the outside.

The owner, who sits in the backroom watching television, hears the gate being closed and runs out to see what is going on. Just as he steps through the doorway, Wustafa aims his gun at the man's head.

"Lay down!" Wustafa shouts.

The man stops in his tracks and raises his hands high in the air. Wustafa reaches over while aiming his gun at the man's head. He quickly pats him down. As he taps his waist he feels a bulge. Wustafa quickly lifts up his shirt and snatches the handgun from the man's waist.

With rage, Wustafa smacks the man in the face with his own gun. Blood spurts almost instantly.

"I wish you would have," Wustafa says with a devilish smirk. "Down!" Wustafa says as he slams the man onto the floor. Wustafa looks over to Anthony. "Hit the register!"

Anthony hurdles over the counter, while aiming his gun at the man's head. He pops the register open and quickly stuffs all the money into his pockets. Wustafa aims his gun at the man while biting down onto his bottom lip.

"Move, and I will bust yo' head wide open," he threatens. Wustafa looks over to Lil Wu and Anthony. "Bring them over. Pat them down," he commands.

"Got one," Lil Wu says as he holds the .380 high in the air.

Anthony shoves the older man to the back of the store, and, once he gets there, he pushes him onto the floor. As soon as Lil Wu gets to the back of the store with his prisoner of war (as Wustafa calls them), Wustafa snatches the young man from Lil Wu's grip. He lifts the gun high in the air before dropping it onto the top of the young man's head.

"You like carrying guns, huh?" Wustafa says as he bangs him on top of the head once again.

Wustafa stares into his eyes through the bifocals. "Y'all hate blacks so much that y'all hope they steal something, so you have reason to kill one of us in here, huh? You're so intimidated by the black man that you want to remove him from the planet, so we become extinct. That way you can have sex with our women and rape our daughters, right?" he asks with a devilish smile before banging him on the head again. "You hate the black man, but you love our women. You can't stand us, and that is why you pollute our communities with this poison. A form of genocide," he says as he points around the store."

He bangs the butt of the gun in between the man's eyes.

Lil Wu, Anthony, and Leonard all watch Wustafa with confusion as he rants on and on. They all wonder what his speech is about. They can hear the rage in his voice and see the passion on his face, but what he's talking about goes way over their heads. The man grasps his face with agony.

"Aghh," he cries.

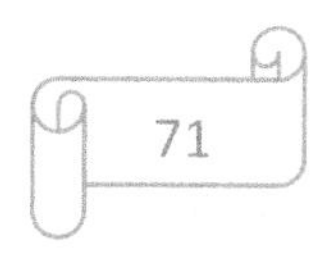

"Shut up and lay down," Wustafa says as he flings the man by the collar and tosses him onto the floor.

As the man lays down, face dripping with blood, Wustafa snatches the owner from the floor. He puts the gun to the back of the man's head.

"Take me to the money!" he says as he forces the man into the back room.

Anthony and Leonard stand over the prisoners of war with their guns aimed at the back of their heads. In less than three minutes, Wustafa reappears with a bag in his hand. He shoves the owner onto the floor as he keeps on stepping past. He stops at the door and taps on it twice before looking back at his crew. The gate lifts up quickly from the outside.

Sameerah snatches the door open for Wustafa to exit. He dashes over to the getaway car, and Sameerah tails him close behind. Just as they get into the truck, Leonard, Anthony, and Lil Wu run out of the store at top speed. The doors are wide open, awaiting their entrance.

"Come on, come on!" Wustafa shouts. "We don't have no time to waste! The police will be swarming the area in no time!"

"You should've let me off them!" Leonard says, enraged.

Wustafa sees a hunger in Leonard's eyes that wasn't there before. Just three months ago, upon meeting each other, Leonard was a timid klutz. Now, in such a short time, he's turned into a beast, who has fallen in love with murder. Wustafa looks at Leonard like his project. He eagerly wants to see just how vicious he can program Leonard to be.

"Nah," Wustafa replies. "Not with no masks. As much as I would've loved to leave them all in there leaking, it's too much of a risk. Never know if they had cameras somewhere in the spot. But don't worry, though; we are just beginning. It's enough of them out there to off. Send them all running back to their country!"

CHAPTER 23

Leonard slips the old sweaty sock over his hand before dumping the bullets out of the box and into his sock covered hand. He wipes each bullet down entirely before loading them into the clip. Once the clip is fully loaded, he grips the sock around it, stroking it up and down to wipe away any fingerprints that may be on it. Speed, Anthony, and Lil Wu are all loading up their weapons as well.

The tapping on the door causes them all alarm. They all look at Wustafa with uneasiness on their faces as they all wonder who could be behind the door. They all sit in silence until a much louder tapping sounds off. Wustafa places his finger on his lips. "Shhh."

He snatches his gun from his waistband and quietly tiptoes toward the door. One by one, they all follow his lead, standing up and drawing their weapons. They all go in separate directions with their guns pointed in the air. They spread out in the tiny apartment with really nowhere to go.

Wustafa peeks through the peephole where he sees nothing at all. He stands there with nervousness and confusion. His heart races as he thinks of who could be behind the door. He stands there for seconds, awaiting another knock but there's nothing. Finally, he tiptoes away from the door.

He becomes nervous as he wonders who could have been there knocking. Did someone track them down? Or worse, has their robbing spree come to a speedy end with the police out there on their trail? Just as he's thinking the absolute worse, another tap sounds off against the door. This time, the tap has turned to an aggressive knock.

They all look at each other with fear in their eyes as they all think the exact same thing. Wustafa tiptoes to the door again. Just as he gets there, another knock sounds off. He peeks through the peephole where it's completely dark. He assumes the person must be holding his hand over the door.

"Open this fucking door," says the person behind the door in a muffled voice.

Wustafa looks around, and, just as he does, he locks eyes with Anthony. A smile spreads across Anthony's face as he nods. Suddenly, ease fills all of their guts. Once the tension has died down, Wustafa winks at them and signals for all of them to come over.

They all stand behind him with their guns drawn. He snatches the door open, and all in one motion, he snatches the person behind the door by the collar. He yanks him inside before slamming the door shut. With ease, he slams the culprit to the floor.

Sameerah looks up with nervousness in her eyes. Her goofy smile has turned into a look of fear. "It's me! It's me!" she says as she stares into the barrel four guns. "It's just me."

As Wustafa is standing up, he hits the lever, and the clip falls out of the gun and drops on Sameerah's forehead. He stands over her with rage in his eyes.

"See, what you get for playing around? Now, get up from there!" he says aggressively.

Sameerah gets up quickly, still wearing the same cheesy grin.

"I was only playing," she says innocently.

"What type of fucking game is that to play?" Wustafa asks. "I'm surprised at you."

At this point, not only is Wustafa surprised, but so is everyone else. Their surprise comes from something totally different than Wustafa's. They all stand there, staring at Sameerah with shock on their faces and lust in their eyes. Their eyes scan her up and down, paying close attention to the tight jeans that are glued to her curvy frame.

Sameerah stands there, tucking her exposed breasts back into her sweater. She adjusts her collar as best as she can, yet her cleavage peeks over the V in her sweater.

"Done stretched my fucking sweater all outta place," she says with attitude.

"You lucky your brains are not stretched all over the kitchen floor with that dumb-ass stunt you just pulled."

Sameerah can tell that he's highly angered by the language that he's using. She, also, realizes how stupid that was of her. As she stands there, she can't believe that she even played a simple game like that. It was all in fun as she did it, but she now realizes how much danger was involved in it.

Sameerah looks around and becomes angered at how they're all gawking at her. She looks down with confusion, wondering what it is that they're looking at. As her eyes set onto her perky breasts, which sit up in the sweater so firmly, she becomes enraged.

"Well, what the fuck y'all looking at?" she asks with fury.

"Y'all act like y'all never saw a fucking girl before," she barks.

As bad as they want to look away, they can't. Their eyes stayed glued on her like metal onto a magnet. It's not that they have never seen a girl before. It's that they never seen her dressed like a girl. Today, the reality has set in that she's really not just one of the guys.

CHAPTER 24
ONE WEEK LATER/ 10:00 P.M.

The intersection area becomes pitch black as the lights from the canopy of the corner store are shut off. A young Hispanic man exits the store and stands on the platform, facing the street. He looks around quite attentively as an older Hispanic man comes stepping out onto the platform. The older man grips a shopping bag in his hand tightly. After peeking in both directions, he turns around and stands on his tippy toes to reach for the gate.

Suddenly, out of nowhere, a Lincoln Navigator bends the corner. The back passenger door swings wide open. The young Hispanic man backs up with surprise as he watches a masked man attempting to hop out of the truck. He stands there nervously for a second or two.

The sight of the chrome handgun snaps him out of his fear. He reaches under his waistband, grips his semi-automatic weapon, and just as he's about to draw, gunfire sounds off.

Boc!

The man stumbles back two steps. Leonard has been hiding in the next alley for the last twenty minutes, just in case of a situation like this. Wustafa was sure that they would be strapped and how correct he was.

A masked up Leonard hops onto the platform as the young man falls to the ground. His gun falls to the ground at his feet. Leonard kicks the gun away from him as he stands over the young man. Anthony runs over with his gun aimed high.

"Papi, don't move, or I will blow your fucking brains out!" he threatens.

The man raises his hands high in the air.

"Here! Take it," he cries with fear. "It's all here. Take it," he says as he extends the shopping bag toward Anthony.

The man stares into the barrel of the gun with hopes that it won't sound off.

"Please," he cries. "Please don't kill me."

Anthony snatches the bag, forces the man onto the ground, and backpedals away.

"Let's go," he says to Leonard.

Leonard kicks the young man in the face before dumping one into his skull.

Boc!

He reaches over and fires twice more.

Boc! Boc!

Both shots sink into the older man's face. His breathing stops automatically. Leonard races to the backseat of the truck and hops in. Speed pulls off recklessly, leaving the two men splattered on the platform.

CHAPTER 25

Wustafa and the crew are spread out comfortably in the big and spacious Ford Expedition. It's the middle of the summer, and the heat wave has everyone miserable, except for them. They've been riding around the city all day with the air conditioner on full blast. The cold air has them all tranquil and ready to fall asleep.

Speed turns down 5th Street in order to get to Route 280 en route to Jersey City. They haven't been over there in quite a few weeks because of the busy workload that they've had right here at home. After riding around locally for hours and lucking up on nothing, Wustafa decided to head over the bridge. He's sure that they will be able to get into something over there.

"Hold," Wustafa shouts as Speed rips through the narrow block.

At the sound of his voice, all of their tranquility has been broken. They sit on the edge of their seats, wondering what has caught his attention.

"What?" Speed asks innocently.

"Come back around the block," Wustafa says as he turns around.

He sits on the edge of his seat with anxiety displayed on his face. He watches closely as a young man, who hopped out of a small compact car holding a shopping bag, climbs into a Land Cruiser that is parked right behind the small car.

"Hurry, hurry!"

Speed cruises off slowly, trying not to draw any attention to themselves. The second he bends the corner, he floors it at top speed. The big truck bounces around awkwardly. In less than a minute, the truck is coming back around the corner. Just as they approach the corner, they all watch the young boy get back into his car.

"Awl, man," Wustafa sighs. "I wanted to catch them in the act. It already went down."

Both the car and the Land Cruiser pull off at the same time. Speed sits at the corner without a clue of what to do.

"Now what?" he asks.

"Follow them," Wustafa replies.

Just as he speaks, the car makes a right turn, and the truck makes a left shortly after.

"Which one?" Speed asks as he cruises the block slowly.

"Follow the money," Wustafa replies. "The Toyota," he adds.

"You sure?" Speed questions. "How do you know that's where the money is?"

"I can smell money. I have a nose like a bloodhound when it comes to sniffing out money," he says arrogantly. "The kid got into the big Toyota with a grey plastic bag and got out with a black one which means the grey one has the money in it. Don't follow him too close and draw attention to us, though," Wustafa says as the Land Cruiser makes the right turn onto Central Avenue.

Speed slows down and allows the Cruiser to get some distance on them before turning behind it. Speed's heavy foot causes him to catch up with the Cruiser in no time at all.

"Fuck that! I'm just gonna cut this motherfucker off," Speed says as he sits on the edge of his seat impatiently.

"Nah, nah. This street's way too wide," Wustafa says. "We can't take the risk of him getting away from us."

"Oh, he won't get away. Trust that," Speed claims. "I will push his ass into a building somewhere," he says with a smile. "Damn," Speed sighs as the Cruiser crosses the Newark/East Orange borderline. "We could be following this motherfucker forever," Speed says with agitation in his voice.

Just as the words seep through his lips, the right blinker starts to flash. The Land Cruiser veers to the right and turns into the Hess Station.

"Here we go," Wustafa says. "See what patience will get you?"

The Cruiser cruises into the lot before coming to a complete stop. The driver's door pops open quickly. They all watch as the foot of the driver extends out of the truck. As both feet land onto the ground, he turns to walk away from it. He steps toward the small building a few feet away. He peeks over his shoulder once before continuing to step.

"Oh, he a cocky one, huh?" Wustafa says with a smile. "Leaves his door wide open with no worries. I wonder who he thinks he is," Wustafa says, feeling slightly disrespected. "Babygirl, let's get it," he says as he peeks over at the man, who is now standing in the line with his money in his hand, waiting to pay for his gas. The man looks around again, and this time he locks eyes with Wustafa from the passenger's seat. Wustafa turns his head quickly away from the man.

Sameerah gets out of the truck on the back passenger side. She closes the door quietly behind her. She peeks at the man through the back window just to make sure he's still in the same place.

"Now?" she asks as she passes the front door where Wustafa is sitting.

"Yep. Now, Babygirl."

Time is running out. The man is now making his way back to his vehicle. A look of concern pops onto his face as he watches Sameerah cut across the front of the Expedition, which is sitting a few feet away from his vehicle. As he spots Sameerah walking toward his truck, he picks up his pace a little.

"Now!" Wustafa shouts.

At the sound of his voice, Sameerah takes off like a bat out of hell. She hops into the driver's seat and slams the gear into drive without even closing the door.

"Yo!" the man shouts as he races toward his truck.

He runs behind the truck, attempting to hold onto the door. Sameerah mashes the gas pedal, dragging him a few feet before he decides to let it go. Once he lets go, he tumbles onto the ground and rolls over onto his back. He stands up, looking around with a cheesy look on his face.

The man stares, in confusion. The action has stolen the attention of every customer in the lot. He feels embarrassed, as well as enraged. He watches his truck bounce out of the other end of the parking lot with a look of despair on his face. The Ford Expedition follows a few feet behind.

"Instead of standing there looking at me fucking stupid, somebody call fucking 911!"

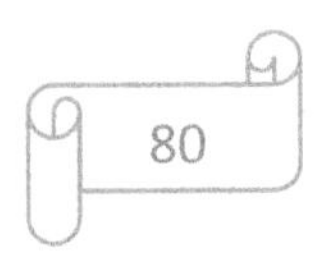

CHAPTER 26

Speed cruises slowly through the car wash. It's hard for him to see on account of the dark tinted windows coupled with the soap suds that are covering the entire windshield. Huge rubber wipers bang against the Range Rover violently. If this was his truck, in no way would he put it through this type of abuse.

Finally, they reach the last phase of the wash where the sprinkler system rinses all traces of soap from the truck. After a two minute rinse, the sprinkler shuts off. Speed pulls up a few feet and stops short. The Mexican man hurries over, dragging a small vacuum cleaner behind him.

The man grabs the passenger's door and snatches it open. Wustafa dashes out of the seat, charging the man like a raging bull. He grabs the man by the collar and yanks him toward him. As he wraps his hand around the man's neck, he puts the gun to the man's temple.

He pulls the drawstrings of his hoodie tightly as he peeks around. He sees that his entire crew has jumped out as well. All of their faces are covered with their hoods, drawn tight. Sameerah stands over two Mexicans that are on their knees with their hands on their heads. Anthony has two of the Mexicans lying face down in a puddle of dirty water, while Leonard has the boss man at gunpoint.

The man hands the huge wad of money over to Leonard with no hesitation. Leonard snatches the man by the collar and walks him over to the glass cubicle. A woman sits behind the glass with a fearful look on her face.

"Tell the bitch to open the door."

"Abra la puerta. ¡Rapido! ¡Rapido!" the man cries.

The woman opens the door quickly, and Leonard pushes the man inside.

"Hand me the money," he says. "Or I'm murdering both of y'all in here," he says with a convincing demeanor.

"Le diera el dinero," the man says fearfully.

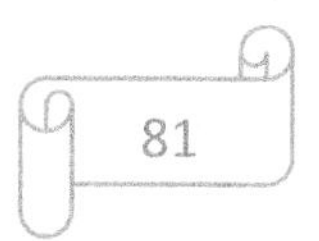

The woman opens the cash register clumsily, and nervously she scoops all the bills from the register and hands them over to him.

Leonard quickly stuffs the money into his pockets.

"Papi, I swear to God you better give me everything or you a dead motherfucker," he says as he stares into the man's eyes.

"Darle todo todo!" the man shouts with fear in his voice.

The woman reaches underneath the countertop and grabs a brown shopping bag. She hands Leonard the bag as she stares at the gun with tears in her eyes.

Leonard snatches the bag from her.

"Y'all motherfuckers lay the fuck down."

The man dives onto the floor with no hesitation, while the woman stands there petrified. Leonard aims the gun at her.

"Bitch, lay the fuck down!"

The woman holds her hands in front of her with fear as she cries hysterically.

"¡Fijar en deponer!" the man shouts.

At his command, the woman drops to her knees before lying face down. Leonard backs out of the small cubicle and pulls the door closed in front of him. He races to the Range Rover and hops into the backseat, sliding over to the middle.

Sameerah runs to the truck, leaving the Mexicans lying face down and so does Anthony. They both hop into the truck. Wustafa slams the man he has in custody to the ground abusively. He drops a kick to his ribs before backpedaling a few steps and climbing into the truck. Speed peels off, dripping a trail of water on the asphalt.

CHAPTER 27
SEPTEMBER 12, 2002

They say time flies when you're having fun. The crew must be having tons of fun because a whole summer has blown right by them. They've worked the entire summer away, day and night with not even the least amount of enjoyment. They didn't attend not one amusement park, carnival or even get the chance to bounce a ball, not once this whole summer. Wustafa has kept their minds occupied with work, work, and more work.

The more work that he had lined up for them, the more work they looked forward to putting in. Now that school is back in session, they do realize all the things of the summer's past that they missed. Sitting in school for all these hours makes them wish they would have, at least, had some enjoyment over the summer, just to break up the monotony.

Today marks the second week that school has been back in session. After an action packed summer, sitting in classes all day has become even more boring to them. Late nights and early mornings, they stayed on the prowl. Now, the ripping and running will have to slow down because school has to be incorporated into their schedules. If it was up to them, they would rather be out making money, but in no way would Wustafa allow them to miss a day of school.

The school cafeteria is packed with kids. The room is full of chaos and horseplay. The room resembles a playground more than a cafeteria because of the way the kids run around, roughhousing. Even the girls are wrestling around with the boys. The only peace in the entire room seems to be at the table that Lil Wu and the crew is sitting at.

They have the entire table to themselves. No one is even standing in the same area as them. It's like they're in their own little world. They're used to being alienated from everyone else. Only difference is, before they were alienated because they were not part of the cool crowd and considered geeks or misfits, now they're alienated by choice.

It's funny how much things changed over the course of a summer. They all noticed a difference their first day back at school. The treatment that they've received from other students tells them that somebody must know something. It's like they're treated like royalty, instead of like the rejects that they were treated like just a few short months ago.

Through all of their years in high school, all they ever wanted to be was accepted. Now, in what seems like overnight, they have no interest in being a part of that crowd. In fact, those that they once looked up to don't seem half as cool today as they did a few months ago. After being around Wustafa, a living legend, they could never be impressed by a bunch of nobody high school kids who have never done or seen a fraction of the things that they have been exposed to in such a short time.

Now, they don't seek to be a part of the cool crowd because they have become the cool crowd.

Somehow, the word has spread throughout the school about some of the activity that they have indulged in. The more bells that their names ring, the more royal treatment they receive. The tables have turned now. They no longer want to be a part of the people. The people want to be a part of them.

The attention and the treatment is all new to all of them. The girls all seem to be attracted to them, and the dudes do almost anything in the hopes of being accepted by them. The dudes who may have mistreated them over the years now try their hardest to get on their good sides and stay clear out of their way. As much as they love the attention, they manage to contain themselves. Wustafa told them that it would be like this, and he, also, taught them how to handle themselves in this situation.

Wustafa made them take an oath to never repeat the things that they have done or witnessed in the organization. How the word has spread throughout the school? He has not a clue. He's sure one of them had to have leaked some things, but he's not sure which one of them. The reality is it's been leaked, and they are now receiving the perks that come with it all.

Wustafa has instilled in them all the values that he believes they need to navigate through it all. He's taught them to stay humble and respect all, even the ones who don't demand respect. He's emphasized over and over his hate for an oppressor, and it has rubbed off on them. That hate for an oppressor makes them mindful to never oppress anyone.

He tells them that, just because the people fear them, they should never force the people into oppression unless there's something to gain from it. He's told them to never misuse their newfound power unless there's a dollar sign attached to it.

"Right there, coming in the now," Anthony says as he barely moves his lips. "He don't talk much around me now, but, last school year, he had a lot to say."

Leonard and Lil Wu look the kid up and down, sizing him up. From head to toe, he looks like money. His crispy white sneakers and his gleaming jewelry tell a story of their own. He diddy-bops through the cafeteria as if he owns it. That is until he notices Leonard looking at him. He tones his walk down instantly. Leonard notices his discomfort and looks away immediately.

"He loves to flash that cash," Anthony says. "Be having crazy knots in his pockets. One day, in homeroom, he counted out three thousand dollars right on his desk in front of the teacher. He claims he been getting money since he was eleven years old."

"Oh, yeah?" Leonard asks. "What's that? A six year run? Well, he should have more than a few dollars put up somewhere then. Maybe, it's time to see just how much of that we can get our hands on," Leonard says with a devilish smirk on his face.

Anthony nods his head up and down with a smile of his own.

"My thoughts exactly."

CHAPTER 28
TWO DAYS LATER/ 4:27 P.M.

The young barber turns the chair around slowly as he stares at the head of the customer who sits in the chair. The barbershop is packed, with not an empty seat, and everyone listens as the loudmouth man shouts at the top of his lungs.

"It's crazy!" he shouts from the chair in the waiting section. "They pushing up on everything and everybody! From drug dealers to businessmen, they ain't picking and choosing. If a motherfucker's getting a dollar, they want in! I heard they're walking into businesses telling motherfuckers they want a cut. My man got a lil dollar store, and he said they came to him."

"And what he do?" the barber in the first chair asks.

"He cut them in. Shit," the man replies. "Every Friday, he gives them an envelope. He says he don't want no trouble."

"That shit sound stupid as hell," the barber spits with rage. "I can't believe that motherfuckers are actually going for that crazy shit," he says as he spins the chair around.

"They ain't got no fucking choice!" the man says with his eyes stretched wide open.

"But who are they?" another customer asks, interrupting the conversation.

"Old Head Wustafa," the man replies with no hesitation. "A stone cold killer," he adds. "He don't play no games. Just came home from beating a quadruple homicide. Now, he's running around with a bunch of wild juveniles. Reckless, young motherfuckers!" he barks. "Call themselves the Young Gunz!"

"Man, fuck that!" the barber shouts angrily. "Motherfuckers got a fucking choice. They just ain't run up on the right motherfucker yet. I tell you one motherfucking thing, if they come in here with that dumb shit, it's gonna be a problem. I'll be got damn if I bust my ass all week in

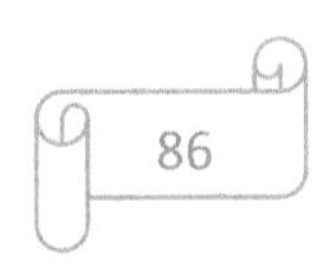

this shop, and then I'm just gonna hand them my hard earned money at the end of the week for nothing! I wish the fuck I would!"

"It won't be for nothing," the man interrupts. "It will be to save yo' motherfucking life," he says while laughing hard.

"Man, fuck Wustafa, whoever the fuck he is!" the barber shouts. "And fuck his Young Gunz!"

The middle barber spins his client towards the mirror and lifts the chair up. Anthony looks in the mirror, examining his haircut. He gives the barber a head nod, and the barber loosens the cape from around his neck. Anthony stands up, and, while digging into his pocket for his money, he looks over at the barber, who has been doing all of the talking.

The barber looks up, and they lock eyes. The cold look that Anthony sends him doesn't spark the least bit of attention. He just continues to babble on and on and on.

"Motherfuckers act like they stop making guns after they made theirs. They ain't the only motherfuckers with guns! And mines bust!"

Anthony pays the barber and makes his way towards the door.

"I'm telling you," the customer shouts. "They on a mission!"

"Man, like I said, fuck them! Bring that shit my way, and I'm gon' be on a mission!" the barber shouts.

Anthony peeks back at the barber one last time as the door closes behind him. The barber doesn't lift his head. He just continues to shout loudly.

"I wish they'd come my way with that shit!"

CHAPTER 29
THREE DAYS LATER

Lil Wu stands at the front of the long line as he watches the pretty, young girl through the glass freezer. The girl packs the butter pecan ice cream tightly into the half gallon container as she peeks up at him with a goofy looking smile on her face. Lil Wu smiles back at her, and his smile causes her to pack even more ice cream in the container.

"Damn! How much ice cream you trying to make fit in there?" the man who stands behind her asks angrily.

The girl looks away from Lil Wu with shame as she places the top onto the container.

"Give it here," the man says angrily as he snatches the container from her.

He walks over to the other side of the store. He steps to the side, where no one can see him behind the column in the middle of the floor. He snaps a brown paper bag open and drops the container of ice cream into the bag.

He peeks around cautiously as he reaches into his pocket. After making sure that no one is looking, he drops a stack of money into the bag and folds the top of the bag over. He walks over to Lil Wu, who has stepped out of the line. Over the counter, he hands Wu the bag.

He looks Lil Wu square in the eyes.

"It's in there," he whispers faintly as he points to the bag.

Lil Wu nods his head before turning around and making his way to the door. The man exhales a huge sigh of relief as he watches Lil Wu exit the store.

Twenty Minutes Later

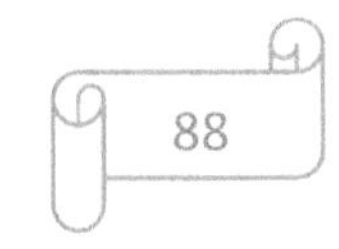

Leonard walks into the small store. The loud music is eardrum piercing. Leonard walks around just skimming over the CDs that are lined up throughout the glass cases. The storeowner looks up from the few customers who stand in front of him, and he and Leonard lock eyes. Leonard acknowledges him by way of a head nod.

The owner's face show signs of slight agitation as he reaches into the glass case and retrieves a CD.

"You need a bag?" he asks.

"Nah, that's alright," the man says as he hands his money over.

In return, he's given the CD. The group of men walks towards the door, passing Leonard. As they exit the store, Leonard looks up. The man raises one finger into the air.

"One minute," he says as he steps behind the cash register.

He opens the register and lifts a stack of twenties from it. He sifts through the stack and parts the stack in half. One half of the stack, he places back into the register, while, the other half, he holds in his hand as he walks back to the middle of the counter where Leonard stands.

"Here," he says as he hands Leonard the stack of money.

He lowers his head in shame as Leonard quickly counts through the twenties.

"It's all there," the man says with a slight bit of attitude.

Leonard finishes counting the money, looks up to the man and lifts his fist in the air. With no energy exerted, the man lifts his hand in the air and taps Leonard's fist.

"I'm out," Leonard says as he turns around and starts stepping. "Peace!"

CHAPTER 30

DAYS LATER/ 11:42 P.M.

The narrow street is pitch dark because one of the streetlamps is busted out. The curbside is flowing with activity. Three men stand side by side, serving the customers who walk up, as well as the ones who pull up in their cars like it's a drive-thru. Wustafa studies the area and comes up with a quick observation.

"Listen. It's too much going on out there. The fast flow of money has them distracted. We pull up, hop out, bumrush them, lay everybody down, and keep it moving. In and out," he says with confidence. "Speed, as soon as that little car moves," Wustafa says as he looks over at Speed.

In the backseat, everyone is preparing for the jump out. All of them are on the edge of their seats, watching ahead of them with caution. Silence fills the air. Wustafa watches as the man trots to the car, which is parked alongside the curb.

He hops into the car, and the lights come on as the car slowly pulls away from the curb.

"Here we go," Wustafa says as he hits the window button. The window slides down slowly. "Action."

Speed steps on the gas pedal lightly. They all watch ahead, just imagining how all of this will play out. They all are envisioning themselves in action. Leonard, who sits in the back passenger seat, grips the door handle, preparing to make his move. He understands that the initial jump out is the most impactful part of it all. It sets the tone for the rest of the job.

Sameerah, who is on the opposite side, grabs hold of the door as well. She's trying to figure out which direction she should come in from. As much as she loves to have her details in order, she always ends up

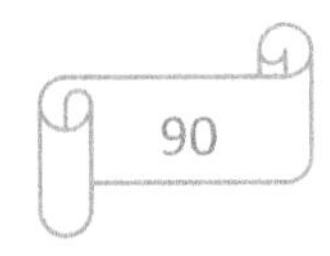

going against her plan and doing the opposite of what she planned to do. She's learned that the best thing to do is to let her gut lead her.

Speed mashes the gas pedal, causing the huge Lincoln Navigator to jerk before accelerating sluggishly. The men standing curbside notice the big truck coming in their direction, but it's already too late. Leonard forces the door open and hops out of the truck aggressively with his gun aimed at the men on the curb.

"Don't nobody fucking move!"

They all stand in place just as instructed.

Anthony slides out right behind him, covering him from the back. He's following Leonard's lead. Their chemistry is in sync. They seem to move at the beat of the same drum. If Leonard aims to the left, Anthony aims to the right, always covering everything in the area. Sameerah runs behind the truck coming toward her teammates when the sound of gunfire rips through the air.

Boc! Boc!

Leonard and Anthony stop in their tracks as they peek around, wondering where the gunfire has come from. The three men on the curb take off running in different directions. The sound of gunfire rips through the air again. Sameerah backpedals to the driver's side of the truck where she hides.

Both Anthony and Leonard duck low to the ground, while backpedaling to the truck. They peek around in confusion. Their guns are held high, but, without knowing where the shots are being fired from, they have no target. Another shot rips through the air.

Boc!

"Let's go! Let's go!" Wustafa shouts as he holds his gun out of the window.

Anthony slides into the backseat at the same time that Sameerah slides in from the opposite side, causing their bodies to collide into one another. Finally, Leonard manages to climb into the backseat backwards.

"Go! Go!" he shouts.

Speed mashes the gas pedal, but the big truck seems to take forever to pull off.

Boc! Boc! Boc!

The last set of shots has the most clarity of all of them. They sound crisp and clear, as if they're right behind them.

"Oh, shit!" Speed shouts as he looks into the rearview mirror. "He right behind us!"

Boc! Boc!

The man fires as he chases behind the truck.

Leonard holds the door open as he leans outward firing a shot with no aim whatsoever. His goal is just to back the gunman up.

Blocka!

Wustafa grabs onto the roof of the truck and lifts himself out of the seat. He hangs his torso out of the window, and, with very little aim, he squeezes.

Blocka! Blocka! Blocka!

The sound of the retaliation gunfire stops the man in his tracks. He squeezes again as he stands still.

Boc! Boc!

Just as Wustafa returns fire...

Blocka! Blocka!

The back window caves inward, and glass shatters everywhere.

"Aghh!" Lil Wu screams from the back of the truck. "I'm hit! I'm hit!"

CHAPTER 31
THE NEXT MORNING

Lil Wu's mother walks away from the hospital bed where her son lays. He has just spent the night here for testing. Although the bullet wound was labeled minor, they still have him hooked up to an IV because of the amount of blood that he lost. Outside of the excessive amount of pain in his shoulder, he's fine.

She managed to keep her composure while in front of him, but, every second that she's not in his presence, she breaks down. She's expressed to him over and over her fear of losing him to the streets. She prays that he sees this as a wakeup call and stays clear of anything that could lead him back into this situation or even worse. All in all, she just hopes that her words have not fallen on deaf ears.

Lil Wu already had his story together, long before even calling his mother. Wustafa had prepped him on exactly what to say. He made him rehearse the alibi over and over again until it sounded convincing. Wustafa knows how persistent his sister can be, so he was sure to cover every question that she could possibly ask.

Lil Wu's mom breaks out into tears the very second she exits the room. She lifts her head just as Wustafa is approaching. Wustafa inhales a deep breath. This is the very last person that he wants to see right now. He knew he would have to face her, but in no way is he prepared.

They stand face to face as she stares into his eyes with pure hatred.

"Hey, big sis," he says as he reaches out to hug her.

He's attempting to break the ice, but she resists by planting her hand in the center of his chest. She pushes him away coldly.

"Don't 'Hey, big sis' me," she says with rage. "How could you?"

"How could I what?" he asks as if he hasn't a clue about why she's reacting like this.

"My only son, your only nephew," she says as the tears flood her eyelids. "That boy idolizes you. He's the only person in the world who sees no wrong in you. Knowing all that you have been through in life, how could you lead him into the same lifestyle? I would think that you would want better for him."

"Of course, I do," he replies. "Where is all this coming from?"

"Grover Watson, don't give me that innocent look with your beady, little eyes. You know what the hell I'm talking about. My child is laying in a hospital bed with a bullet lodged into his shoulder, a few inches away from his heart. Just a few inches more, and I wouldn't be here in this hospital. I would be standing over him in a morgue, identifying his body."

"You're talking like all of this is my fault. The boy was at the wrong place at the wrong time."

"No, he was with the wrong person, who had him at the wrong place, at the wrong time."

"Sandra, we were walking down a public street, and the boy got hit by a stray bullet. This the ghetto, sis. I have no control over that."

"Only y'all know if that is the truth or not," she says sarcastically. "What I do know is that my son is laying in there. I pray that you have the decency to keep him away from all your wrongdoings," she says as she stares into his eyes.

She steps around him while still speaking. "The last thing I want to do is bury my son or visit him in prison." She peeks over her shoulder at him as she's walking away. "And if you truly love me, that should be the last thing that you want as well."

CHAPTER 32
TWO DAYS LATER

Wustafa steps into the barbershop. It's empty, except for five barbers. As soon as he enters, three of the barbers stand up and stand behind their chairs.

"Right here, bro," the third barber says desperately.

"Over here," the fourth barber says with aggression.

"Let me tighten that up for you, ol' head!" The barber behind the fifth chair smiles. "Guaranteed to bring your youth back."

"Nah, I'm good," Wustafa says as he rubs his hand over his peezy hair. "I'm looking for the owner. Is that you?" he asks as he points to the fifth barber. "You?" he asks as he points at the third barber.

The first barber sits in his chair with a look of arrogance spread all over his face. Wustafa knows that he's the owner of the shop. Anthony told him exactly what chair he would be in and described him down to the tiniest detail. Wustafa is just playing the game to see what their response will be.

"What is it pertaining to?" the owner asks.

Wustafa peeks around before taking a seat in the second barber's chair right next to the owner. "It's pertaining to the madness that has been taking place all over the city. I know you heard about it, right?"

"What madness?" the owner asks cockily.

"Business owners are being robbed, and some have even been killed."

"Alright, and what that got to do with me?"

"I just been running around, trying to bring order back to these streets. It's crazy to me that hardworking business owners out here, trying to make a legitimate living, have to worry about being robbed. Shouldn't be like that, and that's why I'm out here providing security for the hardworking businessman."

"Security?" the owner interrupts. "Who the fuck you supposed to be? A fucking guardian angel? A vigilante?"

The barbers all fall out into laughter. Wustafa cracks a smile of his own and answers, "You can say that."

"Listen. This what I need you to do," the owner says before pausing a few seconds. "Get the fuck outta my shop. That's what I need you to do. Come in here talking that bullshit."

"Pardon me," Wustafa says as he extends his hand toward the owner. "Maybe, we got started on the wrong track. Let's try this again. How are you doing, brother? I'm Wustafa," he says with a grin. "And what's yours?"

The owner tenses up with nervousness at the sound of Wustafa's name. All of the barbers tense up as well. They remember that name specifically from the conversation the other day. Fear pumps through all of their hearts. All except for the owner.

"Kareem," he says as he reaches over and shakes Wustafa's hand. "Hayes Homes, all day," the owner says with a cocky look on his face.

Wustafa cracks a smile.

"Hayes Homes," he says as he nods. "Okay. Good to know, but what does that have to do with the price of tea in China?"

The barber stands up with aggression and arrogantly states, "It don't have shit to do with the price of tea in China. We ain't in China. We right here in fucking Newark, and I'm just letting you know that that extortion shit ain't working over here. You can take that shit somewhere else. I work too hard for mine."

Wustafa places his hand in the air, interrupting the man.

"Extortion? Where did you get that from? I'm not extorting anyone. I'm providing a service. For a small fee, I can guarantee that nothing will happen here and that you can continue business with no worries. It's security."

The man slowly reaches under his shirt and withdraws a long .357 Magnum from his waistband. He stares into Wustafa's eyes, looking for a sign of fear. To his surprise, he sees nothing close to fear.

"Do it look like I'm worried or even need security?"

Wustafa grins.

"Okay. I see that you are prepared," Wustafa says as he puts both hands, palm up, into the air. "I see you got it covered and don't need my service."

The door opens up, and Wustafa looks over his shoulder. He's not surprised to see Leonard standing at the door. Leonard backs up against the door and leans on it as he draws his .9mm. The barbers stand there in fear and suspense.

"So, you're not in need of my services?" Wustafa asks.

"Not at all," the owner replies with no hesitation. "I'm a man. I make my own money, and I'm willing to die for mines."

"Understandable," Wustafa says as he nods his head with his lips sagging downward. "Point well received," he says as he turns around and walks away.

Leonard stands on alert, just in case the man gets the balls to fire.

"Good day, gentlemen," Wustafa says as he stands at the door.

The barbers watch quietly as Wustafa and Leonard exit the barber shop.

"Get the fuck outta here," the owner says as he tucks his gun back into his waistband. "Fuck he think he talking to?"

"Yo, you see how he looked when you drew that big-ass cannon?" the second barber asks, while laughing. "Backed his goofy-looking ass right on up."

"That's Wustafa?" the third barber asks. "I wasn't expecting him to look like that. I was expecting some treacherous-looking motherfucker, not fucking *Revenge of the Nerds*," he says before chuckling away.

"Word to mother!" the fourth barber says.

"Ay, man! I told y'all I ain't have that shit," the owner says. "He got the game fucked up. He think he bigger than life. Told him, I'm a fucking man just like you. And I'm willing to die for mines!"

"Yep," the second barber shouts. "That's exactly what you told him."

The owner sits back, accepting the praise.

"You damn sure did!"

CHAPTER 33
THE NEXT NIGHT/ 9:37 P.M.

Speed sits behind the steering wheel of the luxurious Cadillac Escalade as the gas attendant plugs the nozzle into the truck. Wustafa sits in the passenger's seat, deep in thought, as he always is right before they go out on their missions. Sameerah sits directly behind him, and Leonard sits on the other end. Anthony sits cramped up in the middle. Sameerah has elevated her status from the middle rider to always getting a window seat. Her work ethic has earned her a better seating arrangement.

Lil Wu isn't present. In fact, he hasn't gone out with them since his injury. Lil Wu thinks he has been given some time off for his injury. Little does he know that Wustafa has plans of giving him permanent time off. After analyzing all that his sister has said to him, he feels guilty for even dragging his nephew into this mess.

The clicking sound of the gas pump tells them that the tank is full. Wustafa looks behind him at the pump. He squints his beady eyes in an attempt to read the huge numbers on the display.

"How much that say?" he asks as he digs into his pocket.

"Seventy-eight, twelve," Leonard reads from the display.

The attendant walks toward Speed's window. He left the nozzle plugged into the truck as a measure of security. Wustafa extends his hand over to Speed. In his hand, he holds four twenty dollar bills.

"Here," he says as he dangles the money at Speed.

"Seventy-eight, twelve," the man says as he stands at the window.

Speed looks the man directly in the eyes as he sneakily slams the gear into park. He mashes the gas pedal almost simultaneously. The tires screech as the rubber burns the pavement. The nozzle is snatched out of the socket of the pump as the truck peels off.

Speed laughs hysterically as he watches the attendant stand there with a foolish look on his face. He quickly reaches over to the top of the

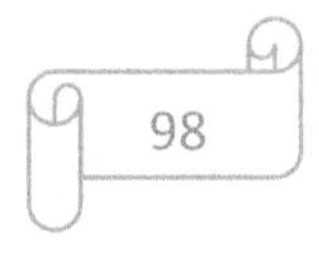

gas pump where he grabs a brick. He runs behind the truck for a few steps before launching the brick into the air. All the kids in the back are laughing hysterically as well.

All of their focus is diverted to Wustafa who sits there with rage plastered onto his face. He stares at Speed for seconds in complete silence. He slowly looks away from Speed and looks back, into the backseat. The anger that is displayed on his face ceases all laughter immediately. He looks back over at Speed still not saying a word.

As Speed cruises down the street, he looks over to Wustafa.

"What?" he asks with a goofy smirk on his face.

"What?" Wustafa barks. "What in the world would make you do something so idiotic?" Wustafa asks with confusion on his face. "Do you use your head? I look at some of the retarded things that you do, and, before, I just thought you got off on doing stupid stuff, but, now, I'm convinced that you are officially retarded."

"What?" Speed asks again.

"What would make you pull off when I have the money right here in my hand, trying to give it to you?"

"Wu, why the hell would we pay to gas up a stolen truck? Being in here is illegal. What part of that you don't understand?" he asks with an angered expression on his face. "This truck has been carjacked. You do remember, right? Or did you forget? Everything we do is against the fucking law. We carjacking motherfuckers for eighty thousand dollar cars and trucks, and you worried about stealing eighty dollars worth of fucking gas? You tripping!"

Wustafa sits there quietly for seconds as he analyzes everything that Speed has just said. He's ashamed to admit that, as stupid as he thinks Speed may be, he actually makes sense, but, in order to look bad in front of the crew, Wustafa speaks in his defense.

"Now, every cop in the city will be looking for the truck before we even make a single dollar. You got us hot for nothing!"

****45 Minutes Later****

Wustafa stares at the porch of the raggedy house in deep concentration. They're parked almost a half a block away, where they

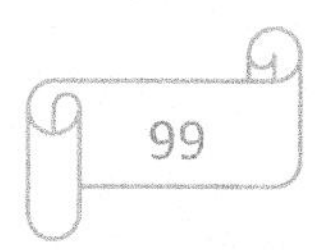

have been sitting for ten minutes already. The heavy flow of traffic caught Wustafa's attention.

"That's the money man right there with the Yankee hat on," Wustafa says. "See how he's in the backdrop? Kind of out of the way, just overseeing everything?" They all watch as customers approach the porch consistently without a second in between. "Judging by the people, it has to be crack money. Heroin doesn't move this consistent this late at night. All the heroin users are home right at this hour, sleeping and preparing for their early morning wake up."

Wustafa sits quietly for seconds before he comes up with a plan.

"Okay. I got it. Here's the plan."

They all sit quietly, awaiting his instructions.

"Babygirl, you gonna have to set this one off. They too alert to let one of us walk up on them. You and Anthony walking as a couple won't cause any alarm. Once y'all get to the porch, they will be paying so much attention to you that they won't see anything else. That will give Anthony the opportunity to draw without them seeing it coming. Anthony, you concentrate on the tall one in the back. In all the time that we've been sitting out here, he hasn't moved a muscle outside of puffing on that cancer stick. That tells me that he could easily be the muscle out there. Not sure, but we can't take a chance. Babygirl, once Ant has the big man covered, you are to follow up and cover the one in the Yankee hat. That's the bank. The last thing they want is for the bank to get hit. Threatening to hit him will stun all of them and leave them in total fear. With him in danger, they will all submit," he says with certainty in his voice.

"By that time, we will be on the scene to back y'all up. Leonard, you hop out, lay everybody down, score the goods, and we out. As usual, y'all stay on point until the money is secure in the truck. Anthony, you hold it down until Babygirl makes it to safety. Ladies first," he says with a smile. "This is an in and out situation. Everything is laid out right in front of us," Wustafa says to build their confidence. "Now, let's get it!"

Sameerah takes her baseball cap off and shakes her curly hair loose before forcing the door open. She slides out of the seat quickly, and Anthony gets out right after her. He quickly slams the door shut. They both take deep breaths before starting on their adventure.

Like a seasoned veteran, Sameerah thinks on her toes. She grabs Anthony's hand tightly. Together, they stride in perfect rhythm like a happy couple. For the first time in all the time that they've been sitting here, the area is clear of customers. With no customers in the way, it makes it easier for them to concentrate on their focal point.

As they near the porch, all of the talking ceases. Just as Wustafa said, all concentration is on Sameerah. The attention makes her heart pound in her chest with nervousness. She squeezes Anthony's hand for comfort.

With no particular strategy in mind, Anthony has decided to just follow her lead. He has total faith in her that she has it all figured out. Just as they're about a foot away from the porch, Sameerah whispers without moving her lips, "You keep walking. I'm gon' act like I'm tying my shoe."

She pulls her hand away from him as she drops to the ground. She fiddles with her shoestrings as she peeks over her shoulder just to get a feel of where everyone is positioned. Anthony continues, stepping slowly as he pretends to keep his eyes straight ahead. Sameerah turns her body at an angle, giving the porch full of dudes a full view of her perfectly rounded bottom. They all watch with perversion.

"Let's go," Wustafa instructs.

With the lights out, Speed pulls out of the parking space and creeps up the block. Wustafa rolls the window down and rests his gun against the door, just in case things get messy.

Sameerah grips her gun in her hand and slowly stands up all in one motion. She locks eyes with Wustafa as they're pulling up. All their focus is diverted from Sameerah to the Cadillac Escalade.

"Who that?" one man asks.

Just as they all stand on full alert, Sameerah spins around with her gun aimed high. She points at the big man standing at the back of the porch. Anthony takes two giant steps and is right in front of the Yankee hat wearing man that Wustafa had referred to as the bank. He slams his forearm into the man's chest as he shoves him backwards. He presses the gun against the man's temple.

"Don't move!"

The man stands there, frozen, stiff with fear.

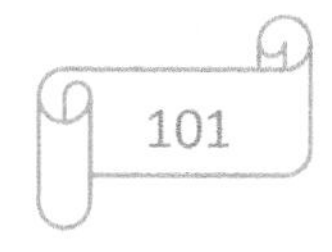

Leonard slides out of the backseat and runs full speed ahead with his gun out as well. “Everybody, lay the fuck down!” he shouts as he grabs the first man and runs through his pockets. He slams the man to the ground before running up the steps to the next man. He quickly pats his pockets and flings him down the small flight of steps.

“On your knees, big man,” Leonard shouts as he aims the gun at the man’s head.

The big man drops to his knees with no hesitation. Leonard feels a huge bulge at his waist side. Just as Wustafa had assumed, this is the muscle. Leonard snatches the .9mm from the man’s waist and clunks him across his head with it. As the man falls backwards, Leonard fires two shots at him.

Blocka! Blocka!

The shot to the shoulder and chest forces the man backwards. He rolls over onto his back. Leonard jumps down the small flight of stairs. He, then, searches the man that Sameerah’s is holding captive. He quickly locates a small, neat stack of hundred dollar bills.

Leonard backpedals quickly in long strides back to the truck. Anthony stands there, waving his gun from person to person in a threatening manner as he peeks over at Sameerah.

“Go,” he instructs.

Sameerah loosens the grip of her captive and pushes him with all of her might. As he’s stumbling backwards, she backpedals to the truck.

“All good,” she shouts from the truck as she slides into the seat.

Anthony waves his gun from man to man as he backpedals. He gets into the truck. He grips the open door with his left hand as he aims the gun with his right hand. Speed mashes the gas pedal and speeds off. As they get a few houses away, Speed slams the door shut. After a block of high speed driving, Speed slows down and begins driving at a moderate speed.

The crew is hyped from the action. They’re all on the edge of their seats, talking loudly with their adrenaline still racing until Wustafa interrupts their moment.

“Babygirl!” he shouts with authority.

The sound in his voice brings them all to silence. They can sense in his voice that something is wrong, but what they have no clue. They all wait in suspense for him to speak again.

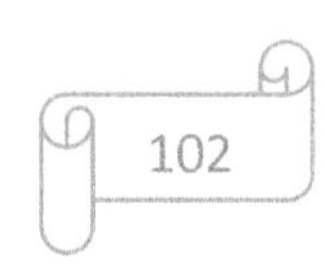

"Babygirl, you totally went against my instructions."

Sameerah sits back, quietly trembling in her seat. "Huh?"

"Oh, now you're hard of hearing?" he says with sarcasm. "My instructions to you were for you to cover the man with the Yankee hat and let Ant concentrate on the big man. Y'all did the total opposite. Do either of you have any reason for why you went against my instructions? Going against my call could have easily cost us." He looks back into the backseat, staring at the two of them. "Well, I'm waiting for your reason."

Sameerah and Anthony sit there, staring at each other. Neither one of them know the right thing to say. Wustafa stares at both of them coldly. He, then, turns his head to face the road ahead of them.

"I'm waiting."

"I take full blame," Sameerah whispers. "By the time I spun around, all in my sight was big man. Something told me that he was holding. I could feel it in my gut. That's why I went against the plan. I'm sorry," she says as she lowers her head with shame. Anthony shakes his head from side to side with sadness on his face as well.

"Sorry?" Wustafa repeats. "Babygirl, that was the best decision you could have ever made. From where we were seated, I couldn't see the area clearly. Y'all know I'm blind as a bat," he says with a smile. "The fact that I couldn't see clearly affected my judgment and my call, but, thanks to you, it all played out well. You improvised. That's what makes you a strong soldier— the ability to improvise and think on your toes as you did. And that's why you're going to go far out here. You got what it takes!" he says as he extends his fist into the backseat.

A smile pops onto Sameerah's face as she looks over at Anthony. She bangs her fist against his. "And that's why you're my Babygirl!" Wustafa shouts.

CHAPTER 34
ONE WEEK LATER

Wustafa opens the door slowly. He's somewhat shocked as he stands behind the slightly opened door. He stares into Lil Wu's eyes with deep compassion.

"Peace," Lil Wu says as he attempts to step into the apartment.

Wustafa blocks his entrance with his body. He pulls the door closed behind him as he steps out

of the apartment. Lil Wu stands there with confusion on his face. He gazes deep into Wustafa's eyes.

"What's up?"

Wustafa stands in silence for seconds before finally speaking.

"What you doing here?" Wustafa asks. "You are supposed to be resting up."

"I been resting up for a week. I got all the rest I need. I'm ready to get back to work."

Wustafa looks away from Lil Wu as he collects his thoughts.

"Oh, about that," he says as he stares back into Lil Wu's eyes. "I been doing some thinking. After talking to your mother that day, I've had a change of heart. She was heartbroken. She told me, if anything was to happen to you, she wouldn't be able to live. She, also, said that she will blame me forever. That's my only sister. She's one of the only people in life that I actually care about. Outside of you and my mother," he adds. "I thought about it, and I agree. If anything was to really happen to you out there, I wouldn't be able to live with myself."

"So, what you saying?" Lil Wu interjects.

Wustafa stands quietly for a matter of seconds.

"I'm saying, I don't want to be the blame for anything else that can happen out there. Them streets are wicked, and you know that. I know I led you to this, but now I want to lead you away from it," he says with sincerity in his eyes.

"But what if I don't want to be away from it?" Lil Wu asks. "I'm not letting one incident turn me away from getting money. This is me," he claims. "This is what I'm about."

Wustafa shakes his head from side to side.

"That's not true. That life really isn't you. Them streets are for guys who don't have a way out. You have a way out. You're an intelligent dude. You can do anything in life that you choose if you put your mind to it."

"It is true!" Lil Wu shouts defensively.

"Nah, nephew, this life isn't you. After thinking about it, you barely even fit in. You stick out like a sore thumb. Your heart is not even into it."

Lil Wu drops his eyes with sadness. Wustafa hates to tell him this, but he refuses to lie to him and be the cause of him doing something that his heart is not into. After listening to his sister, he realized that Lil Wu only does this because he looks up to him so much. Once he realized that, the guilt kicked in.

A hateful smirk pops onto Lil Wu's face.

"So, basically, you're saying that I'm not built for this?"

Wustafa stands there with no reply.

"I'm just as built for this as any of them are," Lil Wu says as he points to the door.

"Nephew, this ain't about them. This is about me and you, my only nephew, who I love from the bottom of my heart. I love you enough to steer you away from this and point you in the right direction. I don't want to see you jack up your life as I have."

"Nah," Lil Wu says as a smirk pops onto his face. "This ain't about me and you. It's about you and only you. No, let me switch that up. It's about you and your little girlfriend Sameerah. It's about y'all."

Wustafa stands in silence. Lil Wu's words come as a shock to him.

"Neph, where did all that come from? What do you mean? What are you saying?"

"I'm saying, I'm just as built as any of them are."

"Neph, I'm not talking about them. I'm concerned with you right now at this moment. I mean, all I can do is ask you. In the end, you are

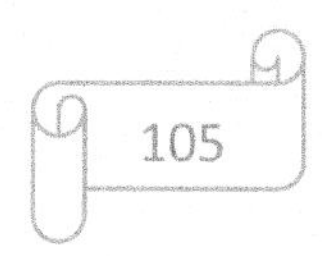

going to do what you want to do," he says with pity in his eyes. "But you just won't do it with me."

They stare into each other's eyes for seconds with neither of them saying a word for before Wustafa extends his hand.

"Nephew, I hope you understand that the decision that I've made is for your own good."

Lil Wu looks at Wustafa's hand as it dangles in the air. He looks back into Wustafa's eyes with disgust before nodding his head.

"Humph," he grunts before turning around and walking away from Wustafa. "I'm not built for this life, but I guess your Babygirl is, huh?" Lil Wu asks as he turns around and walks away. "Is that why you banned us from fucking her, so you can keep all the pussy to yourself?" Lil Wu asks as he walks away.

Wustafa stands there, in total confusion. He can't understand why Lil Wu is saying these things to him. He watches as Lil Wu gets further and further away from him.

"Nephew, don't walk away from me like that," Wustafa shouts out.

Lil Wu continues stepping without once turning around.

"Nephew! Nephew!"

CHAPTER 35
THE NEXT DAY

Anthony hops out of the backseat of the stolen Acura, in broad daylight. As he walks close to the building, he pulls his skullcap low over his eyes. He peeks around cautiously. As he approaches the corner, he peeks around even more. He turns the corner and puts his hand into his army jacket pocket as he passes the first storefront on the corner. He stops at the second storefront and peeks inside.

He peeks around once again before pushing the door open. The chime on the door causes the barber to look up from the floor full of hair that he's sweeping. He automatically recognizes Anthony as one of their customers.

"We closed," he says arrogantly.

He looks up to his right, raising his right hand in the air. He presses the power button on the remote, and the huge screen television shuts off.

"You didn't hear me? I said, 'We closed'," he says as he looks back over at Anthony.

To the man's surprise, Anthony has his gun aimed directly at his head. Anthony has the gun gripped tightly in his latex covered hands.

"Heard you the first time."

"Hold," the barber says with complete shock on his face.

He drops the broom and slowly raises his hands high in the air.

"Yo, what's up?" he asks.

The door chime sounds off again as Wustafa steps into the shop. His hands are covered in latex gloves as well. He quickly locks the door behind himself before walking over to the huge picture window. He draws the shades closed tightly. He, then, flicks the light switch, making it quite dark in the shop.

A bright smile pops up onto Wustafa's face as he walks toward the man.

"What's up, tough guy?" The man's face looks as if he's seen a ghost. He watches Wustafa walk toward him as he stands there, frozen stiff. "Where's that cannon you had on you last time?" Wustafa asks as he gets within reach of the man. A demonic smile appears on Wustafa's face. "Go ahead and draw."

"Come on, man," the man pleads.

"Come on, what?" Wustafa asks. "Draw."

With rapid speed, Wustafa hauls off and pimp slaps the man, causing his head to twist sadistically. While the man holds his face, Wustafa reaches for the man's waistband where he finds the same gun that he drew on him. Wustafa snatches the gun from his waist and smacks him across the face with it.

"I knew you wasn't like that," he smiles.

The man backs up fearfully.

"Please don't. Whatever y'all want, y'all can I have. Please don't kill me?" he begs.

Wustafa laughs hysterically. "Now, it's 'please don't kill me', huh? Not too long ago, it was 'I wish they would come in here with that 'F' Wustafa and his Young Gunz'," he says as he snatches the man by the collar.

He points the gun at the man's face as he digs into his pockets and takes all the money that he has in them. He snatches the man's watch from his wrist and his necklace from his neck.

"You put on one heck of a show. Had all your workers falling out with laughter. You should do stand-up comedy," Wustafa says with a half a grin. "Any other money in here?"

"No, that's it. That's all I got."

"Where are the keys to the pretty BMW you got parked around the corner?"

The man digs into his pocket and hands the keys over with no hesitation.

"You stood up to me, though. I respect that. I have no choice," he says with a grin. "You told me to my face that you are willing to die for yours. At least, you will die as a man of your word," he says as he hands the gun behind him to Anthony.

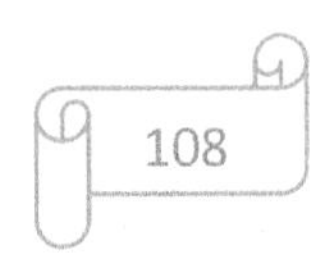

"Please! No, please!" the man cries.

Anthony tucks his own gun into his waistband as he holds the .357 Magnum in the air and aims it at the man's face. Anthony steps closer to the man as Wustafa steps back a few steps.

"At least, you will go down in history as a man of your word. You were willing to die for yours, right? Now, die," Wustafa says as he steps out of the way.

Boom!

The man drops to his knees. He lies twisted on the hardwood floor. Anthony stands over him and dumps one more.

Boom!

Wustafa taps Anthony to awaken him out of his zone. He reaches for the gun slowly. Anthony turns it over to him with no hesitation. Wustafa bends over and lays the gun on the man's dead body.

"Let's go," Wustafa says as he leads the way. Once they get to the door, he stops and looks back at the body once again before stepping out of the door.

"Let's see how funny his employees find this when they come to work tomorrow."

CHAPTER 36

THREE DAYS LATER/ 10:42 P.M.

Speed peeks from side to side quickly, before dashing through the intersection. The cars that are coming at him from both sides slam on their brakes in order to avoid a collision with him in the huge Suburban. Speed looks into the rearview mirror, and the bright red lights make him step on the gas pedal that much harder.

He quickly reaches the next intersection. As he's approaching it, he quickly thinks of the best route to take.

"Go! Go!" Sameerah shouts with fear as she's turned around in her seat. Her eyes are glued onto the flashing lights that are behind them.

For no other reason but boredom, a policeman decided to tail them. As the car followed them for three whole blocks, Speed obeyed the traffic laws, hoping they would eventually turn off, but they didn't. After running the license plates, the truck came up stolen, so the officer called in for backup.

The sight of the second car was the incentive Speed needed to take off. They've now been speeding through the city recklessly in the midst of a high speed chase for the past ten minutes. Those ten minutes seem like an eternity to them. Speed has done everything in his power to get away from them, but, for the life of him, he can't seem to shake them. He's taken risks that would normally make them back off but to no avail.

"Two more cars jumped on it!" Anthony shouts.

Lil Wu sits in the very back of the truck with his head buried in between his legs. His eyes are closed because he doesn't want to see a thing. The more he sees, the more terrified he becomes. The sight of the police cars are enough to send him into cardiac arrest.

Lil Wu's persistence got him accepted back into the organization. Even after that night, he didn't give up. He came back every day as if Wustafa hadn't said a thing to him. He explained to Wustafa that he would continue on with or without the organization. He explained that he would form his own crew and use everything that he'd learned from Wustafa. Wustafa could see the sincerity in his eyes.

The last thing that he would want is for Lil Wu to go out there with no knowledge of the game and jam himself up. He figured, at least, under his wing he could protect Lil Wu. Of all the days for Wustafa to take him back in, Lil Wu has asked himself over and over tonight during this chase, "Why did it have to be tonight?"

Speed makes a quick right turn onto South Orange Avenue.

"We got a stretch on them!" Leonard shouts. "Go! Go!"

"I'm going as fast as I fucking can!" Speed shouts with frustration. "This big shit slow as hell!" Speed makes a sloppy right turn onto 6th Street and almost bangs into a parked car. He catches the turn and regains control. He mashes the gas pedal, hoping to gain more speed. He reaches yet another intersection in a matter of seconds. He peeks to his right where he sees a cop car parallel to him the next block over. He peeks to his left, and, there, he sees a cop car on that block as well. He realizes that they're trying to trap him off. He knows that it's a matter of time before a car comes across and cuts him off.

"They every fucking where! We ain't getting away from them!" he shouts with despair as his momentum dies. He slows the truck up as he tries to figure out his next move.

"What you mean we ain't getting away from them?" Wustafa asks. "We gotta get away from them! You better drive like you never drove before," he says in a threatening tone.

Speed makes a quick left onto Springfield Avenue, and his eyes set onto three cars, which are coming up the hill. He watches them with caution, expecting them to cut in front of him. To his surprise, they let him pass them. Speed watches in the rearview as the three cars make U-turns in the middle of the street. Those three cars jump in line behind the other four cars that were already tailing them. As Speed makes the right turn onto Bergen Street, he spots another car's lights behind him in the intersection.

"We got the whole force on us!" Leonard shouts fearfully. "Go, motherfucker, go!"

Lil Wu sits upward. For a quick second, he gets the urge to open his eyes to see just how messy it looks. He squeezes his eyes tighter to

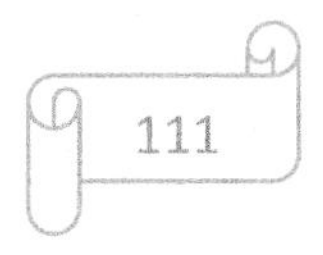

refrain from doing so. He can't see a thing, but the sound of the loud sirens is scaring him to death. He braces himself in the seat as Speed's reckless driving bounces him up and down.

The sound of the blaring sirens and the sight of the blazing lights bring great alarm to Wustafa. He needs one moment of serenity, so he can try and put a plan together. He closes his eyes for a brief second in an attempt to block it all out. In that brief second, he pictures himself in handcuffs. He, then, pictures himself standing behind prison bars. He opens his eyes as he snatches his gun from his waist. He looks over to Speed as he grips his gun tightly.

"I'm not going back to prison," he utters. "Nah, I can't!" he says as he shakes his head. "Load up, y'all!"

They all look at him with great surprise. Speed peeks over at him for a quick second.

"What you mean?"

"I mean, load up!" Wustafa shouts. "I'm not going back to prison!"

"You talking 'bout banging out with the cops?"

"We don't have no other choice," Wustafa says as he looks behind them. "Y'all ready?"

Leonard and Anthony look at each other with their eyes stretched wide open. They hold their guns limply in their hands. Sameerah looks at Wustafa as if he's crazy. Lil Wu sits in the back, frozen stiff. He's terrified.

"Gun in hand!" Wustafa shouts. "Follow my lead!" he says as he rolls the window down slightly. "Roll the windows halfway down."

"Wu, hold up," Speed pleads. "Don't move yet. Let me just get us out of this mess," Speed says as he damn near mashes the gas pedal through the floor of the truck. All he can picture is a gun battle and that makes him drive even faster.

Speed makes a quick right turn followed by a short left onto a one way street. He races against the traffic as cars swerve to the side to get out of his way. Speed looks up the block, and, to his surprise, two blocks away, he spots two police cars coming in their direction. He looks in the rearview mirror where he sees three cars coming behind him.

He realizes that they are trapped.

"They got us trapped," Speed admits as he realizes that it's over.

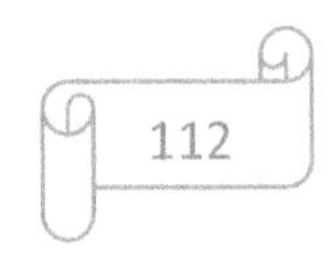

A tear slides down Lil Wu's face. He quickly wipes away the evidence of the tear. He looks up at Wustafa to see what his command will be. Whatever the command is he's sure that he's not prepared to do it.

"Listen," Speed says. "We gonna have to bail," he says as he looks at Wustafa, awaiting his response. Wustafa looks around and realizes that there really is nowhere from there to go. "What you think?"

"I'm with you," he replies to Speed's surprise. "Just get us a head start and we gone from there," Wustafa says.

"Ain't no head start," Speed replies. "They coming from every direction. Look up there. They got the block blocked off already. When I hit the middle of the block, we gotta bail out from there."

They all look around nervously as they think of a getaway route. "Ready, y'all?"

"Listen. We all gotta separate," Wustafa commands. "First chance you get, stash your gun, but remember where you stashed it at, so we can come back for it."

"Now!" Speed shouts as he slams on the brakes and slams the gear into park. He busts the door wide open and sprints like a track star. All the other doors pop open simultaneously, and they all take off in different directions. The sound of the sirens has them running faster than they have ever run in their lives.

Neither one of them has a particular destination in mind. They're just running, hoping for safety. Where will they end up? They have no clue. All of them are running in different directions, but they have the same goal. None of them want to end up in a jail cell.

CHAPTER 37
4 HOURS LATER/2:30 A.M

Extreme silence fills the air. It's so quiet; one's thoughts can be heard. Wustafa paces around the room with his head hanging low. It took him almost three hours to make it home after bailing out of the truck. He hid in a backyard a few blocks over from where they bailed out at. He laid there for over two hours, while the police searched high and low.

He listened as sirens sounded off for many blocks. Once the sirens finally stopped, he crept out of his hiding place and made his way home. When he got there, he was happy to be greeted by Lil Wu and Leonard. They stated that they stayed together, side by side, the entire time. Together, they hopped a couple of fences that led them right to safety. They claimed that they had been sitting on the porch waiting for him for over two hours before he got there.

Anthony was the most fortunate of them all. He slipped into an alley, climbed one fence, and hid in an abandoned building until all the commotion was over. Speed had the worst experience. Almost every officer seemed to have targeted him. He's no foreigner to foot chases with the police. He has a great deal of experience in that field and that worked to his advantage.

His expertise, coupled with his extraordinary foot speed, got him out of the hole. He got away scott-free, but he lost a gun. At one point, things got so crucial that he just knew he was about to get caught. He, then, ditched his gun the very first opportunity that he got, just as Wustafa instructed them to do.

Wustafa stops in the middle of the room. Everyone looks at him to hear what he has to say.

"We are here safe and sound, but I been thinking," he says before hesitating for a few seconds. "From here on out, in case this ever happens again, we are not to meet here. This is the headquarters, our safe haven. We are to treat this as if it's sacred. Our money and our

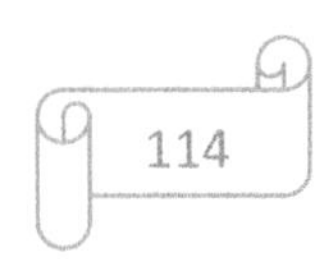

artillery are in here. We have to keep that protected," he says as he starts pacing again.

He bangs his fist into the palm of his hand.

"Four hours have passed. We must accept the reality that Babygirl isn't coming. She must've gotten caught," he says with sadness plastered onto his face.

"Maybe, she's still out there hiding," Anthony says with his face covered in hope.

"Impossible," Wustafa says, crushing all hope that he had. "There's no way that they're still out there looking for us. It's not like we committed a murder. Babygirl got pinched," he says as he stares into Anthony's eyes. "I just hope that she can hold water," he says as his eyes penetrate through Anthony's soul.

They all feel a great deal of sympathy for Sameerah, especially Anthony. The fact that she's his very best friend makes him feel more than the rest of them. They all realize that it could have been them, instead of her. Only one in the room feels very little sympathy, and that's Lil Wu. In fact, a part of him couldn't care less. The way his uncle praises her makes him a little happy that she's been nabbed.

The look makes Anthony feel quite uncomfortable.

"Wu, we don't have nothing to worry about. Don't worry," he says with confidence in his voice.

"Worry? I'm not worried," he lies.

In fact, Wustafa is more than worried. With his jacket, a stolen car and eluding will get him sent away for the rest of his life. He has everything to worry about; wherein, they have very little to worry about. With them being juveniles, they will get a mere slap on the wrist. He's glad that the car was only stolen and not carjacked, or the situation would be more severe.

"You should be worried about her rolling over because, if she does, you will be held accountable," Wustafa says. "After all, you brought her into the organization, which makes her your responsibility. On that note, meeting adjourned," Wustafa says as he continues to stare into Anthony's eyes.

"Tomorrow is Sunday," Wustafa continues. "So, our normal reading and studying will take place. We will just sit back and regain our composure after tonight's close call," he says as he relives the entire experience. "All are to report here at the regular time. Hopefully, Babygirl will be here, as well."

Wustafa grabs the duffle bag from the table and holds it open. They all get up, snatching their weapons from their waistbands. They all make their way over and drop their weapons into the duffle bag, except for Speed. He looks into Wustafa's eyes with pity on his face.

"Sorry 'bout that, Wu."

"Ay, man. That's nothing. We can always get more guns. Your freedom is more important. I hope all of y'all learned a lesson from this," he says as he looks around the room. "Now, do y'all see the importance of being gloved down all the time?" They all nod their heads. "Okay, next day, y'all," he says as he zips the bag closed.

He watches them as they all make their way toward the door.

"Peace!" he shouts.

"Peace!" they all shout simultaneously as they exit the apartment.

Wustafa walks over to the door and opens it slightly. He peeks his head out and watches as they all exit the alley. As soon as they are out of his sight, he quickly steps out and locks the door behind him. He hooks the straps of the duffle bag over his shoulder like a backpack. He walks toward the backyard quickly.

Once he's in the yard, he hurdles over the little fence into the next yard. He peeks around cautiously before climbing over another fence. He looks around at the neighboring houses, just to see if he's being watched. After seeing no trace of anyone, he steps onto the fire escape of the abandoned building. He runs up the fire escape at a moderate pace. After a few minutes, he finally steps onto the roof.

He looks around at all the junk that is scattered around, and, immediately, he locates what he thinks is the perfect hiding spot. He runs over to the edge, and, right in between a few garbage bags, filled with only God knows what, he drops the bag onto the ground. He lifts the garbage bag and plants it right on top of the duffle bag. As much as he doesn't believe that Sameerah will bring the heat to him, he can't afford to take the risk.

****Meanwhile****

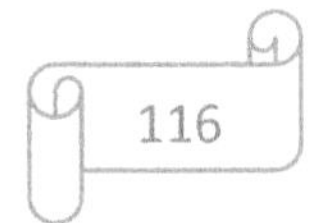

The white robbery/homicide detective sits on the edge of the desk directly in front of Sameerah. He stares at her with extreme hatred in his eyes without saying a word. Watching her sit there with her lips puckered up is infuriating him to the point that he wants to beat her to a pulp. All his tactics of attempting to pump fear in her have failed. As he sits here, he tries to figure out a better approach to get what he needs from her.

"Listen, Sameerah. I'm gonna work with you. You seem to be a smart, young woman. I don't want to see you throw your life away. I'm gonna do everything in my power to help you," he says with a false look of compassion on his face. "But you have to be willing to help me out as well. The bottom line is this, I know that you were not the driver. If you give me the name of the driver, I will see that you get set free. I'm not gonna lie to you. I'm not really concerned with you. You're a juvenile, and I would hate to mess up your life. With a record, you will never be able to get a job. Ever," he adds with emphasis. "You don't want that do you?" he asks. "So, give me the name and the whereabouts of the driver and all of the adults that were present in that vehicle," he says as he looks at Sameerah, hoping that he has gotten through to her.

Sameerah looks up at him with her big, beautiful eyes. She doesn't say a word to him for seconds. As he stares into her eyes, he sees a sign of tears that seem to be ready to drip. He feels a sense of satisfaction.

"Got her," he mumbles to himself.

He watches her mouth closely as she opens it, getting ready to speak. *Come on*, he thinks. *Come on. Give me what I need*, he thinks as he watches the tears build up in her eyes.

Sameerah yawns loud and rudely.

"Can you come on and get me to the youth house? I'm tired as shit," she says as she rubs her eyes. "I can barely keep my eyes open. I need sleep," she says as she watches the detective look at her with disgust. A smile covers her face. "Ain't you tired, too?"

CHAPTER 38
THE NEXT NIGHT

The snow white Cadillac Escalade floats through the darkness like a ghost. All are present in the truck, except Sameerah. Even in her absence, the show must go on. They have not heard a thing from her, and they all are worried about her.

The only one who isn't affected by her absence is Lil Wu. With her not being present, he gets a seat instead of being crammed up in the back like luggage. He sits in between Leonard and Anthony. He hasn't ridden in the seats of the civilized in so long that he had almost forgotten what it felt like.

Today, Wustafa decided to stay local. They have been cruising through the city with no particular destination in mind, just hitting random spots. Although Wustafa likes to have his work planned out, he's found that, sometimes, freestyling can be quite lucrative. Outside of the financial benefit, there are other benefits as well.

He realizes that, sometimes, there isn't enough time to make a plan and one must be prepared to make a rational decision under pressure. He feels that freestyling through the city, every so often, will teach his crew to spot a good vick and, also, teach them to be able to respond without putting very much thought into it. He wants them to be able to think on their toes.

"What's that up there?" Speed asks as he points to the corner store, which is a half a block away.

The store is closed, which means the lights of the canopy are out, and it's pitch black in the entire area. On the corner, little activity seems to be taking place. A few young men stand posted up on the platform of the store, leaning on the gate.

As they get closer to the corner, Wustafa is able to make out the images in the darkness. He sees three people posted up, standing on the platform as they serve a few customers that stand in front of them. Just as they get closer to the intersection, the customers all disperse in different directions.

"Don't look too heavy out here," Wustafa says as he peeks around, observing the surroundings. "But it's right here in our lap, so we may as well get it. Lenny and Ant in and out, y'all," Wustafa says with no real interest at all. "Don't drag this out and turn this into a long drawn out story."

Wustafa looks at the men and realizes that they have their full attention on them.

"They on us," says Wustafa. "You gonna have to be quick," he says as he looks to Speed.

Speed steps on the gas pedal lightly, trying to cruise through the intersection as normal looking as he can. The young men watch the truck closely as it approaches them.

"Slide a little past them," Wustafa commands.

Speed creeps past them and slams on the brakes abruptly. Before the truck makes a complete stop, the back doors pop open, and Leonard and Anthony hop out with their guns drawn and aimed at the corner. Lil Wu slides over from the middle seat to the seat behind Speed in order to make room for their return.

"Don't even think about it!" Leonard shouts as he races toward them. "Touch the fucking sky!"

Anthony comes running from the other side of the truck to cover his partner. Leonard gallops over to the first man and immediately runs through his pockets. All three men stand there stiffly with their hands high in the air. Anthony runs over to the third man, spinning him around before he rips through his pockets.

Leonard slams his gun onto the side of the man's face, sending him stumbling off of the platform.

"Lay the fuck down!" Leonard shouts as he aims at the man. He looks over to the third man. "On the ground!" Anthony frisks the middle man and rids him of every dollar that he has in his pockets.

After the last two men dropped to the ground, Leonard backpedals away, taking giant steps, while Anthony gallops sideways with his gun still aimed. They both hop into the truck, and Anthony closes the door behind them. As they're about to pull off, Lil Wu sees a shadow through his peripheral, causing him to zone in on the shadow.

What he sees causes him alarm— a man creeping out of an alley on his side, a few houses ahead of them. In almost slow motion, he watches as the man lifts a chrome handgun in the air and aims at the truck. Lil Wu wants to warn the crew, but the words won't leave his mouth. Finally, he's able to murmur, "Yo!"

Quickly, he rises up in his seat, fumbling with his gun.

"Watch out!" he shouts before the sound of a single gunshot rips through the air.

Boc!

Seconds later, heavy impact smacks into the body of the truck. Speed and Wustafa both duck, not knowing where the gunshot came from.

Lil Wu hangs his gun out of the partly cracked window and fires a shot of retaliation.

Blocka!

The gunman ducks low in fear, while Lil Wu mashes the trigger.

Blocka! Blocka! Blocka! Blocka!

With surprise, Lil Wu watches as the man falls onto his stomach.

As they're passing the gunman, Wustafa sees him lying in a submissive position and assumes that he has been wounded.

"Finish that!" Wustafa shouts. He looks over at Speed. "Back up!"

Speed backs up sloppily, swerving onto the other side of the street. With a few seconds of hesitation, Lil Wu pushes the door open and hops out of the truck, leaving the door wide open. With his adrenaline racing, he runs over to the man, who lies there, peeking upward helplessly. His gun lies a couple of feet away from him. Lil Wu aims at his dome and fires.

Blocka!

He watches as the man's body caves in and his head bangs against concrete. Lil Wu stands directly over the man and squeezes.

Blocka! Blocka!

He stands there, in shock, for a few seconds until the sound of Wustafa's voice snaps him out of his zone.

"Let's go!" Wustafa shouts.

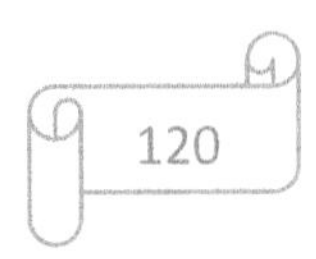

Lil Wu turns around and runs to the truck as fast as he can with his heart banging through his chest. He climbs into the truck, slams the door, and Speed mashes the gas pedal as hard as he can. The truck speeds up the block.

"Good eyes, nephew! Good eyes!" Wustafa cheers as he holds his fist into the backseat, awaiting a return dap from Lil Wu.

Lil Wu sits back with a shocked expression on his face. He is breathing heavily. He finally catches his breath and realizes what has just happened. He returns the fist dap by banging his against Wustafa's. Wustafa pounds the dashboard with his fist.

"That's what I'm talking about, Lil Wu! I knew you had it in you! Just had to bring it out of you!" he shouts with joy.

Hearing Wustafa say the name Lil Wu sounds like music to his ears. Leonard plants his hand on Lil Wu's shoulder. Lil Wu looks over to Leonard, who is wearing a huge smile on his face.

"You back, baby!"

A huge smile slowly covers Lil Wu's entire face.

"I'm back," he whispers. "I'm fucking back!"

CHAPTER 39
THE NEXT MORNING/ 11:46 A.M.

"Oil and vinegar, Papi?" the beautiful Spanish woman yells over the sound of the loud guitars that blare through the little radio.

The woman dances sexily as she dresses the sandwich up with all of the toppings. As she dresses the sandwich, Lil Wu undresses her with his eyes.

"Oil, vinegar, salt and pepper?" she asks as she shakes her body like she's having a seizure.

Lil Wu stares over the counter at her tiny waist and her perfectly sculpted figure. As she sways her full hips from side to side, Wu watches closely, hypnotized.

"Papi," she says in order to get his attention. He snaps out of the lustful hypnotism and looks at her face. Her thick and sexy lips trap his attention.

"Papi, oil, vinegar, salt and pepper?" she repeats.

Without realizing it, Lil Wu has his lips puckered up and moving them in rhythm with hers. She has him mesmerized in her beauty.

"Everybody, lay the fuck down! Move, and I'm blowing your fucking brains out!" shouts a voice from the front of the store.

"Owwww!" a woman shouts from the front of the store.

"Papi, I ain't bullshitting! I mean business! Shut that bitch up before I do!"

"Owwww!" the woman screams again.

The sharp sound of the woman's screams snaps Lil Wu out of the daze that he's been in for the past few minutes. He peeks to the front where he sees Leonard and Anthony running around like madmen. He looks back to the woman behind the counter. She quickly ducks down behind the counter. She presses her index finger against her full lips.

"Shhh," she whispers as she grabs the phone from the table.

She peeks upward to the front of the store as she lifts the receiver from the base. Lil Wu watches with surprise before finally hopping over the counter. He attempts to snatch the phone from her, but she snatches it back from him. They play tug of war for seconds, and, without Lil Wu noticing it, she manages to press the number 9 and the number 1.

He realizes what she's doing, and, right before she presses the 1 again, he slaps the phone out of her hand. Before the phone can even land on the floor, the woman jumps up and charges Lil Wu like a raging bull. With the strength of three men, she flings him around violently. Like a cat, she claws his face with one hand. With the other hand, she bangs a frying pan over his head. Fear inspires her to fight her hardest.

"Oww! Oww!" she screams as she fights for her life.

It takes Lil Wu a few seconds to finally realize what has taken place. It all has caught him totally off guard. Through one eye, he peeks up to the front where he spots Leonard in clear view. Leonard stares at him, while he stands over three Dominicans with his gun aimed.

"Man, blow that bitch's brains out!" Leonard shouts, enraged.

Lil Wu thinks about how all this may be looking. He, then, thinks of how long his lay-off lasted. The last thing he needs is for Wustafa to hear this, and he's finished. He's just gotten accepted a couple of nights ago, and now this. He can't afford another strike. The thought of that causes him to black out.

When he awakens, both of his latex covered hands are clasped around the woman's neck. He's face to face with the beautiful woman, yet her beauty means nothing to him at this point. He stares into her bulging eyes as she gasps for air. He squeezes her neck tightly as he shakes her violently. The tears well up in her eyes like a flood.

He lets her neck go, but, just as he does, he turns over a short left hook onto her face. As she stumbles backwards, he follows up with a punishing straight right. She falls onto her back, staring up at him with fear. He lifts his leg high in the air.

"Please, no," she begs.

"Shut up," he says as he stomps her abusively.

She screams at the top of her lungs. He's never hit a girl in his life and always felt sorry for any woman that was hit by a man. In this case,

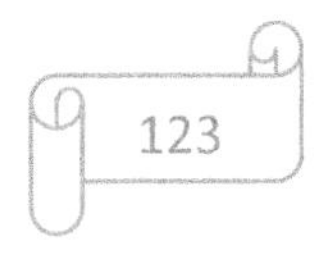

he feels no compassion. It's either mash her out, or be chastised by Wustafa, or, even worse, be kicked out of the organization for good.

He realizes he must do something to redeem himself. He snatches his gun from his waistband. He aims at the center of her forehead as she stares at him with pity in her eyes. As much as he doesn't want to do this, he feels that he has no choice. He takes a deep breath and closes his eyes as he slowly taps the trigger.

"No!" Leonard shouts from the front of the store. "No! Let's go! Let's go!"

Lil Wu snaps out of his zone and peeks to the front of the store where he sees Anthony making his exit. In his hands, he holds a shopping bag.

"Let's fucking go!" Leonard shouts as he jumps up and down impatiently.

Lil Wu quickly thinks of how the woman has embarrassed him and possibly gotten him kicked out of the crew. With all of his might, he kicks the woman in her chest. She gasps for air as all of the wind is knocked out of her body. Lil Wu hops over the counter and runs to the front.

He hops over the two Dominican men and the Dominican woman who all lie face first on the floor. Leonard holds the door open for him to exit, and he does. Together, they run to the Suburban that is waiting for them a few feet ahead. They hop into the truck, and Speed peels off with no hesitation.

"Yeah!" Anthony shouts with rage. "Fuck that!" he shouts as his adrenaline races full speed ahead.

"How y'all make out?" Wustafa asks curiously. Lil Wu sits back nervously, just hoping his situation isn't brought up. He's sure if Wustafa hears this it will be the last straw for him. He prays silently that it's not brought up. "So, I take it that everybody did what they were supposed to do?" Wustafa asks as he looks at Anthony.

"On the real, Big Wu, I was in my zone, just doing what I do! I wasn't even paying no attention to nobody else. My eyes was on the prize!"

"Dead right," Wustafa replies with a slight grin. He quickly looks over to Leonard. "Everybody was on point?" he asks as he peeks over to Lil Wu and back to Leonard. "Everybody do what they were supposed to do?"

Lil Wu sits back in silence, while his heart bangs through his chest.

"Nah," Leonard replies slowly.

"Nah?" Wustafa asks. "Tell me all about it."

Lil Wu closes his eyes as he lowers his head with shame. He opens his eyes and looks over to Leonard with a look of hatred in his eyes. He can't believe that his best friend would go against him like this. Just to think, he brought him into the organization. Now, he's about to sell him out. This breaks his heart. After all the years that they have been together, side by side, through thick and thin, he can't believe that it has come to this.

Lil Wu shakes his head slightly.

"You motherfucker," he mumbles under his breath.

"What happened?" Wustafa asks anxiously. "Who wasn't on point?"

He looks over at Lil Wu with displeasure plastered all over his face. Lil Wu can't even look his uncle in the eyes. He lays his head back against the headrest.

"Man, Lil Wu was back there wilding the fuck out! The Spanish bitch tried to put up a fight till he beat that bitch like a man! She tried to play hero and grab the phone! He stomped the bitch out and everything! When I looked back there, he was standing over her with the gun on her dome 'bout to blow her brains out. I had to beg him not to," Leonard says as he looks at Lil Wu with a slight grin.

"That's right, Lil Wu," Wustafa cheers. "A dame wanna play hero? Then, she supposed to be a dead hero," he laughs. "But I'm glad you didn't murk her with no mask on. You did the right thing, beat the brakes off that dame. Heroes get splattered," he says as he turns to face the front.

A smile pops onto Lil Wu's face. Leonard looks over to him and winks at him. Lil Wu exhales slowly as he wipes the sweat from his brow. He reaches over and sneakily holds his fist in the air. Leonard bangs his fist with a smile.

"Thanks," Lil Wu whispers. "Thanks."

CHAPTER 40
HOURS LATER

Mustafa stands in the hallway of the Newark Youth House, leaning against the wall. This place brings back so many memories for him, and surprisingly most of them are good memories. This is where his life of crime started. He still remembers the very first time he was brought here.

All the other kids that came in with him that day were crying from being scared and homesick, but not him. He immediately kicked off his shoes, made himself at home, and went right to sleep. His lack of a fear factor way back then is the cause of his lifelong criminal career. He didn't care or fear anything back then, and, as he stands here, thirty-five years older, only one thing has changed.

Back then, he didn't care about going to jail. Being away meant nothing to him. Even before his last bid, he still didn't care about going to prison. It was during that fifteen year stretch that he just completed that he started to have a change of heart. Today, the last thing he wants to do is go back to prison.

Nervousness fills his gut as he considers the possibility that Sameerah may have given him up. The thought of that almost deterred him from coming here. With all that he has at stake, he still felt that he had no other choice but to come. Sameerah called him before she called her own mother.

He suggested that it would be better if her mother came for her, but she explained that, if it was left up to her mother, she would be sitting in jail for the rest of her life. She, then, concluded with "Please, I need you." Hearing those words come out of her mouth melted through his stone-cold heart. Something about Sameerah brings out a soft side that he never knew he had in him.

Even though he's not sure if all this is a set-up, he's willing to risk it all. If she has rolled over on him, he loses it all, but, if she's stood her ground and he doesn't come for her, he still loses it all. If he doesn't show up, he's sure that she and the rest of his soldiers will lose faith in him. He emphasizes to his soldiers the importance of being able to depend on each other, and, if he fails them the very first time they are in need, he's sure they will see him as all talk.

He feels that, if they get the feeling that they can't depend on him, they will be less apt to put it all on the line as they have been doing. He's earned the trust of each of them and something as simple as this can tarnish all that he has built. Knowing all of that, he realizes that he has no other choice but to take the risk.

The opening of a door down the end of the hall captures Wustafa's attention. His heart skips a beat as he sees Sameerah being escorted down the hall by a detective. The sight of the detective confirms his thoughts. *A set up*, he thinks. He quickly looks at Sameerah who drops her eyes to the floor with what appears to him as guilt. *I can't believe she done this to me.*

He rises up from the wall. He quickly looks to his right for an escape route, but, to his surprise, he spots another detective coming toward him. For a quick second, he thinks of making a break for it, but he realizes that it's already too late. The two detectives already have him cornered. He flashes a cocky smile as he backs up against the wall. He's already envisioning how it's all going to go down.

"If they foolishly believe that I'm just gonna turn around and let them put the cuff on me, they're sadly mistaken," he mumbles to himself.

In no case ever has Wustafa just given up without a fight. Every one of his charges is accompanied by an assault on a police officer charge. He refuses to let his story end like this. He realizes that, with his rap sheet, a simple car theft charge will get him sent away for the rest of his life, not even including anything else that she may have given up. He backs up against the wall placing his left foot forward. He spreads his legs shoulder width and plants his weight on his right leg. He clenches his fists tightly at his side.

The detective places his hand on Sameerah's shoulder for comfort as they get closer to Wustafa. Just as the other detective gets to his right,

Wustafa takes a step forward, and he prepares to fight his way out of this situation.

"Mr. Jackson?" the detective says as he extends his hand for a handshake.

Wustafa and Sameerah lock eyes for the first time. She gives him the signal, letting him know to agree to the Jackson last name, as if he's her father. Wustafa looks at the detective's hand, which is dangling in the air. He turns away as if he doesn't even see it.

Wustafa despises police so much that he hates everything about them. He hates the way they walk, talk, and even smell. He looks at a handshake as a gesture of peace, which makes shaking the detective's hand out of the question. He could never be at peace with a cop. He doesn't trust cops under any circumstance. His uncle was a cop, and he never even trusted him. Now, as a retired cop for over twenty years, he still doesn't trust him.

He looks deep into the detective's eyes before looking him up and down once. He pays close attention to his stance and his posture. His body language doesn't send off a signal of attack, but Wustafa still doesn't let his guard down. Wustafa gives the detective a simple nod.

"Yes, I'm Mr. Jackson," he says.

Lying to a cop with a straight face is something that Wustafa has mastered over the years.

The detective finally realizes that Wustafa isn't going to shake his hand and withdraws it from the air.

"Mr. Jackson, I'm Detective Ross from Robbery and Homicide." Hearing the word homicide sends chills up Wustafa's spine. "I don't know if your daughter has informed you of all of the specifics but allow me," he says with a stern look on his face. "Your beautiful daughter was involved in a high speed chase in a stolen vehicle throughout the city. It ended with all the suspects fleeing the vehicle, all of them getting away but her. The vehicle had been reported stolen many days ago. Just two nights ago, that same vehicle was reported to have been used in a string of robberies and a possible homicide," the detective says as he looks away from Wustafa for a few seconds.

Wustafa reads the signal and realizes that the detective is lying through his teeth. Wustafa knows, for a fact, that the truck was stolen that morning and that was the very first time they pulled it out. He understands now that the detective has nothing because he's reaching. He's pouring it on thick in an attempt to instill fear in them.

"She claims that it was her first time in the vehicle, and, honestly, I believe her. I believe that she jumped in the truck, maybe, not aware that the truck was stolen. My problem with her is, she may have not known the truck was stolen, but she knows who was driving the truck. No way in the world did she get into a truck with complete strangers.

For almost two days now, I've had her at the headquarters, trying to convince her to tell who was in the truck, to save herself from getting a criminal record. Maybe, you can get her to save herself?" he asks with desperation in his eyes.

Wustafa looks over to Sameerah.

"Babygirl," he says with a sneaky wink of the eye. "If you know something, now is the time to save yourself. I'm gonna ask you one time and one time only," he says sternly. "Who was in the truck with you?"

Sameerah looks him dead in the eyes and with a stubborn look on her face she speaks. "I didn't know them."

"You are a liar!" the detective shouts with rage.

"Detective, please," Wustafa interrupts. "True, my daughter is stubborn and a bit unruly at times, but I've never had a problem with her lying. If she says she doesn't know them, I believe her. I can't stand here and watch you attack her like this."

"Okay. Well, then, watch her go to prison for the rest of her life." He looks over to Sameerah. "You better tell us something." He looks back over to Wustafa. "Mr. Jackson, her court date is next month. You have one month to convince her to tell what she knows if you want to save her future."

"Mr. Ross, correct?" Wustafa asks. "Can I speak to you over here?"

He steps away from them. The detective follows him to the side where they stand face to face. "Detective, it's all my fault. Ever since my Babygirl was in kindergarten, I always taught her not

to be a tattle-tale. Of course, I wasn't talking about a case like this, but I didn't specify. It's my fault, and I will fix this. I will work on getting you all the answers you need to crack this case. It won't be an overnight process, though. It will take some reprogramming. Give me your card and, anything that she's willing to tell me, I will tell you," he says as he holds his hand out for the card.

The detective wears an agitated look on his face as he reaches inside of his suit jacket. He drops the card in Wustafa's hand.

"I will be in touch, sir."

The detective walks off without saying a word.

"Sameerah Jackson, let's go. You are in big trouble," he says as he looks over to Sameerah. "Let's go now," he barks.

Wustafa places his arm around her shoulders as they exit the building. He looks her in the eyes as he drops the card onto the ground. He flashes a smile at her with a wink of the eye.

"That's my Babygirl!"

CHAPTER 41
3:30 P.M.

It's a bright and sunny Saturday here in the Washington Heights area of New York City. It's rather warm for this November day. The sun shines brightly, exposing the beautiful autumn colors. As bright as the sun may be shining, Wustafa has found the perfect spot in the shade. The dark, tinted out, huge Ford Excursion sits parked discreetly under a gigantic tree. The gold color of the truck makes it blend in perfectly under the overlapping extra leafy trees.

They've been sitting here for close to an hour now, just camping out. The target of interest is the apartment building at the corner, half a block away. Today is a big day for the crew. Today is the first day that the youngsters have ever been to New York City.

"Yep, this is it right here, y'all!" Wustafa shouts. "New York City, the big city of dreams," he sings. "Bright lights, fast cars! This is the big league right here! All the local robberies we got under our belt are just foreplay to what we can obtain over here," he claims.

His speech motivates them on a different level. They listen to his every word as they watch all that is going on around them. They all sit on the edge of their seats, watching the heavy activity around them as if it's one big movie. They've never seen anything like this in their lives. Dominicans stand posted up on every corner and on damn near every square foot of the block. Some sit discreetly on porches, stoops, and cellar steps.

"It's money being made out here on a big level," Wustafa says. "This ain't that nickel and dime penny pinching stuff that be going on back at home," he explains. "We are talking about millions and millions of dollars being made a day." Wustafa shakes his head. "There's a lotta money in that building. A lotta, lotta money," he adds. "Y'all can't imagine how many spots are in there."

"Just look at all the *Doe*-minicans," he says with mispronunciation. "And just to think, they all work for the same one or two guys. All the money they're raking in goes in only one or two directions. What direction? I don't know, but we are going to do our research, and we will not only get in that building, but we will get to that money," he says with great confidence.

He points to the corner where two young black men are walking. He watches as the Dominicans surround them and start pulling and tugging on them.

"Look, nothing but skeezers," he barks with disgust. "They all being pimped like whores while the big man sits high on the horse, probably sitting somewhere on a big yacht sailing in the Atlantic Ocean," he says with rage. "They come over here and destroy our country, selling that poison. Then, they send all their money back over to the Doe-minican Republic to build their country up," he spits with anger. "Now, watch closely. Watch how that money moves. See, they following that little Doe-minican into the building," he says slowly. "Now, pay attention to the old man that's sweeping in front of the store. See how he's watching around him?"

The old man digs into his pocket on the sneak tip. He quickly places a walkie-talkie to his mouth.

"See, I told y'all," says Wustafa. "They're all together. The old man just made the call alerting them that the two customers are on their way up." Wustafa watches the old man as he steps into the corner store and posts up right behind the door. "Now, you see, the average person would overlook the old geezer, but now we know not to sleep on nobody. When we make our move, we must pay attention to any and everybody."

A police car creeps through the intersection.

"Look at the pigs. The rollers stay rolling, but they're on the payroll as well. They know exactly where the drugs are, but why don't they go in and get them? I will tell you why. Because they'd rather wait on the outside to catch the niggers red handed. Excuse my language. Y'all know I don't ever use that word, but that's exactly what they are. Only a nigger would sell that poison to his own people. But it's all a conspiracy. The police and them Doe-minicans have a pact," he claims.

"The police take the hush money. Let them live and make money, while they lock up all the niggers as soon as they leave the building. They're all working together," he says. "Look!" he shouts as he points to an elderly woman on the corner. She stands behind a hot dog cart, selling food from it. As the police pass her, she places a walkie-talkie to her mouth. She speaks into it inconspicuously as she peeks down the block, in the direction where the police car went into.

"Even got old Nana on the payroll," he laughs. "Everybody is eating off of us! Look, every customer who has went into that building was black. All that poison is coming over to our community, killing us off. The ones they don't kill off with this poison, they open liquor stores off of the drug money they get and kill the rest of our people off with that legal poison. That's why I have no compassion for them," he barks.

"Look, look," he says excitedly. "Nana is back on the walkie-talkie as the two young boys exit the building. Nana is giving them the green light that the coast is clear. Nana is making real money. Don't let that little raggedy food court fool you. It's a mere front. Her son probably runs the business."

"Jump on them?" Speed asks as he keeps his eyes on the two young men.

"Are you kidding me?" Wustafa asks with attitude. "Them two penny-ante, good for nothing dudes ain't got nothing. They ain't got no money. The lil coins they probably spent in there, I'm sure addicts spend more on their habit. Anyway, they already spent their little money already. We can get nigger pennies all day back at home. We in the big city, the land of opportunity," he says. "We have the opportunity to get some real money. Ain't wasting my time over here on some bum for nothing niggers."

Suddenly, Wustafa's attention is diverted to the left of him. The New Jersey license plates on the champagne colored Lexus Coupe stick out like a sore thumb. As the car approaches on the opposite side of the street, Wustafa's eyes penetrate through the thirty-five percent bronze tint. He sees a young man, laying low in the driver's seat, while a beautiful young woman lays back, reclined in the passenger's seat.

"Uh oh, y'all. I smell money," he says as he watches the car pass by them.

They all turn their heads and zoom in on the license plates before examining the beautiful, luxurious car. The car is parked, and the passenger's door is popped open immediately. The door is wide open for minutes without anyone getting out.

Finally, the beautiful, young woman steps onto the concrete. She stands there for seconds, using the window as her full body mirror. She plays in her hair before turning around and fluffing her butt up in her jeans. Finally, the driver's door opens. The tall and lanky young man hops out, holding a shopping bag in his hand.

"Voilà, y'all!" Wustafa shouts. "The old, faithful sneaker box," he says with a smile. "We got one! Yeah, babbbby!" he says as he watches the man walk behind the car.

The man and the woman meet at the curb. He looks around as he hands her the shopping bag. She grabs the bag and starts stepping up the block toward the apartment building. The man crosses the street and walks along the opposite side of her.

"We gotta hurry, y'all," Wustafa says as they approach from both sides of the street. "We can't let them get to that corner. Lenny, you go behind the girl, and, Ant, you secure the dude," Wustafa says anxiously. "As soon as they pass, don't waste a second."

Just as the man passes the truck, Anthony opens the door as quietly as he can. He closes it even quieter. Leonard does the same on the other side. Anthony tiptoes behind the man, while Leonard takes giant strides with his long legs. The man sees Leonard crossing the street before he actually realizes that Anthony has crept up on him.

"Yo!" he says as he tries to get his girl's attention.

He attempts to take a step, but Anthony pulls him back by the collar. Just as the woman turns around, she spots Anthony wrapping his arm around her boyfriend's neck.

"Owww!" she screams fearfully. Leonard holds the gun at her side.

"Move, and I will blow your head off," he threatens.

She stands completely still as instructed. Once she's in arm's reach, Leonard pulls her to him. He wraps his arm around her shoulders, and they walk as if he's hugging her. He presses his gun against her side. "That's it. Just walk with me, and you won't get hurt."

"Please don't hurt me, please," she begs. "Here take the money."

"Shhh...be quiet. Just wait a minute, and we will get to that. Do as I say, and you won't get hurt."

From the truck, Wustafa watches as it all unfolds.

"That's right, my boys. That's how you get that money!" he shouts with great satisfaction.

Lil Wu sits in the very back of the truck with rage bleeding through his pores.

"Babygirl, you rubbed off on them. Ever since you came to the organization, everybody stepped their game up! You inspired them. Now, look at them work!"

Anthony backs the man into the nearest alley where he can no longer be seen.

"On your knees, nigga," Anthony says as he aims his gun at the man's head. The man drops to his knees without hesitation. "Hand me that watch," Anthony says as the gold Rolex catches his attention. The man quickly unfastens his watch and hands it over. "And the keys to the Lex." The man fumbles in his pockets and hands the keys over as well. Anthony, then, digs into his pockets, where he finds a couple of neat stacks of money.

"Now, listen and listen closely," Anthony says. "I want you to lay down and don't move. Move and your little girlfriend out there gets murdered on the spot. You hear me?" The man nods his head without saying a word. "Now, lay the fuck down," Anthony grunts.

He backpedals out of the alley and turns to walk toward the Excursion. He peeks across the street where he spots Leonard and the girl sitting on the stoop. The way Leonard has his arm wrapped around the girl's shoulder, one would think they were a happy couple. Anthony opens the back door and tosses Sameerah the car keys. "Here, Babygirl!"

"What's that?" Sameerah asks.

"The keys to the whip."

"That's it, my boy!" Wustafa cheers. "Now, you're using your head. It's starting to be second nature for you. I didn't even have to instruct you."

The words of praise infuriate Lil Wu to no end.

Sameerah hops out of the truck and walks over to the Lexus. She gets in, and, in seconds, she's making a U-turn in the middle of the street. She pulls behind the Excursion, which is now pulling out of the parking space.

As Leonard sits there, his eyes happen to land on her wrist. The gold Rolex is the total match to her boyfriend's. Leonard reaches over and unfastens the watch from her wrist. Tears well up in her eyes as she watches him put her watch into his pocket. He reaches over and takes her tennis bracelet from the other wrist. The tears now drip down her face.

He grabs her hand to take the ring that sets on the ring finger of her right hand. She balls up her fist with resistance.

"Please," she cries. "This came from my mother. It's the last thing that I have as memory of her. She died when I was a baby."

Leonard looks into her eyes with a stone cold look in his eyes. He lets her hand go slowly without taking the ring from her.

"Okay. Listen. I'm gonna get up, and we are gonna go our separate ways. You're gonna walk that way," he says as he nods into the opposite direction. He gets up and helps her from the stoop. He plants a kiss on her cheek. "I'm sorry for all this, but you just got caught up in the mix," he says as he looks into her tear filled eyes. "Go ahead and don't look back."

The young woman walks off, and so does Leonard. He picks up his pace and starts to jog over to the truck. He gets in, and Speed pulls off as normal as possible. Sameerah tails them with a few car's distance in between them. As they pass the alley where the man is, they see him still lying face down as he was instructed.

"Easy as pie. What we got?" he asks as he holds his hand out. Leonard hands the bag over to Wustafa.

Anthony hands the watch over to Wustafa. "A gold Rolex."

"Oh, here is her watch, too. It's the exact same," he says as he hands the watch over. "And a bracelet."

Wustafa fumbles anxiously with the shoe box as they all watch. The suspense is killing them all. The box is opened, and what sets before their eyes makes their mouths water. Stacks and stacks of money fill the box. Wustafa quickly skims over the stacks.

"We are looking at, at least, twenty-five large right here! Twenty-five grand, a Lexus, and his and her Roleys. Today is a great day. I told y'all

New York is the land of opportunity. Opportunity has knocked, and we are answering. This is just the beginning!"

CHAPTER 42
LATER THAT NIGHT

Only a few hours have passed since the New York robbery, and Wustafa and the crew are up to their shenanigans again. Wustafa eats and sleeps with stings on his mind. His greed is taking over. He's gone from going out every two days to going out everyday, even two and three times a day. The more he gets, the more he seems to want.

Wustafa makes his way through the crowded strip bar. With the Doll House being the most exquisite strip bar in the area, Wustafa is sure all the heavy hitters in the city must come through here. The aisle is packed, making it a big task for him to get by. He turns sideways to get past the man, who is sitting a stool, receiving a lap dance from a thick and voluptuous half naked dancer. The ratio is about fifteen to twenty men to every woman.

Wustafa keeps his hands tucked tightly in his pants pockets. He is fearful of touching anything. The thought of the many body secretions, germs, and bacteria that are all over this place skivvies him. Men sticking their fingers and hands into the women's private parts or even fondling themselves with perversion and then touching items makes him mindful not to touch anything. Door knobs, bar stools, and even the walls, he's sure are covered with germs. He looks at the whole bar as one huge arena of disease.

He finally makes his way to the back of the bar where he melts into the cut, hoping not to be noticed. He peeks to his left where a woman is bent over a stool, while a man rubs his hand up the crack of her rear. He gropes her perversely with one hand while holding a few dollar bills in front of her face as bait. Further to his right, he sees another woman bent over a stool as a man stands behind her, dry humping her, doggy style.

Just when he thinks that it can get no worse, it does. He watches as a beautiful, plus size dancer crawl around the bar top seductively. She stops in the center of the bar, and all her seduction goes out of the window as she turns around and raunchily spreads her cheeks wide open. She backs up, giving the man sitting there an up close and too personal view.

With no apparent shame, the man palms both of her cheeks before burying his face in between them. To Wustafa's disgust, the woman reaches behind and grips the back of the man's head. She force feeds her asshole to him while rotating her hips and grinding all over his face. The sight of this turns Wustafa's stomach. He turns away with annoyance.

Wustafa's attention is suddenly caught by the most conservatively dressed woman in the room. The pretty barmaid stands right in front of him. From across the bar, she points at him. With her index finger, she waves him closer to her. He steps to the bar with an inquisitive look on his face.

"What are you drinking?" she asks politely.

"No, thank you," he replies defensively. "I don't drink," he says as if he sees nothing wrong with saying it.

"Sir, we have a two drink minimum. No drinking, no hanging out," she says with attitude.

Wustafa sends her a look of pure hatred across the bar before speaking. "Well, in that case, give me two Diet Cokes," he says with a fake smile.

The woman walks off, and Wustafa peeks around the bar. He watches as the men give their money to the woman all for the sake of lust and perversion. He laughs to himself as he thinks of the fact of how these men consider themselves pimps when, in all reality, they're being pimped. They're spending their hard earned money for a touch of flesh in return.

"Johns," he mumbles to himself. "A room full of tricking Johns."

The barmaid steps before him, placing two glasses onto the bar. For the first time, he takes his hands out of his pocket and hands her a ten dollar bill. She turns around, and, like magic, she turns back around, holding a single dollar bill instead of the ten dollar bill that he gave her. Wustafa looks down at the bill with surprise.

"Nine dollars for two glasses of watered down Coke?" he asks with confusion on his face. He's ready to have a fit but quickly remembers what he's here for. He can't afford to shine any light on himself. He charges the outrageous price as an investment. "And give me my change," he says as he snatches the bill from her hand. "Get your tip from your boss since he's robbing his customers like that."

The woman walks away with an attitude, leaving him standing there, staring at the two glasses. He has no intention whatsoever of putting his lips onto those disgusting glasses. The thought of that gives him the urge to vomit. He quickly tucks his hands back into his pockets and leans forward against the bar. His scanner goes up, and he slowly starts searching for the money.

He immediately locates the big boys in the building. They stick out amongst the rest of the broke dudes. Wustafa zooms in on a dude who sits across the bar from him. Wustafa sees a ton of potential while looking at the man who sits there laced in jewelry. His cocky demeanor agitates Wustafa to no end. Mounds of money sit piled up in front of him.

Wustafa is so busy eyeballing the dude that he doesn't see the stripper slide up on him from his right. He turns toward her with a look of great surprise.

"Hey, handsome," the tall, thickly built, Amazon of a woman says as she reaches to put her hand on his chin. Wustafa jumps back with an unpleasant look on his face. He withdraws his hand from his pocket with the quickness and grasps her wrist in mid-air. He grips her wrist tightly, almost squeezing the life out of it.

"Aghh," she sighs. "Easy, big fella," she says with seduction in her eyes. "Don't hurt me."

Wustafa loosens his grip but still he holds her wrist.

"What are you doing in here all by yourself, looking all horny?" she asks with a sexy smile. "Is there anything that I can help you with?"

"Nah, I'm good," he replies, still gripping her wrist.

She spins around and backs her gigantic load against him. The smell of funky sweat mixed with Victoria's Secret lotion seeps into his nostrils. She's so much taller than him that her ass rests on his chest. Wustafa looks down at her sweaty, shiny skin and gets even more sickened.

He pushes her away with extreme force, but she doesn't budge the least bit. Still, she doesn't give up on him. She turns and faces him, once again, grabbing hold of his waist. She grinds on him seductively. "Loosen up, pop. Why you so uptight?"

Wustafa becomes enraged. "I ain't your pop. And I said I'm good," he says as he plants his hand onto the center of her chest. His hand melts into her sweaty cleavage. He digs deep into his pocket, retrieves his money and hands her a five dollar bill.

"Just go, please," he says as he waves her off.

The woman rolls her eyes resentfully before stepping away from him. Wustafa grabs a napkin from the bar and wipes her sweat from his hand with disgust before tucking his hands back into his pocket. He immediately locks his eyes back onto his prey.

Ten Minutes Later

Wustafa has managed to get closer to his subject without being noticed. There he stands right behind the man, back against the wall while watching the man's every move. The man sits back arrogantly as every dancer in the bar makes their way over to him. They treat him like royalty as he treats them like dirt.

He smacks them on the ass and gropes them disrespectfully before peeling off a few singles and sending them on their way. From across the room, Wustafa thinks he saw potential, but, now that he's up close, he's sure that the man is the perfect vick. Wustafa has watched as the man has pulled money from every pocket.

He estimates the man to have, at least, ten grand on him. His Rolex watch and his jewelry, Wustafa estimates to be worth, at least, fifty grand. From the look of it, Wustafa predicts that it will be a good night. Wustafa's attention is diverted to the key ring that sets on the bar in front of the man. The Cadillac logo on the key chain seems to jump up from the bar and reels Wustafa into it.

Wustafa creeps out of the bar without drawing any attention. Minutes later, he hops into the passenger's seat of the Suburban. Speed looks over to him upon his entrance.

"What it look like in there?"

"Looks like we got a live one in there," he says as he looks around as if he's in search of something. "About ten grand in liquid cash and fifty grand in valuables." Wustafa squints his eyes tightly. "We are in search of a Cadillac. Y'all see one anywhere in the vicinity?"

"Car?" Sameerah asks.

"Nah," Wustafa replies. "He doesn't appear to be a Caddy car type. Has to be a truck," he says with certainty.

"Burgundy Cadillac Escalade parked right there, across the street," Anthony says with excitement.

Wustafa looks over and spots the truck immediately.

"Bingo," he says as he looks over at Speed. "Pull over there and park behind it. Not too close, though. Can't blow this. I spent too many hours in that disease-infested, grime ball spot. I'm gonna need quarantine after that. I would hate for all the time I spent in there to be in vain."

After close to two long hours of camping out, the bar is finally letting out. They all have been dozing on and off, except for Wustafa. His full attention has been on that door, so he doesn't miss a beat, and he hasn't.

"Y'all up?" he asks. "It's finally show time."

The crowd of people making their exit goes from packs of three and four to one and two at a time. A great deal of the cars in the area clear out. Five minutes pass without anyone coming out of the bar when, finally, Wustafa's prey staggers out of the bar. Behind him are two dancers. The man stands on the corner, rocking back and forth like a drunk, lighting a cigarette, while the two women post up on both sides of him. They both have duffel bags strapped over their shoulders.

"We up, y'all," Wustafa says. "That's him right there on the corner in between the two whores." They all watch as the man and the two women step onto the street. They're eagerly awaiting Wustafa's next command. "Looks like somebody about to get a ménage. This will be like taking candy from a baby. He's intoxicated and his senses are off. The only thing on his mind is those two filthy whores that he's with.

"Nice and easy," Wustafa continues on to say. "We lay 'em all down. Strip him of the jewels, and, hopefully, he has some money left. The dames get it, too. They made a lotta money in there tonight. I know they're loaded," he says with certainty. "Anthony and Leonard, it's on y'all. Lil Wu, I want you on this one, as well."

Anthony and Leonard prepare themselves. Lil Wu's heart bangs through his chest. He's happy to be called in and plans to go out with a bang. He feels he has something to prove, and he plans to prove it. Lil Wu sits in the very back, on the edge of his seat, awaiting Leonard's exit, so he can hop out right behind him with no hesitation.

As their target makes his way into the intersection, to their surprise, the man heads in a direction that they had not expected. He raises his hand in the air, pressing the alarm. The lights of a Cadillac Deville shine brightly.

"Awl, man," Wustafa sighs. "I was off. I'm entitled to one mistake." He looks over to Speed. "We have to get closer without him seeing us."

Just as Speed starts the car up and begins to pull off, Sameerah blurts out, "No!"

They all jump nervously.

"The heat just pulled up," she says as she points up the block.

On that very corner, an Irvington Police car sits with his lights flashing.

"Whoa," Wustafa sighs. "Good eyes, Babygirl."

"Now, what?" Speed asks.

"We are going to have to put the tail on him," Wustafa replies. "I'm not letting this one get away. Hopefully, he will lead us to something bigger, like his house where all his money is," he says with a spark of joy in his beady eyes.

The man gets into his car, and so do the women. He pulls off, swerving slightly.

"Give him a little time before you pull off behind him," Wustafa commands.

Once the Cadillac reaches the corner, Speed pulls off behind it.

****Twenty Minutes Later****

A highly agitated Speed tails the Cadillac, less than a half a block behind it, on Route 1&9.

"Where the fuck is he going?" Speed asks with rage in his voice.

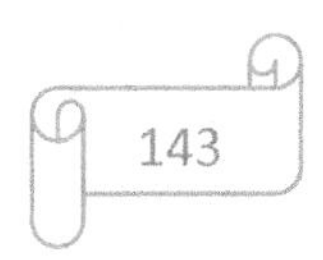

"Hopefully, he's leading us right to his doorstep," Wustafa replies. "Patience, young grasshopper. I'm sure it will be worth the wait. Uh oh, blinker," Wustafa says as he watches the Cadillac swerve recklessly into the first lane. "He's stoned!"

The Cadillac makes the quick left and follows the bend in the road as Speed follows behind it. At the intersection, he makes the left, followed by a quick right into the first parking lot.

"Benedict Motel," Wustafa says, reading the brightly lit sign.

The Cadillac quickly disappears into the darkness. In minutes, the man staggers toward the lobby of the motel. As soon as he's inside, Speed pulls into the lot and finds an empty parking on the opposite side of the parking lot behind the Cadillac.

"Babygirl, I need you," says Wustafa. "You and Lenny Love gotta pull this off. The chemistry between the two of you is crazy and will play out well in this situation."

Leonard and Sameerah look into each other's eyes. Leonard looks at her with a goofy smirk on his face until Sameerah finally looks away from him. Wustafa continues on.

"Y'all work good together, like the perfect couple," he teases. While everyone else is laughing away, Speed looks away with hatred on his face.

"How you want it done?" Leonard asks as he's placing the latex gloves onto his hands. He, then, pulls his skullcap down over his eyes.

"Just follow Babygirl's lead. Now, y'all go on and get out before he comes back out of the lobby. Pretend to be getting something outta the back of the truck," he instructs.

Both Leonard and Sameerah get out from both sides at the same time. Once they get to the rear of the truck, Leonard lifts the hatch while Sameerah stands right by him. They both peek through the dark tinted back windows, watching the man inside of the office.

Finally, he comes staggering out of the lobby. He takes a quick peek in their direction but continues to keep it moving, stumbling every few steps. As he's approaching his car, the two women get out of it, still carrying their bags on their shoulders. The man slowly passes them, leading them toward the staircase.

"Let's go," Sameerah says as she starts to walk away from the truck. Leonard slams the hatch closed and trots quickly behind her. They reach

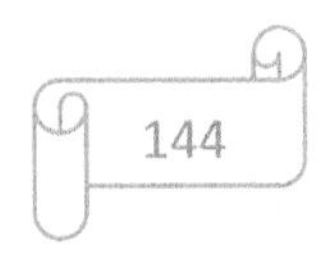

the staircase just as their targets are in the middle of it, thanks to the man's staggering.

One woman holds his hand, leading him up the stairs, while the other walks behind him with her hand planted on his back for reinforcement. The woman, who is pushing him, hears them coming up the stairs behind them and peeks over her shoulder at them. She watches them with a look of alarm in her eyes. As they reach the top of the staircase, the woman slows down her pace and says, "Y'all can go ahead."

Damn, Sameerah thinks. *She's on to us. Now, what*? Sameerah looks the woman up and down with a seductive look in her eyes.

"Damn, ma. You thick as shit," Sameerah says bluntly. "Y'all look like y'all about to have a ball," she says as she bites down on her bottom lip. "I wanna go with y'all."

"Word," Leonard agrees, just following her lead.

"Uhmm," Sameerah grunts, while licking her lips and looking at the woman like a delicacy.

The woman melts like putty in her hands. The cautious look on her face is replaced with bashful blushing. She loosens up her tense demeanor and continues to walk ahead of them. She puts on a sexy show for Sameerah as she switches her huge hips from side to side.

"Damn right! We about to have a ball," the man slurs. "It's a butt naked party 'bout to go on in Room 211, you heard?" the man shouts loudly.

Room 211. Both Leonard and Sameerah grasp in their minds as they look at exactly what room number they're in front of that very moment. "Oh, damn! We in the room right next to y'all," Sameerah lies as she looks at Leonard and gives him the head nod.

The man looks back at Sameerah and gives her the once over.

"You a pretty lil something," he says disrespectfully as if Leonard isn't even standing here. "You invited to the party, but you gonna have to leave your friend," he chuckles. "It's only gonna be one dick swinging in that room, and that's mines!" he says, before falling into laughter. "Ain't gon' be no sausage party in that motherfucker!"

Leonard looks at the man with pure hatred in his eyes, but he doesn't say a word. He continues on past Room 211. He stops right in front of Room 212 and turns his back, pretending to be fumbling with the door.

The man looks back at Sameerah as he stands at his room door.

"So, what is it gonna be, lil mama? You with us or against us?" he asks with a cocky demeanor.

"Nah, I'm gonna have to take a rain check. I got some business to handle over in 212," she says with a smile.

The man looks over at Leonard and looks him up and down with arrogance.

"Ma, that ain't no business. This big business right here," he says as he taps his chest. "But, okay, though. If you hear yelling, screaming, and the headboard crashing through the wall, don't worry; it's just us," he says with obnoxiousness. "If shit gets too quiet over there for you, don't hesitate to knock," he smiles.

"Nah, not tonight," Sameerah replies. "Anyway, I'm selfish and would want her all to myself," Sameerah says as she stares into the woman's eyes.

The other woman opens the door and drags the drunken man inside.

"Bye," the woman says.

She waves sexily as she backpedals through the doorway. The look in her eyes tells Sameerah that she's hoping that she will say more.

"Hold up," Sameerah says.

The woman stops in her tracks as she looks deeper into Sameerah's eyes. "Let me get a number on you," Sameerah suggests as she digs into her pocket.

She retrieves an ink pen from her pocket and hands it to the woman.

"Here. Write it down for me."

Just as the woman reaches for the pen, Leonard turns around with his gun already drawn. He aims at the woman's head as he snatches her by the collar, yanking her toward him. He places his latex glove covered hand over her mouth as he walks her inside the room. Sameerah steps in behind him and closes the door behind herself. Her gun is drawn as well.

The man has collapsed face first onto the queen sized bed. The other woman turns around, and her eyes bulge out of her head as she sees her friend being held at gunpoint. She screams at the top of her lungs, "Oww!"

Sameerah runs over and points the gun in her face.

"Shut up and lay down," she says aggressively.

The man hears the commotion and looks up, peeking through one drunken eye.

"What the fuck?" he slurs.

Leonard pushes the woman over to Sameerah.

"Lay them bitches down," he says as he runs over to the man.

He snatches his head back by his chin as he jams his gun into the man's mouth.

"You know what the fuck," he says as he forces the gun down the man's throat, causing him to gag on the barrel. "It's a butt naked party in Room 211, right?" he asks with a sarcastic grin on his face.

"Ain't that what you said? Now, strip! Everybody strip!" he says as he looks over at the women who are on their knees. "I'm 'bout to make it easy for you, player. This foreplay 'bout to get these bitches naked and ready for you," he says with an evil look in his eyes. He looks back over at the women. "Strip, bitches, strip! Y'all can't hear?"

The women immediately start to peel their clothes off.

"It's a butt naked party, nigga. Get naked, nigga," Leonard says as he strips the man of his watch and jewelry. He lays it on the table before digging into the man's pockets. He has money in every pocket, just as Wustafa stated.

Leonard stacks the money on the nightstand as well.

"Throw me one of those bags," Leonard commands as he points to the women's duffel bags.

Sameerah tosses one of them, and Leonard catches it in midair. He unzips it and loads all the valuables into the bag full of lingerie and perfumes and lotions. Dollar bills are scattered around the bag as well.

Leonard digs into the man's back pocket and finds his car keys. He sticks his gun further into the man's mouth, causing the man to choke.

"You got two seconds to get your drunk ass together and strip before I pop your motherfucking melon."

Fear causes the man to get it to together in one second. He quickly starts snatching his clothes off with fear in his bloodshot red eyes. Leonard looks over to the women, who are both completely naked, with their faces covered in tears of fear.

"Dump their clothes in that bag," Leonard instructs.

Sameerah looks at Leonard for a quick second and is highly impressed by his actions. He always holds his own but never has he taken total control as he's doing at this very moment. She has gotten used to being the leader in every situation. It's not that she wanted to be the leader; it's more like none of them stepped up, so she had no choice but to lead. It's kind of awkward following his lead but still she does since he's already on a roll.

Sameerah dumps the clothes into the bag as she's instructed to. Leonard looks at the women's huge Gucci bags that are on the floor.

"Don't forget them bags," he says. "Watches, jewelry, everything in the bag. I want them butt fucking naked."

Sameerah strips them of their necklaces, tennis bracelets, and rings.

The man sits on the edge of the bed with only his boxers and socks on. He peeks up at Leonard with fear and humiliation in his eyes.

"Ass naked, I said, nigga," Leonard barks with rage.

The man stands up and slowly drops his underwear to the floor. The man lowers his gaze, embarrassed. Leonard holds the duffel bag open.

"Dump 'em in the bag."

The man drops his underwear into the bag, and Leonard snatches him by his throat.

"Let's go," he says as he forces the man in front of him.

As the man is walking, Leonard lifts his leg high in the air, and, with all of his might, he donkey kicks the man up the ass. The kick is for no other purpose but to further humiliate the man.

"Walk faster. Pick up your fucking feet."

Leonard aims his gun at the women, just as he gets to them.

"Let's go. Y'all, too."

They step toward him with no hesitation. He forces the three of them in front of them, pushing them toward the bathroom. His adrenaline is racing so fast that he doesn't even pay attention to the beautiful nudeness of the two women.

Once they're all jammed into the tiny bathroom, he snatches the shower curtain wide open. With confusion on their faces, they all step into the bathtub. Each of them is wondering exactly what is next for them. Leonard reaches over and turns the shower on at full blast.

"Now, y'all go ahead and get yo' butt naked party started," he says with a huge smile as he backpedals out of the room. He leaves them all standing in fear, soaking wet. He slams the door shut and runs past Sameerah. "Let's go."

He allows Sameerah to exit the room first. He slams the door shut, and they fast trot toward the staircase. They hit the staircase and damn near skip the whole flight, only touching two steps.

"Here," Leonard says as he tosses Sameerah the keys to the Cadillac.

Sameerah hands Leonard the duffel bags before sprinting to the Cadillac.

The lights of the Suburban come on as Speed creeps toward Leonard. Leonard hops into the backseat and slams the door shut. They all watch as Sameerah backs the Cadillac up, cuts in front of them, and pulls off. They tail her closely.

Wustafa looks down at his watch.

"Twelve minutes flat," he says, before looking back at Leonard. "Not bad at all. I must admit that I'm quite impressed. Y'all are getting better and better with it," he says as he nods his head. "Pretty soon, we are gonna be ready to get some major, major money."

CHAPTER 43
DAYS LATER/DECEMBER 2, 2002

Wustafa's apartment is pitch black, except for the light created by sixteen candles. The candles set on the cake, which reads 'Happy 16th Anniversary, Babygirl.' The cake is compliments of Wustafa. Sameerah stands over the cake with embarrassment on her face as they sing to her.

This is the absolute best birthday that she's ever had. The fact that she had money to buy herself something for her birthday is what made it so special. Earlier today, she spoiled herself rotten.

She took her two little sisters to breakfast, and she, also, took them for manicures and pedicures. After dropping them off back home, she took herself on a mini-shopping spree, buying herself anything that she wanted. Most of the money that she's made with the organization has been spent on taking care of her baby sisters, who are in need of any and everything imaginable. She has been able to buy herself a few things here and there but not to that magnitude of what she did for herself today. She spent without a care. Today was her day, and she wasn't going to set any limitations for herself.

Today, she stands in front of the crew with a tight fitted mini skirt on and high leather riding boots. To everyone's surprise, today is the first time ever that they have smelled perfume on her. Over the past couple of months, they have witnessed her go from a soggy looking tomboy, who wore the same three outfits over and over, to a fashionable sex symbol of a young woman. She still wears those same three outfits but only to go out and work in.

In her downtime, she's laced in the finest name brand garments. Sameerah has always been fashion forward, but, without money, she was always left fashionably behind. Now, thanks to Wustafa and the organization, she no longer has to stay behind. The fact that she had no clothes is the main reason that she dropped out of school.

As a younger child, she was a tomboy and didn't care much about clothes. Once she got into high school and started transforming into a mature, young woman, it was then that she started finding attraction in the opposite sex. It was then that she developed a complex.

She alternated the few articles of clothing that she had the best that she could. She mainly wore the same three or four blouses with the same two pairs of jeans over and over again. She did that for as long as she could before other students started noticing it and spread the word. After hearing it a few times, she became so ashamed that she just stopped coming to school altogether.

Now, keeping up with the best dressed girls in the school is easy for her. The real task is the best dressed girls in the school attempting to keep up with her. She's gone from the worst dressed in regular school to the best dressed in night school. That's a big title to hold with all the competition of the night school girls, who are a tad bit older and faster than the average high school girls.

"Happy Born Day to you!" they all sing in perfect harmony. "Happy Born Day to you! Happy Born day, Babygirl!" Wustafa says as everyone else says Sameerah. "Happy Born Day to you!" Leonard drags slowly as he hits a deep baritone note. They all fall out in laughter.

Wustafa stands beside Sameerah with his arm around her shoulders.

"Go ahead, Babygirl. Make a wish and blow out the candles."

Sameerah blows out the candles, and Anthony flicks the lights on. As soon as the lights come on, Sameerah places her hand over her eyes and turns away from them. She walks away from them quickly.

"What's up, Babygirl?" Wustafa asks as he stands there in complete shock. "Where are you going? Come here."

Sameerah stands there for seconds, fumbling with her face before turning back around toward them. Her glassy eyes and wet face tell her story. Wustafa walks over and wraps his arms around her.

"What's the matter?" he asks with genuine concern.

"Nothing," she says as she wipes the last tear away and tries to put her tough girl demeanor back on. "I'm gonna be late for school. Thanks for everything, but I have to go."

All this has hit a soft spot in Sameerah's heart. In all her years on earth, she's never had a birthday party or even a cake. She doesn't even know how to accept a gift.

"Don't worry. Speed will get you there in no time at all," Wustafa says, "but you can't leave until I give you your gift," he says as he walks over to his bedroom area. "Babygirl, you know, I was just thinking about what that pig said. He said he had you under pressure for two whole days, and you wouldn't crack. I wanted to tell them two more days, and she still wouldn't have cracked," Wustafa says as if he was certain that she wouldn't. He figures, if he tells the team how she held it down, they would all follow her suit in case they were in a situation like that. With her being the only girl and she didn't crack, they would feel like less than men if by chance they even considered cracking under pressure. "Had them crackers vexed with her!" They don't know we don't breed stool pigeons in this organization?" he says as he walks back over toward Sameerah. He holds his hands behind his back. "Close your eyes."

Sameerah closes her eyes tightly while Wustafa grabs her wrist. Gently, he slides the watch onto her wrist.

"Open them."

Sameerah opens her eyes and almost falls into pieces as she looks at the gold Presidential Rolex. Even though she knows the watch is stolen, it's the thought that counts.

"For me?" she asks with shock on her face.

Wustafa nods his head.

"Yep. Who deserves it more than you? I had it appraised, too. It's worth almost twenty grand. You're worth every bit of that and more, Babygirl. Don't ever let anyone tell you different," he says with sincerity in his eyes.

Tears start to trickle down her face all over again. They're all in shock because they have never seen this emotional side that she's displaying tonight. Secretly, they're all loving every second of it. Seeing her like this makes them all want to be her knight in shining armor who comes to her rescue and wipes her tears away.

Wustafa looks over at Speed.

"Go on and get our birthday princess on to school," Wustafa says as if Sameerah is five years old.

The strange part of it all is that, at this moment, she feels as if she's actually five years old. She turns away with embarrassment. She hates the fact that they're seeing her like this, but she can't help it. She stands at the door with her back facing them as she waits for Speed.

"Babygirl!" Wustafa calls out. She turns around partially, just peeking at him through her peripheral.

"It's okay! This us. You can show your true emotions with us. We are all family. It's all love in here. It's the outside world that you have to guard your feelings against," he says with a solemn look on his face. "Don't ever forget that!" he shouts. "Ever!"

CHAPTER 44
1:23 A.M.

It's the coldest day of the year by far with the temperature barely reaching seventeen degrees. This is what Wustafa calls hustling weather. He loves the winter months because there are fewer distractions on the street in the winter. Everyone who is outside is outside for a purpose, unlike the summer when everyone is outside just for the sake of the nice weather. Also, he likes the fact that everyone is bundled up with layers of clothes, so it's normal for one to have a skull cap and hood on his head. That makes his job that much easier.

"It's loaded out here," Wustafa says as Speed turns into the White Castle parking lot here on Elizabeth Avenue.

The skating rink in Branch Brook Park is the Wednesday night spot, and White Castle is like the after party. White Castle is more of the place to be than the rink is actually. People who weren't present for the rink make sure to be here.

This is the place for all the hustlers to show their worth. Most have spent a great deal of their day at the detail shops, getting their pride and beauty shined up for tonight. The luxurious cars that are spread out in the parking lot makes it resemble a car show. Under the bright lights, the automobiles shine like glass. Beautiful, young women stand around in packs as the young hustlers cruise around the parking lot. Each woman desperately hopes that she's chosen by her Mr. Right.

Wustafa has never seen this many fur coats in his life. The coats vary by fur, color, and style. He's sure he could just rake in the furs and make a decent coin tonight.

"Boy, I wish it was a way that I could freeze time, so I could lay all these suckers down at once," Wustafa says as he looks around the parking lot. "It's a lotta potential out here. Right there, right there," he says as he points to a car, which is backing out of a parking space. "Back up in there."

The car backs out, and Speed blocks the parking lot as he backs the Tahoe into the parking space. They all sit quietly, just observing the activity which is taking place all around them. The windows of the Tahoe are tinted so darkly that it's impossible for anyone to see inside. So much is going on that it's impossible to see it all. Each of them has their own focal point in the parking lot.

Wustafa watches as a group of young girls migrate to the parking space to the right of them. One girl opens the door to the small Honda, and, in seconds, loud music is bleeding into the air. Wustafa watches with disgust as the women start dancing and putting on a show. He shakes his head from side to side.

"Attention whores," he barks. "Look at them. Anything for attention. Don't have a clue that they're in for a rude awakening. Need to be home getting ready for school or work to better themselves. Instead, they're out here trying to bait one of these good-for-nothing niggers. Everybody wants a big willy," he says sarcastically. "Only to get him, get pregnant by him, and get left for the next young tenderoni. All the stories end the same. Fly chick ends up with a bunch of babies on welfare. I can see their future, and all of their destinies are the same," he says sadly. "But not yours, Babygirl, not yours. I'm gonna see to that."

Wustafa's attention is captured by the prestigious black on black Corvette that crosses in front of them. The bright interior light is on, making it quite easy to see inside.

"Look at this show off," Wustafa says with hatred.

The driver stares at the group of girls as he passes them. The chrome rims on his tires shimmer like a disco ball. The driver stops right in front of the girls, begging for their attention. It doesn't take long for him to get exactly what he set out to get. The girls all stand still, posing like they're in a photo shoot. Their extra friendly demeanors transcend into competitiveness amongst each other. They each set out to outdo each other with hopes of being the chosen one.

Once he realizes that he has their full attention, he cruises off with a look of arrogance on his face.

"Hey!" the girl shouts with desperation. The brake lights of the Corvette shine brightly as he stops on the dime.

"Come back!" the girl shouts as he steps away from the crowd. She looks over to her friends and smiles, saying, "Fuck that! A closed mouth don't get fed. Y'all can stand here looking pretty if y'all want to. Shit! I'm trying to get to the money."

"You hear that whore?" Wustafa asks with anger in his voice.

The driver holds his hand out of the sunroof, waving, signaling for the girl to come to him. "Meet me halfway," the girl says as she starts to step toward the car.

The driver's side door pops open slowly and a Timberland boot sets onto the asphalt. The driver

gets out with a huge snorkel coat on, looking like an Eskimo. With an extremely cocky demeanor, he slowly walks toward her. His door, he leaves wide open.

Wustafa sits on the edge of his seat with anticipation.

"That's it, dummy," he says. "Come on, come on," he says as he calculates the space between the man and his car. "Perfect," he says as the man stands in the middle of the parking lot, awaiting the girl. "He got big balls," Wustafa says sarcastically. "Leaving his door wide open like it can't get taken from him. Babygirl, it's on you."

Without hesitation, Sameerah opens the back passenger's door of the Tahoe and gets out. She closes the door and slowly walks to the front of the truck. "Meet us at the headquarters," he says through the opened window, leaning over Speed.

Sameerah struts slowly through the parking lot. With their full attention on the girl and the dude, she's able to pass the girls without being noticed. Just as she's approaching the man, he feels her presence behind him. He looks over his shoulder at her and double takes. He looks her up and down twice before charging her off as a little, dirty girl and goes back to his conversation.

Adrenaline races through the veins of the entire crew as they watch Sameerah creep toward the car. Just as she gets a foot away from the rear bumper, she peeks over her shoulder one last time. Then, she takes three giant steps. She swings on the door and drops herself into the driver's seat.

"Yo!" the young man shouts. He dashes over to the car, just as Sameerah is shutting the door.

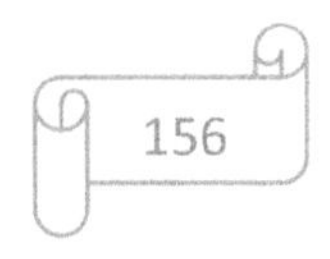

In four steps, he's at the bumper of the car. He latches his arm onto the wing on the trunk as the car peels off. He's dragged a few feet before he releases his grip.

"Let's go," Wustafa commands.

Speed pulls out of the parking space nice and easy. They all watch as the man continues to chase behind his car. Suddenly, he stops in the middle of the parking lot. To their surprise, he raises his arm high in the air and...

Boc! Boc! Boc!

The many people in the parking lot look around in shock as they try to figure out which direction the shots came from. Some locate the gunman, while others don't, but safety is what is on all of their minds. Eardrum piercing screams sound off as the young women run, fearing for their lives. The people duck low and run for cover. They scatter all over the parking lot chaotically.

"Whoa!" Wustafa shouts as they slowly approach the man who starts to run after the car again. He fires once again.

Boc!

Suddenly, the sound of a higher caliber gun rings off.

Blocka! Blocka! Blocka!

The man's body jerks forward violently before he falls, face first, onto the asphalt.

Speed pulls up closer, and Wustafa leans out of the window. Before Wustafa can fire, he hears shots being fired behind him.

Blocka! Blocka!

Wustafa looks into the seat behind him, where Leonard's torso hangs out of the window. He has beat Wustafa to the punch. He lowers his gun closer to the man's body and squeezes two more shots into the back of his head to seal the deal.

Blocka! Blocka!

CHAPTER 45
FOUR DAYS LATER

It's a typical Sunday here at the headquarters. The crew has been reading, studying and memorizing for hours. Today, their reading selection is from *Behold a Pale Horse*. Wustafa has read that book over fifty times already over the years. He has it memorized both forward and backwards. He feels that every citizen should read it, which is why he's sharing it with the crew.

The book speaks of the New World Order and government corruption. Each member of the crew has read a portion of the book aloud. Right now, it's Sameerah's turn. Her soothing voice has rocked them all into tranquility. That is until she gets to a line in which she feels deserves heavy emphasis. So, she shouts loudly, breaking their serenity.

They're all sitting up with their full attention on Sameerah. They look deep into her mouth with their eyes stretched wide open like little children who are being read a bedtime story by their mothers.

"Malachi began fumbling through the contents of the wallet," Sameerah reads in her low, sweet voice. "His eyes widened with surprise and recognition," she says with more energy.

"Wait!" she shouts, causing them all to jump with surprise. They all sit up in suspense. "He barked to Titus," she says as she changes her voice again. "Take them back to the remnant!" she shouts with a sense of rage in her voice.

Loud clapping sounds off from the back of the room.

"Very good reading," Wustafa says while still clapping his hands loudly. "Very, very good!" Wustafa looks over at Speed, who is slouching low on the couch. "You're up next."

Speed shakes his head negatively. "Let somebody else go."

"Everybody else already went. It's your turn," Wustafa explains.

"I don't feel like reading," Speed says.

A smile of anger mixed with sarcasm covers Wustafa's face.

"You don't feel like reading? Since when has it been about what we feel like doing? I'm sure it has been days that we all don't feel like doing things, but, as members of this organization, we all know that we have an obligation to fill," he says with a stern look in his eyes.

"Like I said, I don't feel like reading," he replies with attitude.

Wustafa nods his head up and down with rage, while the other members of the crew watch with expressions of shock on their faces. They all wonder what will be next. Wustafa is livid. This is Speed's second time going against him.

He realizes that he can't allow this to keep happening. He fears that allowing Speed to go against his command can tarnish his image and make the others feel that they can go against his command as well. He understands that, if he doesn't put his foot down, this problem will cause an even greater problem in the future.

If they feel that there is no punishment for their actions, what will prevent them from overstepping boundaries? Also, what will keep them loyal to the organization if no fear is present? He truly believes that love and respect only go but so far without the accompaniment of fear. He's afraid that, if they believe that there are no repercussions to their actions, he could lose total control.

Wustafa steps closer to Speed. They stand face to face.

"I'm commanding you to read from the book," Wustafa says with a threatening look in his eyes. "This is a command, not a request," Wustafa says as he tightens up his hand, causing it to be as stiff as a board. His arm seems to lift itself. He's preparing for a backslap, but he manages to restrain it. He holds his hand tight at his thigh, fighting the urge to backhand Speed.

Wustafa understands that the organization needs Speed. He, also, feels that, maybe, Speed knows this as well and that could be the reason for his arrogance. He has a good mind to slap fire out of Speed, but realizes that that may not be the answer. Humiliating him in front of the crew, especially Sameerah, will spark hatred in Speed that he may never get over. That hatred can later turn into an even bigger issue.

"I already told you, I don't feel like reading today," Speed says as he stares Wustafa square in the eyes.

Wustafa's hand pops up before he catches it at his waist. He quickly envisions his backhand crashing into Speed's face and Speed falling backwards. He quickly shakes the vision from his mind in order to keep himself from carrying it out. Speed notices Wustafa's hand and backs away slightly with his hands at his side ready to block himself.

He backs away slowly. Wustafa follows him step by step until finally Speed bumps into the wall. Wustafa stands there with a look of rage in his eyes with his fist clenched tightly at his waist. Speed quickly raises his hands in the air to prepare to defend himself against any blow that Wustafa may throw.

Wustafa notices the fear that lies in Speed's eyes. Wustafa flinches, and Speed balls up in defense. After realizing that he hasn't been hit, he peeks through his guard only to see Wustafa standing there with a devious smirk on his face.

"Get outta here! Go!" Wustafa shouts.

Speed steps around Wustafa slowly. Still, he is prepared for defense. Once he gets past Wustafa, he walks toward the door. The further he gets away from Wustafa, the cockier his bop gets. He bounces with arrogance as if he wasn't just scared out of his mind. He's embarrassed, but, still, he manages to keep his head high.

The rest of the crew sits quietly as they watch Speed walk past them. Wustafa turns around and watches Speed with anger spread across his face. The arrogant demeanor infuriates him more. To him, it's almost the equivalent of a smack to the face. He charges it off as Speed covering up his embarrassment.

Speed pulls the door open with force.

"And don't come back until you are ready to adhere to the rules of this organ—" Wustafa says before Speed slams the door shut with all of his might, "—ization!"

CHAPTER 46
THREE NIGHTS LATER/9:20 P.M.

It's pitch black outside, and the rain is pouring in abundance. Speed stands at the huge barbed wire fence with giant bolt cutters in his hand. He squeezes them with all of his might until the lock falls onto the ground in two pieces. He peeks around nervously as he pushes the gate open wide. He runs back and jumps into the passenger's seat of the Nissan Maxima. As soon as he's seated, the driver cruises through the entrance. Rows and rows of brand new cars fill the huge parking lot. This is like heaven for a car thief. Here at the Port is where Speed and his car thieving friends have been car shopping for some time now. That is until he linked up with Wustafa and started carjacking.

Speed misses moving around at his own leisure. He's always been his own man, moving at his own pace. Ever since he's been under Wustafa, though, he feels as if he's given up his freedom, as well as his manhood. For the past few years, he has been generating a dollar for himself.

He's never seen the amount of money that he's seen while with Wustafa and the crew, but he's always made enough money to satisfy himself. He feels that he doesn't need the organization to get money. He's thankful for what he's learned from Wustafa because now he can incorporate all that he has learned and keep all the money to himself.

"Security right over there," Speed says as he points to the guard who walks three rows over from them.

Speed's scanner is on high alert, seeking the perfect vehicle. The white stickers that cover each car in entirety are for protection against scratching and damage during shipping. The white stickers would make it difficult for the average person to determine which cars are which but not Speed. His trained eye makes it quite easy for him.

He pays attention to the front grill of the vehicles to determine the make. He sizes each vehicle up to identify the exact model. Cars are shipped here from all over the world before being shipped to car dealerships. Every car made is here on the lot, from Ford to Mercedes Benz, and all of them are for the taking. Speed equates the feeling to being filthy rich and having the ability to go to the lot and pick any car that you want.

"Right there! Right there!" he says anxiously as he points to one of the last cars in the row.

His eyes light up with joy as they set onto the Mercedes SL600. Butterflies fill his gut and sweat fills his palms as they slowly approach the vehicle. His accomplice stops directly in front of the car, and Speed hops out of the car.

Speed looks to his left where he sees a couple of employees walking in his direction. He ducks down low to prevent them from seeing him. In seconds, he's inside the Mercedes. He looks to the floor mat of the car where the keys are laying. He quickly grabs the keys, sticks them into the ignition, starts the car, and he's ready to go.

He gives his accomplice the signal, and the Nissan cruises off. Speed turns in the opposite direction of the Nissan to avoid the security guard. In a minute flat, they meet at the entrance, and, right behind each other, they make their exit.

"Sweet as pie," Speed says to himself. "Sweet as pie."

CHAPTER 47
ONE HOUR LATER

Speed sits parked directly in front of West Side High School as the many students exit the building. The rain has stopped, and it's quite foggy outside. Even through the thick fog, the beauty of the brand spanking new SL600 is evident. The students gawk at the vehicle as they approach it. It is the center of everyone's attention.

Speed sits back with a look of arrogance on his face, accepting the praise as if he really has the right to. He peeks through the fog, where he spots Sameerah coming towards him. His heart skips a beat as he watches her prance sexily down the alley. He swallows the lump that forms in his throat at the sight of her.

Speed has always had eyes for her, even dressed in her boy clothes, but his heavy infatuation came into play the very first time that he saw her dressed like a young woman. The first time that he saw her dressed like that it took him weeks to shake that vision from his mind. After seeing her the day of her birthday, the spark was rekindled.

Speed looks her over closely. With her three quarter plaid trench coat, plaid rain boots, and tight jeans on, she prances like a model on the runway, modeling outerwear. Speed has noticed that even her walk is different when she's dressed in her true element. She displays a sense of confidence that she doesn't display on a normal basis.

The closer Sameerah gets to the car, the more nervous he gets. As close as they have gotten over the months, he still feels like she's a stranger to him. He knows the gangster-ride-or-die-chick side of Sameerah, while the soft and girlie side of her is completely foreign to him.

Sameerah gets to the end of the paved alley and walks to her left. Speed mashes the horn to get her attention, but, to his surprise, he gets more than just her attention. The distinct sound of the European horn causes everyone to look over in his direction. Sameerah peeks over and turns away quickly.

Speed lowers the window quickly because she's getting away from him.

"Sameerah!"

She continues on as if she's never heard that name before.

Her guilty conscience sometimes gets the best of her. With all of the dirt that she's done over the past few months, she often feels like some of it will eventually catch up with her.

"Babygirl!"

Sameerah immediately turns around. She wears a baffled expression on her face as she wonders who could be calling her that. She knows it can only be one of two things. One: it's somebody from the crew, or two: somebody they have done something to who knows about her nickname. She zooms in on the driver's face and exhales a deep breath as she recognizes that it's Speed. She stops short before turning around and walking toward the car. She stops at the passenger door as she looks the car over from the tires to the roof before leaning her head inside of the window.

"Boy, I didn't know who you was calling my damn name," she says with a grin plastered on her face.

"Get in," Speed demands as he reaches over and forces the door open.

Sameerah grabs hold of the door and gets in.

"What you doing around here?" she asks as she closes the door shut.

Speed pulls off slowly. All the students watch in awe as if they're celebrities. Speed thinks carefully before speaking. He knows what he wants to say, but he's too nervous to actually say it.

"Huh? What you doing around here?" she repeats.

"Looking for you," he whispers in a fake sexy tone that comes across all wrong. He turns his face to the left with shame.

"What?" she asks. "What did you just say?"

A sudden burst of courage rips from within him.

"Looking for you," he says loud and clear.

"Looking for me?" she asks with doubt. "Yeah, right. You up here trying to catch."

"Nah, no bullshit. Yeah, I'm trying to catch alright," he says as he looks over at her. "Trying to catch you."

"Catch me?" she asks with evident confusion. "What you talking about?"

"It's the truth. I came here looking for you."

"Looking for me? For what? Wu sent you here?"

"Wu?" Speed barks with aggression. "I haven't seen no fucking Wu!"

Sameerah realizes that she has hit a hot spot. It's evident that Speed still has animosity about that incident. Fear quickly covers Speed's face.

"Nah, Wu or nobody else don't know I'm here. I haven't seen nobody. Honestly, I ain't looking for nobody." He looks deeper into her eyes. "But you," he adds. "And I need you to promise me that you won't tell him. Promise?"

"Huh?" she asks, confused. She wonders what the big secret is. "What's the big deal? You just picking me up from school, right?"

"Yeah and no," he replies with a bashful look on his face.

"I'm lost. Break it down for me. Yeah and no what?"

"Yeah, I'm here to pick you up, but no, that's not it."

"Well, what else are you here for then?"

Speed sits in silence while he musters up the courage to say what is on his mind. He clears his throat. "I really don't know how to say it, but fuck it! I'm gon' say it how it comes out. I'm really digging you, and I came here to talk to you in private to let you know how I feel."

"Digging me?" Sameerah barks with a goofy smile on her face. "Digging me? How? You can't dig me. We are like brothers and sisters."

"Fuck that sister and brother shit! We just met. I ain't looking at you like a sister. Yeah, we part of the same crew," he says before he pauses. "Well, we was part of the same crew, but that don't stop the fact that I'm liking you."

"Hold up! Back up! What you mean 'was part of the same crew'? What is that supposed to mean?"

"It means what I said. Was," he says.

"Psst," Sameerah sucks her teeth. "Need to let that go and come on back," she says as she stares over at him. "It's money to be made."

"Ay, I'm always gon' get money. I don't need him. I been getting money long before I met him, and I'm gon' keep getting money. Anyway, I don't do the group thing. I don't fit in that organization. I'm my own boss. I follow my own rules. I'm a solo act. I roll dolo. But anyway," he says louder. "Fuck all that. That ain't what I'm here for. Yeah, I'm liking you."

"Liking me? Wow!" she asks in total shock. "Where did all of this come from?"

Speed inhales a deep breath. "It's like it just came out of nowhere. I can't even explain it. I just know how I been feeling." Sameerah sits back with a perplexed look on her face. "So, what do you have to say?"

"I don't know what to say," she replies with all honesty. "I'm confused."

"Nothing to be confused about really," he says as he brushes it off as nothing big. "Either you digging me like I'm digging you or you're not," he says with uncertainty in his yes. "So, are you digging me?"

Sameerah hesitates before replying. "I mean, I never looked at you like that. I looked at all y'all like family," she says before Speed interjects.

"Yo! Stop associating me with them. I ain't part of them. I really never been part of them. I just met them a few months ago, and we ain't no family. It was business for me," he says as he pulls in front of Sameerah's project building. He slams the gear into park and zooms in on Sameerah up close and personal. "So, what is it going to be?"

"Speed, I don't know about that. I need some time to think about this. Like what do you want from me honestly?"

"I'm digging you I said. I just want to know if you digging me."

"Hmphh," she sighs. "I have to think about this."

"Okay. Think about it then."

Sameerah opens the door and makes her exit.

"Thanks for the ride," she says as she slams the door shut.

She's in total confusion. All of this has taken her by surprise. She takes a step away from the car with her head hanging low.

"Sameerah!"

She stops short, turns around, leans over and peeks inside the car.

"You gotta promise me something though?" he says with pleading in his eyes.

"What's that?" she asks.

"Please, whatever you do please don't tell Wustafa about any of this." His ego disappears as he thinks of how much danger he could have just placed himself in. "If he finds out about this, he will kill me," he says with a look of fear in his eyes.

"Kill you? Why?" she asks with an oblivious look on her face.

"Because you are off limits. He made it clear to us that we are not supposed to fuck with you like that. We are supposed to look at you as one of the fellas and never cross that line. I tried, but I can't look at you like one of the fellas. I can't," he says with a sad look on his face. "Anyway, I ain't part of yo' organization, so I don't have to look at you like one of the fellas no more," he says as that ego pops up on his face once again. "So, you promise?"

Sameerah hesitates before replying. "I promise."

CHAPTER 48
HOURS LATER

Wustafa paces back and forth with frustration. He's been sitting back quietly with high hopes that Speed would come knocking on the door. As bad as he wants to call Speed back, he will not do so. He refuses to let the crew see him go against his word.

"This is his fourth night not reporting," Wustafa barks. "I can't believe that this is the game that he wants to play," he says as he bangs his fist into the palm of his other hand. "He's selfish and cares nothing about the organization. He only cares about himself."

Wustafa continues to pace throughout the tiny apartment.

"He just ups and leaves us high and dry. Selfish!" he shouts. "Later for the fact that he has an obligation here. He's taken an oath with us."

"Wu, we don't need him," Leonard says. "We got the Navigator parked in the stash. You can drive it, and we can move on without him," he suggests. "Or even Babygirl," Leonard says as he looks over at Sameerah.

Wustafa stops in his tracks. His body tenses up as he stands there with a starry look in his eyes. He snaps out of his zone.

"Nah. It's the principle. He was brought into this organization as a driver. That's his assigned position. Everybody got a part to play, and he's going to play his, whether he wants to or not," Wustafa says with rage in his eyes. "If he thinks he's going to leave this Organization knowing all of our secrets, he has another thing coming. He knows things that can get us sent away forever. To think that he's just going to walk away from this thing with all that information stored is absurd," he says as he stops short.

"Not him," he says as he looks around at each one of them with coldness in his eyes. "Or not anyone else will walk away from this organization. We in, and there is only one way out. We made the oath till death do us part, and that's the only way we will part," he says with a demented look in his eyes. "Has anybody seen him since that night?"

They all look around at each other, shaking their heads, all except Sameerah. Her facial expression is somewhat of a dead giveaway. The guilt is showing all over her face. She hates to get in the middle of this. After hearing how Speed feels about all of it, a part of her feels like she's supposed to tell Wustafa what he's said. The other part would hate to tell and be the cause of Speed losing his life. She's caught up in the middle, not knowing what to do.

"You, Babygirl? Have you seen him?"

Sameerah sits in silence for a few seconds, just weighing it all out. She wants to tell that he picked her up earlier, but that may lead to other questions. Also, after hearing how Wustafa deemed her off limits, she fears that him crossing the line may add more fuel to the fire. Sameerah understands how serious Wustafa is about his rules and his guidelines being crossed. She then thinks back to the promise that Speed made her make to him.

"Huh, Babygirl?" Wustafa asks as he steps closer to Sameerah. Something tells him that she knows something that she isn't telling. Her body language is giving her away. "Have you seen him?"

Sameerah hates to lie to Wustafa, but she's a woman of her word.

"Nah," she replies as she stares straight into his eyes.

I hope this don't backfire on me, she thinks as her and Wustafa's eyes intertwine for seconds before he finally looks away.

"You sure?"

Sameerah nods her head before looking away from him.

"Positive."

CHAPTER 49

Speed zips through the narrow residential block as the speedometer exceeds 110 miles an hour. He mashes the gas pedal, and the speed increases another ten miles. He looks in his rearview mirror, where he sees, at least, five police cars coming at him at top speed with the sirens blazing. They're speeding up the block, driving just as recklessly as he is.

After dropping Sameerah off, he got caught up doing something that he hadn't done in a long time. Surprisingly, he missed joyriding more than he knew. As he stopped through his stomping grounds, showing off his newest prize, they all were happy to see him. The attention inspired him to put on a show for them as he used to.

He went on to show them what the Mercedes was capable of doing. Performing his stunts gave him an adrenaline rush that he hadn't felt in a long time. The stunts not only gained the attention of his peers, it, also, got the attention of the police that just happened to be patrolling the area. At the very first glimpse of them, he darted off and took the chase.

He's now been ripping through the city at top speed for over twenty minutes. Every time he's thought that he's gotten away from them, like magic they reappear out of thin air. No matter what he does, he can't seem to get away from them. He's done life threatening things that normally make them back off. He's sped against heavy traffic, darted through intersections, driven up one way streets, and still they tail him closely.

It's pitch black out, and the only light comes from the flashing sirens that are behind him. The feeling of victory sets in his heart as he watches the cars behind him fall back. He figures they must have finally gotten tired of chasing him. Despite the fact that they have slowed down drastically, he continues up the block at top speed.

As he nears the corner, his heart skips a beat. His eyes set on a huge black Bronco that's parked horizontally across the intersection.

"Oh, shit!" he says aloud. He lets his foot off of the gas pedal to decrease the speed. His heart races faster than the engine of the Mercedes.

The car seems to not be slowing down the least bit. He peeks in the mirror, and terror fills his heart as he sees cars still coming behind him. With less than a hundred feet between him and the Bronco, he grabs the emergency brake and snatches it upward with all of his strength. In a quick flash, he notices cops standing on both sides of the street with their guns drawn.

Police cars crowd the entire area. The Mercedes skids a few feet before slamming into the door of the Bronco.

Craaassshhh!

The airbag blows up just as his head snaps forward. The airbag swallows up his face right before it all goes blank.

CHAPTER 50
1:13 A.M.

In the basement of Green Street Precinct, it's cold and dark. It's so dark that Speed can't protect himself from the painful blows because he can't see them coming. The police have been taking turns beating on him for the past ten minutes.

Speed sits propped up in the corner of the empty room. His hands are cuffed together behind his back, making it impossible for him to defend himself even if he could see the blows coming. He just sucks it up like a man and takes the abuse that they are giving him. His screams can't be heard on account of the dirty sock that has been stuffed and taped into his mouth.

The lieutenant bends over and leans closer to Speed, who twists his body, turning his shoulder toward the man. He tenses his body in defense. He can't see the blow, but he's sure it's coming. He can't see the man in front of him, but he's so close he can feel his breath whizzing across his nose.

"We crashed three cars chasing behind your stupid ass!" the lieutenant says before he fires a short uppercut in the air.

The punch crashes into Speed's chin, snapping his neck. His head bangs onto the cement wall and ricochets forward. The lieutenant catches him by the collar and begins banging his fist into his face over and over until he's huffing and puffing with fatigue.

The lieutenant finally stands up. He drops his boot on top of Speed's head before walking off. As soon as he's away from Speed, another fills in his place. The sergeant drops a heavy stomp onto Speed's head upon his arrival.

Speed grunts with agony. He screams so loudly that he can be heard even with the sock in his mouth. He whines and whimpers like a sad puppy.

"Shut the fuck up," the sergeant says before forearming Speed on the nose bone.

His eyes water on contact.

Speed manages to roll over in an attempt to block his face. He rolls over, face first, on the hard cement floor, which may have been the worst decision that he could have possibly made. He lays there helplessly as five men stomp him out brutally.

CHAPTER 51
THE NEXT MORNING

Wustafa peeks through the peephole and snatches the door open upon sight of Sameerah's face. He stands there with confusion as he stares at the two huge garbage bags that Sameerah has in her grip. Fury covers her face as she storms right past him without waiting for an invitation.

"Good morning to you, too," he says sarcastically as he closes the door.

He turns around at the door as he watches Sameerah dump the bags onto the floor before plopping onto the couch with despair. Wustafa walks over to the stove and continues banging the pots and skillets as he was doing before she arrived. The more he shakes the pots, the stronger the aroma becomes. As Wustafa stands, there he can feel her tension from across the room.

She hasn't said a word to him, which is an indication that she doesn't want to be bothered. As bad as he wants to know what the problem is, he refuses to ask. He's finally learned how to deal with her. He now understands that he gets better results from her when he lets her talk when she's ready to talk. He's known her for only nine months, and it's taken all of the nine months to finally understand her and how she operates.

She's a stubborn fireball who keeps most of her problems bottled up inside, but, once she finally starts talking, she lets it all out. She hides behind a rock hard exterior, but, underneath it, she's as soft and sweet as cotton candy. Wustafa equates dealing with her with a game of poker. He pretends that he isn't interested in hearing what's going on, and, in return, she tells it all.

Wustafa loads up two plates with French toast, cheese eggs, and home fries. He walks over and sets them on the table as he sits down.

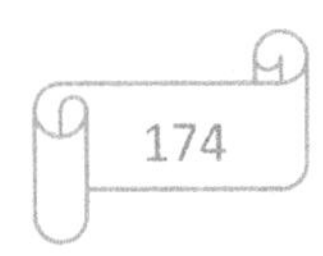

"You eating?" he asks as he picks from the bowl of fresh fruit.

Sameerah gets up, still without saying a word. After washing her hands at the sink, she walks over and plops into the chair. She picks at the food with her head hanging low. Wustafa bows his head and says his grace. He opens his eyes slowly.

"I'm ready to listen when you're ready to be heard. No pressure," he says with a mouthful of food.

Minutes pass without her saying a single word. He keeps his eyes on his plate, instead of looking at her. He feels that zooming in on her will only make her clam up even more, but the anxiety is getting the best of him. He hates to see her like this. He can't refrain himself any longer.

"What's up?" he asks.

"Nothing, just the same old shit," she replies. "My fiend-ass mother's up to her same old shit," she says as she shakes her head from side to side. "You know those shoes that I bought for my birthday? The brown ones you like? Well, I ain't got 'em no more," she says with pity in her eyes. "They just walked away. Let her tell it. I know she sold them, just like she sold everything else that's missing. I can't wait to get the fuck outta that house! Some of the clothes that I bought, she stole those, too. I just don't get her. She never bought us shit, but everything we get she takes. None of us have shit, and the lil shit we got she fucking steals from us and fucking sells it for fucking drugs?"

Wustafa is glad that she's opening up, but he can't take anymore.

"Babygirl, please! With the language, please?" he begs.

"Sorry, but I'm just pissed! I got all my shit in those two bags. She ain't taking nothing else from me. Can I leave it here?"

"Of course," he replies.

Sameerah looks Wustafa square in the eyes.

"But why me?" she asks as she desperately awaits an answer.

"Babygirl, life is jacked up."

"But why mines have to be jacked up?"

Wustafa looks at her as he thinks of a good answer for her, but he has none.

"It is what it is, Babygirl. May not be fair, but it's the hand that you've been dealt. All you can do is play out your hand. As jacked up as it may seem, you living. As long as you living, you have the opportunity to change your circumstances. Follow me? When you think of giving up, think of your two little sisters who are depending on you and keep it pushing."

Sameerah nods her head.

"That's my motivation right there. That's what keeps me going every day," she says as she continues to nod her head. A faint smile appears on her face. "Just when I be thinking about giving up, you recharge the battery in my back. It's like you have all the answers."

"Not true, Babygirl. I just take life as it comes with no complaints. I deal with life and everything for what it is, not what I would like it to be. I never ask why things are the way they are. I just accept them for what they are. I'm what you call a realist."

Sameerah looks at Wustafa with a spark in her eyes that he's never seen in them.

"What?" he asks.

"Nothing," she replies as she looks away bashfully.

"What's up? It's something. I never saw that look in your eyes. Tell me?"

"Nah, I don't wanna come across all mushy, girl like," she says with a smile.

"But you are a girl. A young woman, I mean. Go ahead. I told you, there's no need for the mask when dealing with me. Whatever you say is off the record," he says as he flashes a smile at her.

"It's just crazy," she says as the smile becomes brighter. The smile disappears quickly and turns into sadness. "You know I never met my father, right? But all my life I've had this thought of how my father would be. Like this perfect father," she says as she looks away. "The crazy part is I always imagined him being like you."

Those words melt away at Wustafa's ice cold heart, yet he doesn't let it show.

"That's deep," he says as he looks away.

He twirls the fork around in his food as her words replay in his head over and over.

"Wu, why come you don't have any kids?"

Wustafa sits in silence many seconds before replying.

"Babygirl, I made a promise to myself many years ago that I would never bring a child into this jacked up world," he says with a look of disgust on his face. "As a young dude, I had already made my mind up that a life of crime would be the life that I would be living. I've been in and out of jail my entire life. I didn't have time to make babies, nurture them, and raise them. That would mean that I would have to do something that I rarely do," he says with sincerity in his eyes.

"And what's that?" she asks.

"Get attached," he replies. "I made it my business to never get attached to anyone or anything because, with the life I live, everything is temporary. You're up today, and you're down tomorrow. You got money today; tomorrow, you're dirt poor. Knowing that everything is temporary, I refuse to get attached to something that may not be here tomorrow."

Sameerah squints her eyes tightly.

"But what about me, I mean us, the crew," she rephrases. "Do you see me, I mean, us as temporary, too?"

Wustafa sits in silence as he thinks of the best possible answer. Her question has him stunned.

"Babygirl, in this life, I've seen sons turn on their fathers, brothers kill brothers, and best friends become strangers. I've learned to enjoy people for the moment that you have them."

Sameerah nods her head as she soaks it all in. "Makes sense," she mumbles.

"Babygirl, I've spent twenty-five years of my life in prison. In twenty-five years, I got maybe two or three visits from my mother and my sister. That's it. No attachment to anyone or anything outside of that. I did twenty-five years of thinking and getting to know me. The biggest thing I learned about me is that I don't need people to make me comfortable or complete. I'm totally comfortable with me."

"But don't you wish you had a wife and children? You would make the perfect father, I think."

"Babygirl, I'm a criminal. I've been a criminal all my life. Have a wife and children? For what? To have them visit me in the penitentiary on the weekends. Nah, absolutely not. One thing you have to do is keep it real with yourself. Bullshit the people if you must, but you should never bullshit yourself. Excuse my language," he says with sincerity. "I always knew I wasn't going to do right. I've never misled anyone or even myself to believe that I was going to do right. Even while incarcerated, I kept it true with myself. While others were convincing themselves and others that they would do better when they got home, I kept it real. Instead of lying to myself, I spent my time trying to perfect my craft. I'm a criminal. I do crime. That's all I know. As I've said, I don't question why I am the way I am or why things are the way they are. I just accept life for what it has been and what it is," he says as he looks onto his plate.

A minute or two of silence passes before he speaks again.

"Babygirl, just to let you know," he says as he stares into her eyes. "The feelings are mutual. You would make the perfect daughter as well. If I had a daughter, I would hope that she had your spunk, your charisma, your heart, and your intelligence. Whoever your father is has cheated himself more than he's cheated you by not being in your life. It's his loss, not yours."

Wustafa's words penetrate through Sameerah's soul as they always do. Her eyes begin to fill up with tears. Just as the tears begin to flood her eyelids, she speaks.

"Okay. Okay. Enough of the mushy shit."

She smiles as she wipes the tears that have dripped down her face.

"Back to business," she says."I been planning out something real big for us. I don't want to talk about it until I put it all together though."

Wustafa's eyes light up.

"Oh yeah? How big?" he asks with great curiosity.

"Big, big," she replies. "I guarantee you it will be our biggest sting yet."

"Yeah, like that?" he asks as she slides onto the edge of the chair with anxiety.

"Calm down. Calm down," she teases. "Yeah, like that, like that," she says as she nods her head up and down. "I'm working on it, and the minute I have everything in order, I will lay it all out in front of you."

Wustafa smiles a huge and bright smile. "That's my Babygirl!"

CHAPTER 52
TWO DAYS LATER

"I don't know all the details," Sameerah says as she looks away from Wustafa. "All he said was Speed got locked up in a stolen car."

Wustafa stares right through her. "So, his man, who you don't know, just came up to your school to tell you? Why you? Help me to understand this."

Sameerah realizes that all this may sound strange, but, truly, this is how it happened. The only part that she's left out is the conversation that she and Speed had hours before he got locked up that night. She knew Wustafa was going to dig deep for every detail, which is why she didn't want to tell him in the first place, but she just couldn't allow Speed to sit in jail, knowing that he was depending on her.

"Wu, what is it to understand?" she asks with frustration in her voice and on her face. "You always looking in too deep," she says, while rolling her eyes away from him. "Shit! He got locked up, and he sent his friend to my school to tell me. He probably didn't want to send a stranger to your crib. I don't fucking know why," she barks. "Ask him when he comes home why he didn't come to you."

The rest of the crew watches with no surprise. This isn't the first time that she has chewed Wustafa's ass out in front of them, and they're sure it won't be the last. Each time that she's blasting him, he sits back like an innocent, little puppy with his tail up his ass. He never raises his voice back at her.

He just sits there like a child being chastised by his mother. None of them understand why, but they're sure that they would never be able to get away with it. They don't look at him any differently, though, because, sometime or another, she has chewed all of their asses out. Over the time, she has become like a mother to all of them, and she tolerates bullshit from none of them.

"I'm not going to ask him nothing because I don't care why he didn't come to me," Wustafa says with rage but still he hasn't raised his voice. "I don't even care that he's locked up. What he's locked up for has nothing to do with us," he says. "So, please, excuse my language when I say, fuck him!"

CHAPTER 53
THE NEXT DAY

Sameerah sits behind the steering wheel of the Cadillac Escalade. It's still running as it sits parked in front of the Essex County Jail. After sitting back, Wustafa's anger disappeared, and he started feeling guilty for leaving Speed sitting in jail. Sameerah didn't help ease his guilt by continuously telling him that it wasn't right. She told him that he should just get him out and cut him off but not just leave him sitting.

After an hour of waiting, Wustafa comes strolling out of the building. He gets into the truck and Sameerah cruises off.

"What happened?" she asks.

"The bail is paid. They said he will be out before midnight," he says as he looks straight ahead. "You know, a part of me wanted to let him sit in jail, so he can learn a lesson. You see he went against the organization and look what happened. He didn't care about how we were making out, so I shouldn't have cared about him and his well-being. That mess he got caught up in was senseless and had nothing to do with us. It was his situation that he got himself into, and I should've let him get himself out of it. He's the type that has to learn the hard way. I should've let him learn his lesson."

"Then, why didn't you?" she asks.

"Because I know what jail feels like and I don't wish a day of it on my worst enemy. Jail is a cruel place. Babygirl, it ain't for everybody," he says with a starry look in his eyes. "Just being here brings back memories and gives me the chills. Jail will either make you or break you. I've seen it break the strongest and most upright men. It's no joke, Babygirl. Jail is for savages, the uncivilized," he says with hatred in his voice. "And with us being civilized, we must do our very best to stay out of there. One thing is for certain," he says with his top lip snarled with rage. "I'm not ever revisiting that place, not ever! No way, no how! And anything that gets in between me and my freedom, I'm taking it out! Understand me?"

CHAPTER 54
HOURS LATER

Wustafa opens the door and stares outside. Wustafa says not a word. He just stares at Speed, who stands there with his head hanging low.

"Peace," Speed whispers as he lifts his head up slowly. "I just came by to thank you for bailing me out," Speed says, while looking Wustafa in the eyes. "Just give me a couple of days and I will be able to get your money paid back to you."

Wustafa says not a reply, but he opens the door wider, inviting Speed inside. Speed accepts the invitation and steps inside. He stops at the door, waiting for Wustafa to lead. Wustafa closes the door quietly and leads the way over to the living room area.

"Sit," Wustafa says as he takes a seat himself.

Speed takes the seat across from Wustafa. Wustafa looks over the table at Speed, who sits there with his head hanging low. They sit in silence for, at least, five minutes before Wustafa cracks the silence.

"So, what do you have to say for yourself?"

Speed shrugs his shoulders arrogantly. "I already said what I had to say. I thanked you for bailing me out."

Wustafa shakes his head.

"Hmphh," he sighs. "You don't get it, do you? It's no need for thanks. We are supposed to be a team, and that is what teammates do. We put money to the side after every score, so, in a case anyone gets nabbed, the bail money will be on deck. You don't have to thank me. That money is just as much yours as it mines or any other member of the crew."

Wustafa stares deeply into Speed's eyes. As bad as he wants to let Speed know that he knows he stole from them in the beginning, he knows that he can't on the count of the promise he made to Lil Wu.

"Letting you sit in jail would have been cheating you because you worked for that money just like everyone else. How fair would it be to cheat you? I would never allow you to be cheated, just like I'm sure you would never allow me to be cheated. Correct?" he asks as he zooms in on Speed.

Speed lowers his eyes onto the coffee table. For the first time ever, Wustafa is able to read him. He lifts his eyes up and looks Wustafa right in the eyes without blinking.

"Correct," he says with a straight and convincing face.

"A senseless case you caught, for what?" Wustafa asks with signs of agitation all over his face. "To ride up and down the street? Joyriding? Not a dollar was made through all of that. The only thing you gained was a new charge," he says as he shakes his head from side to side. "I'm sure you are aware of how much money we missed while you were booked for joyriding, right? How could you leave the crew deserted like that?"

"Deserted? I didn't leave y'all deserted. It was a car in the stash. Why didn't you take it out and do what you had to do?" Speed asks with arrogance.

"Because that's your job. That's why. When you signed onto this squad, you signed on as the driver. Never have I put you up to do anything other than drive. We hop out and get the money. We cover you and make sure you can concentrate on driving, and then we bust the bread down evenly. Even though you never once drew a gun on anyone. You know why?"

"Why?" Speed asks.

"Because you're the driver. Without you, we can't get anywhere. It takes all of us to make this team and all of us have a position to play. Seems to me like you have a problem playing your position."

"I don't have a problem."

"Sure, you do," Wustafa says. "All this started because I asked you to read and you refused to."

Speed puckers up his lips with attitude. "I told you I didn't feel like reading."

"But see how much confusion that caused. You could have just read the chapter, just as all of us did. You alienated yourself, which caused confusion between me and you. Then, you stayed away from us, and, after staying away from us, you got yourself in a bunch of trouble. It's all cause and effect."

Wustafa looks onto the coffee table, and coincidentally the book *Behold a Pale Horse* is laying right there, dead and center. Wustafa leans over and grabs the book.

"It was simple. All you had to do was read," he says as he hands the book over to Speed. "Now, read." Wustafa's stubbornness and his love for control won't let him leave it alone.

"Humph," Speed sighs with frustration.

Wustafa understands it all more clearly after thinking about it all. Speed has a problem taking orders. Wustafa has a problem with his orders not being carried out. He's had the right mind to cut Speed off because of the fact that he sees him as a problem, but he can't because he needs him. He realizes that the only way they will be able to work together is if Speed understands who is in control. In order for Speed to see that Wustafa realizes that, he will have to tighten up on him and break him down. From here on out, he plans to have his foot on Speed's neck, giving him no room to breathe. Before it's all over, he will understand his position in this organization.

"You said you want to pay me back? Well, that's how I want to be paid. You owe us a chapter of reading," Wustafa says as he holds the book in the air.

Speed shakes his head from side to side with anger before snatching the book from Wustafa. He pauses, just staring at the cover for seconds before finally opening it. He stares at the open page for longer than he stared at the cover.

"What chapter?" Speed asks.

"Any chapter is sufficient. Wherever your hand is right now just start from there."

"Hmphh," he sighs again before beginning. Speed studies the pages harder and harder. "Nick," he says as he stares at the page. "S, s, s, qu, ints," he says, sounding the word out in totality, piece by piece. "Squints," he says as his eyes light up. "Nick squints his eyes slowly and sw, sw, sw," he repeats over and over. He becomes more frustrated each time he says it.

Wustafa knows the book back and forth.

"Swallowed," he says as his heart sinks.

"Swallowed," Speed repeats. "With some dif," he says before he goes silent. "Dif, fi, cccul," he says, sounding out the word. "Ty. Dif-fi-cult-ty," he says, sounding the word out like a second grader. "Difficulty. Nick squints his eyes slowly and swallowed with some difficulty," he reads slowly.

Suddenly, it all makes sense to Wustafa. It wasn't about Speed being unruly and going against his command. Speed was ashamed for the others to find out that he could barely read. Wustafa now feels bad that he didn't pick up on it that night, instead of exposing him the way he did. Wustafa's heart is saddened as he sits back, listening to Speed struggle with simple words and sentences. It breaks his heart to see a damn near grown man reading on a second grade level. This is no shock to him, though. He's met many in prison who could barely read. Some were totally illiterate. No matter how many times he has witnessed this, it still doesn't take away the sympathy he feels each and every time he sees it again.

As Speed struggles, Wustafa sits back patiently.

"A whole chapter at this pace," Wustafa mumbles under his breath as he leans his head back on the chair. He kicks his slippers off. "It's gonna be a long night."

CHAPTER 55
DAYS LATER/NEW YEAR'S EVE

"One minute!" the woman shouts in a nasty tone. "Hold your fucking horses," she says as she snatches the door open with attitude. "Who the fuck ringing my—" she manages to say before a black glove covers her mouth.

"Shhh," the masked man says as he puts his fingers against his lips. The masked gunman behind him snatches her by the collar. They all enter the apartment, and Anthony closes the door behind them.

"Yo! Who was that?" a male voice shouts from the back room.

The masked man with the gun aimed at her head shakes his head, signaling her to say not a word. He grabs her by the arm and flings her in front of him. He pushes her toward the back room.

"Lena, who the fuck was that?" the man asks again.

They finally make it to the backroom. The nerve-wracking sound of razor blades scraping across plates can be heard loud and clear. From the doorway, they see Sameerah sitting at the table and her two little sisters, both in their early teens, sitting across from her. They all have plates in front of them with a pile of fluffy white cocaine on them. They're packaging the cocaine into little glass vials. The masked men give each other a head nod before bum rushing into the kitchen.

"Don't nobody move!" the man says as he holds the gun against the woman's back.

The sound of eardrum piercing screams rips through the air as the little girls scream their hearts out. The other two gunmen both aim their guns at the only man in the room.

"Please, please," Sameerah shouts. "No," she says as she grabs hold of her two sisters and covers their eyes.

A masked up Wustafa grabs the man and places the gun against his forehead. He looks over to the masked up Anthony and gives a command.

"Take the women and the babies into the next room."

Anthony grabs Sameerah and her mother by the arms and forces them out of the room. The two girls follow close by Sameerah as she keeps their eyes covered the whole time.

Once they're in the living room, Anthony allows them to sit comfortably on the couch. His gun is tucked away and concealed. Sameerah discreetly looks over to him and gives him a wink of satisfaction. She looks over to her sisters, both of whom are crying their eyes out.

"Shhh. Stop crying, y'all. It's gonna be alright," she says in an attempt to calm their nerves.

"Don't worry, y'all," Anthony says. "This don't have nothing to do with y'all. Just be quiet, and we will be outta here in a minute," he says in his calmest and most soothing voice.

He looks over at Sameerah's mother, who is a nervous wreck. She's rocking back and forth. She's staring straight ahead in a trance-like state.

In the kitchen, Leonard empties the cocaine from each plate and dumps it into a Ziploc bag. From the center of the table, he grabs the remainder of a brick of cocaine. He rewraps the tape around it and dumps it into the Ziploc as well.

A tapping on the backdoor steals all of their attention. The secret knock tells them that it's Speed. Leonard runs over and opens the door.

"Let's go," Wustafa says as he shoves the man toward the door.

For the very first time, the man speaks.

"Oh, hell no," he says as he braces himself. "I ain't going with y'all, so y'all might as well kill me right here," he says bravely with challenge in his eyes.

"Man, shut up," Wustafa says as he pushes him with all of his might. "Tape his mouth up," Wustafa commands Leonard.

Leonard quickly unrolls the tape and slaps it onto his mouth as the man attempts to put up a fight. As he gets to the doorway, he stretches both arms across it and holds on for dear life. Wustafa hits him in the back of the head with the gun, causing his knees to buckle. Then, with all of his might, he kicks the man in the back. The man stumbles forward before falling down the three steps. Wustafa jumps down behind him and snatches him off of the ground.

Wustafa grabs him by the arms, while Leonard and Lil Wu grab his feet. The man squirms and fidgets like a fish out of water. He screams underneath the tape, but he can barely be heard. Together, they toss the man into the backseat like a piece of luggage.

Wustafa and Leonard seat themselves on opposite sides of the man, while Lil Wu climbs into the driver's seat. Speed backs out of the alley immediately. Wustafa peels the corner of the tape from his mouth.

"Help! Help!" he screams.

Leonard shoves two inches of cold steel down his throat. "Shut the fuck up! The only thing I wanna hear from you is directions to the money."

"Help! Help!" he screams, totally disregarding the threat.

"Tell my driver where to go," Leonard says as he grabs the man by the throat.

"Help!" he screams.

At this point, the man would rather be killed right here on the spot than take them to the money. In fact, he's purposely trying to infuriate them in the hopes that they will kill him right here. They realize the game that he's playing, so they realize that they must play a game of their own.

"So, you're not going to take us to the money?" Wustafa asks with a smirk of sarcasm. "Okay. I got you."

CHAPTER 56
ONE HOUR LATER

The basement of the abandoned house is dark and cold. Wustafa and the crew all kneel down around the half-naked man. The only things he has on are his boxers and a slab of duct tape over his mouth. He's sitting on the floor, up against the wall with his hands tied together in front of himself. His ankles are tied together as well.

His face and head are full of lumps, the result of many blows from the pistol. Blood covers his face and eyes, making it hard for him to see clearly. He's taken a lot of abuse, yet he still hasn't given in. He's determined to die before taking them to his hard earned money.

Wustafa is determined to break him and make him take them to the money. He's enjoying the challenge.

"You a tough cookie, I see," Wustafa says accompanied with a demonic smirk. "I got something for you, though."

Wustafa digs into his jacket pocket and pulls out a pair of jewelry pliers. He came prepared just in case of a situation like this.

"Hold him down," he says as he grabs onto the man's foot. The man tries to put up a fight, but he's too weak from the continuous abuse. Leonard is able to hold him down with very little effort.

The man looks down at the pliers, wondering what he's about to do with them. The first thought that comes to his mind is his precious jewels. He gets a sudden burst of energy. He starts kicking and squirming. He tries to shake his foot out of Wustafa's grip, but Wustafa has the claw on him.

"Uhhmmm, uhhmm," he mumbles underneath the tape.

Wustafa locks the tip of the pliers onto the nail of the man's big toe. He grips the nail, and, with all of his might, he yanks it as hard as he can.

"Uhhmmmm," the man whines like a sad puppy.

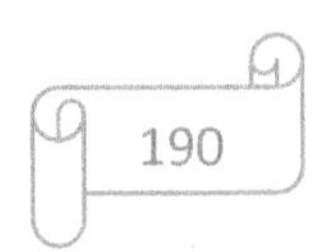

Wustafa locks onto the nail and yanks once again.

"Uhhmmm," the man cries.

The man's attempted screams have turned to crying and whimpering.

"No need for tears now, tough guy. You should've taken us to the money, and we wouldn't have to do this to you. Now, you have to suffer." Wustafa lifts the pliers into the air, so the man can see the tiny fragment of his nail in between the pliers. "That was just a little chip. We are going to rip the whole nail down from the cuticle of each nail," he says with a sinister grin.

Meanwhile

"She's hungry and thirsty," Sameerah says as she points to the smaller of her two sisters. She gives Anthony a quick wink of the eye.

"Cool," Anthony replies as he points to the kitchen. "Go ahead and eat. I'm not holding y'all hostage. I told y'all, this ain't got nothing to do with y'all. We got our man. In a minute, y'all will be set free, and I'm gonna be outta here."

Anthony's purpose here is not to harass the family. He was instructed to stay here with them just until they get to the money. They figured, if they kidnapped him and didn't get to the money immediately, they could possibly lose out. If they left them alone, Sameerah was quite sure that her mother would inform his people, who would notify the authorities or even go on a manhunt of their own. Wustafa wasn't worried about the manhunt. He was more worried that his people would get to the money before them.

Anthony looks over at Sameerah's mother.

"Let's go," he demands with aggression.

"Please, please," she cries. "Please, just let us go. Me and my children have nothing to do with any of this."

Anthony smirks underneath the mask.

"Nothing to do with it, huh? You got your beautiful teenage daughters at the table bagging up drugs, but you say y'all don't have nothing to do with it?" he barks. "I bet you put your children up to this for your own selfish reasons, didn't you?"

Anthony knows the answer to the question. He and Sameerah have been friends for years, and she's shared things with him that have broken his heart. He could go on and on, but he doesn't want the mother to realize that he knows as much as he does.

"I told you, I will be outta here in a minute. Until then, you will do as I say. Now, let's go," he says as he shoves her toward the kitchen.

Anthony has a deep hatred for Sameerah's mother. Sameerah thinks that he's putting on a hell of a performance, but she doesn't realize that it's no act. The hatred is real. She has no clue how the stories that she's told him have affected him.

Finally, they're all in the kitchen. Sameerah goes to the refrigerator, while the two girls sit at the table. Anthony forces the woman into the chair, and he takes a seat right next to her. He stares at her with pure hatred.

****One Hour Later/11:59 PM****

As the ball drops and a new year comes into existence, the crew is hard at work. As cold as it is here in the basement, Wustafa's forehead is covered with beads of perspiration. He got bored with snatching toenails, fragment by fragment, from the cuticle, so he let Leonard and Lil Wu take over. Both of them have been assigned to a foot of their own.

For the first half hour, he snipped tiny chunks of skin from the man's face with huge toenail clippers. His face is still a bloody, smeared mess, covered with hundreds of tiny open sores. The sores burn and hurt at the same time. He's in so much pain that he's almost become numb to it. Just as he got used to the pain of his face being clipped away, Wustafa changed up on him. For the last half hour, Wustafa has been concentrating like a skilled surgeon, snipping away chunks of the man's back.

"How many y'all got left?" Wustafa asks.

"I got three and a half nails left," Leonard replies as he digs his pliers deep into the man's cuticle. With no compassion, he snatches the last fragment of nail from the pinky toe. "Two more to go."

"I got three," Lil Wu says as he's in deep concentration.

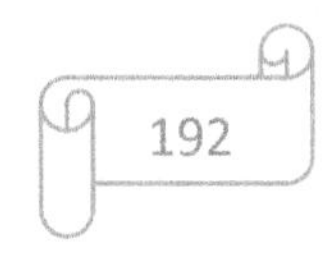

Wustafa thinks of Sameerah's little sisters back there in fear and under pressure and realizes he must speed up the process. He's, also, starting to wonder if anybody could possibly be looking for the man by now. He wonders if Anthony is okay back there.

"Y'all can go back to that," Wustafa says. "Grab those toenail clippers, and y'all work on his legs while I operate on his chest. Once we're all done, it will be time for the best part," he says with a smile. "An acid bath," he says as he picks up a bottle from his bag.

The man thinks of the pain, and he quickly starts to shake his head from side to side. Submission is in his eyes as he mumbles, "Mmm, mmm."

"What?" Wustafa asks. "You trying to say something? Speak up," he says sarcastically. The man nods his head up and down. Wustafa snatches the tape from his mouth. "Speak."

"That's enough. I give up," he says with defeat in his eyes. "No more," he says as he lowers his eyes. "If I take y'all to the money. Just please spare my life. Y'all won."

CHAPTER 57

THE NEXT MORNING/ JANUARY 1, 2003

He held it down for as long as he could," Wustafa says as he looks Sameerah in the eyes. "Once he saw that acid, he gave up. He took us straight to his crib."

"Where did he live?" Sameerah asks nosily. She's known the man for so many years, yet he remains a mystery to her.

"In Union. Had a nice little crib, too. Laid out," he says with his eyes stretched wide open. "Thanks to you, this has been one of the biggest come ups we ever had. Just as you promised. He had watches, jewelry, and a hundred and twenty-seven thousand dollars in cash."

"What?" she asks in shock. "I knew he had a couple of dollars. Been getting money for a long time. I'm sure that wasn't it. I bet he had more at his baby mother's house. I know that nigga was a millionaire with his tight stingy ass," she says with rage in her eyes.

"Had three more kilos of coke at the crib, too."

Sameerah's neck snaps quickly as she turns to look at Wustafa.

"Wu, you not throwing away no three kilos of coke. I know you think it's a poison and it will destroy a community, but fuck that," she barks. "That's too much money to throw away."

"Calm down. Calm down," he says with his hands in front of him. "I got a plan. Don't worry. We gonna get the worth of it. But just this time, though, 'cause, like you said, it's too much money to throw away. Once we off the coke, we will bring all the earnings to the table and divide it up from there," he claims. "But between us, you got extra coming to you. The finder's fee on a buck twenty-seven alone is twenty five grand. It's only right that you get that. I mean, I don't know if you want to stash it here or not, but you can. I want you to take care of those two pretty, little sisters of yours. How are they doing anyway?"

"They still a little shook up, but they will be alright. The little one had a nightmare last night, but that ain't nothing compared to the nightmare she been living all of her eleven years here. I know it was too much for them to see, but I rather them see it and that chapter be closed in their life than to be living it forever. Feel me?"

"Nah," Wustafa replies. "Break it down for me."

"I been at that table bagging up for him since I was twelve fucking years old. That's how we were able to eat. Bag up for him, and he pays us a couple of dollars, but the bigger part of it is paid to my mother in crack," she says with sadness in her eyes.

"As bad as it may have looked, we looked forward to him coming by because we knew we would eat that night. You can't imagine how many nights we weren't able to eat. Wu, as much as I hated him, we needed him."

"If he made a way for y'all to eat, then why do you hate him so much?"

Sameerah shakes her head from side to side. What she's about to say she has never told anyone. Her comfort level with him makes her feel at ease in telling him this. Besides, she wants to get it off of her chest.

"Wu, I lost my virginity to him at twelve years old," she says as she lowers her eyes with shame.

Wustafa squints with fury at the sound of those words.

"Twelve?" he asks. "How old was he?"

"Yeah, twelve. I don't know. I'm sure he was, at least, thirty. My mother sold me to him, so she could get high. She would make me do it. Not just him, though. All the local drug dealers would come by, and my mother would make me have sex with them. I was young, and, even though I knew it wasn't right, I did it because I had no choice," she claims.

For the first time ever, Sameerah sees water building up in Wustafa's eyes. Seeing that causes water to build up in hers, as well.

"I'm all cried out," she says with a smile. "I'm good. None of that shit don't faze me no more," she claims. "Between me and you, I've had over thirty sex partners from twelve years old to fifteen years old. Diseases? I've had them all except AIDS," she says. "Thank God. Over thirty something partners and not one of them were by choice," she says with a fake smile. "That's why I don't know if you noticed or not," she says, "but I have no respect for men."

"Nah, I never noticed," Wustafa says sarcastically. He knows this is no laughing matter, but he's just trying to ease the moment a little.

Sameerah flashes a smile back at him. "But seriously, though. In my life, you are the only man that I ever respected. I feel comfortable with you. You never looked at me sexually or came at me that way. It's like you look at me like a daughter," she says as the tears build up again.

Wustafa nods his head.

"I do," he mumbles.

"All other men are perverted dogs and all they wanna do is stick their dicks up in something. Excuse my mouth," she says with sincerity. "And that's why I have no problem dumping six hot ones in their face every chance I get. I wish I could have seen him die for all that pain and shame I been living with because of him. Every time I dump in one of their faces or watch y'all dump in one of their faces, I feel like I've gotten even with what mankind has done to me since I was an innocent, little girl." She looks Wustafa deeper into his eyes. "I remember the first time you saw me get busy. You said I was a cold bitch. I wasn't always a cold bitch, though. At one time, I was a sweet and innocent little girl, but them niggas took that from me. They made me a cold bitch," she says with a smile. "It's cool, though. I went through all of that so my little sisters don't have to. I refuse to sit back and watch them go through the shit that I been through. I will murder a motherfucker before they take my sister's virginity, and I will murder my mother if she tries to force them," she says with coldness in her eyes.

"That's what most of our beefs be about. My sisters ain't fucking, and my sisters don't have to bag up to eat no fucking more. That's why I get out here and do what I need to do every night, just so they don't have to do that shit no more. My mother's beef is I don't give her money to get high with, and she has no way to get high if I don't let my sisters bag up for him. And that's where all me and her arguing come from. Wu, my sisters ain't going through all I been through. I mean that shit from the bottom of my heart," she says as the tears drip down her face. "That's my mother, and, as fucked up a mother as she is, I still got love for her," she says as she wipes a tear from her cheek. "But before I let her fuck up my sisters' lives, I will take that bitch outta here. And I mean that shit from the bottom of my heart."

CHAPTER 58
TWO DAYS LATER

Wustafa sits in the small kitchen in the apartment here in Passaic. Across from him sits his old cellmate, Eddie. He and Eddie lived together in the same cell for six years before Eddie was released from prison. While living together, they built a tight bond despite the two strikes Eddie had against him.

One of the strikes he had against him was that he's Spanish. In Wustafa's experiences with the Spanish race, he's learned that they stick together, and he feels that they could care less for anyone outside of their race. The second strike comes from the fact that Eddie was a drug dealer. After several late night talks, Wustafa really got to know him and considered him a solid dude. They consider themselves more than friends or old cellmates.

"My black brother from another mother," Eddie shouts with a smile. "So, what's up? How's our mother?"

Eddie and Wustafa haven't spoken in close to a year now. The last time they spoke was when Wustafa first came home. It's all courtesy of Eddie that Wustafa even has a roof over his head. Eddie paid the rent for Wustafa for a whole year in advance. He, also, put a few thousand in his pocket to live off. For that, Wustafa has genuine loyalty to him and feels as if he owes him forever.

"Life is good," Wustafa replies. "Mom is good as well."

"So, what's up? What you up to?"

"Hey, man! You know me and what I do. Some things are just a given and don't have to be said," he says with a smile.

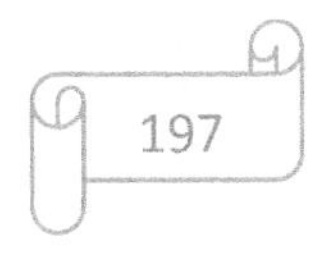

"And I know exactly what that means," Eddie replies as he flashes a smile in return. "But what brings you here? You need something? Is there anything I can help you with?"

"Nah, my brother. I'm happy to say that I need nothing at all," Wustafa replies with great pride. "In fact, I'm doing better today than I've ever done in my entire life," he says as he pulls an envelope from his pocket. "Here."

"What's that?" Eddie asks.

"That's ten grand. The eight you loaned me and two grand interest."

Eddie shakes his head as he shoves the envelope back across the table.

"That wasn't a loan. I told you that. I gave you that because I wanted you to have it," he says as he gets up from the table and walks away. "Is that what you come to my home for?" he asks. "To insult me by throwing a gift that I gave you back in my face?"

"Nah, not really," Wustafa replies. "I mean, that, too, but I, also, came here to talk business with you."

"Business?" Eddie asks with surprise. "Wu, you know what my line of business is. The last I knew of you, you despised drugs and drug dealers."

"Yes, I did, and I still do," Wustafa says with a sincere look on his face.

"Then, what kind of business can we do?"

"In my travels, I run across all types of things out there. I've come across something that I think you may be able to use," Wustafa says as he unzips the bag that's in front of him.

"And what is that?" Without answering, Wustafa shoves a sealed kilo in his face. "Whoa!" Eddie says as he fixes his eyes on the brick. "How many of these you got?" he asks with greed in his eyes.

"About three and a half."

"And how much you asking for them?"

Wustafa smiles charmingly. "I'm no drug dealer as you know. I don't have the slightest idea how much they go for, so I'm going to ask you what you're willing to pay. All I can do is hope that, as my brother, you wouldn't beat me," he says, while staring deep into Eddie's eyes. "You name the price."

Eddie immediately starts to peel the tape off the brick.

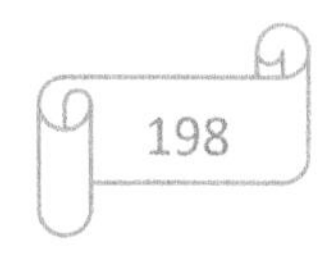

"Beat you? I would never," Eddie says as he stares back into Wustafa's eyes. "Right now, I'm getting them straight from Colombia at fifteen a kilo. If it's the right work and you got the price, I will take them all off your hands right now," he says as he looks at the fluffy white brick with the shiny interior.

"Yep, it's the right work. Name your price."

"You said you get them for fifteen grand. As my brother, you can have these for thirteen apiece. I would do better than that if it was just me, but I have a whole crew to bust the bread down with."

"I understand. We have a deal," he says as he reaches out to shake Wustafa's hand. "And anymore that you come across in your travels, don't hesitate to bring them to me. I will take as many that you have."

As much against drug dealing that he is, he feels no guilt in selling the poison to Eddie. Selfishly, he doesn't care that this cocaine will destroy Eddie's community. He feels that dumping this poison in this predominantly Spanish city is payback for all the lives that the Spanish have destroyed by dumping their poison in his community. *Payback*, Wustafa thinks. Wustafa returns the handshake.

"Good to hear, and I most definitely will." A smile is pasted onto his face. "This will be my first stop."

CHAPTER 59
LATER THAT NIGHT

The crew sits around the kitchen table, while Wustafa stands front and center. He drops the duffel bag onto the table before speaking.

"Today is a big day. It's sorta like a celebration. Does anyone know what we are celebrating?" he asks as he looks around the room. He points to Anthony.

"You?"

He, then, points to Sameerah.

"How about you, Babygirl?"

While Sameerah shakes her head from side to side, Wustafa looks over at Leonard.

"You have any idea?"

All of them shake their heads negatively before Wustafa continues on.

"I'm going to tell y'all what we are celebrating."

Wustafa looks back over to Anthony. "What's the most money you have ever seen in your lifetime? I mean, touched with your own hands?"

"I, I don't know," Anthony replies. "I guess that fifteen grand we scored at the liquor store. That's the most I touched at once."

"How about you, Leonard?"

"The shoebox the other night in New York," he replies. "That was seventy-five grand."

"Okay, so I'm sure it's safe to say that none of you have ever seen three hundred grand, correct?" They all shake their heads simultaneously. "Well, I'm gonna show you all what three hundred thousand dollars looks like," he says arrogantly as he unzips the duffel bag. He opens it wide and tilts it for them to view inside. "Three hundred and twelve thousand to be exact."

Bundles and bundles of neatly stacked bills are piled up inside the bag.

"This is what a three hundred large looks like," he says as he stares into the eyes of each one of them one by one. He passes the bag to his right where Lil Wu sits. "Put your hand in the bag," he demands. "Touch it, so that you know what real money feels like. When you're done, pass it along.

I want every one of y'all to feel what real money feels like."

Wustafa sits back with satisfaction on his face as he watches Lil Wu dig his hand into the bag and lift the stacks and shuffle them around. Wustafa hopes that showing them the money will inspire them to want to see more. The more they see, the more he hopes they will want.

Lil Wu passes the bag over to Speed, who doesn't dig in one time. He wears a nonchalant look on his face as he just peeks in one time before passing it over to Leonard.

"What? You don't like money?" Wustafa asks with a grin on his face.

A false smile pops onto Speed's face.

"Nah," he says as he shakes his head. "I don't like money. I love it."

Wustafa smiles, but, in all reality, he doesn't see this as a laughing matter. He sees a look in Speed's eyes that makes him feel uncomfortable. What he sees is hate, and he doesn't like it one bit. Wustafa watches him for seconds as he fidgets in his seat uncomfortably. Speed realizes that Wustafa is paying close attention to him, so he tries to act like he doesn't feel him watching.

Wustafa switches his attention over to Anthony, who has picked a stack from the bag and placed it up to his nose. He sniffs it for seconds with his eyes closed tightly.

"Appreciate the money," Wustafa says. "But never worship it. Money is a tool. Money makes money," he says loud and clear.

"Although that may seem like a lot of money, it isn't. If we use it properly, it will bring us more money. We have a great situation right now. We had a beautiful year last year, but I'm looking forward to an even more lucrative 2003. Just nine months of rocking and rolling, and we have managed to put away three hundred grand. Look at this as a cushion. A launching pad," he adds. "We got money, so we are not under pressure. With no pressure on our backs, we can take our time and plan our attacks instead of going out every night hunting desperately like skeezers. Now, we can pick our battles and choose situations which make sense. No more desperate decisions. Every Friday, we get approximately twelve grand for nothing, for work that we put in months ago," he adds. "That's a guaranteed twelve, which is more than enough for us to live off a week," he says. "All we have to do is keep the pressure on them, and that money will continue to come in. Of course, twelve is not a lot divided up between six of us, but it's enough for us to live off every week with no pressure until we make our next move," he says.

"The Washington Heights Heist will be major. Once we secure that, I'm sure we will have more money than we can count. So, what we are gonna do at this point is just sit back and plan our attacks. The petty everyday lurking must now come to a cease. These next stings will put us on an altogether different level. I hope that y'all are ready for what is in store for us from this point on. Welcome to the Big League!"

CHAPTER 60

Wustafa and Sameerah walk side by side along Market Street, while the rest of the crew tail slowly behind. All of their arms are filled with bags. They've been shopping for hours. They all have bought themselves, at least, three or four pair of sneakers and many outfits. Wustafa is the only one who has spent sparingly. He bought himself only one pair of no name work boots and three Russell cotton sweat suits.

As they're walking up the block, nearing Broad Street, Wustafa notices a pack of young men posted up against the storefronts. The young men all have their attention on Wustafa and the crew. Wustafa pretends to not notice them, but he keeps watch on them from the corner of his eye. The closer they get, the more tense the young men become.

They all stand quietly with their full attention on Wustafa and the crew. They stand there petrified. Wustafa notices each of them take their last breath as if they're not sure what to expect next. As they pass the young men, the tension in the air becomes thinner.

"You seen them scary motherfuckers?" Leonard asks. "Shaking in their boots."

Wustafa is quite used to this treatment. All of his life, he's watched as people damn near fall into pieces whenever he stepped into a room. The fear factor is basically all new to the rest of them. It started out on a small scale, but, over the months, it has gotten greater. Now, the majority of the people fear them the same. Those that don't fear them still respect them.

The one thing that makes Wustafa feel uncomfortable is the fact that they are marked. People that they don't even know them recognize them long before they even realize it. It's like they can barely shop in peace without people thinking they are up to something. Everywhere they go, as soon as they're spotted, people start to evacuate the area. They have the city walking on eggshells, and that can be a curse, as well as a gift.

Wustafa never rejects the opportunity to educate his crew about the fear they have instilled throughout the city. He never wants them to think that they are untouchable. Although they listen to him and claim that they understand, it still doesn't take away from the huge ego that they all now have.

"But a scared nigger will kill you fast," Wustafa says as he peeks over his shoulder. "I need you to understand that. You ever see how scary a cat is? But have you ever seen how a cat reacts once you back him up in the corner? It's the same mindset. Back a coward up in a corner, where he feels he has to fight, and his fear and desperation will make him fight like he's never fought before.

The fact that they know us and we don't know them is something that isn't to be taken lightly either. It means we are marked. Even when we are up to nothing, they believe we are up to something. That's something that we shouldn't take lightly," Wustafa says as he steps off the curb. He looks to his right, then his left, before proceeding to cross the street.

Wustafa slides to his left to allow the crowd of pedestrians to pass by him.

"Grover Watson!"

Wustafa stops short at the sound of his name. Hearing his government name sends chills up his spine. The last time he heard that name in public was ten years ago. He hates the name so much that he changed his name legally while in prison.

The only people who he still allows to call him that are his mother and sister. The rest of the world is restricted from calling him that. In his eyes, Grover died many years ago. He turns around slowly, wondering who could be calling him.

As soon as he turns around, he spots a heavyset woman, waving her hand in the air. He zooms in on her, squinting his eyes tightly.

"Grover Watson?" she asks if she isn't sure.

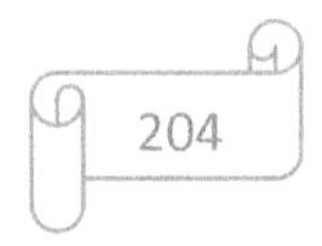

The obese woman waddles over to him as fast as she can. He stands in the middle of the intersection, waiting for her to come over. She gets within a few feet from him.

"You're Grover Watson, right?" she says as the words seep from her thick, cherry red lips.

Her voice sounds so familiar to him. Just as she gets closer, it all comes back to him. His beady eyes turn to googly eyes as he looks at his Mary Jones. Mary Jones, his childhood crush. He hasn't seen her since he went away to Jamesburg Boys Home over twenty-six years ago.

Outside of all the thick, pasty make up that's painted on her face, she looks the absolute same. As far as the weight, she appears to have lost five or ten pounds as opposed to gaining. Even with the weight loss, she still appears to be about 300 pounds. The only difference is her salt and pepper colored hair.

"Mary Jones?" he asks with a huge smile.

"Yes," she replies as she leans in for a hug.

Instead of being receptive to the hug, Wustafa reaches out for a handshake. His cold demeanor causes her to step back away from him.

"I knew that was you. How have you been?"

The loud sound of constant horn blowing reminds the both of them that they are standing in the middle of a busy intersection. Wustafa grabs her hand and fast walks across the street, opposite of the direction he was going in. He attempts to pull her faster, but she's going as fast as she possibly can with the heavy load that she's carrying. Finally, they make it to the curb where they stand face to face.

"How long has it been?" she asks. "So, tell me what have you been up to?"

"Twenty-six years, two months and seven days," he replies accurately.

"Wow," she replies, quite impressed. "What are you doing with yourself? Married? Kids?" she asks, firing question after question.

"Nah, not married," he replies. "No kids."

"So, what are you doing with yourself? Where are you working?"

Wustafa can't think of a lie quick enough. He decides to switch it up and take control of the conversation.

"How about you? Married? Children?"

She lowers her gaze and shakes her head with shame.

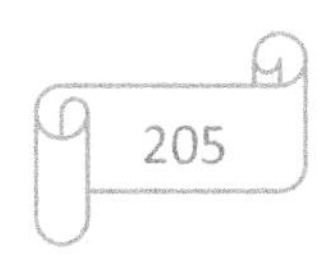

"No. Single," she says as she points to her ring finger. "Never was lucky enough to find Mr. Right. And no, no kids," she adds.

"So what are you doing with yourself?" he asks.

"I work for the state. Other than that, I've dedicated my life to Christ. I do a little preaching at a small church in Irvington. That's the highlight of my life. I live for Sundays," she says with a bright glow on her face.

The woman peeks to her left.

"Oh, Lord! My bus," she says as she looks at the 25 Springfield Avenue Bus. "Listen, I gotta go. It was good seeing you," she says as she pats him on the shoulder. She takes two steps away from him with slight hesitation. It's evident that she's hoping for him to say something, but he doesn't. "You take care of yourself now, you here?" she says as she runs toward the bus.

Wustafa watches her for a few steps before walking off and stepping across the street. He stops at the corner where the crew is standing waiting for him. He peeks over his shoulder once and notices the bus pulling off as Mary is running toward it. He watches as Mary stands there at the curb, watching the bus leave her.

He turns back around and just stands at the curb.

"What's wrong?" Sameerah asks with concern.

"Nothing's wrong. Why you ask that?"

"Because I never seen this look on your face before."

"What look is that?" he asks defensively.

"That googly eyed, goofy, I'm in love look," Sameerah teases. "Who was that?" Wustafa blushes from ear to ear. He's not able to even look Sameerah in the eyes. "Look at you blushing like a little kid," she teases. "Who is that woman?"

Wustafa traces little circles on the ground with his foot while he hangs his head low. He continues to act like a bashful little kid with a crush.

"My childhood sweetheart," he says in a goofy voice. "Boy, I was sweet on her."

Sameerah has never seen him like this before. He's totally out of his element. He's loose and not so uptight as she's used to seeing him.

"So, what she talking about? Did you get her number, so you can call her?"

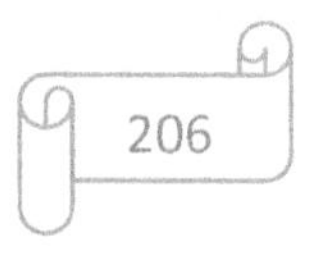

Wustafa looks up, and his face becomes saddened. His stern demeanor presents itself.

"No," he replies rather firmly.

"Why not?" she questions.

Wustafa shrugs his shoulders.

"I don't know," he says as he peeks over his shoulder at the woman, who is standing on the corner, waiting for the next bus. He quickly turns around and begins walking.

Ant, Leonard, and Lil Wu walk ahead, while Sameerah is glued to his side. She refuses to leave it alone.

"Why you didn't get her number? Is she married?"

"Nah, she ain't married."

"Then, why you didn't get her? Wu, I never seen you like this. When was the last time you saw her?"

"I haven't seen her in twenty-six years."

"Twenty six years, and you still are crazy over her? You better go on back and say something," she demands as she stops in her tracks.

Wustafa stops as well. He looks at Sameerah with a baffled look on his face.

"Say something to her like what?" he asks. "What should I say?" he asks as he really awaits an answer from her.

"Ask her, 'Can I have your number, so I can give you a call sometimes?'"

"That's it?" he asks as he takes a step away from Sameerah.

"Yeah, that's it, unless you got some other fly shit you wanna say," she says with a smile.

"Nah, I ain't got nothing fly to say," he says with a smile. Just as he takes a step, he stops short. "Nah, I can't do it," he says.

"Why?" she questions. "You want me to go over and ask her for you?"

"Would you really do that for me?"

"I will do anything for you," she says, while gazing deep into his eyes. She then dashes off and trots across the intersection.

Wustafa stands behind the hot dog cart, peeking around it as he watches Sameerah approach the woman. The closer she gets to her, the more butterflies fill his stomach. Nervousness seeps through his veins as he watches Sameerah standing there and talking. He turns his head, for

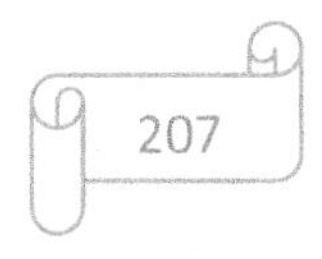

he can't stand to watch. The suspense causes him to look back over at them.

Although he and Mary never had an official relationship, she was the closest thing to a relationship that he'd had in his whole life. They only kissed once, and that was a peck that she gave him on the cheek. He remembers that day like it was yesterday. Through the years, he's thought about Mary, and, because he's not had any relationships, he has made their little crush into more than it actually was.

Wustafa has met a few girls throughout his life but never has a built a solid relationship with any of them. He's never had anyone in his life that he could call his own. Every time he even got close to building a relationship, he was arrested and shipped off to prison. That's the story of his lonely life.

Wustafa finds himself caught up in thought, thinking about that peck she gave him almost thirty years ago. Each time he thinks of it, he makes it more romantic. A simple peck on the cheek has turned into a wet passionate tongue kiss with a tight hug.

"Wu!" Sameerah's voice snaps him out of his daze.

He looks over to her, and the look on her face causes his heart to beat. She wears a saddened expression while looking away from him. She doesn't say a word, but her demeanor leaves him in suspense. She starts to walk ahead of him in the direction of where the other crew members are standing.

"So, what did she say?" he asks with great curiosity.

Sameerah shakes her head from side to side with a look of despair on her face. "She said..." Sameerah says as she pauses for a second. She looks away from him. "She said call her anytime," she says as she hands him a tiny matchbook. A huge smile spreads across her face. "She said she's on her way to bible study, but she will be free after ten," she says with joy in her eyes. "Seems like she's just as sweet on you as you are on her."

Wustafa raises his hand high in the air and yanks the air downward. He loses all self-restraint as he cheers like no one is watching. He tries to retain his stern and upright demeanor, but an uncontrollable urge charges through his body.

"Yes," he cheers as he jumps so high that he can touch the sky. "Yes."

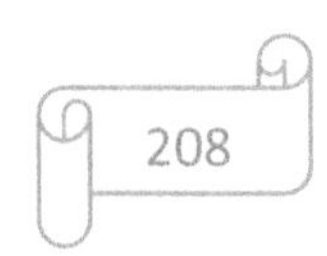

CHAPTER 61
DAYS LATER

The midnight blue 7 Series BMW creeps through the quiet block. The chrome wheels gleam through the darkness. The driver of the BMW remains a mystery to Wustafa and the crew, who have been tailing a block behind it now for the past twenty minutes. They were just cruising along Springfield Avenue when the BMW, which was cruising in the opposite direction, caught Leonard's attention.

The twenty minute game of follow the leader has led them into Maplewood. Wustafa has gone against his word, claiming that they would no longer chase the small situations, but he has a problem letting opportunity pass. Whenever he sees a potential situation, the thief in him makes it hard for him to let the opportunity pass him by.

"We can't be playing around up here," Speed says. "Maplewood cops don't be bullshitting. We gotta be in and out."

The BMW slows down before coming to a complete stop. The car, then, turns into the driveway.

"Okay," Wustafa says as he rubs the palms of his ashy hands together. "Home, sweet home. Y'all ready?" he asks as he looks into the backseat where Leonard, Anthony, and Sameerah are seated.

"Yep," Leonard confirms.

"Lil Wu, you fall back," Wustafa says.

Lil Wu shakes his head angrily. The car stops short at the small gate.

"Okay. Perfect," Wustafa says. "As soon as he gets out, we pull up on him and make our move," Wustafa says, giving strict instructions. "Hmphh, judging by the size of these houses, this may be one of them big willies. You gotta sell a lotta drugs to be able to afford to live here. Might have to go in and see if he got something for us in there," Wustafa says as he considers the thought.

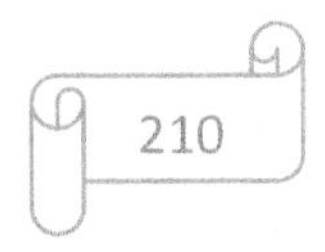

"We going in?" Leonard asks anxiously.

"Nah, nah, slow down, killer," Wustafa smiles. "Let's just go with the original plan. It's not planned out, so it won't be right," he says.

The driver's side door pops open as they all watch in suspense, wondering who will get out. The suspense is over once the tall, athletically built man steps out of the car.

"Looks like one of them ball players," Wustafa says. "Gotta be, at least, six foot ten."

The man walks toward the gate, leaving the door wide open.

"Now," Wustafa commands.

Speed slams on the gas pedal, and, in two seconds, they have the BMW blocked in. The back doors of the Navigator flies open, and Leonard hops out from the back passenger's side. Anthony climbs out behind him, while Sameerah hops out from the opposite side. The man's instincts cause him to turn around just as Leonard and Anthony are creeping up behind him.

The man's eyes stretch wide open with shock as he sees three masked bandits coming at him. He steps back with fear, and, like magic, his hand appears gripping a .40 caliber handgun.

"Oh, shit!" Leonard shouts. "He got a gun," he says as he crouches his tall, lanky frame low to the ground.

Leonard sends two shots at the man.

Blocka! Blocka!

The man sends three back at him.

Blocka! Blocka! Blocka!

The sound of the gunshots has broken the peace and quiet of the beautiful neighborhood. By now, all the neighbors are peeking out of their windows.

"Somebody call 911!" the man shouts at the top of his lungs.

As Leonard and Anthony run for cover, the man chases behind them. Anthony sends a shot at him to back him up.

Blocka!

Wustafa extends his arm out of the window and fires two shots of his own.

Blocka! Blocka!

The man's attention is diverted to Wustafa, causing him to not see Sameerah creeping up behind him.

Blocka! Blocka! Blocka!

The man tilts forward and crashes onto the concrete like a tall tree. Sameerah doesn't hesitate to run over to the BMW and hop into the driver's seat. It's become second nature to her. Sameerah slams the door shut behind her and honks the horn for Speed to move out of her way. Speed backs the Navigator up as Anthony and Leonard run toward it. As Leonard passes the man, he dumps two more bullets into his lifeless body.

Blocka! Blocka!

Police sirens can be heard from many miles away.

"Go! Go!" Wustafa shouts after Leonard and Anthony have gotten into the truck. Speed follows the speeding 7 Series BMW up the block as close as he can.

"Yo! What the fuck?" Leonard shouts with rage as he nags his fist into the palm of his hand.

"He caught us lunching," Wustafa replies. "That's what!"

Twenty Minutes Later

At the hiding spot, they all crowd around the BMW, while Wustafa looks inside a small duffel bag that he found sitting on the backseat. His eyes stretch open with fear at what he sees.

"What the?" he blurts out. "A cop, y'all," he whispers with nervousness. "A sheriff's officer," he says as he lifts the handcuffs and the badge up for them to see. They all stand with terror in their eyes and their mouths stretched wide open.

I killed a cop, Sameerah thinks. *A fucking cop*.

"Awl, shit! Now, what?" she asks frantically as she stares at Wustafa for an answer. "What the fuck are we gonna do?"

"Calm down. Calm down," Wustafa says with a false sense of comfort. "Just relax," he says as he paces back and forth around the backyard.

An hour has passed, and Wustafa is still pacing back and forth around the yard. He doesn't have much room to pace because the Navigator and the BMW are both parked in the center of the yard. Wustafa is sure that every cop in the county is probably on a manhunt searching for them. He's, also, sure that every news channel is covering this story. His mind is so cloudy that he can barely think straight.

Sameerah, who is in total shock, hasn't said a word in an hour. All she can think of is spending the rest of her life in jail. Leonard and Anthony sit side by side on two cinder blocks. Neither of them have said a word either.

Finally, they are able to breathe a little as they watch the huge Ford Excursion pull into the backyard. Lil Wu hops out with a gas can in his hand.

"Come on, hurry," Wustafa demands as he runs over and opens the door to the BMW.

He snatches the gas can from Lil Wu and pours gas on the floors and the seats. He, then, runs over to the Navigator and empties the entire gas can inside.

"Here," Wustafa says as he hands Lil Wu a t-shirt that he found in the trunk of the BMW. He, then, throws one to Anthony as well.

"Matches?" Anthony asks.

"Right here," Lil Wu says as he pulls five books of matches from his pocket. He hands two over to Anthony.

"Come on," Wustafa says to Speed as he runs past him.

Leonard and Sameerah run behind them as well. Once they're in the truck, Speed backs out of the yard. Before they even reach the street, the bright orange flames are sizzling inside of both vehicles. Anthony and Lil Wu sprint at top speed. They hop in, and, before pulling off, Speed waits for the command.

Wustafa watches as the flames grow bigger and even fiercer.

"No trace whatsoever," he says. "Rest assured that there is no way that this can be linked back to us. Let's go."

CHAPTER 62
ONE MONTH LATER

In Wustafa's day to day travels, it's becoming more and more normal to run into his jail associates. It's like, the more he's out roaming, the more of them he runs into. He's starting to feel like it's not by chance that he's running into them and that it's more like on purpose. He feels as if they're in search of him.

Every one of them wants a piece of the action. They all seem to have some type of plan for them. What they all seem to have in common is that they claim to have been sitting back patiently because they didn't have anyone on their side that they can trust. Wustafa translates that as they saw the opportunity but didn't have the heart to move on it.

Most of the people who have come to him with a plan have been totally disregarded because he didn't trust them. The others, he disregarded because the money at hand wasn't enough to get him motivated. Years ago, even months ago, he wouldn't let a single dollar get past him, but, today, the money has to make sense. He's grateful that, after all these years, he's finally in a position where he can pick and choose what vicks to take. For so many years, starvation sent him out on vicks that could barely feed him for the night.

Last week, Wustafa bumped into one of his old accomplices who goes by the name Reesie. Reesie propositioned him with a sweet deal that he claims is foolproof, but, after hearing the amount of money that was on the table, Wustafa lost the drive immediately. Hearing his man rant over a few measly grand bored him, yet he heard him out anyway. He reminds himself to stay grounded and never forget where he's come from.

Just months ago, he would've jumped at a sting worth a few grand, but, today, it's not that interesting to him. Despite the minute amount of money on the table, Wustafa still agreed to roll with his man Reesie.

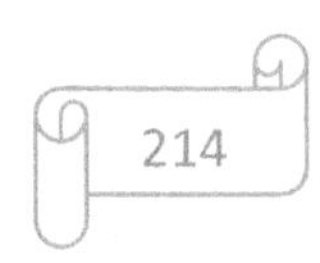

It wasn't about the money for Wustafa. His reason for agreeing was for the sake of him and Reesie's history with one another.

They've done many jobs together in the past and always threw each other a bone if one of them was in need. Most importantly, Reesie saved Wustafa's life many years ago. After committing a burglary, the word got out, and a bounty was placed on Wustafa's head. Because Reesie was one of the only people that could get to Wustafa at the time, the bounty was offered to him. Instead of murdering Wustafa and cashing in on the bounty, Reesie did the total opposite. He not only told Wustafa about the bounty that was on his head, he, also, pleaded with the people who put the money up. Needless to say, the bounty was revoked, and Wustafa lived to commit more burglaries and more crime. Because Reesie saved Wustafa's life, Wustafa feels like he owes him his life. With Reesie being down on his luck, Wustafa feels that the least he could do for him is help put a few dollars in his pocket.

Reesie sits in the driver's seat of the Acura Legend, while Leonard and Wustafa sit in the backseat. In the passenger's seat sits the owner of the Acura. He sits there, sweating bullets. What started off as a drug deal has turned into a robbery that they plan to turn into a kidnapping, a robbery, and two homicides.

Reesie called the man in the passenger's seat and placed an order for 250 grams of cocaine. The man's greed prevented him from questioning the rapid increase of his purchase. He's been dealing with the man for three weeks now and has placed four orders with him. The first order was for twenty-eight grams. The next order was fifteen grams. The third order was seven grams, and the fourth order was for 250 grams. The spurt would have alarmed a thinking man but not a greedy man.

The man delivered the order, but no money changed hands. Instead, Reesie aimed his .9mm at the man's head and held him at gunpoint until Leonard and Wustafa hopped into the backseat. The original plan was to leave him dead in his own car, but Wustafa came up with a more interesting and more lucrative plot to the story. He decided to force the man to take them to his home in the hopes of obtaining some real money.

After a brutal pistol whipping session, the man continues to stick to his story, stating that he has nothing. He claims that he's a mere middle man, working off the point system with his connect. Once an order is placed with him, he places an order with his connect. Once the deal is solidified, he scores a dollar for every gram that was purchased on that deal.

Hearing that only frustrates Wustafa. He quickly comes up with an even better plan. He forces the man to call his connect and place an order for half a kilo. Their plan is to have him deliver the work and then force him to take them to the mother load.

Wustafa places the gun against the back of the man's head.

"So, you're sure this is gonna be worth our while, right? Your life depends on it."

"I'm positive," the man replies in a high pitched squeaky voice. "This nigga loaded. He had a ten year run, straight, without going to prison, so I know he got money."

"What's the most you ever ordered from him?" Wustafa asks.

"The biggest order I ever brokered was for two and a half kilos," he states.

Wustafa nods his head slowly. "Okay."

"Here he come now," the man says as he sees his savior coming toward him from the far end of the block in the hunter green Range Rover.

"Showtime," Wustafa says.

He nudges the barrel of the gun against the back of the man's head.

"You know the plan. If you give him even the slightest indication, I'm leaving you for dead," he threatens. "Go ahead and get out."

The man gets out quickly and sits on the hood of his car, waiting, while they all hide behind the dark tints. The lights of the Range Rover brighten up the pitch dark area as it pulls up. The driver attempts to maneuver into the parking spot. The man stands up from the hood of his car and makes his way across the street as the Range Rover is backed into the parking spot. He walks in front of the truck on his way to the passenger's side.

"Now," Wustafa says as he busts the back door open.

Leonard and Reesie bust their doors open and get out at the same time. Both of their guns are aimed at the driver as they run across the street.

"Don't even think about it," Leonard says as he approaches the truck. He snatches the door by the handle with aggression. "Get the fuck out!"

"Alright! Alright," the man stutters as he speaks through the opened window. Fear covers his face.

As the man is being dragged out of the truck, he peeks over at Wustafa, who is running toward him with his gun in hand. The man's eyes open up and shine brightly as if he's just seen God at the pearly gates.

"Wu!" he shouts. "What's going on, Wu?"

Wustafa is caught by total surprise. Hearing his name being called shocks him tremendously. Leonard looks over at Wustafa as he continues to manhandle the man. Reesie, who is standing at the passenger's side of the truck, stares at Wustafa, as well. In fact, they all are staring at Wustafa. Four sets of eyes all on Wustafa as his two sets are zoomed in on the man trying to see who it is. As Wustafa gets closer, the face becomes more familiar.

"Rashawn?" he asks with uncertainty.

"Yeah!" the man replies with uncertainty as well.

Wustafa and Rashawn did time together almost twelve years ago in Northern State. Wustafa is about a decade his senior, but he always admired how Rashawn moved. He didn't spend his time watching videos and wasting time. He maneuvered like an old head. He spent his time in the library reading and studying. That immediately won Wustafa's heart.

They had a decent relationship in prison, but Rashawn knows Wustafa's M.O. He, also, understands that was a long time ago. A lot can change in twelve days, let alone twelve years. Rashawn stares at Wustafa, wondering what it will be.

"Let him go," Wustafa commands. Wustafa gives Leonard a head nod. "Y'all take him back over to his car."

"Yo, Wu! What's going on? What is this all about?"

Wustafa shakes his head from side to side with a look of aggravation on his face.

"I'm about to explain it all to you," he says as he walks around to the passenger's seat of the Rover and climbs in. "We gonna have to pull off from here," Wustafa says as the man positions himself in the seat.

Fear is displayed on his face and so is doubt. He's still not trusting any of it, but he realizes that he really has no choice but to move at Wustafa's command. Wustafa yells at Reesie through the opened window.

"Follow us!" He looks at Rashawn with a look of trust in his eyes. "Pull off."

Rashawn pulls off and watches the rearview mirror as Reesie makes a k-turn in the middle of the street and cruises right behind him. He then sees the lights of a Suburban with dark tinted windows shine on brightly. As he passes the Suburban, he pays notice to it, making a k-turn in the middle of the street as well. Seeing the cars behind him makes him more fearful of what may be about to happen.

"Yo! What's up, Wu?" Rashawn asks nervously. "Talk to me," he says in the calmest voice that he can. "What is it? Money... that y'all want? Just let me know." At this point, he's ready to negotiate in order to save his life.

Wustafa looks over at Rashawn with stone-cold eyes.

"Dig. The bottom line is this," he says as he bangs his fist into the palm of his hand. "Somebody brought me in on the sting. Apparently, he copped off your man a few times in the past. He came to me with a plan to grab your man up and make him take us to the house. He placed the order for the work, and your man shows up with it," Wustafa explains in full detail.

"We tell 'em what it is, and, immediately, he starts talking like a parrot. He tells us you rich and so forth and so on. To make it brief, he called you up to bring you in. He gave you up to save his own life," Wustafa says as his face becomes slightly saddened. "He never said your name, and I never asked. I didn't even recognize it was you until I got up on you. You know I'm blind as a bat," he says before flashing a smile.

Rashawn listens attentively, and, as he thinks of how blindly he walked into all of this, he becomes even more terrified. He can't believe that this entire situation was based around him. The suspense of wondering what will happen from here is killing him.

"So, now what?" he asks with sad puppy dog eyes. "I mean, how much is it gonna cost me to walk away from this situation? Name the price," he says as he cruises the block at five miles an hour.

"Ay, man. In a nutshell, I done some creepy things in my life, but I'm no creep," Wustafa claims. "Me and you had a good rapport down the way. I considered us to be alright."

"We was," Rashawn confirms in a further attempt to save his life. "I mean, we are."

"Money don't mean that much to me to go against the people I consider to be alright with me. We can walk away from this like it never happened," Wustafa says as he stares deep into Rashawn's eyes. "Or you can tell me what you wanna do?"

****Minutes Later****

Reesie watches from the driver's seat of the Acura as Wustafa walks away from the Rover, which is parked a few feet away from them. Leonard and the other man sit in the backseat with their eyes on Wustafa, as well. Everyone is watching with suspense, wondering what the next move is.

Wustafa walks up to the window.

"Ay, Reesie, get out for a minute. Let me holler at you."

Reesie gets out quickly, while Leonard peeks through the window at Wustafa. Wustafa nods his head three times before he leads Reesie to the Suburban, which is parked a few feet away. As Wustafa and Reesie get into the truck, the sound of muffled gunfire rips through the airwaves.

Blocka! Blocka!

Leonard hops out of the backseat of the Acura with the blazing gun still in his hand. He hops into the truck, and Speed peels right off. The Range Rover follows behind them, leaving the Acura parked with the dead man lying stretched out on the backseat behind the tinted windows. It was all because of honor and integrity that Wustafa gave Rashawn a pass. Rashawn was so terrified that Wustafa is sure that he could've gotten any amount of money that Rashawn had, but he didn't act on it. Instead, he gave Rashawn the price of twenty grand to off the man who attempted to have him set up. In the end, it all worked out. Reesie got the 250 grams he was in search of. So, another twenty grand is contributed to the organization, and Rashawn lives to make another dollar. All is well that ends well.

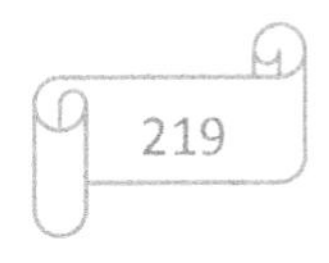

CHAPTER 63

The smell of oxtails, collard greens, and baked macaroni and cheese graces the air of Wustafa's apartment.

"What's going on?" Leonard asks. "You keeping secrets from us now?" he asks with a smile. "First you tell us we not working at the very last minute, and now it is nine at night, and you cooking like it's Thanksgiving or something. And you saying we can't get a plate," he teases. "This is crazy!"

Wustafa doesn't say a word. He ignores Leonard and stirs the pot of collard greens. The phone rings and interrupts Leonard's teasing.

"Babygirl, answer that for me."

Sameerah picks up the phone from the end table.

"Hello?" she answers.

"Yes, please hold. Uncle Grover," she yells in mockery.

She knows just how much he hates that name.

Wustafa walks over, snatches the phone from her, and walks away before putting it to his ear. Once he's far enough away from them that they can't hear him, he finally speaks into the phone.

"Hello," he says as he nods his head up and down. "Yes, just tell the cab driver 98 South 10th Street. I will be listening for the horn to come out and pay," he whispers. "Okay. See you then," he says before hanging up.

"Oh, now, I see," Leonard blurts out. "You got company coming over. So, tell me who the unlucky lady is?" he says with a smile.

"Alright, y'all. The party is over," Wustafa says. "Y'all don't have to go home, but you gotta get outta here," he says with a grin.

"You choosing a woman over the organization?" Leonard asks with more sarcasm.

Wustafa stands at the door, holding it wide open for them to exit.

“Tonight, yes,” he replies. “Now, out, out, out,” he says as he literally pushes them out.

As Sameerah approaches the door, he puts one finger into the air.

“Babygirl, you hold up for a second,” he says as he closes the door.

Wustafa walks over to the kitchen and opens the cabinet door.

“I picked these up earlier today,” he says as he holds a bouquet of roses in his hand. His face shows shame. “Is this corny?” he asks with a cheesy grin. “Flowers? Corny, played out, or what? You know I don’t know,” he says as he stands there with a goofy look on his face.

Sameerah laughs rudely in his face.

“What?” he asks with signs of confusion on his face. “Okay. No problem,” he says as he steps over to the trash can and opens the lid.

“No! Don’t throw them away. I mean, to me, it’s corny,” she admits. “But I don’t think she will think it’s corny.” She shrugs her shoulders with doubt. “I mean, most chicks like flowers. I just don’t,” she says with a look of disgust on her face. “It’s funny seeing you like this.”

Wustafa flashes a smile back in return. “Oh, okay. How about these?” he asks as he pulls out a vase full of flowers. “This cool, too?”

“Yes,” she replies, while shaking her head. “They’re perfect. Now, if you’re done with me, I’m out. I don’t want them to leave me,” she says as she awaits his okay.

“Okay. Cool.” Sameerah walks over to the door and snatches it open. She closes the door behind herself after making her exit.

“Babygirl!” Wustafa shouts. She peeks back at him through the tiny gap. “Thanks for everything!”

She pushes the door open. “No need to thank me. It’s nothing. Just give me all the details in the morning.”

****Two Hours Later****

Anthony, Leonard, and Sameerah have been roaming the streets with no destination ever since Wustafa kicked them out. It’s freezing out, but the liquor has them heated up and not even thinking about the below freezing temperature. Sameerah takes a huge gulp of the Hennessey just as they pull up in front of Anthony’s house.

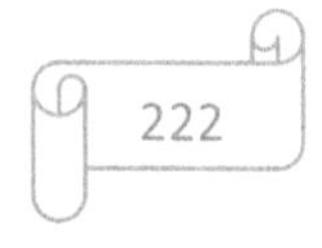

"Aghh," she grunts as the liquor sets her insides on fire. "Here," she says as she passes the bottle over to Anthony. "One last hit before you go in."

"Nah, I'm good," he slurs as he holds onto the railing for security. "I will see y'all tomorrow," he says as he pulls himself up the steps.

It would break Wustafa's heart to see his crew like this, drunk off of the "poison", as he calls it. Also, if he were to find out that they were roaming the streets intoxicated with their guard down, they would never hear the end of it. He has no idea that any of them even drink. They are sure it will be frowned upon by him, which is why they are sure not to let him know. They know what he thinks of those who do drink, and they would never want to be looked at in that same light.

Once Anthony is inside, Leonard and Sameerah get to stepping. Sameerah extends the bottle in front of Leonard's face as they walk side by side.

"Here," she offers.

"Nah, I'm good. Go ahead and neck that."

Sameerah stops short, turns the bottle up to her mouth and leans her head back. She guzzles the alcohol in totality.

"Aghh," she growls as she shakes her head, trying to shake away the burning sensation in her throat. She drops the bottle onto the ground and continues walking.

"It's getting late, and I'm drunk as shit," Leonard says. "I'm 'bout to call it a night. I'm walking you home, and I'm going in," he says as he looks over to her.

"Nah, just go on in and do you," she replies sadly. "My fiend-ass mother was bugging earlier. I cursed her fiend-ass out and bounced. I ain't going back there tonight. Fuck her!" she says passionately. "I'm 'bout to spark this blunt up and burn it down. I'm out here!" she shouts loud enough to wake all the neighbors.

Leonard looks at her and can see through the false smile that she's wearing.

"Hell, no! I ain't leaving you out here walking the streets by yourself."

"Good," she says. "'Cause I woulda been lonely as shit out here by myself. I guess it's me and you against the world," she smiles as she pulls a fat blunt from her cargo pants pocket. "I'm tired of walking, though. Let's go sit in the graveyard and smoke these three blunts I got. Get them dead motherfuckers high as shit," she says as she falls into laughter.

"Nah, I'm going in."

"But you said you wasn't leaving me."

"I'm not leaving you," he replies quickly. "You going with me. I ain't gon' have you out here with nowhere to stay."

"Nigga, you barely got somewhere to stay," she laughs. "Your mother ain't going with that shit."

"Just trust me," he replies. "I got this."

15 Minutes Later

Sameerah walks through the alley between the two raggedy houses. She stops short at the pitch black backyard. She peeks around nervously before stepping into the darkness. Finally, her eyes adjust, and she's able to see faintly.

She steps behind the house and waits impatiently. In a few seconds, her attention is caught by a light flashing on. She watches the window until Leonard slides the curtain to the side. He, then, opens the window slowly and quietly.

He leans his torso out of the window with his arms extended.

"Come on," he says as he reaches for her.

She grabs hold of his hands, and he pulls her up with all of his might. After very little struggle, she grabs hold to the window pane and pulls herself inside. Leonard closes the window quietly.

"Told you I would get you inside. Told you to trust me," he says with charming smile. "A little trust goes a long way."

CHAPTER 64
DAYS LATER

Wustafa is back in Passaic. Eddie called him up and said he needed to get with him. He wouldn't talk over the phone, which meant that it was either something serious or illegal.

It could easily be both. The only thing that keeps popping into Wustafa's mind is maybe the work wasn't any good, but, with that being over a month ago, he doubts if that is the reason for the call. He hopes that isn't the case because he would hate to have to give Eddie forty-five grand back.

Wustafa steps into the apartment, and Eddie closes the door behind him.

"What's wrong?" Wustafa asks before the door is fully closed.

"Wrong?" Eddie asks with confusion on his face. "Nothing's wrong. You brought business my way the other day, and I want to bring some your way," he says as he puts his hand on Wustafa's shoulder and leads him to the living room area. "Keep the money in the family, right?"

"Absolutely," Wustafa replies.

"Oh, before I forget. I talked to Mickey the other day, and I told him that I saw you."

"Oh, yeah?" Wustafa asks with a bright smile. "What's up with him? What he up to?"

"He's good. He's just working and staying in my pocket," Eddie smiles. "I see him whenever he's short on cash. That's my man, though."

"Yeah, Mickey is a beautiful dude," Wustafa says.

"Yeah. When I told him I saw you, he went crazy. He told me he needs to speak to you. He's been calling me two and three times a day asking if I talked to you."

"What about, though?" Wustafa asks.

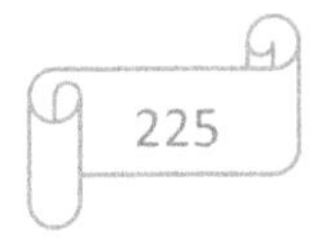

"I don't have a clue. He acts like it's top secret. He wouldn't tell me anything. But later for that," Eddie says. "That's you and his business. If you want to find out what it's about, I will give you the number. If not, it's no sweat off my back. I gave you the message, and now I'm out of it. My job is done. But my business is this," he says as he looks Wustafa straight in the eyes. "I got a problem. Actually, I got a few problems. I been letting a lotta things slide," he says with despair on his face.

"You know, with me getting married and having the baby, things changed.I had to slow down if I wanted to keep my family together. You know what I mean?" he asks as he flashes a smile. "Guys know what's going on in my life and think I won't do nothing to them. Understand?"

Wustafa nods his head as if he agrees, but, in all reality, he knows that Eddie was soft long before his wife and baby came into the picture.

"Yeah, yeah," Wustafa replies, feeding his ego.

"It's like, since they know I have something to lose, they been trying to take advantage. They don't know me, though. I will just say fuck everything and go on a wilding spree," he says in a not so convincing manner.

"Nah, nah, you got way too much to lose," Wustafa says just to shut him up. "That's what you got me for. What's up? Who on the list?"

"Shit! I got a long list of motherfuckers I wanna see one by one."

"Okay," Wustafa says. "Who first?"

"First on the list is a Dominican dude that I knew for a long time. I hate to do it to him, but he been in my pocket for a hundred grand for like three years now. Every time I see him, he crying broke. I just got the word, though, that he just bought a little bar, so he ain't that fucking broke."

"Hold up, hold up," Wustafa interrupts. "You let somebody owe you a hundred grand for three years? No wonder they're taking advantage of you out there. The word has spread."

"Nah," Eddie interjects. "Some things happened, and he wasn't able to pay me back. I know that for sure."

"I don't care what happened," Wustafa says with no compassion at all. "He could've, at least, gave you back one dollar a week. That would show you that he, at least, wanted to pay you back. It's the principle of the matter," Wustafa barks with rage. "So, what do you want done to him? Want me to scar him up?"

"Nah," Eddie replies. "I want him whacked," Eddie says with sternness in his voice. "How much will it cost me?"

"My brother, I hate talking money with you."

"Don't do that," Eddie says. "This is business here. Has nothing to do with our brotherhood. How much?"

"Eddie, you're putting me in a tough spot." Wustafa pauses before speaking. "Something like that would normally cost a guy about twenty-five cash," Wustafa says as he looks in Eddie's eyes. He wants to see how he will react to that price. "But, for you, I will do it for ten. I'm not even gonna eat off it. That will just feed my crew," he claims.

"Ten it is, then," Eddie says.

"Eddie, you do know, once you put that money on his face, ain't no coming back from that, right? I'm not going to stop until he's no longer breathing. You do understand that, right?"

"Perfectly clear," he replies.

"Okay, then. Get your list ready. Your reputation is ruined out here, but I'm gonna rebuild it for you. I promise you that."

CHAPTER 65
10:47 P.M./THREE DAYS LATER

It's late, and, although the Washington Heights area of Manhattan seems to be peaceful, many moves are still being made. As dark as it is, Wustafa still manages to see almost every move that's being made out here. Wustafa's main reason for being here tonight is to watch the building, so he can formulate a plan based around his studies. They've been sitting out here for three hours already, and he's noticed some things that he hadn't noticed the other times that they've been here.

In the three hours that they have been sitting out here, many potential vicks have been in sight. He let them all get away because he didn't want to blow their spot up. Within the past hour, he decided that he'd studied the building long enough and that it was time to go. He would never leave without scoring a few dollars here to make it all worth their while.

He's been sitting back, patiently waiting for the right vick to present itself. Something about the snow white S500 Mercedes with the Boston license plates tells him the right vick has presented itself.

"Now," Wustafa commands as he watches three men walk away from the Mercedes. Leonard, Ant, and Sameerah exit the truck and start off behind the men.

Not even five steps have been taken before the man on the end peeks behind and notices them. He turns his head, facing forward before looking back to take another peek.

"They on us," Leonard whispers.

Now, all three of the men turn around at the exact same time. Trying to be as discreet as possible, the men pick up their pace. Their focal point is the busy intersection in which they all believe to be the safety

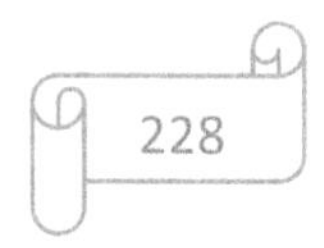

zone. Leonard picks up his pace and so do Anthony and Sameerah. In a flash of an eye, the three men take off in flight.

The man on the left dashes across the street, while the other two men stay on the sidewalk, running side by side. Anthony dashes across the street after the man who already has him beat by many steps. Leonard and Sameerah run side by side. The intersection seems to be approaching fast, and the men seem to be getting away when the sound of gunfire rips through the air.

Blocka! Blocka!

Leonard throws two shots at the man in the middle. He's the target because he's the one with the bag in his hand. The man buckles, indicating that he's been hit. He slows down, but his accomplices run that much faster.

Sameerah and Anthony try desperately to catch up with the other two but to no avail. They're now both a few feet away from the intersection. The man drags himself for as far as he can before he trips and falls onto his face. Leonard catches up with him no time at all.

The man is on his knees, trying to crawl onto his feet. Leonard snatches the bag out of his hand before pushing him onto the ground. He stands over the wounded man with the gun aimed at his head. The man covers his face.

"Please, please don't kill me," he pleads.

The sound of blaring police sirens breaks Leonard's concentration.

"Let's go!" Wustafa shouts from the passenger's seat.

Leonard backpedals to the truck and climbs in behind Anthony and Sameerah. Speed pulls off at a normal speed.

Just as they reach the intersection, they spot police cars coming from every direction.

"Oh, shit!" Speed sighs with extreme fear. The blazing sirens flashing in their faces frighten them all nearly to death. A total of five cars stop in the middle of the intersection.

"Nice and easy," Wustafa coaches. "Don't panic. Just drive. Panic and we go to prison."

Speed cruises through the intersection just as another car pulls into the intersection. Now, all six cars sit in the middle of the street with no sense of direction.

"They're clueless," Wustafa says as he looks behind them at the cars. "They know what direction the shots came from but not a clue of who did it."

Wustafa watches as all the cars zoom down the block to the intersection.

"They're going down the block now. Them niggers gon' tell what we in. In less than five minutes, every cop in the borough will be looking for us. We have no time to waste. Step on it!" Wustafa says as he turns around in his seat.

A few blocks later, they all exhale as Speed turns onto the ramp of the George Washington Bridge. They all take a quick peek behind themselves just to make sure no cops are in sight.

"Phew," Wustafa sighs. "That was a close call," he says as he opens the bag for the very first time.

His heart pounds anxiously. He hopes that all the risks they just took weren't in vain and that what is in the bag is worth all the hassle. He cracks the shoe box open, and his eyes bulge out of his head.

"It was a close call," he repeats, "but it was well worth it!" he shouts as he lifts the opened box for them to see inside.

"We are looking at a hundred grand at a minimum," he says as he flicks through the many stacks. "The reward was greater than the risk! I'm a trained specialist," he says with arrogance. "I can spot a good sting a mile away! One more for the history books!"

CHAPTER 66

Wustafa, Speed, and Sameerah sit at the table of the Greek diner, finishing up their food, when the waiter makes his way over to them.

"Desert?" he asks.

Both Wustafa and Speed refuse but not Sameerah.

"Yes, can I get some strawberry cheesecake?" she asks with greed in her eyes.

She looks over at Wustafa with a big smile on her face.

"My favorite," she says as she licks her lips.

A Mexican man comes over, pushing a cart full of dirty dishes. He stops at the table and begins snatching the empty dishes from their table. As he stands next to Wustafa, he leans his head over and, without looking at him, he whispers, "Meet me outside at the back of the diner," he says. "Alone," he says with emphasis before getting behind his cart and rolling away.

Wustafa looks over at Sameerah and Speed and nods at them before peeking around the room cautiously. He wipes the corners of his mouth with the napkin before laying it down.

"Excuse me," he says politely as he gets up from his seat.

He steps casually through the diner and makes his exit coolly and calmly. Once outside, he walks to the back as he's been instructed. Once in the back, he stands there, waiting patiently. Minutes pass, and his patience wears thin. He begins pacing back and forth. He decides to stand to the side, just so he doesn't bring any attention to himself.

Finally, the back door opens, and the Mexican steps out, carrying two large garbage bags. As he passes Wustafa, he whispers, "Walk inside and wait for me by the door."

The Mexican makes his way back quickly. He and Wustafa stand face to face at the back door. A huge smile spreads across the Mexican man's face.

"What's up, my man?" he asks as he hugs Wustafa tightly. He steps back. "Long time no see."

"I agree," Wustafa replies. "Good to see you on the outside," Wustafa says with sincerity. "Eddie said that you wanted to rap to me. What's up?"

"Follow me," the man says as he closes the door behind himself and tiptoes away.

Wustafa follows close behind him, tip toeing as well. He wonders exactly what is going on. As they reach the door, the man puts his hand on Wustafa's chest holding him off. Wustafa stands completely still as a waitress cuts across their path.

"Wait one minute," he says before walking across the room.

He peeks around carefully to make sure that the coast is clear. As he gets to another door, he peeks to the left and to his right before waving Wustafa on. Wustafa runs across the room as fast as he can.

The man sticks his key into the lock and opens the door. He allows Wustafa to step inside before him. Wustafa steps into the darkness with caution and suspicion. The man closes the door before flicking the lights on. What lies before Wustafa's eyes leaves him quite confused.

Rows of slot machines, two poker tables, and one pool table fill the room. For a brief moment, Wustafa forgets that he's in the basement of a restaurant. Instead, he feels as if he's in a casino in Atlantic City.

"This is what you wanted to talk to me about?" Wustafa asks with signs of agitation all over his face. "I don't gamble."

"Psst," the man sucks his teeth in reply. "I know you don't gamble."

"Then, why did you call me all the way over here for this?"

"Once a week, every week, this room is filled with a bunch of Greek millionaires. They gamble till, sometimes, five and six in the morning. Millions of dollars at a time in this little room," he says with his eyes stretched wide open.

He now has Wustafa's undivided attention.

"Millions?"

He nods his head many times before speaking. "Yes, millions."

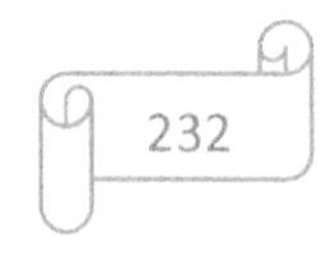

"Mickey, don't bull jive me just to get me all excited, and it's a dud. I will be extremely angry," he says with a threatening demeanor.

"I would never do that. Wu, you know me better than that."

"So, tell me, how are you so sure that it's millions involved?"

"I've been working here for three years, ever since I came home. I've been sitting back watching patiently for over a year now. They just started allowing me down here this year. They trust me, I guess," he says with a smile.

"They see me as a harmless Spick. Me no speakie no Ingles," he says with a broken accent. "So they think," he smiles. "I'm working here under the table for less than minimum wage. Last year, just when I was about to quit, they started letting me in on the action. I decided to hold off and get something outta them before quitting. After all the years of working for less than minimum wage, just one sting will make it all worthwhile. I knew I needed someone that I could trust to pull it off.

Eddie telling me that he heard from you was like a blessing in disguise. It's like you were sent here as an answer to my prayers," he smiles. "All I'm asking for is thirty percent of the earnings. I think that's fair. What do you think?"

Wustafa stands there with greed in his little, beady eyes. "If there's millions involved, then thirty percent it is. Give me the details."

The man shakes his head no. "Only after you give me your word that you won't move without me and count me out."

"Mickey, I'm insulted. You've known me for over ten years. You know that I'm a man of my word."

"Of course, I do, and that's why I asked for your word because I know you would never go against that." The man extends his hand for a handshake. "So, do I have your word?"

Wustafa reaches out and squeezes his hand with a tight grip. He looks the man square in the eyes. "You got my word," he says as he stares deeper into the man's eyes.

"Good," Mickey says with a smile. "Every Thursday, Greeks from all over New Jersey and even New York and Connecticut come here to gamble. Big money is at stake. Millions," he says once again to get Wustafa more motivated. "They carry their money in brown paper bags. Greasy paper bags," he adds. "The bags could be charged as bags of takeout food, but, in all reality, there are hundreds of thousands of dollars in the bags."

"What about guns?" Wustafa asks. "I know they're not carrying that type of money around with no protection."

"They feel they don't need security," he replies. "They all trust each other. They're all related some type of way. Some are blood relatives and some are related through marriage," he explains. "Anyway, they will never set foot near a gun. They're softer than drug store cotton," he smiles. "And by the middle of the night, they're all pissy drunk."

"But what about police and video cameras?" Wustafa asks.

"I control the camera every Thursday. I shut it off before they start showing up. The same way I just accidentally shut it off before you came back here," he says with a devilish smile. "And as far as police, they will never make the call. They're not stupid. They can't make a report of hundreds of thousands of unreported tax dollars. That will only open up other doors that they don't need opened. They will just take the loss," he says before flashing a smile.

"You make it sound way too easy," Wustafa says as he thinks of anything else that can possibly go wrong.

"And it's even easier than it sounds. I just been waiting on someone that I can trust. No gimmicks. I promise you."

Ten Minutes Later

Wustafa, Speed, and Sameerah exit the diner. Wustafa gallops fast. Speed and Sameerah gallop fast as well, just to catch up to him.

"Wu, talk to us," Sameerah says with great curiosity. She wonders what all this is about. "What's up?"

Wustafa looks over at them as they approach their Lincoln Navigator.

"We are about to be so rich," he says slowly. "Filthy rich. Mark my words. We pull this off, and we will never have another money problem for as long as we all live."

CHAPTER 67
DAYS LATER/3:30 A.M.

It's pitch black out, but sitting behind the dark tinted windows of the Cadillac Escalade makes it seem even darker. The block is dimly lit, which gives the block a creepy, eerie feeling. Wustafa and the crew sit a car length away from a small, rundown bar. More people have left out of the bar than one could imagine could even fit inside. They watched as the lights went out almost forty minutes ago.

Suddenly, the flashing of a single bulb over the doorway of the bar catches all of their attention.

"Here we go," Wustafa says as he reaches into the backseat and taps Leonard's knee. Leonard lifts up to the edge of his seat as he pulls the mask down onto his face. As the door opens, Leonard prepares to open his door.

They all watch with disappointment as a bright white stiletto steps out of the door. The short, stacked, skimpy dressed Spanish woman steps out totally unaware and uncaring of her surroundings. Without a single glimpse of the area, she aims her hand at the Honda that's parked directly in front of the bar, and the lights flash. The door opens once again, and a tall, slender Spanish man steps out partially.

"That's our mark, y'all. Lenny, don't hesitate because my man Eddie says he's known to carry a gun from time to time. Says he's extra scary, so you know what that means. Don't give him a chance to let his fear take over." Wustafa analyzes the situation. "Better yet. Ant, you go with him, just in case he's holding and decides to draw."

"Nah, nah," Leonard denies. "I got this. Trust me."

The man looks around before stepping all the way out of the bar. He, then, turns around and pulls the gate down.

"Now," Wustafa commands.

Leonard pushes the door open and jumps out. Before taking even two steps, the man turns around and faces Leonard. The sight of the masked up, gun toting Leonard causes both the man and the woman to scream like girls. Leonard races toward them with his gun aimed precisely at the man.

"Owwwww!" the man screams as he snatches the woman and pulls her in front of him.

He uses her as a shield as he hides behind her for cover.

The woman now screams louder than him as she looks back and forth from Leonard to the man. She shakes and squirms as she tries to get out of his tight grip. Their loud screams pierce through the peaceful airwaves. Finally, the woman manages to snatch away from him.

She backpedals away from the man, giving Leonard a clean shot, and he takes it with no hesitation.

Blocka!

The slug crashes into the man's chest, sending him back a few steps before he falls and lands in a seated position. Leonard stands over the man as he holds both hands high in the air.

"Please, please," he cries.

Leonard squeezes the trigger.

Blocka! Blocka!

The man's body folds like a chair before lying there with no movement at all. The woman's loud scream can be heard from many miles away. Leonard looks over at her, aims his gun at her, and the screaming ceases automatically. As he slowly squeezes the trigger, Wustafa's words sound off in his head.

"No women, no babies," he hears Wustafa say over and over again.

He backs away from her, leaving her standing there very much alive, unlike the sack of death that lies there a few feet away from her.

CHAPTER 68
8:45 A.M.

The streets of North Newark are packed. The rush hour traffic accompanied by the four inches of soft and fluffy snow on the ground is frustrating Speed gravely. The heavy downpour of snow flurries is blinding. He bosses his way through the streets in the Chevy Tahoe, cutting cars off and damn near running them off of the road.

"I'm not really understanding where you coming from?" Leonard says from the passenger's seat. "What you saying, though?"

Speed honks the horn with rage.

"Get the fuck outta my way," he says as he swerves around the car that is cruising in front of him. He looks over at Leonard. "What I'm saying is, we don't need him. The same shit we doing with him is the same shit we can do without him. What we need him for? To take the money, break us off peanuts, and keep the rest for his self when he didn't do none of the work? Huh?" Speed asks with aggression. "Is that what the fuck we need him for?"

Leonard sits back, just absorbing all that Speed has said.

"Y'all don't see nothing wrong with that picture?" Speed asks as he looks into the backseat at Anthony.

Anthony sits back in silence as he always does.

"Probably not," Speed continues on. "'Cause he got y'all minds."

"Don't nobody got my mind," Leonard replies defensively.

"Yeah, whatever," Speed challenges. "Y'all don't see nothing wrong with the fact that he don't put none of the work in, but he keeps most of the money? Talking 'bout that money belong to the organization. I don't need the organization to hold mines. I'm a grown-ass man, so I can hold my own money. I mean, think about it, all the vicks we have done, how many of them did he put work in? I will tell you how many," he says. "Barely none of them! Law number seven," Speed says slowly.

"Get others to do the work for you but always take the credit. Do that sound familiar to y'all?" Speed asks. "How about law number twenty-six? Learn to keep your hands clean," Speed quotes.

Both Leonard and Anthony sit back and, finally, see where he's coming from. They both start to think back to certain situations where Wustafa has commanded them to do things while he laid back watching from afar.

"He's brainwashing y'all using tactics from the book," Speed claims. "The crazy part is he's teaching y'all the same tactics from the same book, but y'all so damn brainwashed that y'all don't even realize what he doing," Speed says with agitation. "He got y'all brainwashed, but he ain't got me brainwashed. We doing all the work, while he don't do shit, but y'all feel like y'all need him. That's law number eleven," he says. "Learn to keep people dependent upon you," he says as he stares at Leonard. "Y'all read, study, and memorize the book, right?" he asks with sarcasm. "Then, why the fuck y'all don't see what's going on right in front of yo' fucking eyes?" he shouts with anger. "Or are y'all that fucking stupid?" he asks as he further attempts to belittle them and hopefully turn them against Wustafa.

They're both pissed off right now, but, because they realize that he does have a point, they both sit back and take the verbal abuse. Speed continues. "Using us, that's all! Oh and his nephew, punk ass Lil Wu," he says with rage.

"When is the last time that he got out the truck and put some work in?" he asks as he looks at them both, awaiting a reply. "Can't remember back that far, huh? Been a long, fucking time, but still we break that bread off even with him. He's just getting a free ride, while we put our lives on the line. All he doing is riding in the truck," he says as he pulls in front of Barringer High School.

Speed hits the lock button. He looks over at Leonard.

"Just think about what I said. We don't need him or his punk-ass nephew. We can do the same shit by ourselves. Think about it and let me know," he says as turns to look in front of him.

"Oh," he says with a sudden burst of energy. He looks at Leonard, then looks in the backseat at Anthony. "And whatever y'all do, don't tell Sameerah because Wustafa all in her head. He got her brainwashed like a motherfucker. This stays between us three and us three only."

CHAPTER 69
MARCH 1, 2003

Lil Wu stands in front of the middle-aged Spanish man as the man drops a pile of rock cocaine onto the triple beam scale.

"Fifty grams," the man utters as he points to the scale. Lil Wu pays close attention to the numbers to make sure that they're accurate.

The spot is crowded with so many customers. There are too many in the room for everyone to have a seat. A total of about fifteen customers are standing around, posted up, waiting for their turn. With today being the first of the month, the spot is extra busy. Dealers are here preparing for the first of the month rush.

Lil Wu, Anthony, and Leonard have been sitting in here for over an hour, just waiting for their turn. This has been the longest, most worrisome wait of their lives. With every knock on the door, they considered the possibility that maybe it was the law coming to raid the spot. In the hour before, they watched as the Dominicans busted open, at least, six kilos.

Before witnessing this with their own eyes, they never realized that it was possible to score a hundred and twenty grand in sixty minutes. They felt that type of score was only possible in their line of work. They both now bear witness to what Wustafa said about millions of dollars a day being made in this spot.

Leonard sits on the couch with his eyes on the man, standing at the door, holding a .9mm in his hand like he's guarding Fort Knox. He scans the room attentively with a keen eye. Leonard sits across from Anthony with his eyes on the kitchen area where two men stand. Quickly, they bust open another two kilos.

The plastic sandwich bag filled with rocks is handed to Lil Wu at the same time as he hands the man the money.

"A thousand dollars," he says proudly.

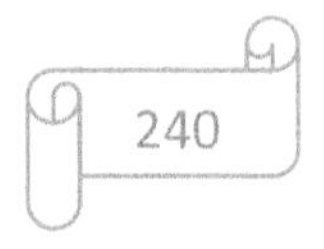

The man quickly counts through the bills and gives Lil Wu a head nod for confirmation. As Lil Wu turns around, both Anthony and Leonard get up from their seats. The attention of all the men is on them as they make their way to the door. The gunman opens the door for them to exit. Leonard takes the lead, and Anthony follows close behind. Lil Wu tucks the cocaine into his pocket before stepping out into the hall.

They take the stairs instead of the elevator as Wustafa instructed, just so they can observe their surroundings. Once they finally get to the downstairs lobby, they pass another man standing in the doorway. He nods at them as they approach, which is an indication that he's part of the operation as well. He stops them before opening the door.

He peeks his head out and yells out a few words of Spanish before finally looking back at them and giving them another head nod. He opens the door and steps back as they make their exit. Anthony and Leonard walk the busy block, cool and calm, as Lil Wu trembles with each step. The busy block coupled with the bag of rocks in his pocket makes him a nervous wreck.

Every few feet a few words of Spanish are yelled out. Finally, they make it to the corner where they notice the old woman with the food cart looking around attentively. She looks over to them, giving them a nod that the coast is clear. They pass her and cross the busy intersection. A few feet away from the corner the Escalade is parked and waiting for them.

Once they're seated inside the truck, Speed pulls off with no hesitation.

"So, give me all the details," Wustafa says with no patience at all. "Every little detail without leaving anything out."

In not even ten minutes, as they cruise the George Washington Bridge, Wustafa has questioned them over and over, so that he's sure that he has everything covered.

"The hardest part of it is over, y'all. We're on the inside now. Now, we have to infiltrate. It's gonna take some time, but patience is what this game is all about. We cop a few more times, increasing the amount gradually, and, before we know it, we will have them fully comfortable with us," he says before pausing. "And bam!" he shouts. "We make the biggest score of our career," he says with passion in his eyes. Wustafa reaches his hand into the backseat. "Give me that poison."

Lil Wu drops the bag into his hand.

Wustafa rolls the window down and tosses the cocaine over the bridge.

"Damn, Wu," Sameerah says with disappointment in her voice.

"What?" he replies.

"You just threw a thousand dollars into the water like it's nothing."

"It is nothing," he replies. "We will get that back a hundred times over once we make our move. Look at it like a small investment. Anyway, that little bag of cocaine is enough to destroy an entire community, so look at it as we have done a good thing. That's fifty grams less that will touch our community."

Sameerah shakes her head with aggravation.

"You bugging," she mumbles.

"Babygirl, I've done a lotta foul things in life, but poisoning my community will never be on my slate," he says as he shakes his head slowly. "I got way more than enough to answer for as it is. You don't understand now, but, one day, you will. Just trust me."

CHAPTER 70

The young man peeks into his rearview mirror as he pushes his Lexus past the limit. More fear pumps into his heart as he sees the huge Ford Expedition coming up the block behind him. He has not a clue as to why the Expedition started tailing him fifteen minutes ago. After making a few turns and the truck staying behind him, he attempts to get away from it but to no avail.

The driver looks ahead and becomes frightful as he notices the cars in front of him, piling up due to the red light at the intersection. Quickly, he steers to his left in an attempt to pass the sitting cars but the heavy flow of traffic coming in the opposite direction rules that out. He peeks back in the mirror, and, there, he sees the Expedition getting closer. The driver of the Lexus steers his car to the right and sets his car on an angle, so the Expedition can't creep alongside of him to his right.

The man peeks into the rearview mirror as the Expedition gets closer. He tries to see into the front windshield to see the faces of the driver, but the dark tint makes it impossible. Stuck in limbo, he looks from side to side, thinking of an escape route. As he looks to the front, he sees the car in front of him pulling off slowly. Honk! He mashes the horn like a lunatic.

"Go! Go!" he shouts.

Just as he's pulling off, the Expedition bounces onto the sidewalk and pulls alongside of him. The back window catches his attention because it's wide open. Just as he attempts to see the face of the back passenger, a ball of fire is tossed from the back window. The man's eyes stretch open with fear as the ball of fire comes flying into his passenger's side window.

"Owwww!" he screams with fear. All he can think is that a bomb has been thrown into his car. He screams with even more fear as the flaming, gas drenched white t-shirt lands onto his lap.

He takes off at top speed. Speed is glued onto the bumper of the Lexus. They all watch as the Lexus swerves from side to side up the block. Cars have to swerve in order to prevent from being hit by the Lexus.

The driver of the Lexus is a young man known as Nino. The streets have given him the name after Nino Brown. He's an above mid-level drug supplier who supplies, at least, ten blocks throughout the city. He was given up by a rival who can't compete with him, so he figures the best way to get rid of him is by putting the wolves on his heels.

The rival is a dude that Wustafa took under his wing many years ago down in Rahway Prison. Wustafa hadn't seen him in many years until last week when they just so happened to run into each other on a Newark street. Wustafa asked him if he knew anything good, and he didn't hesitate to throw Nino under the bus. Wustafa saw it as his man looking out for him, but, in all reality, his man was really only looking out for himself.

He told Wustafa everything that he knew including the man's place of residence, his mother's place of residence, and the place of residence of each of the man's three babies' mothers. Wustafa had planned on running up in his house at the right time, but, today, while cruising the city, looking for something to get into, they ran into Nino. It was then that Wustafa decided that the right time had presented itself.

With such short notice, he didn't have time to put much of a plan together, so he decided they would just cut him off and snatch him out of his car. The plan from there on out was to force Nino to take them to the money. That plan fell through when Nino managed to swerve around them and get away from them.

"There we go," Wustafa says as he watches the Lexus bounce onto the sidewalk before crashing into a light pole. "Showtime, y'all! Hurry, Speed! We gotta snatch 'em."

Before they can get to the corner, the driver's door of the Lexus pops open. The driver jumps out of the car with his pants on fire. He takes off running for his life, still attempting to pat the fire out.

"Man on fire!" Leonard says, laughing like he's watching a live comedy.

The man darts out into the street, not paying attention to traffic. He sprints up the street like a track star. The running ball of fire and the car crash has now got the attention of everyone on the street. People are watching in awe as they walk the streets. Throughout all of this, Wustafa doesn't notice the people. All he sees is the money getting away from him.

"Lenny, he on your side. Hawk 'em down." Speed cruises side by side with the man.

He cuts over to his right in order to get away from the truck. Just as it seems that he's about to get away.

Blocka! Blocka!

Leonard hangs from the window, ready to fire again. The people duck low and disperse at the sound of the loud gunshots. Anyone in his path attempts to get clear of him.

The man tumbles over and pops back up all in one motion. The fear keeps him in the race. The man crashes into the glass door of the liquor store, and, with his shoulder, he forces entry. Leonard forces the door open and prepares to jump out.

"I'm going in."

"Nah," Wustafa replies without a second thought. He looks around at all the witnesses and thinks of all the time that has been wasted and realizes that there is no way that they can pull it off.

"We can't. Police will be here any minute now. Damn!" he shouts with rage. "We blew it!" he says with anger and frustration. "Back to the drawing board."

CHAPTER 71
DAYS LATER

So, how are y'all making out?" Sameerah asks.

She's been prying from day one, but Wustafa has been holding out on her. He's extremely private as it is when it comes to everything in his life, but he treats this like top secret information.

"We been making," he says with a stone-cold expression on his face. He then dazes off as if he's in deep thought. "Babygirl, let me ask you," he says before pausing a few seconds. He's not sure if he wants to let her into his business, but he's gotten comfortable with talking to Sameerah about the situation.

She's been extremely helpful to him and given him valuable tips that he will never forget. He's actually happy that he had her in his corner to coach him because, if not, he feels that he would have blown the situation a long time ago.

"What does it mean when a woman just keeps staring at you without saying a word? I mean like in a deep daze," he explains.

Sameerah smiles. All this is kind of cute to her. To see Wustafa, a man that she sees as a very knowledgeable man, who knows a little bit about everything but girls, is funny to her.

"It means that she's head over heels in love with you."

Wustafa blushes like a teenage boy. He tries to wipe the cheesy grin off of his face.

"Yeah?" he asks with disbelief. "You think so?"

"Yep, and guess what else I think?"

"What is that?"

"I think that you're head over heels in love with her, too."

Wustafa waves one finger in the air. He shakes his head slowly with his lips sagging in a pouting position.

"Absolutely not," he says as he looks away from her.

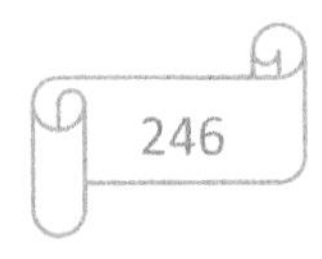

"Look at you," Sameerah teases. "You can't even look me in the eyes when you say that. You're in love. Nose wide open," she teases.

"Babygirl, I just don't go around falling in love with people."

"Have you ever been in love?" she asks.

Wustafa shrugs his shoulders.

"I can't even answer that. I don't know what it feels like to even know if I ever been in it."

"Me, either," Sameerah admits. "But, from what I hear, it's like butterflies in your guts. Like feeling fireworks when you see this person. Like they're the missing piece to your puzzle. Like you just want to be with them forever. You're always thinking of them every free second of the day," she says as she looks at Wustafa, who is dazing off into space.

With each example that she's given him, he's dazed off further and further.

"Yep, you're in love," she says. "I can see it in your eyes."

"Babygirl, I can't love her. We're from two different worlds. She's a die-hard Christian, and I'm a stone cold criminal. I'm just pretending to be something that I'm not when I'm around her. We read from her Bible, and I teach her things about it that she didn't even know. She says that she's in love with my mind," he says with a confused expression on his face. "She has no clue that the same mind that breaks those scriptures down for her is the same mind that strategically puts capers together that end in murder. She has no idea what I really do."

"What does she think you do?"

"She thinks I'm a temp worker for a construction company. She doesn't have an idea about my past and all I been through since the last time we saw each other. She thinks I done fifteen years for mistaken identity," he says, while shaking his head in pity. "She wants to sue the state of New Jersey and all. Sometimes, I feel like a hypocrite when I'm with her. Living a total lie," he says before going silent. "Remember last week when I told y'all I had business to handle with Moms? Well, that was the first lie that I ever told y'all," he says with sadness plastered onto his face. "I was in church with her all day from morning to night. I was dressed in a three piece suit, sitting in the front row. She even tried to persuade me to join the church and get saved."

Sameerah sits back in complete awe at all that she's hearing. She doesn't say a word because she wants him to keep flowing. She's curious to hear all that he has to say.

"That's not my life," he whines. "I'm a criminal. I been a criminal all my life. There I am, sitting in the church, knowing all the people that have lost their lives at my hands," he says as he stares a blank stare. "And knowing there will be a whole lot more. I don't believe in that mysterious God that most people believe in, and I don't believe in heaven or hell, but still I don't play with religion. I don't agree with it, but I respect it. Every man has to find his own path. One day, while talking, I told her that I have committed a lotta sins in life, and she says, 'God forgives'. Babygirl, I've never believed in religion, but, after talking to her, I just hope my thoughts on religion are correct," he says with eyes stretched wide open. "Because, if there is a heaven and a hell, I'm a roasted ass," he says with a huge smile. "With all the sinister things that I've done in life, nothing I can do at forty-two years old will be able to save me from that fire that she talks about," he says as he continues to stare off into space.

He looks over to Sameerah and the look in her eyes tells him that he's gone too deep.

"Enough of that already," he says in a more upbeat tone. "Where can I take her out to eat?" he asks. "I was thinking a fancy restaurant like Red Lobster or something."

"That would be nice," Sameerah replies.

"Only thing is, I don't know no bus that goes out to Route 22," he says with innocence in his eyes. "Anyway, the bus ain't safe. All the dirt I've done, I can't take the chance of being caught with her somewhere, unless I catch a cab out there."

"That's not romantic at all," she replies. "Why don't you just rent a car? Y'all can spend the whole weekend together. Go over to Times Square."

Wustafa stares off into space once again. He envisions them strolling down 42nd Street, holding hands, just staring at the bright lights. Suddenly, the reality sets in. He shakes his head with sadness slowly covering his face.

"Why?" Sameerah asks. "You got a license right? It's nothing to rent a car," she claims. "Why not rent a car?"

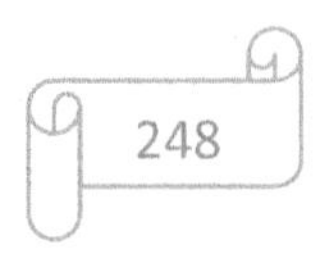

Wustafa stares into her eyes for close to a minute. "I can't drive," he mumbles.

"Huh? What you say?"

"I said, 'I can't drive'," he says shamefully.

"Why? Because of your eyesight?"

"No, because I don't know how to drive. I never learned. I was too busy going back and forth to prison," he says with embarrassment.

This is the first time that he has ever admitted this to anyone. As embarrassed as he is, it feels good to get the load off of his chest. He's been holding onto this secret forever, and it's been weighing him down.

Sameerah looks at him in complete shock. Wustafa's words play clearly in her head. 'Every man has a weakness,' he tells them over and over. All the while that he's been telling them this, she considered him so smart that he was above having a weakness. She's now found two of his weaknesses—women and the inability to drive.

"So, you mean to tell me that you never ever drove a car before?"

"I've never even sat behind the wheel of a car. Not even a bumper car at the carnival," he says with embarrassment. "Honestly, it scares me to death." Wustafa sits back for a second just analyzing the situation. He's never told anyone this until now. He can't understand what it is about Sameerah that makes him feel comfortable enough to tell her anything. It's as if, with Sameerah, he doesn't have to wear the mask that he's been wearing all of his life.

He continues on spilling his guts. "I have nightmares about driving a car, trying to get away from the police. I have no control over the car. It's doing whatever it wants to do, like it has a mind of its own. I wake up in cold sweats."

"Wow," Sameerah replies. She's at a loss for words.

"Babygirl, I trust that my secret is good with you. I always tell you that every man has a weakness. Well, that's mines," he says as he looks deep into her eyes. "I just hope that you don't look at me differently."

"Wu, you've taught me so much about life. I've told you things that I never ever will tell anyone, and you never judged me. How could I judge you?" she asks with sincerity in her eyes. "You've taught me everything a girl needs to know to get through this shitty life. Now, I will repay you by teaching you that one thing."

"Nah, that's alright," Wustafa mumbles. "I'm good without it. I haven't driven in all these years."

"Yes, I will," she says with determination. "That would make me feel so good to be able to repay you for all that you've done for me." She flashes a bright smile. "And I will not take no for an answer."

CHAPTER 72
TWO WEEKS LATER

The parking lot of Kings Restaurant is packed with luxurious, chrome wheeled automobiles. Wustafa sits on the edge of his seat, filled with anxiety, like a kid in an amusement park. They all watch with deep concentration through the heavy downpour of rain that bangs onto the windshield. The rain makes the tempo just right. With the storm being so heavy, people are less likely to pay attention to their surroundings. Their main concern is getting in out of the rain.

There are many vicks to choose from in this place alone, but they have one in the bag already. Wustafa got a lead on a kid from this side of town who is supposedly holding onto a few hundred grand. A scorned ex-girlfriend who told a girlfriend told her boyfriend. The information landed in Wustafa's ears from there.

The work that they've put in on the streets is like advertising and marketing. The more business they do, the more people want to do business with them. Now that the Young Gunz are a brand, it's like everyone brings vicks to them. Wustafa no longer has to go out and search for work because it finds him. Whether it be a scorned woman, a jealous friend, or a competitor they know they can count on the Young Gunz to even the score.

They sat in front of the gym this morning, waiting for their prey to exit. At 9:30 on the dot, he leaves the gym just as the sources said he would. They, then, follow him here. Before going inside of the restaurant, he parks beside a BMW. The driver of the BMW gets out with a shopping bag in hand and gets into the prey's Mercedes. The man gets out of the Mercedes empty handed, which tells Wustafa that there's a few more dollars in the car. He won't let a single penny get away from him.

They've been sitting out here for over an hour now. They've passed away the time by writing down license plate numbers of all the potential vicks that they've seen. Wustafa instructed them all to memorize each license plate number, so, while out in their travels, they could keep an eye out. That way, they can hopefully get a pulse on some of the potentials.

Just as Sameerah is scribbling another plate number down, the prey makes his exit out of the restaurant.

"There he go," says Anthony.

They all watch as he walks down the stairs and gets right into his Mercedes. He backs out of the parking space and exits the parking lot.

"Give him a block," Wustafa commands.

With them already knowing exactly where he's going, they have room to let him get even three blocks ahead of them.

Thirty Minutes Later

They sit impatiently in front of the prey's home. The two family house sits on the far end of the quiet, secluded dead end block. Because it is a work day, only four cars are parked on the block. Wustafa decided to give the prey a few minutes to unwind, get comfortable, and drop his guard before going in for the attack.

Wustafa looks at his watch.

"It's time. Go on, Babygirl."

Sameerah pulls her baseball cap down low over her eyes and puts her bag over her shoulder. As she gets out, she opens the huge umbrella and uses it as a shield, so no one can see her face. Dressed in sweats, Sameerah appears to be a young girl leaving the gym, not headed to a robbery. She grabs her water bottle from the floor before walking away from the truck. She peeks around attentively before lowering her head and walking up the steps to the house.

Sameerah peeks around cautiously as she's walking up the steps. The coast appears to be clear. Once she gets to the door, she peeks around once more before placing the water bottle up to the lock. She gives it one big squirt. She squirts again and again until the acid is overflowing and is now dripping out of the lock.

She pretends to ring the doorbell. After a few minutes pass, she pulls a key from her purse and sticks in the lock. Like magic, the door opens. She steps inside, and Wustafa and Leonard hop out of the truck. They walk at a moderate pace, to prevent bringing attention to themselves.

Wustafa closes the door gently and tiptoes to the door of the man's apartment. By the time he and Leonard get there, Sameerah is already inserting the key. The acid eats up the metal inside the lock, and any key inserted will open it. This is a trick that Wustafa learned during his breaking and entering days.

As they enter the apartment, the fresh smell of Irish Spring soap, running water, and loud singing tells them that he's in the shower. Wustafa stops in his tracks for a second, just enjoying the sound of his voice. He shakes his head.

"Such a nice voice. He could've been something. Instead, he'd rather be out here selling poison to the community. Typical nigger for you," he says angrily.

Wustafa quickly sends the hound out. They say a woman's nose is sensitive and can pick up anything. Wustafa finds that to be true. He's learned that Sameerah can sniff money no matter how well it's hidden. Sameerah dashes off into the bedroom in search of valuables, while Wustafa and Leonard make their way to the bathroom.

The door is wide open, so they step inside. Just as the man hits another high note the shower curtain is snatched to the side. He opens his eyes and looks at them in shock, mouth open, eyes open. His heart pounds so hard that he can barely breathe. Looking into the barrels of the guns causes piss to trickle down his leg uncontrollably.

Wustafa fades to the back while Leonard takes the lead. Seeing Leonard at work makes Wustafa proud. He can remember the days when Leonard was just a tall, goofy, and clumsy geek. Now, he's a coldhearted killer, and Wustafa is proud of the monster that he's created. He always knew he could bring the killer out of him, and he did.

"Take me to the money," Leonard says with a cool and calm demeanor. The man says not a word. He puts his hands high into the air and slowly steps out of the shower.

"Lead the way," Leonard says as he shoves the man out of the room.

As they're entering the room, Sameerah has her back facing them. She has the shopping bag that the man in the BMW was carrying. She looks through the bag with great satisfaction.

"Babygirl, close your eyes," Wustafa says. "This isn't a respectable sight," he says in reference to the butt naked man. "This ain't for my Babygirl's eyes."

Wustafa and Leonard follow the man as he leads them into the kitchen. He turns around and peeks over his shoulder as he's walking.

"Please don't kill me," he begs.

"Just shut up and keep walking to that money," Leonard says as he pushes the man by his shoulders.

The man stops short at the trash can which sits by the sink.

"It's all in there," he says as he points to it.

"Get it then," Leonard commands.

The man bends over slowly. He dumps the garbage onto the floor and snatches a plastic bag from the pile of garbage. "Here," he says as he hands the bag over quickly.

"That's everything I swear."

Wustafa snatches the bag and opens it anxiously. Inside that bag, there are four huge vacuum sealed bags.

"How much is everything?" Wustafa asks as he stares at all the money which appears to be fifties and hundreds.

"Two hundred thousand," the man says with tears running down his face.

Wustafa quickly calculates how much he will have to break off for the finder's fee of this vick. They agreed on a thirty percent finder's fee, which is sixty grand. The crew walks away with 140k. It's not the three hundred grand that was promised, but, overall, it's still a great sting.

"Please," the man begs. "I swear to you. That's every," he manages to say before...

Blocka!

His body drops to the floor with the words still in his mouth.

Leonard stands over the dead man, who lays there, eyes wide open, as if he's staring up at him. He aims in between the man's eyes. Leonard is sure that the man is already dead, but, still, he must fire one more shot. The shot isn't to seal his death. The shot is for the love of murder.

Blocka!

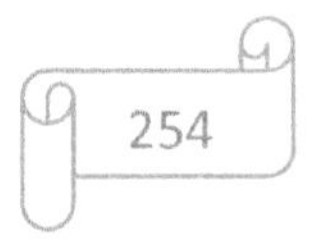

CHAPTER 73
DAYS LATER

Wustafa stands face to face with another acquaintance from his time served in prison. They have no real bond, but they are cordial to and respectful of each other. Pretty much everyone who comes in contact with Wustafa has a great deal of respect for him. It's him that respects very few.

His morals, belief system, and overall perception of life makes him extremely judgmental. He tries to not let his opinions hold so much weight. He tries to allow his energy radar to guide him through. It's like a sixth sense to him, and he tries to roll with that sense in every aspect of his life. When his radar tells him that a person is a good person, he believes that. When it tells him the opposite, he believes that, as well.

Wustafa never got a reading on Sal, the young man who stands here, because they didn't spend enough time together. Some days, he felt him, and, other days, he didn't. It was a wishy-washy situation, which is why Wustafa stands here now, trying to get a better reading on him. By the end of this conversation, he will know if Sal fits into his situation or if he doesn't.

"So, how are you sure that it's a hundred grand in there?" Wustafa questions with disbelief in his eyes.

"I said it's, at least, a hundred grand in there," he says with emphasis. "Might be a few more by now. That was last week. And know because I count the money with him after every flip. I know how much is stash money, and I know how much is buy money."

Wustafa nods his head. "Is that so?"

"Very much so," Sal replies. "I know his whole routine like the back of my hand. I'm with him every day. On Sundays, we have video game tournaments most of the day," the man says as he tries to prove himself to Wustafa. "He cops a bird every Monday night. Every Tuesday, me and

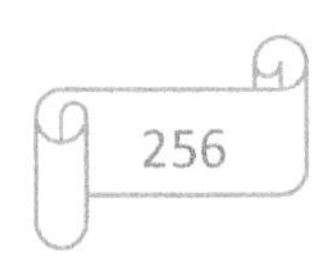

him sit at the kitchen table and bag up all day until we finish the whole bird," he says with his lips puckered up like a girl. "The rest of the week, we out on the block moving the work. If we catch him on Monday night, we can get the money and the work," the man says with a bright glow in his eyes.

"So, you say it's a minimum of a hundred grand in there, right? So, how do you expect it to be broken down?"

"I mean, I was hoping we could bust it down fifty-fifty," he says with uncertainty on his face.

"Fifty-fifty?" Wustafa repeats with sarcasm. "You expect half, and you're not putting in half of the work?"

"But it's my sting," he says in defense.

"So, you take fifty k and keep it to the neck, while me and my squad split up fifty?" he asks with a smile. "That sound right to you?"

"Nah, you right," Sal replies with desperation covering his face. "Let me get a third then?"

"Listen, take twenty grand and the bird. That's all I'm offering," Wustafa says with no room for negotiation.

Sal dazes off into deep thought for seconds before speaking. "Deal."

"But let me ask you, though. If y'all be together every day and he basically keeping food on your table," Wustafa says before pausing for a second or two, "then why you hate him enough to do this to him? I don't care nothing about him," Wustafa admits. "I just want to know."

"This ain't got nothing to do with hate," he replies. "In fact, I love him like a brother," he claims. "And because I love him, I don't want to see him get hurt. Just want you to take the money, not hurt him or kill him," he pleads with his eyes. "The bottom line is I been a lieutenant for him over half of my life. Every bid, it was me taking the fall for him. Still, there's no room for growth for me," he says sadly. "His selfishness won't let him make me a partner, so, instead, he keeps zoning me out," he says with frustration in his eyes. "Basically, I just want my turn."

CHAPTER 74
DAYS LATER/4:45 A.M.

It's been Wustafa's practice every day for the past twenty years to take his morning jog and indulge in his exercise ritual before the sun rises. In all of his years of incarceration, everyone always knew that he was in top physical shape. How he managed to stay fit, no one ever knew, for the simple fact that no one ever saw him actually working out. He never worked out with anyone in all his years of incarceration.

He's always felt, by working out with dudes, that opens the door for them to become too familiar. He felt that working out with them would lead to conversation, and conversation eventually would lead to jokes and horseplay and that eventually would lead to disrespect. He's made it his business to stay away from all of the above. By doing so, he's managed to keep the line of respect bold and clear enough where no one would ever feel comfortable enough to cross it.

He, also, knows that working out is ego driven. It's an indirect way for another man to size you up, testing each other's strength and endurance. They're all in search to find the other one's weakness. Wustafa would rather his strong points and weaknesses remain mysterious and keep them totally off balance.

Right now, he has just jogged into Vailsburg Park. The short run is nothing to him. After a two mile run, his breathing is just a tad bit faster than normal. He runs over to the bench and drops to the ground in a push up position. He digs his bare hands into the moist mud for a better grip as he lifts his legs and places them on the bench.

He quickly knocks out a hundred full extension, slow pushups with ease. He gets up from the ground with his breathing now a little heavier. He paces in little circles before dropping onto the ground once again. He counts aloud to break the boredom. "One, two, three," he says before stopping his count.

His attention is caught by an all-black Jeep Cherokee, which is entering the park. The Cherokee bounces off of the track onto the grass, coming in his direction. He quickly gets onto his feet as the Jeep comes at him at top speed. He backpedals slowly, as he squints his eyes tightly. His blindness coupled with the darkness makes it impossible for him to see.

Boc! Boc! Boc!

Wustafa crouches low to the ground. He backpedals in an attempt to get away from the truck, which is still coming in his direction. Now, the Jeep has gotten close enough for him to see the hooded bandit hanging from the passenger's window. The passenger fires two more shots at Wustafa.

Boc! Boc!

With the Jeep coming at him at full speed, there's no time for Wustafa to be nervous. He barely even has time to react. He draws his gun from his pocket and fires a set of shots of his own.

Blocka! Blocka! Blocka!

The shots echo throughout the park loudly, sounding like a battlefield.

Wustafa quickly darts behind a tree and uses it for cover. As he peeks around the tree, he notices that the Jeep has stopped in its tracks. The driver, then, spins the truck around and speeds off. Wustafa's adrenaline is now at an all-time high. He runs behind the truck, firing repeatedly.

Blocka! Blocka! Blocka! Blocka! Blocka!

As Wustafa watches the Jeep exit the park, he backpedals. Once the truck is totally out of sight, he turns around and sprints as fast as he can. The sound of police sirens in the air makes him run that much faster. As he's running, many thoughts flood his mind.

He wonders who they are. More importantly, he wonders how they knew he was going to be here at this time. He's been coming here for almost a year now and has always thought his movements were low and mysterious. This incident proves that he was wrong all the while. The bottom line is someone came here to take him out. *But who?* he asks himself over and over. With all the enemies that he has created for

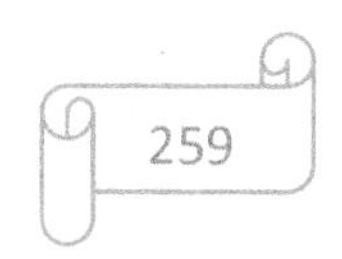

himself, he understands that the hit could have come from anywhere. He respects the game and all that comes with it. The only thing that bothers him is the fact that they know more about him than he knows about them. He, also, wonders what else they may know.

CHAPTER 75
LATER THAT NIGHT

Wustafa and Sameerah tiptoe slowly up the front steps of the house he lives in. Sameerah didn't even knew how the front entrance even looked because they always use his side door. Once they get to the attic, Wustafa pushes the door open for her to enter. As soon as she steps inside, the smell of mothballs and old people smacks her in the face.

Sameerah looks around at the many boxes that are scattered around the tiny room and wonders why he's even brought her up here.

"Babygirl, you know that I trust you, right?" he asks.

Sameerah nods her head.

"No, I mean, I really, really trust you. I trust you like I've never trusted anyone in my whole life. I trust you with my life," he says, while staring into her eyes.

Sameerah becomes nervous. He's coming across as super weird to her.

"What's the matter?" she asks. "What is this all about?"

"Hold your horses, and I will tell you," he says before pausing a few seconds. The look in his eyes indicates that he's debating if he should share this with her or not. "Babygirl, give me your word that what I'm about to tell you will never leave your lips. It's from my mouth to your ears."

"I give you my word," she says with no hesitation.

"This morning, while I was working out, a Jeep Cherokee came speeding into the park, busting shots at me."

Sameerah's eyes damn near pop out of her head. "Who was it?"

"I don't have a clue. I couldn't see their faces. If I wouldn't have been strapped, we wouldn't be standing here talking right now. Whoever it was came there to take me out. What bothers me is the fact that they knew to find me there. I thought that my movements were mysterious and that the only people who knew how I moved were the people that I wanted to know. Meaning y'all," he says. "That's the part that confuses me. Maybe, it was somebody who was supposed to know my movements," he says as he stares at Sameerah, looking for some type of reaction. The first thing that comes to her mind is Speed, but she doesn't want to say something and be wrong, knowing what Wustafa would do to him if that was the case.

"It makes me wonder what else they know about me. Even y'all," he adds. "I haven't told anyone about this but you. I don't want to throw it out there and it circulates around. Once the people get wind that someone had the heart to take a shot at me, then that will build the heart of others who may have been thinking about doing it," he claims. "I'm gonna keep quiet and let it surface on its own. Whoever was behind it will eventually tell on themselves. You follow me?" he asks as he gazes deep into her eyes. "And once they are revealed, it will be an all-out war," he says with determination in his eyes.

"I knew this day would come when they would get tired of us pushing them around and start coming at us to get us out of the way. It's now that day. All this comes with the territory. Occupational hazard," he says with a smile. "I'm sure that today is just the beginning. There's someone, somewhere right now, this very moment who is planning an attack on us. So, we know that we must be prepared for whatever they send our way. Enough of that, though," he says. "Like I said, that's the game."

"The real reason that I brought you up here is to show you something," he says as he digs a chest up from underneath a pile of boxes. "This is where the money is." He stares deeper into her eyes. "That safe downstairs is completely empty. That's the fake out," he says as he looks away with shame. "I want you to know where the money is just in case something was to ever happen to me."

Sameerah shakes her head with sadness in her eyes and on her face. She places her hands over her ears and says, "I don't want to hear that shit about something happening to you."

"Babygirl, stop it," he says as he snatches her hands from her ears. "I don't have no plans of going nowhere no time soon," he says with a smile. "But what I'm talking about is the reality of this lifestyle. I told you that I'm a realist. I just want you to know where the money is at. If I would have been murdered this morning, no one would have ever known where the money is. Y'all worked just as hard as I did and that wouldn't have been fair to y'all. So, if by chance, anything ever happens, you are to come up here and get the money."

"How will I get up here?" she interrupts.

"Don't worry. I will make a way for you," he replies. "The money is completely safe up here. The landlord, Old Man Mr. Jackson, hasn't been up here in years," he says as he looks around. "He can't even make it up the two flights of stairs. Whenever he needs to get something from up here, he asks me, so that isn't a problem," he claims. "Babygirl, I am appointing you second in command, and, in the event of my absence, you are to come get this money and divide it up equally amongst the crew. Can I trust you to do that?"

Sameerah nods her head. "Absolutely," she whispers. "You can trust me to do that and more."

"And that I'm sure of. That's why you're my Babygirl and second in command."

CHAPTER 76
DAYS LATER/ APRIL 1ST

Sameerah steps onto the porch of the small house. She peeks around before pressing the doorbell. As she waits for a reply, she fluffs her bouncy curls over her shoulders. She hears a door opening on the other side, followed by footsteps.

She inhales a deep breath as she tries to calm her nerves. Just as soon as the door is parted, Leonard steps over from the left side and forces the door open all the way. Sameerah steps back to allow Wustafa and Anthony in. Wustafa instructed her to go back to the truck and wait with Speed and Lil Wu once they were inside, but she's totally disregarded that command.

She's fallen in love with the adrenaline rush that she gets during a robbery. She's become addicted to it, and, when she's not called upon, she feels empty. The fast pace, the feeling of dominance and watching grown men turn to scared little boys, all that together gives her a feeling that she's never felt before. For nothing in the world would she miss this opportunity.

Leonard pulls his mask over his face and so does everyone else. Sal looks over at Wustafa and gives him a quick wink of the eye. Wustafa returns the gesture with a head nod.

"Ready?" Wustafa asks.

Everyone, including Sal, gives some type of signal as confirmation. Leonard grabs Sal and turns him around with force before wrapping his arm around his neck. With the other hand, he points the gun to Sal's neck. Leonard walks Sal to the door where they stop until Anthony takes the lead. Anthony stands to the side as Wustafa and Sameerah fall in line behind Leonard.

Anthony looks over his shoulder and nods once before pushing the door wide open. Leonard steps inside, holding the man at gunpoint.

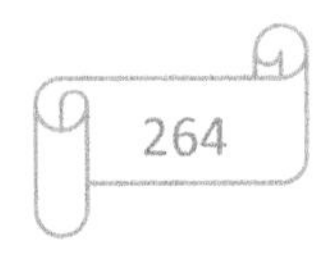

"Don't nobody move!"

Anthony, Wustafa and Sameerah all rush inside, waving their guns around the entire room. The two men who are sitting on the couch with game controllers in their hands look up with fear. Sameerah closes the door. Both men stand to their feet with their hands in the air. Fear covers their eyes, while terror fills their eyes. Wustafa immediately runs over and begins searching them for weapons. Wustafa, then, grabs the man of the hour and wraps his arms around his neck.

"You lay down," Wustafa says to the third man. "On the floor."

The man dives onto the floor with no hesitation. Leonard quickly pushes Sal onto the couch.

"Move and I'll knock your fucking block off," he threatens.

Leonard looks over to Sameerah.

"Hit the apartment," he commands as if he's in control and Wustafa isn't even standing here. "Don't miss a spot."

Sameerah takes off and disappears into the next room.

"Listen," Wustafa whispers into the man's ear. "You're the author of this story. This is the plot," he whispers. "We are here for the trap. This the action right here. Only you can determine if it's gonna be a happily ever after ending or a sad dramatic ending," he whispers in the man's ear with his lips on the man's earlobes.

"What is it gonna be?" Wustafa asks. "Are you going to take me to the money, or do I have to find it myself? The longer I look, the more frustrated I'm gonna get," he says.

"What money?" the man asks innocently.

Sameerah runs back into the room with the duffel bag in her hand. The money was hidden exactly where Sal said it would be.

"Got it," she says with joy in her eyes.

Wustafa looks at her with great satisfaction before rage pops onto his face again. He turns the man around, and, in one motion, he has his hand around the man's neck. He chokes him as hard as he can.

"What money?" Wustafa asks.

Wustafa slams him onto the loveseat.

"What money?" he asks again as he rests the gun against the man's forehead.

"You think we are in here to play games. You think this is one of your little Space Invaders games that you're playing over there. This ain't no April Fool's Day joke. No, this is real life," Wustafa barks.

The man shakes his head from side to side.

"No, sir," the man mumbles. "I know. I know."

Wustafa kneels down, so that him and the man are eye to eye.

"Do you know how you got yourself into this position? I'm gonna tell you how," Wustafa says as he looks at the man with a smirk on his face. "L, bring him over."

Sal sits on the couch, confused. Leonard snatches him to his feet and drags him over. Leonard stops short, right next to Wustafa. He looks at the man on the loveseat.

"Look into the eyes of the man who made all this possible," Wustafa says as he points the gun up at Sal.

The man looks up at Sal with confusion on his face as well. Sal shakes his head. Wustafa looks up at him.

"Am I lying?" Wustafa asks as he stands up. "What did you tell me? Didn't you say that you're tired of being his lieutenant? Tell him all that you told me," Wustafa says with a smile. "Now is the time. After this, you will no longer be his lieutenant. Let him know how you really feel about him before I finish off his selfish-ass life. Tell him to his face like a man, so, at least, he will know why this has happened to him and he can rest in peace. Tell him," Wustafa demands as he jams the barrel of the gun into one of Sal's nostrils. "Tell him that you think he's selfish because he wouldn't make you a partner, so you had him set up."

Sal stands there with a dumb but scared look on his face.

"Tell him, or I'm gonna bust your melon," he says as he sticks the gun even further up his nose. "Tell him he's selfish and that he should've made you a partner or this wouldn't have happened to him."

"You selfish," Sal whispers with sadness in his eyes. In no way did he expect this.

"Louder," Wustafa says.

"You selfish, and you should've made me a partner, and this wouldn't have happened," Sal says as he lowers his eyes with shame.

The man is at a loss of words. He can't believe that all the years that he's taken care of Sal that he would betray him like this. He shakes his head as the tears trickle down his face. Wustafa looks at him with no compassion at all.

"Hurts, don't it?" he asks. "You got anything that you would like to say to Sal?"

The man shakes his head as he shrugs his shoulders. At this point, he doesn't know what to say. Wustafa discreetly nudges Leonard with his elbow, and, two seconds later...

Blocka!

The man's head snaps back and bangs against the wall loudly before his whole body tilts over onto the other side of the couch.

"Aghh, no," Sal cries before Leonard covers his mouth with his latex glove covered hand.

"Shut the fuck up, you double-crossing piece of shit."

The man on the floor lies there quietly, but he shivers like a leaf. He hasn't looked up once, but he can tell, by the sound of things, how this story is about to end. He wonders when his turn is coming. His wondering stops when...

Blocka!

His trembling and shivering stops immediately.

Leonard slams Sal onto the couch where he lands right next to his friend's dead body. Wustafa stares deeply into Sal's eyes.

"No loyalty, no honor," he mumbles. "Been taking care of you all your life and this is how you repay him?" he says as he looks at him with disappointment. "All you ever wanted was your turn, right?" he asks as he gives Leonard the nudge of death. "Guess what, Sal? It's your turn."

Blocka! Blocka! Blocka!

CHAPTER 77

"We can always step into the backyard if you got something you wanna get off your chest," Leonard says. "All that talking ain't never been what I'm about."

"Ain't none of this what you been about," Speed replies, enraged. "You just came off the porch a few months ago. Don't act like you been doing this! I been ripping and running these streets since I was ten years old!"

Leonard flashes a grin filled with anger.

"Yeah, I just came off the porch a few months ago, and I'm still more live than you! So, what?" he asks with the same agitated smile. "I got a mean knuckle game. Always did, even when I was on the porch," he says with a cocky grin as he bangs his fists together. He, then, holds his fingers like a gun and aims at Speed. "And my aim is accurate. What?" he barks with a smile. "Nigga, pick your poison."

"Yo, don't mark me, aiming no fake-ass gun at me," Speed says with rage.

"You already a mark," Leonard smiles.

"You a joke to me, Lurch," he says, using the nickname the school had given him.

Everyone knew how much he hated that name, but nobody cared enough about his feelings to not call him that. It's just recently that they all stopped calling him that name. Now, no one would even dare to call him that.

"I don't even take you serious. Everybody else sees you as some wild boy, but you will always be that tall goofball that I used to see niggas playing out and taking advantage of."

Speed has now struck a nerve. Leonard is burning up inside. He wants to jump up and beat Speed to a pulp, but he must practice discipline. *Law Number 48*, he thinks. *Assume formlessness*. He repeats

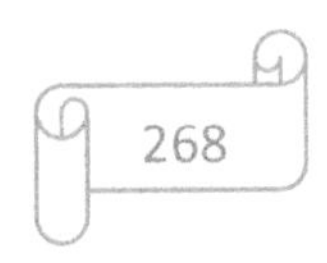

it over and over to erase any sign of emotion that he may be showing on his face. *The objective to this law is to make one's self unpredictable and difficult to understand by their enemies.*

Leonard smiles a big smile of false happiness.

"Like I said," he says in a jazzy tone. "I ain't with all the talking. If you wanna feel the wrath, stop yapping and make it happen," he says as he bangs his fists together again. "All you gotta do is stand up and make your way to the backyard, and I will do the rest."

Wustafa sits back quietly, just listening to them go back and forth. He's noticed the tension in between them building and knew that one day it would come to a boiling point. Everyone stares at Speed, awaiting his reply. They wonder if he will accept the invite that Leonard just threw in his face.

Speed feels the attention on him, and his ego speaks out for him.

"Let's go," he says as he stands up.

Deep in his heart, he hopes that Leonard doesn't get up. His prayers go unanswered when Leonard not only gets up but makes his way over to the door as well.

Speed trails way behind. It's quite evident to everyone that he really doesn't want to go. Leonard opens the door, and, just as he's about to step outside, Wustafa yells out, "Yo! Close my door!"

He walks toward them. He slams the door shut as he stares at them both back and forth. His temples pulsate with rage. He remains quiet for a few minutes before finally speaking.

"What's going on with y'all two? Why can't you get along? Y'all are like two siblings with all this back and forth rivalry. Now, y'all ready to go outside and indulge in a physical fight? Next, y'all will be loading your pistols and going to war with each other. We family! We don't fight each other. What has gotten into y'all?" he asks as he looks at them back and forth.

"Nobody got an answer for me? So, I'm gonna give y'all the answer," he says before pausing for a few seconds. "A siren," he says in an eloquent voice. The moment that he mentions the word "siren", the book *The Art of Seduction* pops into all of their minds.

"A mythical, goddess like figure," he says loud and clearly. "Full of fantasy and allure with a bit of theatrical quality. She is sensual, unpredictable, and ever changing," he says as he continues to stare back and forth at them. "She dazzles her audience with dramatic make-up and dress, her voice oozes with passion and confidence. Her presence alone draws you in and promises you pleasures and adventures, a world of fantasy that takes you away from the lull of daily life."

Sameerah hangs her head low and sinks into the couch. The more Wustafa talks, the lower she sinks. She's fidgeting in her seat uncomfortably. Anthony and Lil Wu sit back clueless, wondering where Wustafa is going with all of this and what it has to do with the point at hand.

"We all are familiar with the story of Cleopatra," Wustafa says. "Women have been the cause of problems and wars dating back to Adam and Eve. Just like the fruit was forbidden, I warned all of you to stay away from the fruit of this organization, but you didn't listen," he says.

As he points to both of them, guilt covers their faces.

"Now, look at the mess that we have here," he says with disgust. "Babygirl!" he shouts. "Look at what you have done to my soldiers. Look at the war you have created. Are you happy?" he asks as he stares at her, displeased.

Anthony looks over to her with confusion and so does Lil Wu. She's so embarrassed that she can't look either of them in the eyes. She feels Wustafa staring at her and feels as if he can see right through her. The visions of her sexual experiences with the both of them run through her mind. She attempts to shake them from her mind as she feels that Wustafa can read her mind.

The experiences meant very little to her, but she noticed a while ago how much it must have meant to them. Once she spotted the change in them, she promised herself that she would never let it happen again, and she hasn't broken her promise. What she didn't realize was that the damage was already done.

Staying at Leonard's house that night was a big mistake. She watched as Leonard changed from a goofy, awkward kid to a cocky, aggressive leader, and she loved every bit of it. She realized that she was developing an attraction for him, but still she was able to resist moving on it and keeping him in the brother basket.

She was able to disregard any feelings she had for him until that night that she stayed at his house. Although it was all done in

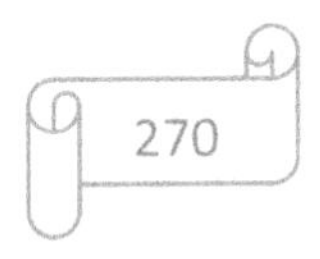

innocence, it ended up being one big mistake. Add intoxication and vulnerability to the feelings that she had for him and that equals hours of sex. The next morning, Sameerah regretted every moment of it and wished she could've taken it back. She made him promise to never repeat it to anyone. The truth of the matter is he never said a word verbally, but his actions told it all. She tried to go back to their normal brother/sister relationship, but his feelings for her made that impossible. He's always touchy feely with her, and he even feels some kind of way when Wustafa calls on her for certain jobs. He steps up and is willing to take the risks, just to protect her.

Speed has noticed the way that Leonard caters to her and that makes him jealous. Although their experience was barely intimate, it still was a big deal to him. His persistence at coming to pick her up from school and saying all the right things to her touched a soft spot in her heart. Then, there was that one day that he picked her up from school and said all the right things, which led to a quickie in the backseat of the truck.

Sameerah hates herself for being so weak. She told herself that she would never allow herself to be that weak ever again in life. She now understands why Wustafa deemed her forbidden to them. She, also, realizes that her giving them sex is not the reason that they're ready to go to war with each other. It's the fact that she's not willing to give them anymore sex that has them ready to go to war. She's learned a valuable lesson.

"So, Babygirl, what do you have to say for yourself? Say something, anything," he says in an attempt to make her feel even worse. "Man is weak, and that's no excuse, but I understand what has happened. Because man is weak I deemed her off limits. But you, Babygirl, I am extremely disappointed in. I'm not going to ask any of you how far it has gone. I'm going to save myself the embarrassment of hearing it. Anyway, the actions of these two tell it all. Sameerah, understand that I am disappointed, but in no way am I judging you."

She realizes that he must be terribly disappointed in her because she hasn't heard him call her by her name in quite some time now.

"Two kings ready to go to war for the love and approval of the queen," he says as he stares into Sameerah's tear filled eyes. "I hope that we've all learned a valuable lesson from this. We just reached our one year anniversary last week," Wustafa says with great pride. "One year of working with each other and watching each other's backs like family. Now, y'all two can't even be in the same room with each other without a squabble. We have come too far for this. We can't fall apart now. We have some major, major situations on the table. The Greek Diner situation alone will have us all walking away with millions. After we land that situation, y'all don't have to get along no more. We will never have to pull another caper in our lives," he says confidently. "The Washington Heights Heist will be a bonus.

I'm sure, with those two stings, we all will be sitting on a cool million apiece. Then, we can all walk away from each other, like we never meant a thing to each other," he says as he stares into Speed's eyes. The deep gaze into his eyes makes Speed realize that he's being singled out. "That is if that's what you choose to do."

CHAPTER 78
HOURS LATER

The meeting came to an end a couple of minutes ago. Everyone else has gone on about their way, except for Leonard. Wustafa asks him to stay for a couple of minutes. To not draw any attention to him, he made up a bogus reason on why he needed him to stay behind.

"I need you to keep your emotions under wraps," Wustafa says as he stares into Leonard's eyes.

"I wasn't emotional," he says defensively. "That was him."

"I'm not pointing the finger on who was wrong or who was right, but both of y'all was wrong. You should've stayed away from the fruit as I told both of you. That's neither here nor there right now. The situation took place, and we can't take it back, but, from this point on, I'm going to need you to be a little less confrontational with him."

"I be trying," Leonard claims. "But he makes it hard, always talking that tough talk."

"I understand, but I need you to just try a little harder. We only need him for a little while longer. Once we make these scores, then his services will no longer be needed," Wustafa says with a stern look in his eyes.

Leonard knows that look all too well.

"What you saying?" he questions with a bright spark in his eyes.

Wustafa nods his head up and down.

"Yeah," he says slowly. "That, I've been watching Speed all this year, and he's full of corruption. He's poison to the organization. He's like cancer that just keeps on spreading and spreading. I don't trust him as far as I can see him."

Leonard thinks of the conversation that Speed had with them about Wustafa using them. He so badly wants to bring it up, but he can't due to the fact that he waited so long to tell Wustafa. He's glad that Wustafa sees it for himself. Leonard nods his head.

"I agree. He can't be trusted. He's a creep."

"Creep is only one of his characteristics," Wustafa says. "He's sneaky, selfish, dishonorable, disloyal, and untrustworthy. All those characteristics are the qualities of an individual who can take the stand on their crew and not think twice about finishing them off for life. It's called the 'me or them mindset'. They only care about themselves and will do anything in the world to save themselves.

A guy like that can be detrimental to this organization. We've done too much dirt to have a person like him have all of that valuable information stored in his memory bank. I will never be able to sleep at night, knowing that he's roaming the land with our lives in his hands like that," Wustafa says with sadness in his eyes. "The only way I will be able to rest at night is if he can no longer hold that over our heads."

"And how is that?" Leonard asks.

"End our worries," he whispers. "After we make these scores, we off him," Wustafa says as he stares deep into Leonard's eyes. "Until then, we make him feel comfortable. Sleepwalk him all the way to the finish line," he whispers. "Then, bang!"

CHAPTER 79
DAYS LATER/1:32 A.M.

It's pitch black out tonight. The only source of light comes from the full moon, which is shining brightly over Wustafa and the crew as they stand on top of the rooftop of the tall building. They have formed a circle around two men. At the four corners of the rooftop, there stand four other men. The four of them all have semi-automatic weapons with extended clips in hand and are prepared for battle if need be.

Wustafa's eyes light up like a kid in a candy store as the dread headed man pulls the guns out of his duffel bag one by one. The duffel bag is filled with all types of guns. Wustafa has always had a deep love for guns. He loved guns so much as a child that he wanted to be a cop, just so he could carry a gun. As a kid running up and down the block playing cops and robbers, surprisingly he always seemed to play the cop. No one really knows what happened in between his early years and his teen years that made him cross over to the other side.

"How many handguns you got in there?" Wustafa asks.

"Not a one," the dread says with a heavy Jamaican accent. "Assault rifles and military artillery only," the man says as he shuffles through the bag. "All exclusive pieces. Uzis," he says as he holds the gun up. "And look at this, a three-hundred round clip," he says as he holds the magazine in the other hand. The members of the crew all watch in awe. Neither of them have ever seen an Uzi in real life.

"Three hundred rounds?" Wustafa asks in a high pitched voice.

"Three," he replies.

"Three," Wustafa repeats. "Wow! So you're telling me we can be packed with nine hundred rounds at one time?" Wustafa says, while shaking his head from side to side with amazement. He quickly envisions an all-out gun battle with the Uzis sounding off in the background. "Now, that's major."

"Oh, and this baby right here is one of my favorites. It's a M14 assault rifle," he says as he pulls the gun out of the bag.

"Ooh," Leonard sighs. He can no longer fight the urge. He stands there, dreamy eyed.

"Yeah, that is a beauty," Wustafa agrees. "How many rounds that hold?"

"Twenty," the dread replies.

"Only twenty? That's it?" Wustafa asks.

"Is that it?" the man asks with sarcasm as he holds one of the bullets in between his fingers. "How many of these do you think you need to finish the job? Superman couldn't stand up to one of these."

"I guess you're right," Wustafa says. "What else you got in there?" he asks anxiously.

"Last but not least, the rarest piece of them all. Y'all ready?" he asks as he stalls them. The anticipation builds as he shuffles his hand around in the bag. "Y'all ready?" he asks again. "Well, feast your eyes on this baby," he says as he slowly pulls the rifle from the bag.

Oohs and ahhs sound off from each of their mouths.

"What the fuck?" Anthony blurts out.

"What the fuck?" the dread repeats. "I will tell you what the fuck. This is the Mp5 Hechler and Koch," he says as he holds the awkward looking rifle in his hand.

"Let me see it," Wustafa says as he snatches it out of the man's hand. He turns it around over and over, examining it from every possible angle.

"And look at this," says the man. "A two hundred round clip." A sparkle sets in Wustafa's eyes. "So, which one you want?" the man asks.

"Which one?" Wustafa asks sarcastically. "I want every piece in the bag, every clip, every bullet and a lifetime refill of ammunition. Promise me that. Give me a reasonable price, and we got a deal." Wustafa reaches over and takes the duffel bag from Sameerah. "Money is not an issue," he says as he taps the side of the bag.

In less than ten minutes, the money has been counted, and the deal has been solidified. The Jamaicans have gone on their way, leaving

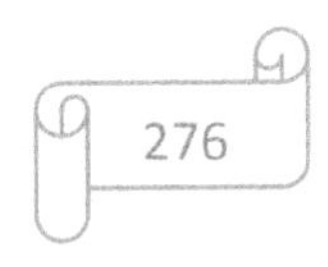

Wustafa and the crew here on the rooftop. Wustafa hasn't parted with the MP5 since he snatched it from the dread. It's like it's glued to his hand.

Wustafa grabs the two hundred round clip and attaches it to the rifle.

"'Bout to see what this baby is made of," he says with a spark in his eyes. They all watch with uncertainty. "Y'all ready for this? We are about to wake the neighbors up from many miles away," he says, while staring at the gun with a devilish look on his face.

They all step away from him as he steps closer to the ledge. He raises the gun into the air and points to the sky. He braces himself and locks his arms tightly against his body. Just as he's about to squeeze the trigger, Sameerah shouts from behind him.

"Wait!"

Wustafa turns around to face her. There, she stands with her hands extended, palms up.

"Can I?" she asks. "Please?" she begs.

"You think you ready for this, Babygirl?"

"It's only one way to find out," she replies.

"Sure. You're right," he says as he hands the rifle over to her.

Sameerah steps up to the ledge, and the other members back away even further. She aims the gun into the sky, planting the butt of it in between her breasts. Wustafa stands to her right.

"Lock your arms," he says. "Right foot behind for balance. I'm sure she got some kick, so hold onto her for dear life, so she don't get away from you."

Sameerah positions herself as instructed.

"Got you," she says as she swallows the lump in her throat and tries to ease the nervousness in her gut.

"Ready?" he asks. Sameerah nods her head without a verbal reply.

"Squeeze," Wustafa says with suspense in his voice. All the others stand behind with their hands covering their ears.

The machine gun sounds off, firing rapidly round after round for fifteen seconds. They're all shocked at the quietness of the gun. They take their hands from their ears and listen for a few more seconds as Sameerah continues to fire away.

"Hold," Wustafa says, causing Sameerah to snap out of her zone. She lets her finger off of the trigger, while she stares at the gun in shock. Although she expected so much more from the gun, the feeling was great. The feeling almost reminds her of her first consensual sexual experience. After the initial time, she wanted more and more.

"Can I do it again?" she asks with joy in her eyes.

Wustafa chuckles. "Nah, Babygirl. That's it. How did it feel, though?"

At this very moment, Sameerah feels like the machine gun is the ultimate high.

"Great," she replies.

The feeling is equitable to having sex with an experienced man when she's only had sex with immature little boys. The little handguns will never do it for her again. She's been turned out.

CHAPTER 80
TWO WEEKS LATER/THURSDAY, APRIL 24TH

The black on black G500 Mercedes truck blends perfectly in between a Range Rover and a Mercedes SL500. With the excess of luxurious automobiles that are spread out in the parking lot, the Mercedes seems to belong here, but it doesn't. Where it truly belongs is in Livingston with its rightful owner.

Two nights ago, Wustafa and the crew caught the owner, a music producer from New York, totally out of bounds. While cruising along South Orange Avenue, he was snatched out of his vehicle at a red light. Speed has taken the liberty of putting a temporary tag in the back window, as well as tinting the windows to personalize.

From the angle that they're parked, they can view the entire parking lot. They can see every car that enters, as well as watch the back door of the restaurant. A few men have sprinkled into the lot and snuck into the back door, just as Mickey promised. They have pulled up in luxurious automobiles, as well as hunks of junk on wheels.

Some are dressed in suits. Others look a step above homeless. The quality of life they lead all appear to be different, but they all have two things in common. They are all Greek, and they all carry a greasy brown paper bag in hand.

As they sit there, a convertible BMW pulls into the parking lot and parks as close to the back door as it can. A young Greek boy who appears to be in his late teens hops out of the driver's side. He dashes over to the passenger's side and opens the door. He leans inside and struggles to pull the passenger from the vehicle.

After a few minutes, an elderly man is visible. The young boy, then, leans inside, and, when he stands back up, he has an aluminum walker in his hand. He stands it up in front of the elderly man. Judging by his frail bent over body and his white hair, he appears to be in his eighties.

As he takes slow baby steps across the parking lot, using his walker, the young man holds his arm tight to keep him from falling. They all take notice the brown bag, which the elderly man holds clasped over the grip of his walker. He grips the bag tighter than he grips the walker. Of all the bags they have seen tonight, this is the biggest one of them all.

"That's what you call old money," Wustafa says with lust in his eyes.

Seeing the bag and knowing what is inside of it makes it hard for them to allow it to get away from them.

"I know he holding on to, at least, a million in that big-ass bag," Leonard says. "Come on, Wu. This too easy," he whines like a baby. "I can run up on him, knock his old ass down, snatch the bag, and keep it moving. We can still double back another Thursday and get more money," he says as he desperately awaits the command.

Wustafa sits there with the same thoughts in mind. He tries hard to restrain from giving the command. He thinks about the money in the bag and can even imagine counting it.

"Discipline," he whispers to himself.

As easy as it may be, snatching that bag that will only blow their chances of getting to the big money. He quickly shakes the vision from his head.

"Nah, why grab one bag with a million in it when we can wait a week and get every bag in the building, which could be three or four million easy, as I was told? Anyway, I gave him my word that I would wait until he gives me the green light," Wustafa explains. "No amount of money in the world can make me go against my word. Patience is the name of the game."

CHAPTER 81
DAYS LATER

Speed stands next to the candy apple red convertible BMW as the African man walks around, examining it.

"They will love this," the man says with a heavy accent. "Come on. Follow me," he says as he walks through the cluttered garage.

Mechanics are busy working on the cars and not paying the least bit of attention to them. The garage here is an auto mechanic shop, but the real money is made from the shipping of stolen cars over to the Motherland.

Speed follows the African into his office. The man quickly counts through a stack of money as Speed counts right along with him. After counting it once again, the man hands it over to Speed. "Seven thousand," he says.

Speed tucks the money into his pocket. It feels good not having to split his earnings with anyone. Better yet, it feels good not turning over his earnings and getting a small percentage. Truly, he can't believe that he's been playing the fool for this long. He doesn't feel like a complete idiot, though, being that he pocketed two grand off of every vehicle sold. That alone makes him feel like he has one up on Wustafa.

It's not that he wants to cut all ties with the organization. He just can't allow anyone to dictate to him when he can eat and how much he can eat. The money that they do get is consistent money that he can count on, but he plans to continue on with his side business as well. The more money he makes, the better off he's sure he will be.

"So, how long do you think it will be before you can get that Porsche that I'm in need of? They've been asking me about it for three weeks. If you can get your hands on it, I'm willing to pay up to ten grand."

"Ten grand?" Speed asks with dollar signs flashing in his eyes. "Say no more. All I need is a day or two."

Meanwhile

Sameerah sits in the passenger's seat of the Jeep Cherokee, which is parked on the secluded dead end block.

"One hand in the ten o'clock position and the other in the two o'clock position," she says as she looks over to the driver's seat.

In the driver's seat sits Wustafa. Sameerah had to damn near force him to get into the driver's seat. He's sweating bullets right now. He wipes his sweaty palms onto his sweatpants to remove the perspiration from them. He, then, wraps his hands tightly around the steering wheel just as Sameerah has told him. His mouth is dry from nervousness, and his heart is pounding like a drum.

"Just like that," she says in a soothing voice in an attempt to calm his nerves. "Now, I'm gonna put it in drive, and you're gonna drive to the other end of the block. Put your foot on the brake and hold it there till I tell you to let it up. Okay?"

Wustafa has a slight panic attack.

"Hold up, hold up," he says as he tries to get it together.

"Don't think about it," she says. "Just do it. Ready? Foot on the brake?" she asks as she slowly drops the gear into drive.

The Jeep jerks, and the engine revs up, but it doesn't move at all. Sameerah realizes that he's using both feet.

"Easy," she says. "Take the right foot off the gas but leave the left foot on the brake."

Wustafa does just as she instructed, and the engine is no longer racing. The quietness of the engine eases her nerves.

"Good," she congratulates. "Now, slowly ease your foot off the brake."

He slowly lifts his foot off of the brake, and the Jeep coasts along slowly.

"Just like that. Let it cruise," she says as she sits tensely on the edge of her seat.

Wustafa grips the steering wheel with all of his strength as the Jeep cruises at about seven miles an hour. It takes approximately five minutes just to reach the other end of the block.

"What to do right there?" he asks with fear as he sees the cul-de-sac slowly approaching.

"Slow down," she says. "Turn the wheel and ease your foot off of the brake."

He stops short, turns the wheel hard to the left, and eases off the brake. As he's turning around the loop, he feels a feeling of great satisfaction. He can't believe that he's actually faced his biggest fear.

"Okay," he says as he gives it a little more gas.

"Easy," she says as nervousness swims in her gut.

She watches as the needle of the speedometer goes up and up. She looks over at Wustafa, who has taken his right hand off of the wheel. He holds the wheel at the top, nodding his head with a look of arrogance on his face.

"Easy, easy."

"I got it," he says arrogantly as the needle goes up a little further.

"Look, I'm four wheeling," he boasts.

"Wu, slow down," she says as they approach the oncoming block quickly.

"I'm trying to," he says with his eyes bugged out.

The look of arrogance has disappeared, and the look of fear has replaced it. He mashes the gas pedal harder and harder, but still it won't stop. The Cherokee zooms through the intersection, swerving from side to side.

"Wu, take your feet off the gas," she says as she reaches over and attempts to lift his leg. His leg feels as if it weighs a ton. Wustafa closes his eyes just as the Jeep bounces onto a divider. It doesn't stop bouncing until it bounces onto the next curb. The Jeep runs over a small fence and crashes into the garage of a beautiful single family house.

Sameerah busts the door open as soon as the Jeep stops.

"Let's go," she says as she dashes out of the vehicle. Wustafa sits there in total shock. His hands are still on the steering wheel.

The house owners are now standing on the porch staring at the Jeep with confusion on their faces. Sameerah runs to the driver's side and snatches the door open. She slaps Wustafa with all of her might and awakes him out of his trance. He sees the owner of the house running down the stairs toward them.

"Let's go," Sameerah shouts.

Wustafa jumps out of the Jeep, and together, side by side, they make their getaway. Sameerah looks over at Wustafa as they're dashing up the block.

"That was your first and last time in the driver's seat."

CHAPTER 82

Sitting here in this tiny room gives Wustafa flashbacks of being in prison. He's suffering from claustrophobia just being in here. He's here at this rooming house visiting a dear friend of his. This man is an old jail buddy that he refers to as the Old Man.

There's no one in the world that Wustafa admires and respects more than him. He met him many years ago in Trenton State Prison where the Old Man was finishing up a twenty year sentence for bank robbery. Wustafa was just a young boy in the Big House. Sure, he had been in a few different jails but none to the magnitude of Trenton State Prison.

The whole experience was different from any other prison that he had been in. The system, the inmates, the officers, and the politics were an altogether different experience. The Old Man took a liking to Wustafa and took him under his wing. Within the eight years they spent together, they developed more than a friendship. Wustafa looks up to the man like a mentor, better yet the father that he never had.

Even after the Old Man's release, they still stayed in contact. Wustafa feels bad that, with all of his ripping and running, he hasn't once came to check on the Old Man until now. Tonight, he made it his business to come here. Being here breaks his heart to see the conditions that the man is living under.

The smell of burning crack vapors seeps into the crack of the door. Wustafa gets frustrated just thinking that the poison is getting into his system.

"I can't take the smell of that poison," Wustafa says as he gets up from the chair.

"No, no, no," the Old Man says. "Calm down. Don't get yourself in no trouble here."

Wustafa has so much respect for the Old Man, but he has lost a portion of that respect. The Old Man battles with a crack addiction.

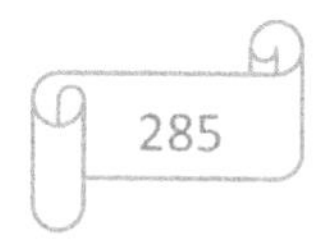

How has he gotten himself hooked onto drugs? Wustafa hasn't a clue, but it breaks his heart to know that he's weak enough to succumb to it. Each time Wustafa speaks to him, he denies the fact that he's still indulging, but Wustafa can see it in his eyes that he's not telling the truth.

The Old Man has been home for close to twenty years, and still he's institutionalized. He has his room set up similar to a jail cell. Everything that he needs is within arm's length from his bed. He can reach a beverage or food from his ice box, his magazine rack, his hot pot and even his piss pail all from the bed without getting up.

Living here in a crack infested rooming house is no way for a man to spend his supposed golden years. The Old Man isn't just old; he's extremely sickly. At seventy-two years old, he has kidney problems and has to go to dialysis three times a week. As if that isn't enough, he's a diabetic. He's been suffering from diabetes for the past twenty-five years.

In prison, he did better with his sicknesses because his medication was brought to him at the scheduled time. Being home, he has to depend on his own responsibility. Since he's been home, he's lost a half of his left leg, and he's lost his right foot due to amputation. Wustafa stares into the Old man's eyes and sees suffering.

"It ain't as bad as it looks, Young Fella," the Old Man says. "I'm gonna be alright. You don't worry about me. Just take care of yourself out there and stay outta that penitentiary."

"That's one place that I'm never going back to," Wustafa says with determination in his eyes. "The penitentiary days are over for me. I will leave that for them young boys," he says as he gets up. The smell of the crack has him light headed and woozy. "I gotta go. I got a crack contact," he says as he shakes his head from side to side.

He digs into the inside pocket of his army fatigue jacket and pulls out an envelope.

"Here," he says as he hands it over.

The Old Man's eyes light up as he sees the stack of twenty dollar bills inside the envelope. "What's this for?"

"It's for you. That's a grand. Get your medication. Stack your refrigerator," he says as he points to the little ice box that sits on the floor. "And get yourself a nice lady to sit on your face," he says with a smile.

"Ah, nah man," the Old Man says with disgust. "I don't eat no pussy. I'm seventy-two years old, never have and never will. I don't know how you young fellas do it," he says, while shaking his head from side to side with disgust on his face. "Did you ever take a good look at a pussy? The ugliest thing I ever seen in my life. Nah, man, never had to eat no pussy. Still don't. The Old man can still get it up," he laughs. "But nah I don't trust these dames around here as far as I can throw them. They will come in my room and rob the Old Man blind," he says with sadness on his face. "Had one in here who was supposed to give me a shot a cock and from here to there," he points to where Wustafa is standing. "She went in my sock drawer and took my whole welfare check. She was like a magician. I didn't even see her and I was watching her. Never even got the cock. Got mad 'cause I took a little longer than expected to get up and started bitching. I paid her and she left. That's when I noticed all my money left with her."

Listening to this story infuriates Wustafa. The fact that he's being taken advantage of hurts his heart.

"Gotta be careful around here, though," he whispers. "The old gal down the hall... they just beat her and stole her check last month. I have to sleep with both eyes open," he says with evident fear in his eyes.

It's killing Wustafa to see the Old Man like this. In his heyday, he was a pure terror, tough as nails. Today, he's just a sickly, helpless, scared old man.

"You don't have to live in fear for nobody, and you don't have to sleep with both eyes open," Wustafa says with rage. "Close your eyes, leave your door open and put your leg up," he says as he points to the footless leg. "You have a problem in here, you call me, and I will set this joint on fire. On my way out, I'm gonna make a prime example outta somebody. I guarantee you won't have a problem," he says with rage.

"Nah, nah, don't go being a hot head. That's where all your problems came from. We worked on that for eight years. Take it easy," the man says like a true mentor. "You've already done enough," he says as he holds the envelope in the air. "If you need me, don't hesitate to call."

"Need you?" Wustafa asks with a smile. "And what you gonna do? How you gonna get around?" he teases as he walks over to the Old Man. "Alright, Old Man," he says as he leans over and plants a kiss on the man's forehead. "I will be here to check on you next week. You be sure to get your medication in order because I need you around for, at least, another twenty years," he says, encouraging him.

"I got about another two for you tops," the man replies with sadness. "I done put mines in. Just happy to be here. With all I been through, I didn't expect to see seventy-two. Wasn't supposed to see twenty-five, let statistics tell it. So, the other forty-seven is a bonus. I'm gonna let you go. I ain't gon' hold you no longer. Just lonely in here and feels good to have company. You go on ahead. And remember, anything that I can do to help you, I'm here."

"Just help yourself and get healthy," Wustafa says. "That's what you can do for me."

"Oh," the man says with a spark in his eyes. "It almost slipped my mind. My old connection dropped by to see me last week, and he's still in business. Well, he's not actually in business. He's old like me. His grandson has taken over the family business. He's got all the paperwork you need, counterfeit money, licenses, government IDs, anything. Can make you an ID that says Secret Service, and I guarantee you can get into the White House with it," he claims. "Can even get uniforms to match the IDs. These boys bad, *mane*! Anything you need, let me know."

Wustafa's wheels start turning. He thinks of all the things that he could do with a connection like that. He nods his head up and down.

"I already got an idea. That's right on time."

"See," the man says as he points at Wustafa. "The Old Man still got some use left. When you can no longer be used, you're finished."

CHAPTER 83

ONE MONTH LATER/TUESDAY, MAY 27, 2003

The streets here in the Washington Heights area are peaceful. At this hour, more elderly people are present than any other time of the day. They feel more comfortable traveling this time of the day. By the time the children are out of school, the elderly are in with their locks on the doors, trapped here, like prisoners, in their own homes.

Very few men are posted on the corners and not one child is present in the entire area. All that can be seen are elderly people pushing shopping carts, strolling, and sweeping in front of their homes. The only movement in front of the Spot is the mail woman who passes by the three Dominicans who stand on guard in front of the door. High up on the telephone pole, a man looks around with nosiness more than he's actually working. He pays close attention to a Federal Express worker who bends the corner with a box in his hand. He steps right into the building as well.

Leonard and Lil Wu step up the block at a moderate enough speed to not stand out but also moderate enough to watch everything that's going on around them. They both take one last look before stepping into the building. They jog to catch the elevator in which the doors are wide open. They manage to slip inside as the doors are closing.

Three flights up, the mail lady taps on the door for the fourth time. Finally, the door is slowly opened. An elderly woman peeks under the chain lock.

"Sí?" she asks.

"Post office, ma'am. You have a package. I need you to sign," she says as she holds the envelope in the air.

She, then, points to the Post Office badge on her cap. The woman quickly snatches the chain off the door and opens it wider.

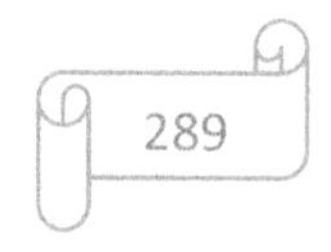

The mail lady bumrushes her way into the apartment, knocking the old woman off of her feet. She quickly slams the door shut behind her as she reaches inside her bag. She draws her .9mm from the bag and aims at the woman while putting the chain back on the door for further security.

"Oh, Dios," the woman cries fearfully. "Dios por favor," she cries as she holds her hands in front of her body submissively.

Sameerah lifts the hat from over her eyes, so she can see clearly. She pulls the wire from her bag as she runs over to the woman. She quickly ties the woman's wrists together before pulling her onto her feet. Gently, she shoves the woman throughout the apartment while holding the gun to her head.

This is the first time that Sameerah has ever felt compassion during a robbery. The look in the poor old woman's eyes melts Sameerah's heart. As much as she hates to do this to her, it's all the nature of the business. *God, please forgive me*, she thinks.

"Anybody here with you?" she asks as she looks around in each room.

"No ingles," the woman cries.

After confirming that the woman is here all alone, she puts the gun to the woman's face. "Where's the money?"

"No habla ingles," the woman cries. "No habla ingles."

Sameerah finally understands the importance of what she learned in Spanish 1, after all the years of thinking that it was a waste of time. Now, she wishes she would've paid more attention instead of sleeping the time away.

"Dinero," she says slowly. "Pesos."

The lady quickly points into the bedroom. Sameerah shoves her in front of her for her to take the lead. She stops short at the armoire. Sameerah opens it, and the woman points directly at a plastic shopping bag. Sameerah's eyes are stuck on the top shelf, not even paying attention to the bag that the woman is pointing to.

On the top shelf, in clear view, there are nine kilos in total, three rows stacked three high. Sameerah gets an uncontrollable adrenaline rush, which causes her to get lightheaded. She dumps the kilos into her mailbag and then feasts her eyes onto the plastic bag. She snatches the plastic bag from the shelf and peeks inside.

Her heart skips a beat when she sees not one but three huge Ziploc bags of money. She lifts the one from the top and carefully examines it. The black marker writing on the top reads $100,000. She looks at the other two and is happy to see that they indicate the same. Her mouth goes dry after swallowing the lump of anxiousness in her throat. She feels like she's holding onto the winning lottery ticket.

She quickly pulls more wire from her bag as she pushes the woman over to the bed. She pushes the woman onto the bed and quickly begins tying her left ankle to the bottom bed post. She, then, ties her right wrist to the top bed post. The woman looks up at her with tears of suspense in her eyes, wondering what's in store for her.

Sameerah grabs a walkie talkie from her bag, holds it up to her mouth as she presses the side button. The alert comes back immediately.

"All good," Sameerah says.

"Copy," Wustafa says loud and clear.

Outside, from the top of the telephone pole, Wustafa looks around attentively. He chirps back at Sameerah.

"Okay. Wait for the command," he whispers.

He looks around at the Dominicans, who are sprinkled around the area. Their nonchalant demeanor tells him that they have no clue about what's going on inside of the building.

Wustafa has planned long and hard for this attack. For ten months, he's staked out in front of here, at least, twice a week. The last three months he's spent even more time out here. He scoped the spot out every day last week from morning to night.

He sent Lil Wu and Leonard in once a week for the past two months, just to scope out the details of the operation. He learned that the old woman's apartment is where the cocaine is held until it's needed. He, also, learned that, every so often, the money is transferred to that apartment as well. He figured there is no better time than now because there are no more details to know.

He's sure that, if he would've waited until the nighttime, he could have landed a bigger score. He, also, realizes that the risk would be bigger as well. In the night hours, there's more action, but there are, also, more Dominicans. Adding all of that into the equation, he figured daytime would be best. He pulled them all out of school today just to go ahead and get the job done and out of the way.

Lil Wu stands at the scale as the man drops a chunk of cocaine onto it. He's tapping his foot with nervousness but trying to play it as cool as he can. He knows that, any second now, he will get the command. His body language could be read from afar if the men were really paying attention to him.

Leonard sits on the loveseat with his head laid back and his eyes half closed. The feeling of peace is in the room because of the comfort level that the Dominicans now have with them. The man stands at the door with his gun in hand but not as tense as he was the first few times that they visited. He's barely even paying attention to them. Leonard is just waiting for the right second to make his move. All he needs is something as simple as a blink of the eye, and the game will begin.

"Three hundred grams," the man says as he points to the scale.

"Hachoo!" The loud sneeze sounds off from behind.

Another sounds off right behind that one.

"Hachoo!" The gunman opens his eyes after the heart stopping sneeze only to stare into the barrel of the Uzi with the three hundred round extended clip.

"Hand it over," Leonard says with a devious smile as he pries the gun out of the man's hand. He doesn't put up the slightest amount of resistance.

"Hands in the air," Lil Wu says as he lifts his Uzi over the table, aiming at the man's chest. The man raises his hands slowly.

"Pat him down," Leonard says as he places the chain lock onto the door.

Lil Wu steps around the table and frisks the man carefully.

"Nothing," he yells out.

"Lay 'em down and tie 'em up."

Lil Wu reaches into his bag and digs out the rope. He quickly ties the man's hands together behind his back. He, then, ties his feet together. Leonard shoves the man over to Lil Wu who slams him on the floor next to the other Dominican. Lil Wu quickly ties the man up.

Leonard bends over and kneels close to the man.

"You ain't that tough now, huh? You got big cahoonas when you're the only one in the room with a gun. Act tough now," Leonard says aggressively.

Leonard puts the gun to the back of the man's head.

"If you even look at me, I will splatter your spick-ass brains all over the floor."

The man trembles with every syllable, expecting to hear the gun sound off. Oh, how badly Leonard wants to bust his head open, but he was commanded not to unless he had no choice. Wustafa explained to him that the sound of gunfire will blow the whole situation.

"I knew it was all an act," Leonard says as he bangs the gun against the man's head. "A bitch hiding behind a gun." Leonard pulls his walkie talkie from his pocket and presses the button. "All good," he says with arrogance.

Wustafa hits back immediately. "Copy."

Seconds later, the Dominican's walkie talkie goes off. The speaker on the other end says a few words of Spanish, but Leonard is clueless to what they're saying.

****

On the outside, Wustafa watches as two young black men walk toward the building. The Dominican in the front speaks into his walkie talkie again, alerting them that they have two customers coming up. The man holds the customers off from entering until he gets the cue to let them in. Frustration covers his face as he hits the button once again.

Wustafa hits the button on his walkie talkie.

"How we looking? They're sensing something fishy?" he whispers into the walkie talkie. "Gotta hurry up before they get onto us. We are running out of time."

"Got you," Leonard replies as he opens the cupboard doors.

He pulls two kilos from the bottom shelf and drops them into his bag. He, then, runs back over to the scale. He grabs the three hundred grams from the table and throws that in the bag along with the remainder of the brick of cocaine.

Lil Wu reaches under the table and grabs hold of a Ziploc bag full of money. He throws it over to Leonard.

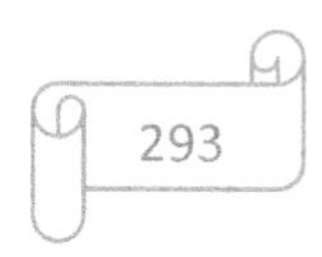

"Here."

Leonard tosses the money into the bag as he makes his way to the door.

"Let's go!"

They make their exit and sprint toward the stairwell. One flight behind them, there is Sameerah, who is making her way down the stairs.

Wustafa planned this entire caper out perfectly. The only thing that he didn't factor in is the fact that today is Tuesday. Today is the day that TNT makes their rounds throughout all the boroughs. Their other day of operation is Thursday.

The initials stand for Tactical Narcotics Team, but drug dealers have associated those initials with Tuesday and Thursday. Dealers from New York know to walk lightly on those two days. Dealers from Jersey even know to avoid coming to New York on those two days. Because Wustafa is not and has never been a dealer, he had not a clue.

A block away, in both directions, unmarked police cars sit parked. Through high power binoculars, they've been watching the spot since it opened this morning. Just like Wustafa has been scoping the spot heavily for the last two weeks, so have they. They know the details of the operation even better than Wustafa.

"Something is going on, Sarge," the narcotics officer says from the driver's seat. "Their sudden movements tell me something isn't right. You see how they're scrambling around?" he asks. "You think someone may have gotten wind of us being out here?"

They watch as five Dominicans form a huddle and appear to be scheming.

"I don't know, but I think it's time that we move in," the sergeant replies. "Get on the radio and tell them we're going in."

Wustafa watches as two more Dominican men join the huddle. His heart is pounding as he wonders what they're up to. His walkie talkie sounds off.

"We coming out," Leonard says.

The Dominicans, all at once, dash across the street toward the building. Wustafa fumbles with the walkie talkie nervously. He hits the button.

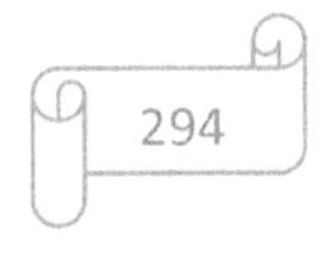

"They're coming in. They're coming in," he whispers as he starts to step down the pole. He hits the button again.

"Speed, come on in."

Seven Dominicans bust through the double doors of the building. Only three of the seven are armed with pistols. As soon as they enter the building, the sound of the MP5 machine gun echoes throughout the empty lobby. Anthony stands there in his FedEx uniform, blasting away from side to side like a seasoned war veteran. Three of the Dominicans fall on their faces immediately. One of the gunmen stands there heroically, firing back as the other two run away with their guns in hand.

Boc! Boc! Boc! Boc! Boc! Boc!

Anthony stops his side to side spraying motion and focuses merely on the one Dominican. Quickly, he pumps the man's body with over twenty consecutive rounds. The Dominican collapses face first onto the marble floor. Two of the other men fire their guns as they attempt to back out of the lobby.

Boc! Boc! Boc! Boc!

Anthony backs them down as he fires from side to side relentlessly. Leonard, Lil Wu, and Sameerah all follow a few steps behind him. The sound of Leonard's Uzi sounds off rapidly, while the sound of Sameerah's .9mm rips in between rounds. The sound of the gunfire echoes throughout the hollow lobby.

The two Dominicans fall onto their bellies, and Leonard and the crew run past them. One man lays at the door, wounded and helpless. He looks up at them with pity in his eyes, and Leonard feels none at all. He dumps four rounds from the Uzi into the man's face. The man rolls right on over and drops dead.

Wustafa watches as the black Suburban comes up the block at top speed. His attention is diverted to the Dominican who is running out of the building. Wustafa holds his gun in the air, he aims and fires.

Blocka! Blocka!

Like a skilled marksmen Wustafa hits his target twice in the head. The man tips over, head first.

Anthony runs out of the building first, beating the crew by many steps. He runs over to the Suburban and snatches the back door open for the crew to enter. He stands on guard at the passenger's door as he watches around attentively. He's ready to start blasting away if need be.

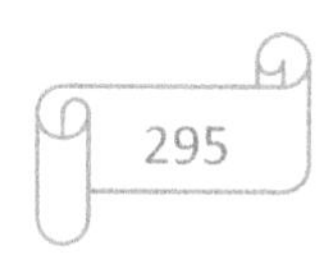

Wustafa stands on guard at the door for anyone else who may be coming out.

"Let's go! Let's go," Wustafa shouts as they pass him.

The sound of police sirens take all of them by surprise. They freeze in their tracks, looking around to see where the sirens are coming from. As they peek around and notice that they're coming from each direction, they begin running again in an attempt to get to the Suburban. The speeding unmarked car is only a few feet away from the bumper of the Suburban. Three more cars are tailing that one.

Speed looks up ahead where he sees two cars coming in his direction. Both are speeding along the wrong side of the street. His heart skips a beat as the sirens blaze all around him. Fear takes over his body, and, without even realizing it, his foot mashes onto the gas pedal. The Suburban pulls away from the curb with no passengers. Anthony holds onto the handle for dear life.

"Hold, hold," Anthony shouts.

The others watch in shock as their getaway car gets away from them. The machine gun falls to the ground as Anthony uses both hands to hold on. Speed swerves and speeds up the block as Anthony attempts to get inside.

"Wait, wait," he begs.

He holds on for as long as he can until he falls off the truck. His pants leg is hooked onto the seat lever, causing him to be dragged upside down.

As Speed gets to the intersection, a police truck darts out at him. He swerves to his right. The sudden jolt forces Anthony's body to fall out of the truck. He hits the ground while screaming loudly.

"Oww, oww, oww!" he cries.

A huge thump sounds off as the back wheel rolls over his head. A loud, bursting noise replaces the screaming as his head busts open like a cantaloupe. Speed continues on with no regard whatsoever. He makes a quick right turn and mashes the gas pedal as hard as he can.

The thought of going back to prison has sent Wustafa off to battle. He backs up against the wall as two detectives hop out of the car.

"Freeze!" the cop says as he aims at Wustafa.

Wustafa sends two shots at them before taking off into flight.

Blocka! Blocka!

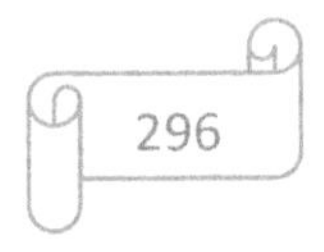

He races up the block as fast as he can with Lil Wu glued to his side. The sound of the Uzi rips through the air from the opposite side of the street. Leonard fires round after round in an attempt to get away. Another cop car cuts in front him in an attempt to block his path. He fires at the windshield with aggression as he dips around the car. The cops duck low with fear.

As he's running up the block, the passenger's door of the cop car pops open, and the cop hops out.

"Freeze!" the officer yells as procedure before he fires nine rounds.

Boc! Boc! Boc! Boc! Boc! Boc! Boc! Boc! Boc!

Leonard falls face first onto the asphalt in the middle of the street. With his gun still in hand, his arms and legs are spread wide. He lays there stiff as a board, dead to the world.

Sameerah runs clueless around the building. The sight of the police car and seeing Speed pull off without them caused her to run back into the building. As she's under the stairwell, looking for an escape route, the sound of walkie talkies sound off.

"Lieutenant, we got five bodies in here. All appear to be dead," he says into the walkie talkie.

Sameerah stands as still as a statue. All of this is playing like one bad nightmare. She keeps closing her eyes and opening them, hoping that she will wake up, laying in her own bed. It was all seeming to go so smoothly. She knew it was all too good to be true. She just can't believe how, in a matter of just seconds, it all went haywire. She begs and pleads with God for the cops to not come back there where she is. As her eyes are closed, a quick vision of Speed pulling off flashes in her mind. *How could he leave us?* she asks herself. As hectic as things were, she believes they would have had a better chance at getting away in the truck.

Quickly, she wonders how everyone else is making out right now. The last thing she saw before running back into the building was Wustafa firing at the police. After that, several different gunshots rang off in the air. As much as she hopes that they're winning the war with the way they were outnumbered out there, she's sure that's not the reality.

Sameerah looks down the staircase and right at the basement level, there's a door. She looks up at the doorway of the lobby where three

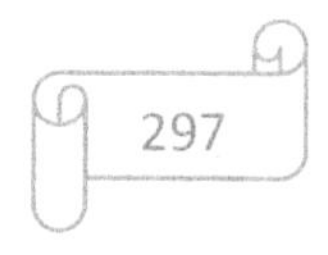

cops are now standing. She's sure it won't be long before one of them plays super-cop and starts roaming the halls looking for leads. She stands there, petrified. She realizes that she must make a move and the move must count. She can't afford to draw any attention to herself by moving, and she definitely can't afford to stand here and wait for them to come get her.

Speed races up Broadway at top speed with the passenger's door swinging wildly on the hinges. The fact that he's left his crew has not even settled into his head. Neither has the fact that he rode over Anthony. There is no room in his mind for those thoughts at this time. From the time that he saw the first set of flashing lights, only one thing has been on his mind, and that's his wellbeing.

He peeks from side to side as he speeds through the intersection. Tears of fear drip down his face. His heart pounds so hard that it's drowning out the sound of the loud music. A string of police cars tail him not even a half a block behind. He looks up ahead, and all he can see is blazing lights coming from every direction.

He's trying his hardest to figure out a solid getaway plan. He understands that his life and his freedom all depend on it. What happens from this point on can change his life forever. For the first time ever, the loud music is interrupting his thoughts.

"Deep concentration," he says loudly as he shuts off the stereo.

An oncoming police car swerves at him. Speed swerves around him with no regard. He realizes that was merely an attempt to break his concentration. He continues on, flooring the truck, pushing it to the limit. He peeks at the speedometer as the needle exceeds well over ninety-five miles an hour. He peeks over at the gas gauge and feels satisfaction in knowing that he's only a tad bit short of a full tank.

"I'm not giving up," he says to himself. "We gon' ride all night."

He feels a little hope as he reads the George Washington Bridge sign which isn't even a block away. Through the rearview, he sees that the closest cop car behind him is about two blocks away. Traffic seems to be on his side. In seconds, he reaches the sign to the bridge.

Just before making the right turn onto the ramp, he peeks behind once again and sees that the cars are still way behind. He slows down slightly as he turns onto the ramp. He bends the curb, and, just as he's about to increase the speed, his heart stops beating. He slams on the brakes as he sees the barricades about a hundred feet in front of him.

Police have the entire area sealed off. All entrances to the bridge have been sealed off as well. All major streets have been shut down, also. The entire highway is bare and empty with no sign of traffic for many miles away.

"What the fuck," he utters to himself as he sees the many police that are standing at the sides of the barricades. "Think quick, think quick," he says to himself. The thought of backing up creeps into his mind, but the sight of the sirens coming behind him cancels that thought. Two police officers pop out in front of him behind the barricade with their guns aimed at the truck's windshield.

"Hands up!" the officer yells.

Speed quickly pictures himself in handcuffs. His mind then goes back to the scene of the crime. He thinks of the robbery and all the gunshots that he heard. He has no clue how many were killed back there. For the first time, he thinks of Anthony. Suddenly, it all plays clearly in his mind. He sees Anthony falling out of the truck. He hears his loud screams and his cries. He, also, feels the squishy feeling he felt as the tire rolled over and squashed his head.

He's sure that Anthony is dead, and that's a homicide that will be added onto the many other crimes that he's sure they will charge him with. He considers all that he's up against, and he mashes the gas pedal as hard as he can. The two officers flee out of his path.

Before the Suburban can even crash through the barricade the shots start ringing off from every direction.

Boc! Boc! Boc! Boc! Boc! Boc! Boc! Boc!

The barricade flies high into the air and lands on the hood of the truck. Glass shatters everywhere as every window is shot out on both sides of the truck. The shots continue to ring off as he passes them. Three officers have their guns aimed at the back windshield of the truck. The sound of rapid gunfire rips through the airwaves.

Boc! Boc! Boc! Boc! Boc! Boc! Boc!

Two slugs enter Speed's head almost simultaneously. His face bangs against the steering wheel as his foot is still glued onto the gas pedal. He is dead as a doorknob but the truck continues to race down the empty highway at above full speed. Finally, a half a mile away, little by little, the truck swerves to the right and crashes into the highway railing.

Sameerah hops over the little fence with ease. Her heart is racing and all types of thoughts fill her mind. In front of her is fence after fence, yard after yard. Where is she headed? She has not a clue. With the fear that's in her at this moment, she could run all the way to a foreign country without getting tired. All she wants to do is to get away from here. She's already made a promise to herself and God that, if she makes it out of New York City, she will never ever return.

As she's climbing over the biggest fence that she's encountered, she hears voices. She becomes startled. She stops climbing and strains her ears to listen. The familiar voice catches her attention. She's wondering if she's hearing right or if her mind is playing tricks on her.

"Go ahead."

She's sure that she's correct, but she listens closer as she holds onto the fence tightly.

"Don't leave me like this. Do what you gotta do and get on back to Jersey."

Sameerah hurries over the fence and tiptoes through the yard.

"Go ahead! Dammit! Squeeze the fucking trigger before they come here and find us."

Sameerah peeks around the house and what she sees brings tears to her eyes. Wustafa sits propped up against the house. He's a bloody mess. Blood has soaked through all of his clothing. The expression on his face shows that he's in massive pain.

Lil Wu stands over him with his back towards Sameerah. Wustafa closes his eyes and flinches as he holds onto his gut. He grabs his stomach once again, holding it a little longer this time.

"I knew you weren't built for this life. I told you, but you didn't want to believe me," he says before closing his eyes and clenching his gut again. "Lil Wu, my ass," he barks. "You nothing like me. You a bitch made motherfucker like your sucker-ass father. Like father, like son," he says as he winces with pain. "You a scared-ass punk," he says in an attempt to infuriate Lil Wu enough to pull the trigger. Lil Wu stands over Wustafa with his gun aimed, but he can't make himself pull the trigger. Tears drip down his face at a rapid pace. "You can't pull the trigger because you don't have it in you."

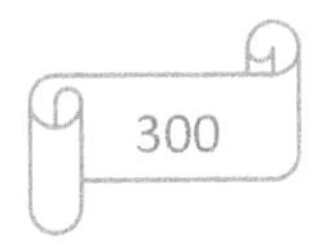

Sameerah finally steps out of hiding. Lil Wu hears her footsteps in the leaves and quickly aims his gun in her direction.

"Babygirl," Wustafa says with a sense of happiness in his voice but not on his face. The only thing on his face is pain. "Good. I'm glad you're here to save me," he says before he winces with pain once again.

"Them pigs got the old boy," he says as he points to his chest. "It's over for me," he says as he clenches his gut tightly. "I gave this bitch-ass nigga the command to take me out of my misery, and he can't even carry out the command," he says with disgust on his face. "Babygirl, I beg you not to leave me like this. Please?" he begs. "Leave no soldier behind," he says in the strongest voice he has at this moment. "Babygirl, don't let them find me like this," he says with sadness in his eyes. "If I go back to prison, I'm done. I'm a career criminal. I will never see daylight again. Please don't let me die in prison, please?" he pleads with all of his heart. "Please," he says with tears in his eyes.

Sameerah isn't sure if the tears are tears of fear of prison or tears of pain, but tears have built up in her own eyes as well.

"Please," he begs once again.

Sameerah pulls her gun from her waist and aims at his head.

"That's right, Babygirl. Take me out of my misery."

Sameerah hesitates. As bad as she wants to, she can't make herself do it. The love and admiration she has for him prevent her from killing him even if that's what he wants. She shakes her head from side to side.

"Wu, I can't," she cries. "I can't do it."

Wustafa clenches his gut tightly with his eyes closed while biting on his bottom lip to ease the pain. He peeks up through one eye.

"Yes, you can, Babygirl. Do it," he whispers in agony. "Pull the trigger."

"Wu, let us just carry you from here and get you fixed up in Jersey," she suggests with desperation in her eyes.

"We will never make it," he denies. "A tri-state manhunt is probably already in effect. Any hospital we go in, they will alert the police. I can't go back to prison, Babygirl," he says sadly. "Please don't leave me to die in prison. Babygirl, you are second in command. I appointed you second in command because I knew I could depend on you. I trusted you over all of the others. You are the only one that I trusted with my life," he says as he looks at Lil Wu with disgust. "You told me that I could trust you with my life, right?" he asks.

Without a verbal reply, Sameerah nods her head up and down. Her face is now flooded with tears.

"My life is in your hands," he says. "Now, I'm here begging you to end it. End it, Babygirl. Squeeze the trigger."

Blocka!

Sameerah opens her eyes and sees Wustafa trembling like he's having a seizure. She steps closer to him. With tears in her eyes, blurring her vision, she attempts to aim. She closes her eyes tightly to flush the tears out of her eyes. She squeezes the trigger once again.

Blocka!

Wustafa's movements stop completely.

Lil Wu looks over to Sameerah with an expression of total surprise on his face.

Blocka!

Lil Wu's body drops to the ground lifelessly. Sameerah stares closely at him to make sure that he's not moving. She, then, looks back over at Wustafa. Neither one of them has any sign of life in their bodies. She tucks her gun into her waistband, turns around, and continues on with her journey.

CHAPTER 84

Sameerah steps out of the clothing store here on Broadway and 192nd Street dressed in tight jeans and a matching jean jacket. The mailbag and uniform is tucked inside of the shopping bag that she holds in her left hand. In her right hand, she holds another shopping bag, which contains a total of twelve kilos and over three hundred thousand in cash money.

She walks hurriedly up the block. Her paranoia has her feeling like all eyes are on her. With all that has just happened, she still tries to carry herself as normal as she possibly can. With every few steps that she takes, she peeks around to make sure that no police are eye balling her. She feels like everyone is watching her. She blames it on her guilt because she's almost sure that no one saw her face. The only description that they should have had is the fact that she wore a mail uniform if any description at all.

Sameerah disregards the traffic light and crosses against it. Heavy horn blowing sounds off as angry drivers speed up purposely. She dips and dodges the moving cars. It's like she's walking around in a daze.

She's in shock, and most of the details of today haven't even settled in her mind yet. All the pieces of today's puzzle are scattered in her head chaotically. Everything is running together at a rapid pace. The vision that sticks in her mind is of Wustafa begging her to end his life.

As hard of a task that was he left her with no choice. She wouldn't be able to live her life in peace knowing that she left him to rot in prison. As far as Lil Wu, she always knew that he wasn't built for the lifestyle, but, today, it was proven. She hated to end his life, but she realized, if she didn't, he could possibly end hers on the witness stand.

Sameerah drops the shopping bag with her mail uniform in it in the trash basket that sits on the corner. Not once does she even look back at it. She steps toward the subway entrance with her attention straight in front of her. As she takes the second step, she steps over to the right side to allow the woman at the bottom of the stairwell room to pass. Sameerah's gut wrenches giving her the signal that something isn't right. The woman lifts her head up, and, in one motion, she flashes her badge. In her other hand, she grips her gun.

"Freeze!"

Sameerah's eyes pop wide open with fear. As she backpedals up the steps, she reaches for her own gun. She gets to the top step and looks at the woman, who stands there with her gun aimed. She spins around, and, just as she's about to dash off, she sees a movie playing in front of her very eyes.

Police stand in the middle of the street scattered all over. Guns are aimed at her from every direction. Cops from several precincts have been called in. Before the shooting of Wustafa and Lil Wu, she was in the clear. Neighbors heard the shots ring out and were able to give a description.

Sameerah was totally ignorant to the fact that they were tailing her all the while. They even sat outside and waited for her to come out of the store where she changed clothes. Instead of just nabbing her, they waited in hopes that she would lead them to an accomplice.

"Drop the gun and get on your knees," one of the cops yells as he aims an assault rifle at her head from the middle of the street.

Sameerah stands there in confusion. She looks around at the many police that are in the area and realizes that she will never make it out of here alive. She, then, thinks of the fact that being slaughtered here may be even better. She looks around as she weighs her options and thinks of what she should do.

"Drop the gun and get on your knees!" he says with a more threatening demeanor.

Sameerah peeks to the left, then the right. She, then, puts her left hand in the air as she kneels down slightly to lay the gun on the ground.

"Now, get on your knees and put your hands on your head."

Sameerah slowly lowers herself onto her knees. As soon as she puts her hands onto her head, the woman cop yanks them behind her back with force as she places the handcuffs on tight. The female cop snatches Sameerah onto her feet and begins frisking her thoroughly. She quickly looks inside the bag and finds all the evidence stacked inside. She holds the bag high in the air.

"We got her," she says with a smile.

Sameerah watches as one of the detectives grab her shopping bag from the trash basket. The woman cop shoves Sameerah toward the unmarked car that is parked near the curb. People crowd the scene, watching nosily as Sameerah is thrown into the car. From the backseat of the car, she watches the police congratulate each other. As she's sitting there, the pieces of today's puzzle start to come together. The reality has now set in. The huge nightmare has come to an end, or has it just begun? Sameerah lays her head against the headrest as the tears pour down her face.

"It's over," she mumbles to herself. "I'm finished. Game over."

THE END

ALSO BY THE AUTHOR

No Exit
ISBN # 0-974-0610-0-X $14.95

Block Party
ISBN# 0-974-0610-1-8 $14.95

Sincerely Yours
ISBN# 0-974-0610-2-6 $14.95

Block Party 2 /The Afterparty
ISBN# 0-974-0610-4-2 $14.95

Caught 'Em Slippin'
ISBN # 0-974-0610-3-4 $14.95

Block Party 3 /Brick City Massacre
ISBN# 0-974-0610-5-0 $14.95

Strapped
ISBN# 0-974-0610-5-8 $14.95

Back 2 Bizness /Block Party 4
ISBN# 0-974-0610-5-8 $14.95

Block Party (Comic)
ISBN# $4.50

Sales Tax .27
Total $4.77
Sales Tax per book title: .89

Shipping/ Handling for 1-3 books Via U.S.
Priority Mail $4.60
Each additional book add $1.00 for shipping
Buy six or more books shipping is free

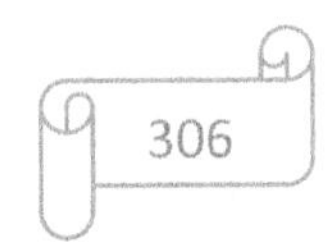

BOOK ORDER FORM

Purchaser Information

Name: ____

Address: ______________________________________

City:______________ State: _____ Zip Code: ________

No Exit ___

Block Party ____

Sincerely Yours _____

Caught 'Em Slippin' _____

Block Party 2 ____

Block Party 3 ____

Strapped ____

Back 2 Bizness ____

Block Party (Comic) ____

Book Total: ______ Total Due: _______

Make Checks/Money Orders payable to:

True 2 Life Publications
PO Box 8722
Newark NJ 07108

www.True2LifeProductions.com

Made in United States
Orlando, FL
28 February 2023